Praise for Somewhere Out There

A new and original fantasy that transports the reader into a world where myth and magic collide. Vampires, ghosts, and the legend of King Arthur. A battle between good and evil, although is it ever as clear cut as that?

E.J Davies, author of The Harbinger

A great debut novel. It's certainly a different take on the Arthurian legend.

Claire Louise, author of Trauma to Truth

If you're a fan of Norse mythology, Arthurian legends, fantasy, supernatural and magic you should give this a try. It keeps you guessing at exactly what is happening.

@krbooks13, bookstagrammer

ABOUT THE AUTHOR

Inspired by anything supernatural, historical, and the myths and legends of Europe, Caroline writes fantasy and supernatural stories that pack an emotional punch. Her work has been featured in Liverpool's Royal Court's 2023 new writing night. When she's not writing, Caroline spends her time helping to bring other people's stories to live on stage, screen and radio. She loves going to gigs, theatre and baking.

Also by Caroline Astiago

Shadows and Regrets series:
Somewhere Out There
Make Damn Sure

Plays
And Then Skull Said ...

Sade,

MAKE DAMN SURE

BOOK TWO IN THE SHADOWS AND REGRETS SERIES

CAROLINE ASTIAGO

*Thanks for continuing on
the adventure.
Happy reading,*

Caroline Astiago x x

Caroline Astiago
hello@carolineastiago.co.uk
www.carolineastiago.co.uk

First published in the United Kingdom by Caroline Astiago, 2024
Copyright © 2024 by Caroline Astiago

Book design by Cover design and illustrations © Scott Eckersley

A catalogue record for this book is available from the British Library.

ISBN 978-1-0685697-0-8
eISBN 978-1-0685697-1-5

Copy edit by Bowland Editorial
Book cover design by Scott Eckersley
Typeset in Garamond by Caroline Astiago

For sales and distribution, please contact hello@carolineastiago.co.uk

To everyone who has asked me to dedicate a book to them, assume this is for you.

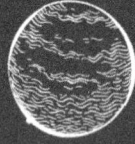

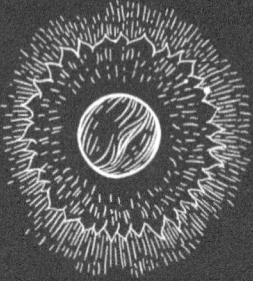

Avalon

Fae

Gaia

Tuonela

Erebus

Styx

Hades

Purgatory

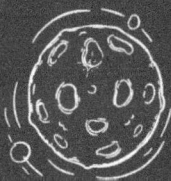

Annwn

Tartarus

CHARACTER LIST

A PRONUNCIATION GUIDE CAN BE FOUND AT THE BACK OF THE BOOK.

Benjamin/Ben – (he/him) A shtriga and Guardian of Gaia. Former court physician to King Arthur and apprentice of Merlin. He was a warlock in his human life and his magic is called Ambrosius.

Jack – (he/him) A vampire and Benjamin's partner.

April – (she/her) A hunter.

Fate – (she/her) The God of time and creator of the universe. She writes history and builds worlds.

Barqan – (she/her) A Djinn Queen and Guardian to Avalon.

Chaos – (they/them) Creator of the Gods and the first universe.

Charon – (he/him) Guardian of Styx, ferryman of the dead.

Hades – (he/him) God of Hades.

Hecate – (she/her) Guardian of Fae.

Artemis – (she/her) Guardian of Hades, the realm.

Arthur – (he/him) Former King of Gaia. Previously in a relationship with Benjamin.

Merlin – (he/him) Advisor to King Arthur. Fate's husband and Benjamin's mentor and best friend. Merlin was responsible for creating the Guardianship. His magic was called Emrys.

Mórrígan – (she/her) Deceased. The God of War. Ex-wife to Merlin. As War, she is responsible for creating and resolving conflict.

Magic – (shares its owner's pronouns). Magic manifests itself in characters with natural magical abilities (Ben, Merlin, for example). Their magic has its own identity and personality which represents the side of the character that others wouldn't see.

REALMS AND GUARDIANS

Avalon – The uppermost realm, inhabited by the Gods. Guardian: Barqan. God: Fate.

Gaia – An upper realm populated by Mortals. Guardian: Benjamin and Merlin. God: Freyja.

Fae – An upper realm populated by witches, wizards, warlocks and mages. Guardian: Hecate. God: Nyx.

Erebus – Destroyed. An under realm populated by vampires. Guardian: Keres. God: Lamia.

Tuonela – Destroyed. An under realm populated by werewolves. Guardian: Kalma. Gods: Tuoni & Tuonetar.

Annwn – Destroyed. An under realm populated by shtrigas.

Guardian: Cerridwen. God: Arawn

Styx – The first level of hell where souls come to cross over. Populated by ghosts and ghouls. Guardian: Charon The Ferryman. God: Mórrígan, prior to her death.

Hades – The second level of hell populated by demons and the damned souls. Guardian: Artemis. God: Hades.

Tartarus – The third level of hell where the most evil souls and disgraced Gods who have broken the law are imprisoned. Populated by night–shades, shapeshifters and tricksters. Guardian: Menoetius. God: Chaos.

Purgatory – A featureless plane inhabited by deceased supernatural beings. It takes its shape around the individual's insecurities, fears and worst memories.

The Nothingness – The centre of the universe where Time resides. It is a vacuum-like state where Gods and supernatural creatures go when they die. There is no return from here.

1

THE WINTER

DECEMBER, OXFORD

T he harsh glare of a security light interrupted Jack's unrelenting tears. His feet had carried his aching body to the
ramshackle house on their own. His hands hovered just above
the splintered gate that led to the path, that led to the front door,
that was marred by scratch marks. Jack shook his head, trying to
erase the long list of things that had changed since – no!
He wasn't going down *that* path. He wasn't so sure that he
wanted to walk up the one in front of him, either.

Jack had gone back to the start.
He'd looked in the tavern, he'd turned his apartment upside
down, he'd yelled his anger from the Bodleian's roof. He'd given
his grief to the bitter wind, but it couldn't carry such a burden.
Jack had taken himself on a tour of the rooms and the places
they'd haunted, desperate to find pieces of *him*.

And now he had reached the rickety gate.

1

The last place to look.

The wind pushed past him, nudging the gate open, disturbing a pile of leaves that skittered across the cracked path. Curls of smoke snaked up from the lifeless body in Jack's arms. Ambrosius oozed to the surface, engulfing the body in a shroud of brilliant, orange embers. The wind cupped its eager hands around the ashes, and *he* was gone.

'Stop it! I don't –' Exhaustion pulled Jack through the gate; he stumbled and fell. He rolled onto his back and found himself staring at a night sky laden with blurry stars. The very same stars had greeted him after he'd awoken from Merlin's enforced sleep. By Jack's reckoning, a year had passed, but that wasn't right. His head was all … His phone insisted that it had been four weeks.

Four weeks. Twenty-eight days down, eternity to go. November had given way to December, and wasn't that just the loneliest thing? Time was careening on, whilst he meandered about, unable to locate the one presence that had always been somewhere.

'Why?' If the stars knew the answer, they refused to tell him. 'He's gone.'

Who? the wind whispered.

'I'm not falling for that! If I say his name, you'll take it … all that's left.' Besides, Jack couldn't stand hearing himself speak it with such pain. It sounded like letting go. And if Jack let go, he would become nothing more than a black-and-white picture. Jack fumbled with his wallet, freeing the crumpled photo. He was side-on to the camera, arms dangling over the railings as he watched the water rush over the edge of the falls, his contented smile a rare treasure. 'That stupid cloak! Did you 'ave to wear it?' He hugged the picture as best he could, pictures being hard to hug. It was hard to believe that one day, Jack would forget the sound of his voice – 'Ah!' A cold, wet nose poked Jack in the neck. 'Hello doggo. Does your human know you're out?'

'A–hem?'

'Merlin?' Jack craned his neck back and was sorely disappointed. 'You're an ordinary human. The dog yours?'

'Oscar. Had too much to drink, have we?'

'Not enough!' After a parting lick, the dog trotted back to its owner. 'Aww, bye Oscar ... Merlin?!' Jack yelled, causing lights to blink on across the road. Sticky tears forced a fresh path down Jack's cheeks. His fingers came away smeared with blood. 'Not again.' Jack had been collecting cuts that he had zero recollection of receiving. Yelling into space had so far achieved nothing. But Jack had nothing better to do, so: 'Merlin!' The clouds drifted about, tucking the stars and moon in. Jack wondered if there was any point in getting up when the heavy feeling in his chest would only drag him down.

'*Warlocks. I don't see what all the fuss is about.*'

The emptiness at his centre taunted him.

'I keep forgetting. You're not there.' Jack lifted his head, looking up at the front door. If he didn't get up. If he didn't go in. If he held his breath, if he stopped another minute from slipping past, then ... 'But you're not running late.'

A cloak swirled around a scrawny figure in the living room

window. Jack scrambled to his feet, dropping the front door key in his haste. The door punched a hole into the wall. Nothing but Jack's heavy breathing came back to him. He tore through the house, broken glass and salt lines crunched underfoot. He burst into each room, clearing them quickly. 'Don't play with me!' Jack's frustration echoed round the empty bathroom. He jumped, rather than ran, down the stairs, skidded round the corner and came across his quarry sitting at the kitchen table on the only upright chair.

'You,' Jack choked, 'should not be here.'

'Were you not calling for me? Beg your pardon, I misheard.' Merlin made to stand.

'Sit down!'

'Oh, don't look at me like that,' Merlin snapped, 'with your how-could-you-kill-him eyes. Of course I could! And look at that, the world has carried on without him.'

Razor-sharp fangs tore at Jack's gums, but he held strong. 'You make it sound like you inadvertently stepped on a bug.'

'That scene in the woods always ends with his death. One way or another.'

'It would be oh-so-satisfying to tear you to pieces, Merlin.' Jack's hands curled into fists, urging him to let go and see where he ended up. 'There's nobody to stop me.'

'So do it. I can't say that he'd approve. Hmph.' Merlin's squared shoulders and straight back insisted that he wanted to fight just as much as Jack. But the torn robe, the stench coming from skin so dirty that Jack could write "clean me" on it, suggested that Merlin didn't want to survive it.

And Jack wasn't inclined to give Merlin what he wanted. 'By the Gods, I should have smelt you coming!' Jack's eyes were watering.

'You're one to talk, lad! I'm getting drunk from the fumes. When was the last time you did something other than moping and drinking?'
Jack's fingernails dug into his palms; he pulled back his fist, but the kitchen started to rock. He swayed to the nearest chair, missed and found it on the second try. 'Why are you being like this?' Jack asked the tabletop.

'Like what?' Merlin pouted, channelling his inner petulant child.

'Like you don't care. Like he meant nothing to you, like, like, it didn't take everything you had to do that?'

'You can't say his name, can you?' Merlin goaded, his eyes roaming over the busted back door.

'And you can?' Jack asked in disbelief. Merlin met his gaze with eyes that were all storm clouds, boredom, and unspoken plans.

'You should board that door up. Anything could get in.'

'Clearly.'

'I suppose he broke it, when the three of you left? Hmph ... You'd like it even less if I said his name, lad. Perhaps I shall never speak it again. What point is there in breathing life into a dead thing?'

The hurricane in Jack's mind stalled. The static that had

plagued his mind for weeks, stopped. Sitting amongst the dust and the debris was Merlin, imploring Jack with bloodshot eyes, to put him out of his misery.

The warlock had seen a great deal in his long life, had double-crossed the best double-crossers and committed atrocities in his service to Fate, and he was stalling for time that wasn't his to grasp.

'I am a Guardian, Jack –'

'So was he!'

'And his service ended. It was for –'

'Don't say it!' Jack jabbed an accusing finger into Merlin's face. At least he meant to, his aim was a tad off.

'You're the second Guardian now, like it or not.' Merlin pushed Jack's hand aside. 'Without your help, the people of this realm will be dead before year's end.' Merlin paused. 'They would have been dead sooner if –' Merlin stifled Jack's protest with a raised hand. 'He would have become distracted and gotten himself killed, chasing after Arthur. Or you. Or the girl. If something had happened to either of you, he'd have ripped worlds apart trying to make it right.' Merlin pulled out a pocket watch that was either invisible or imaginary.

How this lunatic had ruined both of his lives, Jack didn't know.

'Why are you moping, lad – you got what you wanted? He is free of his responsibilities.' The imaginary pocket watch returned to the folds of Merlin's robes.

Laughter that wasn't borne of humour jumped up Jack's

throat. It was his fault, obviously. He didn't specify that the three of them should make it out alive. Jack slumped onto the table, arms folded, head atop them. He had been warned about summoning Merlin. That was on Jack. And that premonition! 'If April had –'

'Where is the girl?' Merlin craned his neck, looking into the hallway behind Jack.

'I'm not sure exactly.' The last time Jack had seen April, she'd been holed up in his apartment. He'd left. Or had April gone first? Jack couldn't remember; everything had blurred into one insignificant event. 'She's safe.' That much Jack had remembered to care about.

'You know,' Merlin interrupted Jack's train of thought, 'that she has magic?'

'I've seen it working its way over her wounds.'

'You didn't see it before?' Merlin laughed. Jack had to sit on his hands. 'Premonitions are my bread and butter. That would explain why she doesn't like me.'

'Sure, that's the only possible explanation.' Jack was going to find her as soon as Merlin left. 'Did you really trap Arthur's soul in the sword?'

'Yes.' Merlin leaned back in his chair, his beady little shark eyes darting over Jack's face.

Jack puffed his cheeks out. 'Is, is, he still in there?' The throbbing in his temples threatened to ratchet up a few notches.

'Stupid questions are a waste of time.' Merlin tossed his cloak across one shoulder for dramatic effect.

'Just asking! I'd have thought you'd have gotten him out already.' Not that Jack wanted Arthur back. If *he* hadn't have made Jack promise –

'All in good time.' Merlin's hands disappeared up his sleeves.

'Oh, is he not done yet? Needs another year?' Jack massaged his temples, not that the stomping headache cared. 'Are you planning on leaving shortly? I'm not drunk enough to deal with this. Or am I too drunk?' There was a flash of silver up Merlin's sleeve and Jack realised with mounting dread that Merlin still had the dagger. 'You've pissed Fate off big time, haven't you?' Jack searched Merlin's eyes and read it in his body language.

'Hmph! You cannot ask tomorrow what it will be. You'll have to wait and see.' Merlin stood, holding his cloak together with one hand. 'Find the girl.'

'You can't pull rank! It's an equal partnership! I think.'

Merlin tipped his head back, laughed with his entire body and vanished.

Defeated, Jack's bones gave up and he slumped forwards, grateful of the table's solid support. Nothing was stirring in the heavy silence but for the persistent tick-tock of out-of-sync clocks. At least six were cuckoo clocks. If they chimed in unison, Jack would burn the house down. April would encourage Jack, but she probably didn't want to talk to him. He'd become uneasy in company that wasn't his own. That's when the drinking had started. Jack pulled his phone out with shaking hands and choked back a sob. He kept forgetting that his lock screen had become torture by photograph. There weren't so many numbers in his phonebook, it wasn't difficult to find April's. Jack exhaled and dropped his head onto his hands. She was going to be furious. In Jack's defence, he had been using all of his energy on functioning. April had stopped trying to phone him over a week ago. He hit the call button.

The dialling tone screamed for so long that when April's stilted 'hello?' replaced it, Jack thought it was her voicemail.

'Jack?'

The concern in April's voice was too much. He ended the call. His phone started buzzing immediately. April's name stared up at him from the flashing screen. Jack just couldn't get his mind to stay focused on one thing for very long, not unless that thing was –

Jack snatched the phone up, 'April?'

'Hi.'

He could feel her searching for something other than *how are you?*

'So ... What have you been up to?'

'Oh, you know, this and that.' Jack searched his surroundings for inspiration. 'DIY.' Great, now he was going to have to fix something. 'How are you feeling?'

'My injuries have healed, thanks to magic that I didn't know I had. And I maybe, definitely, set some of your blinds on fire – it was an accident!'

'Oh?'

'You're not mad?'

'They're just blinds.' Perhaps it would have bothered him

9

before. 'Still figuring your magic out, huh?'

'It's only been a month! If you came home every once in a while, you'd have been able to save your apartment.'

'You haven't burnt it down, have you? Blinds are one thing, but the flat itself ... Magic isn't my thing, it's –'

'Yeah. About that, how are you?' April asked softly.

'I'm not anything right now.' Jack stood and stretched his sluggish limbs, his attention drifted out the window. The garden was torn up from Barqan's fight with –

'And that's alright, Jack.' With no purpose, he wandered through the house. He let his fingers trace over dust-coated objects, the knick-knacks of a life now fled.

'Is it because of the premonition?'

'Gods, no! Of course not!' Jack found himself sat on *his* bed, surrounded by clean washing. The shtriga never had much patience for laundry.

It was the most banal thing, and it crushed him. Jack just about stifled a sob by burying his face in a shirt, relieved that April couldn't see him collapse in on himself. He didn't want to face the world right now, but he clearly still meant something to April. Enough for her to worry. And that made everything worse. Because Jack hadn't been worrying about anybody but himself. Grief's currents were strong, and he'd not been fighting back. He'd lost all perspective, unable to keep sight of himself. Priorities and responsibilities seemed so insignificant. And with Merlin back, Jack had no choice but to pay attention. He stuffed some of the clothes, the watch that *he* usually didn't go anywhere without, and some photos into a holdall. 'He'd sort this stuff out properly another day, when it felt less like Jack was throwing *his* life away. 'He wouldn't be very impressed with me, would he?' Jack's laugh was shaky.

'He'd have gone to pieces if it had been the other way around.'

'I wish it had been.' Jack couldn't rescue it from the awkward silence that caught it with open arms. 'Anyway, how are you?'

'Yeah, I don't think we can sail past that one.'

'Could we try?' Jack threw the bag into the chair by the window. He took a deep breath and forced himself to leave the comfort of their bedroom.

'Don't buy into it too much ... I miss him too, Jack.'Why was April better at this than he was? She deserved better than him. Jack grabbed the bag and left the room without looking back. 'I'm sorry April, I've not –' The door to the office was slightly ajar. Jack hadn't been into the office before. It wasn't that he was forbidden, Jack had just respected his space. He leaned against the doorframe and nudged the door open with his foot.

'Where are you?' A layer of dust had already formed on the desk, as if it had pre-empted its owner's death and had settled into its long stretch of disuse. Stacks of plastic boxes crammed full of envelopes lined the walls, stacked floor to ceiling.

The letters.

Curiosity pulled Jack further into the room where the shortest stack of boxes came up to his shoulder. He mouthed a silent 'What the hells?' as he gave one of the boxes a light kick.

'The house. I have never understood why he needs an office.

What business does he have that needs conducting from an office?' Jack couldn't commit his partner to past tense.

'Shtriga business? Want me to come over and help?'
Jack absentmindedly opened the curtains to let the moonlight filter in. 'It's alright. I didn't come here to sort stuff out.' With his spare hand, Jack dragged a stack of boxes over to the worn leather armchair wedged into the only corner not occupied by boxes. The moonlight bathed the chair in silver. Jack let the windowsill take his weight. 'Oh; watch out, there's a Merlin about. And I'm not talking about the bird.'

'That's what Merlin looks like! A bird!' April said with satisfaction. 'That nose could be a beak. Anyway, did he speak to you?'

'In riddles.' The edge of the top box's lid bit into Jack's finger. He steeled himself and popped the lid off. His hand ghosted over the ridges, plucking one at random. A neatly penned 'M' sat in the centre of the page. Of course. 'Don't open the door.' Jack sat, tucking one leg underneath him, fingers tapping indecisively against the envelope.

'Doors aren't an obstacle for Merlin.'

'Don't go inviting him in, is what I'm getting at. He's up to something.' Jack slipped the piece of paper out, trying to ignore how dirty the guilt felt. Its contents weren't much of a surprise. 'He's in some sort of trouble. I could see it in his eyes.' Hoping to find a letter addressed to him, Jack plunged his hand into the pile and came up with a letter addressed to Arthur. 'Son of a bitch!'

'What?!'

Jack didn't know why the idea that his boyfriend had been writing letters to his 'dead' ex bothered him, but it did.

There was a scandalised gasp from the other end of the phone. 'Are you poking about in his drawers?'

'Of course not!' Jack slid the lid back onto the box.

'Liar.'

'Somebody has to sort this stuff out.' It was a lame excuse, he knew it. 'He wrote to everybody but me.'

'He didn't need to write to you, did he?'

Jack was going to spin it into a conspiracy theory all the same. Outside, a lone bird sang out. If April were with him, she'd have pushed him aside in order to riffle through the boxes first. Her curiosity must have been killing her. Jack slipped his finger behind the crimson seal. The crack raced across the faded imprint of Excalibur. Oh well, he had to read it now. 'Can I call you back?'

'Don't. Read. The. Letters. Jack.' April ended the call.

539AD

Dearest Arthur,

Two years have at once flown and dragged by. Searching for a way to undo that which was so brutally executed, is a fruitless labour. The stars alone understand; to cease would be to sever us from one another. The music of your voice is already fading.

How is it, that the one who meant so much to me, can slip through the cracks in my mind? Memories are troublesome. They dismantle my *entire being. No longer can I tell what goes where. My heart should not keep time when yours does not beat at all. We fitted together seamlessly, and I will never find another as compatible as you.*

It was always you. It will always be you.

Love,

Benjamin

It shouldn't matter.

The ink was so faded it was hard to read.

Jack hadn't even been born at that point.

The room felt rather warm all of a sudden. It wasn't a surprise, but Jack hadn't needed to read about it in *his* own hand. He scrunched up the letter.

A new envelope on the desk arrested Jack. It bore Merlin's spider-like handwriting. Jack broke the seal and tried his best to decipher the mess. 'How, after all of these years, have you not learnt to write properly? A five-year-old could do a better job.' Sufficiently annoyed, Jack began recognising words.

Benjamin,

'Oh gods, Merlin's writing letters to dead people now? I'll have to board up the letter box.'

That which might have been and what is leads to the same place. For us, there was no other scenario. Do you understand now?

There's nothing we can do about the past. Just be thankful it was then, and this is now. You're all the different tastes and flavours you made out of yourself.

You are wiser for it all. Be proud of where you stand. Try not to miss yourself; the person you were before your first heartbreak, before I betrayed you — he's not worth mourning. You allowed the ghosts of the past to wield such power over you. Shame. Mayhap a lesson learned.

It was excruciatingly painful. I want you to know that. I urge you to remember all that I lost. And the losses we shared, such as my daughter.

There is no good. No evil. Just power and keeping that power in balance is me.

Merlin

P.S. You should not be reading other people's correspondence, Jack. I know that you are incapable of stopping yourself, but it is rude, lad.

Poking out from underneath a notebook was the side of another envelope. 'I should have made you go to therapy.' Jack fished it out and noticed it was addressed to him. 'Huh.' He sat back down in the chair with a thud, his phone buzzed furiously in his pocket, forcing him to put the letter down.

'April! I got caught up – not looking in drawers.' He shoved the letters into his pocket and stood to leave.

'Merlin stopped by. Appeared in your kitchen, looking like he'd wandered through a cage fight on the way. Muttered something about them being idealistic young men. Said that chivalrous words and good deeds won't fix every problem. Took off before I could say a word.'

'Woah, April! Breathe. I've got to find a way to keep him out. Draft excluder maybe?'

'Do you think he Flat Stanleys his way into rooms?'

'I don't know what that is, but he's definitely lost it.'

'An unstable warlock is just what we need.' He recognised the clicking sound of a pen and knew that she was fidgeting. 'He's always been unstable, April. With any luck he's crumbling from the inside out.'

'Ouch!'

'If Merlin has the nerve to talk like a shell–shocked soldier, I'll return fire. I have no sympathy –'

'Jack –'

'Merlin picked up the knife. But oh, *Fate's* more persistent than Death; *Fate* can't be denied; there's no creature that can outrun *Fate*; better he die at the hands of a friend. If he doesn't die today –'

'Put the phone down, girl.'

Panic hotwired his mind, forcing him to listen to the footsteps approaching her.

'April?'

The line went dead.

2

ANCIENT NAMES

JACK'S FLAT

April held the phone away from her ear.

The far-too-tall bundle of tattered robes and grey-black cloak stopped barrelling towards her. April's dinner tried to reappear – it needed to wash its rags, because it reeked of decaying flesh and something else that April couldn't name.

'Are you looking for Jack?'

'No.' Skeletal fingers that were almost translucent crept out of its sleeves and lifted back the hood of its cowl. Below the translucent skin, its skull poked through. Behind its sunken, cataract eyes, the sockets were black holes in the middle of its gaunt face. And unless her eyes were deceiving her, there were maggots crawling over its bones. It dropped its head to one side, stretching the skin over its skull, its cloudy eyes seeing her all too clearly. Her dinner jumped back up her throat. April held up one finger and legged it to the kitchen sink. It floated along behind her. She squeezed her hands shut, trying to grab a hold of her magic. It was nowhere to be found.

'Are you looking for me?'

'No.' The blunt reply pricked April's confidence. It was ridiculous; having to stall for Jack because her magic was difficult at best. Living on the fifth floor was all well and good for Jack, but April couldn't jump out the window.

'Are you going to tell me who, or what, you are?'

'No.' It tilted its head to the other side, dislodging a few maggots.

'Are you going to say anything other than no?'

'No.' Another head tilt. More projectile maggots, some of which landed on April's boot. She violently flung her foot about. It bent forwards, hand outstretched. April held her breath. It nudged the maggot into a cupped hand and gently returned the squirming critter to its eye socket.

'There's nobody else here,' April insisted.

'There is more than one way to be present.' It took another menacing step forwards and the cold steel of the sink bit into her lower back.

'Oh child, Jack will not arrive in time.'

April's lungs tried and tried to fill with air, but they couldn't, her skin broke out in goosebumps. April fumbled behind her, seeking a knife in the pile of washing-up. It leaned in closer, seeing right through her. A hand brushed against her cheek, cold as the grave. April swung a butter knife; the skeleton caught her wrist. A silvery light bloomed from the skeleton's hand, transfixing

April. She wanted nothing more than to tumble head-first into the warm, soothing glow, that suggested everything would be alright for the rest of eternity. The light stretched and swallowed the apartment. April relaxed, floating in the comfortable numbness. The skull materialised in the light and April understood that she was staring Death in the face.

'You have nothing I desire. At least, not today. Do not give me cause to harm you.'

She was ejected from the warm, comfortable light. The knife clattered on the ground. The faintest prickle of pins and needles in her arms had April trying to imagine freeing herself from the skeleton, but the pins and needles vanished.

Its knowing smile showed teeth that outnumbered the stars. 'Magic requires a name, child. That is why it refuses you.'

'Thanks?' The clocks in the flat suddenly sounded rather loud. As if time felt itself running out when in the presence of Death. 'I assumed you weren't Fate – you don't look like Merlin's type.'

'No.' Death laughed a laugh that carried for years and years, dropping into a little bow.

The Grim Reaper, death personified had trapped her in Jack's kitchen.

Her magic had nothing to say about it.

A long, flowing turquoise dress rippled past them and into the hallway. 'And who have you brought with you, Death?'

'*I* am Fate, and, you – ' Fate ran her eyes over April, ' – are not at all impressive.'

'And you, are not nearly enough to drive Merlin mad.' April

held Fate's gaze whilst Death choked on a snort of laughter. 'You just missed him. Merlin.'

'It is you that I seek. I shall deal with Merlin and his transgressions in due course.'

'And you brought Death with you because?' She didn't know what was taking Jack so long.

'Death has business with Merlin –'

'He left. Via the door. Over there.' April pointed behind them but neither fell for it. She dug down and screamed internally at her magic.

'You are an enigma.' Death moved to one side to allow Fate better access. Long manicured nails dug into April's cheeks. 'You emerged from nowhere, became tangled in Benjamin's mess. Your proximity to the Guardian is not enough to mask your death, and yet, your path is unknown to me. Why is that?'

'As the only person here who hasn't seen the future, I can honestly say I don't know what I'll grow up to be. A dinosaur maybe. That's what I wanted to be at school.'

Fate pulled April closer towards her. 'It is excruciating, to not have a clear picture. Perhaps the problem was with myself, but I have never been wrong about these things. So, I consulted Death.'

'Thanks?'

Death nodded in acknowledgement, head to one side, realisation in their dawning in the cloudy eyes. April looked away, worried that Death was changing their mind about not being interested in April. She kinda wished that Merlin hadn't left.

'Death could offer no insight. Merlin refused to share his interest in you.'

'Merlin isn't interested in anybody but himself.'

Fate laughed darkly. 'When you have known him as long as I, you shall know that is not true.'

'Will I get that chance?'

'No.' Fate's silver magic glistened in her hands.
A calmness washed over April. From the oldest part of her being, a name punched through the serenity.

'*Vivienne Eilir.*'

'*Vivienne?*' Nothing. '*Vivienne-Eilir?*' April held her breath, but the name wouldn't fit her magic. Death shifted forwards ever so slightly, their frustration wrapped around her, making it harder to focus.

A crash startled them, and Fate arched backwards, her hands swatting at whatever had grabbed her hair, but the unseen entity threw her into the far wall. Death turned their fathomless eyes back to April, that silvery light started to grow again.

'Vivienne Eilir!' The two words felt like ashes from a long-dead fire in her mouth.

'I don't think that's a spell.' Jack's voice couldn't have sounded any better than it did at that moment. 'Try again?'

'Vivienne.' The name felt stronger. The feeling of belonging intensified.

The name was hers. Not her magic's. *Hers.*

'Eilir!' The faintest prickle of pins and needles tingled in the tips of her fingers. 'Eilir – you're called Eilir?!' The pins and

21

needles feeling nodded in April's mind. She looked Death straight in their eyes. 'It's not my time.' The confidence, the certainty, the feeling familiar enough with Death to defy them – that was all Eilir. April wanted to hit pause, to ask questions – so many questions – but Death was reaching for her throat and Eilir rushed forwards to fill her mind. April's hands came up, encased in the jade glow. She blinked, able to see Jack grappling with Fate at vampire-speed, her entire body on fire with pins and needles.

'*When I tell you to, push the spell at Fate.*' Eilir's calm, rich voice made April jump. '*Ready ... and ... now!*' April pushed forwards with all of her weight, wobbling on her tiptoes. Eilir barged into Death's shoulder – the silvery light extinguished itself – and ricocheted off in Fate's direction. The impact reverberated in April's head. She peeked through her fingers, just to check that she hadn't shot off to another realm or something. Death climbed back to their feet with a rattle of bones and dusted off their sleeves. They inclined their head in a small bow and disappeared.

'What. The. Hell?!' April asked of nobody in particular, hands on her head.

'Sneaking up on the kid when she's alone is, by itself, a dick move. But bringing Death for backup? That's out of Merlin's playbook.' Jack huffed as he heaved Fate off of him.

'Death will return.' Fate stood, hair and dress dishevelled, sneering at them.

'Wonderful, I look forward to it.' Jack flashed Fate a quick grin loaded with contempt.

April knew that she'd gotten incredibly lucky, and the ancient beings were talking, but she'd been holding it together for weeks with nobody to talk to. 'What gives you the right to destroy entire worlds?'

'If Merlin had returned home when asked, perhaps I would have allowed this universe another eon. And how the Gods whine about their assignments to those awful realms. I was sick of listening to them. But that's the beauty of drafts, you can scrap one and start another.'

'You can't just kill the Gods because they irritate you! And too bad if the Guardians stop you from getting what you want, you're not two, deal with it.'

'April!' Jack said sharply.

'They'll be reborn eventually.' Fate levelled a pointed stare at Jack. 'All except one.'

Dumbfounded, April looked to Jack.

'Gods are selfish, uncaring creatures, kid.' Jack shrugged, not taking his eyes off of Fate. 'I am monumentally tired and you, Fate, are interfering in my mourning. I'm not giving you the talisman. I'm not giving you April. You're not destroying Gaia. We can talk, we can fight, or you can leave. It's your call, my lady.'

'How gracious of you!' Fate scoffed.
April stepped up beside him, a ball of jade magic pulsing in her hands.

'Don't mistake this as kindness, it's just poor timing. Merlin wouldn't have killed my partner if you hadn't backed that lunatic into a corner. You will pay for that. Not today. I have other

23

business.'

'Poor timing is the coward's excuse. I'll let you have this moment, as there won't be another.' Fate threw open a portal, seeming to dislike the stillness of Jack's voice.

'What took you so long?' April grumbled watching her magic die down and fade.

'I got here as quickly as I could! It's busy out there, lots of people to dodge.' Jack stuffed his hands into his pockets and felt the pointy edge of a letter jab him. 'I need to look for something. Five minutes and I'm all yours.' He turned before April could stop him. Her magic might enable her to slow time enough to follow his movements, but she couldn't physically keep up with him. He shut himself away in the bedroom, dropped the bags of Ben's stuff and took out the letter with shaking hands.

13/02/1999

Dearest Jack,

I had the strangest premonition last night. I saw you, a hundred years from now (at least that's what it felt like). You were sat on your bed, reading a letter. Heartbroken. A huge storm cloud ready to burst. There was nothing to be done.

Whatever upset you so, it's not worth it. Sadness is a funny thing. Time does a wonderful job of removing feeling. Whatever you are feeling right now, it will ease. You'll be able to breathe again. In time. I don't say it enough, but you are all that matters to me.

Wherever you are, wherever you go, I go with you.

I hope I never have to deliver this letter. But if I do, may it bring you peace. I thought I'd known love before. I was wrong. We fitted together seamlessly.

I've said that before, to somebody else.

I didn't mean it. I wanted to, but ...

It was always you. It will always be you.

Love,

Benjamin.

3

TWENTY MILES

The best place to hide was just behind the person chasing you.

The best place for Merlin to hide was in the hallway outside Jack's apartment. Death wasn't going to take April. A little peril would force the girl into connecting with Eilir. And the bundle of fangs and anxiety was going to shoot past him in:

three,

two,

one –

Jack crashed through the front door. The blast of air from the apartment crackled with an energy that hadn't been used in quite some time. The door swung back on itself and hid April from view.

Things were playing out exactly as Merlin had foreseen.

A silver, wispy wraith poked its head through the middle of Jack's front door, its cloudy eyes locked onto Merlin straight away.

'I should inform Fate of your presence.' The rest of Death slid through the door and darted over to Merlin.

Sometimes, the worst place to hide was just behind the person chasing you.

Merlin leaned back against the wall, arms crossed over his heart that beat a little too quickly. 'Are you just going to float there? What if somebody wants to get by? They'd have to walk through you! Hmph. It's hard to take you seriously when you're slithering about like an airborne snake.'

Death's eyes blazed, threatening, well, death, but then they crinkled as a creaky chuckle escaped from the skeleton. 'My presence here surprises you, Merlin.'

'Prophetic sight isn't twenty–twenty. I wasn't with Fate for her sparkling personality. I prefer to be informed.' Merlin shivered and it had nothing to do with the lack of carpet in the brick and concrete corridor. Death knew something they should not.

'Indeed. You have yet to reveal the truth to the girl. Most curious.'

'Leave life to the living, Death. I'll play my hand as I see fit.' Merlin readjusted his robes, Jack's cold voice washed up against the door, but Merlin couldn't make out Fate's reply. It wasn't time for the truth, not just yet. And even if it were, Merlin wasn't sure that he was prepared.

'The trickster's cloak no longer fits you. Set it aside. Deceit is the heaviest weight a heart can carry. We must think of the scales.'

'It's all a matter of what the individual thinks.' Merlin shrugged nonchalantly. 'If you're inclined to feel guilty over the

27

smallest thing, then you've damned yourself before you even reach the scales.' Though required to remain impartial – something that Death was proud of – Merlin was struggling not to bow his head under Death's ready judgement.

'That,' Death said sternly, 'is a matter that concerns my agents. It does not concern wayward warlocks who have forgotten not only their place but have deemed their actions outside of all laws.'

'That's uncalled for,' Merlin grumbled, returning the concerned stare of Jack's next-door neighbour who poked her head around her door, darted out, shut it and half ran down the hallway, past Merlin, and down the stairs.

'Congratulations on fooling your friends, and to a certain extent, Fate.'

Jack detested him. Benjamin had disowned him. And truth be told, so had Arthur.

'I see you, Merlin. Wherever you think to go, I am present.'

'Kindly hurry to the point, Death.' Merlin pushed himself off the wall and came nose-to-nose with the reaper. Galaxies swirled in Death's unamused eyes, suggesting all of the ways they could make the rest of Merlin's existence a misery. He held his breath, his entire body numbed by Emrys' desire to flee.

'Arthur was in my care! I warned you then that I would overlook it once, and once only. The circumstances being as they were. But the fact remained that you'd taken a life before it was due.'

'Benjamin's change –'

'Did not restore the balance! His existence was altered. And then you meddled further!'

'Technicalities!' April's raised voice caught Merlin's attention. Emrys twisted into knots, pulling Merlin towards the flat. Death grabbed Merlin's collar and pinned him in place.

'You cannot leave anything alone for longer than a century!' Death's bony finger stabbed at Merlin's chest. He pushed Death out of frustration. The hallway vanished, causing Merlin to levitate in the depth of space and time. He wrapped his arms around himself, longing for his cloak in the freezing expanse of space.

'Warnings have no impact on you, Merlin, so I will speak plainly.' Death's voice boomed across the universe. Merlin looked down; his stomach tried to follow. Death had him dangling in the nothingness of the cosmos, of time itself, from whence Chaos and Death had come. 'Leave Arthur where he is. Do not place souls into my care before their time. And, if you only remember one thing, let it be this – cease meddling with the natural laws. You are not so clever that you can outmanoeuvre me.'

Merlin scowled at a distant, blinking star, unable to fathom why Death couldn't understand. Merlin was ensuring that there was a universe left in which to enforce the natural laws. The Gods expected him to keep Fate in line but complained when he did. He was damned if he did, damned if he didn't.

'Merlin! Do you understand?'

'Yes! Now if you don't mind, I was eavesdropping.' Death stared long and hard into Merlin's soul – a novel experience given that it was one of Merlin's favourite tactics. With a snap of bony fingers, Merlin's feet mercifully touched down on a solid floor.

'*Thank* you!' Merlin pushed his ear against the door, just so he didn't have to look into Death's displeased face any longer.

'Carry on as you are, and I will deposit you into nothingness for the rest of time,' Death said with unquestionable conviction. From the other side of the door came the tearing of the universe's fabric. 'Fate's departing. Should you be away?' Death stared long enough for Merlin to grow mildly concerned.

'I pray you understand your actions and their consequences, Merlin.' Death darted towards the door but stopped with their nose brushing the chipped wood; cold bone grazed Merlin's cheek. 'You have assembled an odd group.'

'They were here when I arrived.'

'Because you pushed them.'

Merlin turned from the door solely to roll his eyes at Death. 'If you don't mind?' Merlin gestured towards the door. Jack would do fine as a friend, but as a mentor, no. She needed to relearn magic from somebody with magic.

'Ah yes, April.' The certainty in Death's voice chilled Merlin to the bone.

'Yes, April. She's proving to be a challenge.'

'Stubbornness was her only inheritance.' Death said sternly, arms crossed in disapproval.

'She'll be your problem soon enough.' Merlin caught the nagging in Death's silence and softened his tone reluctantly. 'What would you have me say? That I failed her? Because I did. In every respect. Time and time again ... We weren't, Fate and I weren't –

I am no longer fit to be a parent. This is my one chance to make amends.' This was Merlin's greatest secret and now it rested in Death's care.

'I detest being involved in such matters. It is unseemly.'

'Yes, yes, you care only for the natural laws and the balance of the universe.'

Death shook their head in exasperated wonder. 'My involvement is a direct consequence of your decision-making.' Death glanced at the door, deep in thought. 'Fate speaks to me as if I am a hired assassin. Her quarrel with Chaos threatens the natural order of things.'

'How many wars have you endured, Death? How many times have you had your heart broken at the result of utterly mindless destruction? Trust me, please. I'll spare you another war.'

'You are the least trustful creature that has ever, and will ever, be created. Heed my words, Merlin. For the sake of your daughter, if nothing else.' Death looked past Merlin for a moment, nodding in agreement with a voice Merlin could not hear.

'Fate will not learn of your attendance, nor that her daughter lives on, not from me.'

'My unending gratitude. Sincerely.'

Death vanished, leaving behind the echoes of screams and cries of those recently reaped.

Something blunt and heavy collided with a wall inside the flat. So, Jack had read the letters.

***

Avalon

Death had meant every word. Such matters were below them. When time began, Death had been absorbed in how other creatures chose to live. Each one made curious decisions, always tangled up in emotions and fretting about their inevitable ends at the expense of their living. Death soon realised that the living were built to do just that, live and die, but damn them if they could not do so without tearing themselves apart first.

Merlin was no different.

Although he should know better.

The warlock was convinced that he was the righteous crusader, defender of the universe. Prophetic sight. Chaos' gift to mortals. Mortals with such insight tended to grow into irritating inconveniences.

Like Merlin.

Merlin would have benefitted from being wrong every once in a while. Being wrong did a world of good for a soul – shaped it nicely. And now Merlin had reached the inevitable junction that all prophets passed through – the unravelling. His time was coming to an end, and he had foreseen it.

It was safe to say that, without Merlin, Death would not be waiting in Fate's mirror room. A mirror room, of all the things! Death shifted into their human form, paying little attention to the storm wailing outside and slamming against the palace walls, seeking entry. On reflection, perhaps their human form was not as welcoming as first thought.

April was not the first to react in terror and repulsion. Death could not help but catch their reflection with every little movement. A shadow darted between the pillars littering the hall. 'Hurm, perhaps new robes are in order. What say you, Barqan?'

Barqan stepped out from behind a pillar, her footsteps echoing in the room. She was one of the few creatures who had no trouble meeting Death's eyes, but today the djinn's blue flames were burning holes in the floor. Shame and regret were new sensations for Barqan. She rung her hands together, over and over, and yes, she was quite definitely ensnared in a trap of her own making.

'If you were aware of my being here, why not call me out sooner?' Barqan glanced at Death.

Guardians weren't required to live in the shadow of their realm's god, so it baffled Death as to why Barqan skulked around Fate's palace. Avalon was a spacious enough realm; Death had to wonder why Barqan did not send herself away. Fate's presence hurtling through space was a constant bother at the back of Death's mind.

'Fate is arriving, Barqan. May I suggest you seek out a better hiding place?'

Death chuckled at the wave of panic that crashed into them. Death understood the concept of fear – they witnessed it every single day, but they had never felt it themselves. 'Why do you hide from Fate?'

'I failed to kill Benjamin and April. I prevented Gaia's destruction,' Barqan admittedly reluctantly.

'Quite commendable. Guardians are supposed to prevent such events. One could say that you were acting within your remit.' Death settled themself on Fate's ornate golden throne, knowing full well it would incense Fate. Death traced the delicate silver strands and spinning wheels that magic had woven through the gold.

'I defied my God. Questioned her decisions. You would not understand.'

'Loyalty? I expect it from the reapers.' Death crossed to the Guardian and squeezed her shoulder until she looked up. 'Your concern is misplaced. Weaker beings follow orders unerringly. Questioning something immoral, questioning a god no less. That takes strength.' Barqan blinked back tears. 'Keep questioning.' The atmosphere crackled and tore itself apart. 'Go.' Barqan darted off, leaving Death to consider their reflection in the nearest mirror, one eye trained on the space just behind their shoulder. The tiny ripple of silver magic curled in the air, looped back on itself and cut through the air like a white-hot knife. Long fingers forced the sides of the portal to part as an impatient and dishevelled Fate shouldered her way through. She skidded to a halt, dangerously close to a mirror.

'I wonder if it would be seven years bad luck for the likes of us,' Death pondered, keeping their back to Fate. 'Several hundred, perhaps.'

'Why did you leave?!'

'I am only interested in ensuring that the natural laws are observed.'

'Then relieve Merlin of his life.' Fate snapped her fingers, and her magic worked its way up her body, rearranging clothing, hair and makeup.

Death heaved a heavy sigh. 'He has been wilfully disobeying the laws since he was able to crawl. For his faults, Merlin has his uses.' Fate blinked once, her hands clenching fistfuls of her skirt. 'If you won't intervene, why are you here?'

Death reverted to their wraith form and twisted around Fate, staring her down. 'I am here to deliver the same warning that I intend to give to your estranged husband.'

In their vast experience, it was best to let Fate believe herself to be first in all matters.

'Leave Arthur where he is. Leave lives alone that are not yours to end.' Fate stiffened, her hands disappeared up her sleeves out of habit, searching for her still-missing blade. 'Cease your termination of worlds before their proper date, and, if you only remember one thing, let it be this – stop meddling with the natural laws. You are a god, madame; begin acting like one.'

Fate ripped a mirror from the wall and hurled it at Death. They remained still, listening to the roar of the tide on the beach from whence the sand had come, and felt the sway of the tree that had offered the wood for the frame. They allowed it all to pass through them without breaking eye contact with Fate. Death tripled in size, their head brushing the ceiling as they looked down at the now ant-sized Fate.

'Am I a low-level demigod? No. I am Death! I will remain long after you have bid farewell to your plans.' The disrespect alone was enough to rile Death. 'I am woven into the fabric of time and space. It is not so easy to unpick me. Time and I will stand alone whilst the rest of you all drift apart.'
Fate's hands reappeared, engulfed in magic. They were all so tiresome. Everything moved along as it should. Until Chaos created Fate. Her warning shot tinged the air around Death.

'Keep on as you are, and you will have no lives to spin.' Another bolt of silver bounced off Death's shoulder. 'I cannot fathom why Merlin expends so much energy fleeing Avalon.'

Point made, Death took their leave. Perhaps it was an inherent feature of gods, to think they were the single most important entity in existence. They too would eventually answer to Death, of course.

Death was the only thing a soul could rely on.

4

BURY ME

OXFORD

J ack cast a doubtful eye over the scorch marks on the floor, the kitchen cabinets missing their doors, and returned his armchair to its feet, ignoring the acrid stench of smoke and magic that hung in the air.

'So, your magic –' his stomach dropped. 'No, no, no!' He hurried over to the scorched bookcase and ran his hands over the distressed wood. Book covers creased with use now sported black singe marks, some were missing pieces, and some were nothing more than piles of ashes.

'They're just books, Jack.'

'Just books?' He scooped up a pile of ashes and thrust them at April. 'Fix it!'

'Not unless you want to lose more books. I'll replace them. What's the big deal?'

'*He* got them for me.'

'*Oh.*' April's eyes widened with regret. 'Sorry.'

Jack dropped his gaze, his face on fire. The pit in his stomach grew wider. His skin tried to crawl away from him. He carefully returned the ashes to the shelf.

'It should really come with a warning label: CAUTION! Do not use in confined spaces.' There was a laugh in there somewhere, but Jack couldn't find it. His shoulders touched his ears, book ashes tickled his nose. April's arms wrapped themselves tightly around him and that only made the shame cut deeper. 'So, how'd you get your magic to work?'

'Named it,' April mumbled into his shoulder.

'Well, you can't call something if you don't know what to call.' Jack tried to sound like an authority. 'Makes sense.' Whereas the scattered debris of clothes, shoes, bags, scarfs and other assorted crap didn't. 'I have wardrobes, drawers, shelves.' The burst of magic that flared in April's hands sent Jack behind the sofa, trying to decide what to save first.

'How do I put it out?!'

Jack darted for the kitchen, looking for a tea towel. He found them all, in a pile by the washing machine. 'They're not going to throw themselves in for a spin!' He chose to overlook the piled-up dishes in the sink, grabbed a coffee-stained tea towel and ran it underneath the tap.

'You're thinking of fire!' April's magic grew in height and intensity alongside her panic.

'What's the difference? You can't control it!' Jack spun back to face her, yanking the dishwasher open. 'We really need to talk about you putting stuff away.'

'In my defence – ' April sheepishly squashed her magic between her hands until it died down. 'I was going to try cleaning it up with magic. And I didn't think you'd be back so soon.'

'That's a good use for magic.' Jack rolled his eyes, fighting the urge to clean the whole flat, top to bottom. There were crumbs on the countertops. His hand reached for a sponge of its own accord. 'Make yourself at home, I said, and you did. Ugh.' Jack filled the sink, watching the washing up liquid bubble and the water forcing the week-old stains to break apart. 'Should I look in the fridge?' He rammed the plate into the dishwasher and went for another.

April hurried over. A sliver of light illuminated her face; she shook her head. Jack averted his eyes, lest he learn of the horrors hiding in the cold. 'Did, um, did Ben name his magic?'

And there it was.

There was only so far that they could go in conversation before they bumped into *him*. The bubbles popped against Jack's hands, the light making little kaleidoscopes of colour appear. They looked like little specs of magic in every colour. April darted into view, turning the tap off. Jack splashed about in the warm water, surprised that the sink was about to overflow.

'He was aware of his magic from an early age. Ambrosius was just ... there. Magical parents.' Jack shrugged. 'Not sure if he came up with the name or if his parents suggested it.' A plate snapped in half under the water. Jack took it as a sign and dried his shaking hands. 'What did you choose?' Jack's voice cracked.

'It'll be something generic, or something ridiculous! Bob?' Jack dropped himself onto the sofa, resentful of the cheery voices coming from the car park below, accompanied by the constant ding of bike bells. Even in December Oxford was plagued by bicycles. April curled herself up in the oversized armchair as she had on her first visit. Jack caught himself staring at the empty half of the sofa and made an effort to focus.

'It's ... old ... a first and last name, I think. Just popped into my head. I've never heard either of them before. My magic named itself.'

'For the sake of my belongings, I wished it had spoken up sooner. Spit it out.'

'Vivienne Eilir. The magic goes by Eilir. Vivienne didn't do anything.' Vivienne! There was a name Jack hadn't heard in quite some time. 'Back in the day, Vivienne did quite a bit ... with Merlin.'

'What?!' April shot forwards in her chair, her hands flying up to hug herself.

'Calm down! Vivienne hung out with Merlin and eventually trapped him in a tree once she'd learned all of his secrets. There was something about Excalibur as well. Go and ask the internet, like a good millennial.'

It was meant to be a joke, April knew that. But Jack snapped the last bit. April also wasn't buying the fake smile and forced laughter. And of all the names, her magic picked that one? It couldn't be just an uncomfortable coincidence that Jack could have kept to himself. 'I can't believe Merlin did it.' Jack nodded, looking just over her shoulder. She didn't like the faraway look. It reminded her a little of Merlin, just after he'd appeared in the apartment. April hesitated, not wanting to open up her own poorly-healed wounds. Jack snatched his head up, vague recollection washing over his face. April spotted what looked to be the corner of a letter poking out of Jack's pocket. 'I told you not to go poking about!' Jack tried to look guilty, but his face collapsed back into sadness. 'At least he wrote to you. You've got something to hold onto.'

'You're jealous of Jack,' her magic insisted. So far, April wasn't friends with Eilir.

'You've got nothing of Danny's.'

'Nope, just memories.' Since meeting Merlin, large chunks of April's life prior to that night in the park had been lost, replaced by castles and people she'd never met.

'Memories fade,' Jack said with shared understanding of that particular hurt. 'You know – ' He flopped back into the cushions, pulling one into his arms. 'Loving him ... I didn't think it would take a toll on me. I tried drinking. I tried doing nothing at all. I tried to imagine loving somebody else. I tried lying to myself. I even tried thinking about it.'

April nodded in sympathy. None of that was ever going to work.

'Why did *he* put something in a letter instead of saying it to me?'

April swallowed back tears and shook her head. Jack puffed out his cheeks and nodded in agreement.

'Could you have asked Death to, I don't know, bring Ben back?' Not that she'd gotten the helpful vibe from Death. But April's soul/being/whatever was still attached to her body, so it was worth a punt.

'Death doesn't have a return policy.' Jack headed to the kitchen. He gave the kettle a shake, keeping his back to April.

'Sometimes I find myself back at the start ... I'm watching and I can't ... I changed a lot in the first year. Parts of me were tougher, others were torn to pieces ...' April winced as Jack automatically took three mugs off of the mug tree. The look of painful real-isation, though expected, brought tears to her eyes. 'Oh!' Eilir pricked at her skin with the pins and needles feeling. 'I think my magic wants to play.'

'Not indoors.' Jack threw a tea towel at her. 'My apartment has suffered enough.' Jack drummed his fingers on the kettle handle, still not really looking at her.

April stared at a speck of mud on her boots.

If she'd spoken up sooner, then maybe Jack wouldn't be star-ing at the wooden rolling pin as if it were his way out. Pins and needles flared in both arms. Eilir, it seemed, thought April should tell him. Jack and Ben had offered nothing but acceptance and friendship. They had asked her, repeatedly, to talk to them about what was going on. They'd respected her answers. They hadn't pushed her, and now Ben ... She'd been drowning in the weirdness of it all, not that that was an excuse. Jack deserved an explanation, but if he left again, April wasn't sure what she'd do.

It wasn't like she had anybody else left in this world who cared enough to keep her alive. She'd tried to explain that to Jack, right before he disappeared, but she couldn't find the words and he had already hit the self-destruct button.

'I should have told you sooner.'

'Yes. You should have.'

April expected to see her breath in the air from the coldness in Jack's tone.

'The first premonition – I didn't understand it – and I didn't recognise it until we were there.' April's fingers snagged at her hair. She kept finding little knots in it because she kept twisting it round her fingers. She should let it go, but her need to explain, to be reassured, compelled her. 'It came to me when we were sat in Ben's kitchen. Right before Barqan attacked.' April flinched, expecting Jack to yell, to round on her and demand a better explanation, but he stayed as he was, hands braced on the countertop, his head bent over the three mugs.

'Jack?'

His shoulders started to shake with quiet sobs. The guilt gripped her like a vice. April moved towards him, but the sound of Jack calling out for Ben drove her back. She'd let fear and denial rob her of her voice. The mugs crashed to the floor.

'I'm so –'

'He's dead, April!'

'I know, Jack! And I have tried and tried to help you deal with this, regardless of what I've been feeling. Not that you noticed.'

Jack stalked past her and snatched up his jacket.

43

'They don't make sense. I've had more. Merlin is in most of them. It feels like he knows I'm there. Like he's there with me, in that moment, and we're connected. Ben didn't want me to draw Merlin's attention, and now I have magic, and he's in my head somehow? Ben was right to be worried, because me having magic has brought Fate and Death to me.'

Jack put his jacket down but wouldn't look at her. She grabbed the broom and pushed the pieces of mug about. If she did a bad enough job, Jack would have to acknowledge her. He had to listen to her.

'I didn't figure it out until it was happening – I'm so sorry. It's my fault.'

Jack snatched the broom from her. He fetched the dustpan and brush, the pieces of the mugs clinked and clanked as he dropped them into the bin, his hands shaking. He pulled a new bin bag from the roll and swapped it out. He stomped to the fridge, dragging the full bin bag behind him. He peeked into the fridge and promptly shut it, disgusted; he darted to the cupboard under the sink, filling his arms with cleaning products. He looked thinner than usual, his face drawn and eyes ringed by dark circles. He was exhausted to the point of needing to feed.

'Jack? Please talk to me.'

'Let's go to the park and see what your magic can do.'

'Oh, okay.' Relief washed over April. 'Are you sure?'

'You didn't know what you didn't know.' Jack dumped the cleaning products on the side.

'Thank you. For not killing me.'

'If you die, then my only friend will be Merlin. And that's just tragic.' Jack laughed his first laugh that didn't sound forced. 'We're good. Now, mush! I don't fancy being in this apartment anymore.'

5

THAT'S WHAT YOU GET

AVALON

The hair on the back of Barqan's neck jolted to attention; she reluctantly stood, stretching in the shade of the mulberry tree. The dry heat of Avalon's desert region shimmered at the edges of the shade, waiting to embrace her. Barqan had travelled as far as her duties allowed. She'd strode through the djinn's town of red-bricked houses and sandy streets, ignoring the others who darted a variety of glances at her, out onto the sand plains with their golden-brown dunes and ridges. She walked for miles, seeking the mulberry tree, keen to sit and bask in the heat away from inquisitive stares.

If her clan didn't know of Barqan's involvement in the destruction of realms, they certainly suspected it. Djinn were made to protect, an often-forgotten fact. Now that Barqan thought on it, that might, in fact, be the crux of the issue.

They were all trying to protect something.

By gifting that responsibility to gods who once stood unified, Fate and Merlin had nurtured war. They had crafted the perfect excuse for atrocities. After all, that had been her defence when challenged over the realms. She considered herself above Merlin, but at least the warlock had not been complicit in the destruction of realms. Although they now shared the accolade of killing a fellow Guardian. Even if Merlin's murder had been more of a faux pas, a trick. Whereas Barqan's last conversation with Kalma played over and over in her head.

'*Barqan!*' Fate yelled in the djinn's mind. '*Do not keep me waiting!*'

She should have left with Death.

Barqan freed a pouch from her belt. The weight felt comforting and terrifying. Fate would kill Barqan without hesitation if she knew that she still possessed Keres' miniature wooden stake talisman.

Djinn.

The name meant a number of things, depending on the language, but it came down to two words: hide and adapt. It was in her nature, in her bones. Hiding was out of the question, it would leave Avalon free to be terrorised.

Adapting was the only logical choice.

Barqan replaced the pouch. She would wait and see where the cards fell before deciding who to give the talisman to. Fate had been too calm after the fiasco in Gaia. Merlin had done Barqan a favour by stealing Fate's blade. The distraction had provided a much-needed second in which to hide the talisman. With one last longing look at the sun-drenched sand plains, Barqan opened a portal to the throne room.

There was the inky blackness of the space, then the delightful colours of the universe, and then came the blinding flash of light rushing towards her at such a speed it looked intent on impaling her. The light fractured, tearing down the middle in a lazy curve that revealed the hazy glass of the throne room, the light outside turning the windows a dusky pink. The tiles, adorned with spinning wheel motifs, drew the eye to the glass throne at the room's centre. Barqan bobbed her head in a gesture of a bow.

Fate rose to her feet and stalked towards Barqan in one graceful motion. 'Tell me again, what became of the talismans after Mórrígan's death?'

Barqan laced her hands behind her back, lest they wander to the pouch. 'Last I saw, Benjamin held Gaia's and Cerri's. I imagine they're with Jack or Merlin now.'

'I expected treachery from Mórrígan, not from you.'

Barqan knew better than to protest her loyalty, so she dropped her eyes to the ground. Mórrígan hadn't been the god to back. At least Barqan had been able to retrieve some of the talismans. That gave her bargaining power. 'Perhaps you should search Mórrígan's hall.'

'I might just do that. As for your lack of enthusiasm in Wales –'

'Benjamin was defending his realm. I hardly thought it my place to assist War.'

'Did Benjamin chip away at your resolve? Pathetic.' Fate paced back and forth.

Benjamin had called Barqan out for what she was. And wasn't.
Perhaps Benjamin had been the only Guardian who understood
his role and honoured it. Perhaps there was a lesson to be learnt
there. Then again, Benjamin was dead. Fear was a strange thing.
Barqan considered it a river that appeared to flow one way but
was, in fact, moving in the opposite direction. Truth be told,
Fate was drowning. Fear had taken charge some time ago. Fate
remained unaware, destroying what she liked in a misguided
attempt to regain control.

'Chaos was created to meddle. Why resist?' The shadows outside the palace were lengthening. Thunder rolled across in the
distance and Barqan feared she would be trapped in the palace
overnight.

'Each realm was built to take us up and far away from Chaos'
reach. The Gods –'

'They could not build. You facilitated their escape. Alongside
your own. And you expected never-ending gratitude.'
Fate stopped, turning slowly to stare Barqan down. 'The whining was persistent. Eternal. Never a word of thanks.'
Barqan thought better of drawing Fate's attention to the thankless work Merlin and Mórrígan undertook, warding Tartarus to
ensure Chaos' imprisonment. Not that Chaos was alone down
there. They had the company of disgraced Gods and the worst
of creation.

'Whatever I built, Chaos twisted it into something ugly and
angry. I could not stand for that. Even imprisoned, there is not

a corner of any universe Chaos cannot influence. And I have grown weary of ensuring that they have enough new sport to keep them entertained.'

Fate yearned to build without Chaos tarnishing her creations. Millions of lives spun, and Fate had not learned the truth: life manifested chaos. If Barqan paid close attention to the heart of storms, she could hear Chaos roaring, feel them throwing themselves against Tartarus' warding whenever a gust of wind slammed into buildings and tore down trees. 'So much comes from Chaos – love, anger, sorrow, fear, order, excitement. All of your building blocks!'

Fate's heels clicked towards Barqan. 'So, I will design a world with a brief that does not require Chaos.'

'Death issued warnings –'

'Warnings are suggestions dressed in their best.'

To destroy her own worlds was one thing, to kill Chaos and disobey Death quite another. Death was ancient, they were the dust from which Fate created life. They kept the universes in balance. A balance that had to be maintained, for the good of every soul.

'Merlin visits Chaos.' Barqan quite enjoyed the thrill of that first tentative step onto ice that might well break under the weight of her new-found defiance. 'I hear that Arawn was far away from Annwn when Mórrígan and I visited. As a matter of fact, he's nowhere to be found ...' When last in Gaia, the rat of a God, Arawn, had failed at ceasing control from Arthur and Merlin. And Benjamin had died for the first time, so to speak.

'Thinly veiled hints at conspiracy suit Merlin alone.'

'Disregard Death, challenge Chaos and war is what we shall have –'

'There will be no war, no resistance. There are few Guardians left. Jack is subdued. Merlin will be fool enough to resurrect Arthur and when he does, you will be waiting for them, Barqan.'

Barqan sent her magic into the atmosphere, allowing it to subtly unpick the fabric.

'Open a portal and the djinn will find themselves in Death's care. Yourself included.'

Barqan recalled her magic, with great reluctance. 'What would you have me do?'

'Whatever is necessary to break the bonds of the group. Whatever is necessary to discover April's secret.'

6

SO LONG

21ST DECEMBER, OXFORD

'Try, and lift ...'

April *tried* not to huff as Jack pivoted about. Her hands had retreated up her sleeves in search of warmth an hour ago and they had no plans on reappearing until they were safely back indoors The park glistened in that hushed silence that came with fresh snowfall. The cricket pavilion seemed to rise from the snow. She'd begun to notice the hum of magic in the world around her. Traces of Emrys could be found all over Oxford, notably, throughout the park. Merlin had been casting spells. Big spells. April didn't acknowledge any time before ten am. And yet here they were in the frozen park at eight am when everybody else was still inside. Jack had forgotten how to rest. His days didn't so much as start and end as chase each other, nose over tail, into the next. He insisted on including her in his insomnia-driven insanity.

'Oh! That stone. Go on!'

'Fine.' April stamped her feet – for warmth, of course, not out of irritation, and scowled at the ground until she spotted a small rock poking its head out of the snow. April's hand darted out of its shelter to scoop up the glistening grey rock. She dipped into a bow, hand extended to Jack.

'That's not what I meant, and you know it.' Jack's encouragement seemed to be waning.

'It's easier to pick it up!' The last fortnight had spun on for what felt like four months as April wrestled with Eilir, learning how to live with this new being in her head. Eilir had yet to make a physical appearance. For her part, April had been very patient and polite, but Eilir seemed content to dwell deep inside April's mind.

'You're new to this. Give yourself a break, April.'

'Great!' April picked up another rock with her hand. Jack dragged his hand down his face. He had mostly kept his word and stuck around. Sometimes he walked the city streets or the park for hours. Routine eventually deposited him at Ben's house or the library roof. The roof being Jack's preferred spot because April couldn't get up there on her own. With considerable effort, April focused on that bundle of energy that had appeared inside her, at her core. Eilir had zero interest in picking up stones. Eilir preferred running before April could walk. Taking shots at Fate, for example. *The sooner you make it levitate, the sooner Jack leaves me alone, and I leave you alone.*

The rock stayed where it was.

'I give up! I've tried picturing what I want to happen, I tried the spell, I've tried asking it –'

'Have you tried working with Eilir? You know, treating her as part of you?'

'I guess I have been putting all the emphasis on –' The rock shook violently and started to rise. April's eyes narrowed, pins and needles poking at her hands and arms. Jack nearly smiled. And damn it, that was motivation enough. Except that her arms were shaking with the strain of fighting to control her magic. It weighed a ton. The stone plummeted back to the ground. Not that it had far to fall. Jack patted her shoulder. He wasn't disappointed with her, April thought, more his inability to help her. Eilir wrapped around the stone, and it rose a couple of feet above the ground.

'So, have you thought any more about what you want to do for Christmas?'

'Focus on the rock, for Gods' sake!'
April glanced over in shock, Jack caught her doe-eyes and he softened a little.

'I'll think about it, April.'

'We both know that I'm not going to get it any higher. What do I do with my hands? Raise them?' Jack shrugged. The rock wobbled and rose a little more. 'It's this week, you know? Wednesday, in fact.'

'Oh,' Jack replied with little interest, staring at the horizon with envy. 'What day are we on?'

'Saturday.'

Jack nodded, stuffing his hands into his pocket, chin tucked into his chest.

'We don't have to do anything,' April ventured, letting the stone drop and jamming her own hands back into her mittens, 'I need to go shopping either way. And I need to feed my cat.'

'You still have the cat?!' A spark of the old Jack flared up, his attention fixed on her, thankful for this little island of conversation that couldn't hurt.

'Yes! What was I meant to do?'

'Wait.' Jack's hand flew to April's shoulder, turning her to look him in his wide eyes. 'It's not in my apartment, is it?'

'Urm, I think you would have noticed. And *it* is a she.' The cat had, in fact, been in Jack's apartment. April had snuck her out just after Jack returned. 'When you go out, I go back to mine for a bit.'

'Oh.'

And Jack was back in the water whilst she stayed on the island. Eilir twisted herself into knots in April's mind, distraught on Jack's behalf.

'You have feelings?!' Eilir nodded and it felt like somebody had walked over April's grave. It was the strangest sensation, as if Eilir was standing behind April, always out of sight. 'So, what does one get a vampire for Christmas?'

'Ben didn't like Christmas.'

They were still getting through the *can you do the washing up? Ben used to do the washing up*, phase. 'That wasn't what I asked. I'll just get you a book.' Jack scuffed at the ground, wrestling with whatever memory was pushing him towards tears. 'You do have a lot of books already,' April sighed.

'It's not enough. An eternity without books really would be ill-spent.'

'And I guess there's not much to do over Christmas if you don't eat.' A shiver rippled down April's spine. 'I think Eilir just rolled her eyes at me!'

'Probably because you're being insensitive,' Jack scowled.

'I am being nothing but supportive!' A wave of resentment took April by surprise. She knew that Jack had to find his way through this. But she was getting tired of his sudden outbursts of irritation aimed at her.

Eilir surged through her veins, so present that April could taste something metallic. April brought her hands to her face, looking for Eilir's tiny jade embers. Nothing. This was bordering on farcical. *'What do you want to do, Eilir?'* A ball of impatient jade magic flashed into existence in her hands. April tried to squash her magic between her hands, but Eilir pushed back, fed up of being restricted. Eilir surged forwards, dragging April with her. Jack caught April. Eilir burned her hand; she let go and her magic shot off, colliding with a tree in a shower of jade sparks. Smoke plumed from the gaping hole left by Eilir. Seemingly content at having caused mild destruction, Eilir returned and died down to a faint glow in April's hands. She shook them violently, but Eilir didn't take the hint.

Jack let out a low whistle, 'Is that how my kitchen cupboards went?' April shook her head. *That* had been something else entirely. 'Well, I think we're just about done here, don't you?'

April nodded. 'Eilir is super restless, but she won't tell me why.'

'Weird.' Jack's attention was fixed on the cricket pavilion. 'I need to check in on somebody first.'

'Who?' Although April had accepted that she'd never learn all that there was to know about Jack, her trademark curiosity persisted.

'The ghost that lives in the cricket pavilion.'

But of course, what had April expected?

'I haven't seen him in a while. He usually only disappears when –' Jack froze, looking over April's shoulder. 'Put Eilir away.'

Her magic sat like a heavy block in the centre of her chest, alert and refusing to budge. 'Eilir won't –'

'Now!' Jack grabbed her arm and held firm. 'Merlin's watching us.' Jack's face was set in grim line. 'He's heading over.'

It could have been the low, soft light, or it could have been April's imagination, but she swore that she could see Jack's fangs pushing against his lower lip. Merlin's pitch-black eyes locked with hers, and an unseen hand squeezed at her throat.

Merlin stood beside an ancient oak tree in a huge estate that resonated with the power of the mighty forest it once was. Merlin stared up at the tree's branches, seemingly in conversation with it.

'You and I have a lot to do – that's what Merlin said, do you remember?'

'*Hello, Eilir. Nice of you to join us.*'

The branches of the oak tree stretched, the sound of leaves rustling filled the air, stirred by a biting wind. Merlin glanced back at her, his usual aquamarine aura a fuzzy blur of orange-blue-black-silver outlining his scrawny figure. Ben had told her that black auras meant somebody was resigned. Or coming to their natural end. The orange meant purpose. Merlin jumped at something April couldn't see.

'*And thus the whirligig of time brings in his revenges.*' Eilir poked more holes into April's worry. Eilir pulled April from the premonition, back to a reality where Merlin was almost upon her. April's breath jammed in her throat.

The out-of-control warlock caught his foot on April's pile of discarded rock and stumbled the last few steps.

'We're not interested, Merlin.' Jack stepped forwards, shielding April from the crazy. 'Were you dragged through every bush on the way here?' Merlin had lost his cloak, a large chunk of his black tunic had been torn, but not quite severed, from the rest of it, the pale skin beneath littered with angry red welts. His arms, exposed from just above the elbow, were covered in long, fine scratches.

The warlock's shark eyes were locked on hers. Emrys prodded and poked, eager for Eilir's attention. Angry, aggressive pins and needles shot down April's arms.

'Have you learnt much from Jack?' Merlin peered up at her like a lemur on drugs.

'He taught me how to make souffle. I'm still getting the –'

'I meant – ' Merlin pinched the bridge of his nose. ' – with regards to your magic.'

April stood on tiptoes to address Merlin over Jack's shoulder. 'Jack is doing fine.' She'd never throw him under the bus – especially if Merlin were driving – but they'd only found one book on magic at Ben's house. Progress had been slow.

'Then why is that tree on fire?' Merlin raised his eyebrows. 'Wouldn't you prefer to learn from somebody who has magic?' Emrys flared into the palm of Merlin's hands, illuminating his face, the silvery-black dark circles under his eyes glistened.

'Don't use it for evil, keep a true heart. Kids' movie stuff. She's figuring it out – we're figuring it out.' Jack reached behind him to pull April into some weird, defensive side hug.

'There is a great deal more to magic than that, as you well know.'

'You gave me the impression that I wouldn't see you for some time. I was looking forward to that.' If Ben were here, he'd swat the smug smile off of Jack's face and tell the vampire not to wind Merlin up.

'Time!' Merlin scoffed, swaying from foot to foot. 'What an absurd notion. A construct.' Merlin fixed Jack with an intense stare. 'He's running out of it, you know?'

'Arthur?'

It had not escaped April's attention that Jack had stuffed the talismans into a carved stone pot, adorned with knights and dragons, on his bookcase, instead of wearing them. They'd be at the bottom of the murky river if April hadn't intervened one night. Jack had drowned his sorrows and then tried to drown the King.

'I suppose he is as well.' Merlin tilted his head to one side, watching how April tried and failed to keep Eilir contained. Her magic lurched forwards, taking April with it. '*Stop drawing attention to us!*'

'If you do not have patience with yourself, your magic will have none with you.' Merlin grabbed at the air, and when he opened his clenched fist, Emrys was calmly hovering above the palm. 'Focus on one thing. It's no good if your mind is hopping from one thought to the next. Your magic?'

The name sat heavy inside her. In the back of her mind, Ben's voice insisted that if somebody didn't know her name, they couldn't curse it. Merlin edged closer, Emrys swirling around the scrawny warlock. 'Eilir.'

Merlin's bushy eyebrows jumped into his hairline, tears of recognition were quickly swiped away. Jack was right. Merlin had lost the plot.

'Eilir lives inside your intentions and your emotions. She will be getting all worked up because you are. What do you want Eilir to do right now?'

'To stop trying to drag me about and settle down.'

'Very well. Relax your shoulders; steady your breathing. That's it, deep breath in, big breath out. No, breathe from down here. Feel your magic in your core.'

'Have you been doing yoga, Merlin?' Jack stood beside her, out of his depth and searching for a trap.

'Shush you earth-vexing lout!' Merlin shook his head. 'Magic is, by nature, strong-willed but so too are those who wield it. Your task is to out-stubborn your own subconscious.'

April closed her eyes and imagined Eilir, a bundle of irritated embers stuffed inside that knight box. Eilir pushed back, climbing up the edges and forcing April to force the lid on. She counted to five, and Eilir stayed put. Her triumphant smile dropped when she clocked Merlin blinking back tears. His smile was proud and sad and conflicted all at the same time.

'Just so – ' Merlin reached for her shoulder, but Jack pulled her back. 'A few weeks in and already a better student than Benjamin.'

April wrapped her arms around Jack's, worried that he would pounce.

'Word reached me that you have been enquiring amongst the magic-users of Gaia, Jack. There is no need to search for a tutor.'

'For a million obvious reasons you, Merlin, never made the long list. Or any list. But ... it's not my decision.' Jack looked to April, anxious.

Her uncertainty extinguished Eilir. She needed to progress past levitating rocks and setting fire to Jack's kitchen ...

'Hmph!' Merlin peered up at the clouds darkening the sky. 'We're going to be late. You can decide later.'

'Late for what?' Jack asked, exasperated.

'It's the 21st of December.' Merlin released a long sigh that seemed to make the clouds rush by.

'I know. It's Saturday. What of it?'

'It's the winter solstice.' April answered for Merlin and startled Jack.

'And we should care about that, because?' Jack pushed forwards, against April's restraining arms.

'The longest night and, rather fittingly, a splendid storm, is upon us. I always find that a good storm makes spells zing that bit more. And storms are a fine backdrop for tempestuous news.' The warlock's strange, squashed giggle sounded almost nervous. 'Come now, you won't want to miss our only chance to retrieve them from Purgatory.' Merlin said as if he were reminding Jack that the shops shut earlier on a Sunday. 'We must away to Cornwall.'

'Them? Don't tell me that you trapped all of the knights in there too.' Jack groaned and freed himself from April.

'There is a very tight window in which I can perform the spell – April will assist.'

'I'm not leaving this park with you, Merlin, let alone the county. And neither is Jack.' April was going for determined but judging by the quick smile that Merlin shot her, she'd crashed into adorable.

'Miss it and we shall have to wait another year. It matters not to them, a year to us is one day for them. Like dog years but in reverse.'

'One human year equals seven dog years?' April frowned, watching a far-off dog walker collide with a park bench. Maths wasn't her thing, but that was a long time to be in Purgatory.

Jack's suspicious eyes were watching Merlin. 'Tell me who

"they" are. I'm not going into this blind.' Betrayed, April stared at Jack.

'Look, I'm no more a fan of Merlin or Arthur than you are. But if bringing Arthur back means I can hand over the talisman, I'll do it. Besides, I promised.' Jack looked so forlorn his eyes shone with tears. 'I've got a lot of life left to figure out, it'll be easier to do that if I'm not playing Guardian.'

Or worrying about unkept promises, April thought to herself. She had been pushing Jack to buy a Christmas tree when moving on really wasn't that simple. April nodded. If she spoke, she'd babble about oak trees.

'I wouldn't be in such a hurry to move on, if I were you, Jack.' Merlin laughed. 'You never know who or what we'll find in Purgatory.'

Jack stared, frozen in the moment where Merlin had so carelessly deposited hope. April allowed Eilir flare up.

'There's no need for cheap tricks, girl.' Merlin looked to Jack. 'You're so distracted by matters of the heart. Had you been paying attention when I dispatched Benjamin, you'd have noticed the spell.'

7

HAVEN'T YOU?

B en awoke reluctantly to the harsh grey light of a strange new day.

All those hours spent petitioning the moon to stop the sun from rising, and Merlin had done it for him. Ben pressed his fists into his closed eyes as the pain in his head climbed to its crescendo. It felt like a year had passed in a couple of hours. The tragedy of it all was that he couldn't remember what had started it. A battle? The sky rumbled and let go of angry rain that washed over Ben's tilted head; perhaps it would whisk away the dull, throbbing pain squatting in his chest. Through flashes of lightning the rain-darkened grey slate of Tintagel appeared – the gables of the great hall, towers, the grey curtain wall with its archway and turrets, the thatched white and black cottage Merlin had lived in, when not at Caerleon. The island courtyard! Everything was intact. Including the isthmus that the waves and tides had built up, only for it to collapse again.

'*Looks like we're nearly home, Ambrosius.*'

Ambrosius snorted. '*If home had been an illusion in a remote part of Purgatory. And considering that the entire place is remote, that's saying something.*'

His own bark of angry laughter startled him. The next time their paths crossed, he was going to throttle the warlock and then trap him in a tree. Ben couldn't fathom how such a man could have delivered, in such a manner, the fatal blow. Tears forced a new path down his cheeks, streaked red with blood. Careful prodding of his forehead revealed a sizeable cut.

'Merlin?!'

Yelling into space would achieve nothing, but it helped to vent a little. A fresh wave of grief foiled his attempt to stand, sending him crashing to the ground where he lay, curled into a tight ball, already covered in mud.

'When you get lonely, Merlin – and you will – do not seek me out.' He wiped the tears away, taking deep, shaky breaths. As if breathing could calm the raging waters of his soul. He wasn't sure where it came from sometimes, the rage. He felt justified on this occasion. Memories erected flimsy paper ladders that he climbed, forgetting that it was nothing but a cruel trick. Every damn time. Ben should have seen this coming. The signs had been there. He couldn't dwell on that now. If he were in Purgatory, then Ben could find a way out. Jack had to be worried sick. Or worse, Jack was feeling just as Benjamin had after Arthur died.

The sea, furious at Ben for forgetting his second home, swelled and crashed against the rocks, nearly swallowing the sound of the great hall's oak door cracking against the slate, thrown about by the wind. Rain thundered off of the walls, the ground, drowning out the sound of his own breathing. On his most recent visit to this clump of headland, Ben had been dismayed to find that time, the elements, and people had left the weather-beaten foundations to its decay.

The wind whipped past him, dragging icy claws across his exposed skin, intent on pushing him off the edge of the cliff.

Ancient wood groaned in protest as the iron-studded door beside the watchman's hut opened. Another flash of lightning and Ben glimpsed the steps carved into the cliff that descended towards the sea. Steps that would have been suicide to climb in this weather, slippery as they were. Hands darted from the cloak and dragged the hood, heavy with rain, back. The steep climb up the almost vertical stairs had flushed his cheeks, the rain had flattened his golden hair, but Arthur looked just as Ben remembered.

His heart skipped a beat.

His King half-raised a hand in what could have been an uncertain greeting or surrender. 'Benjamin! What kept you?'

The rough-edged slate of the curtain wall bit into his hands as he slammed into it, feeling along the wall for the door hidden within the stone. Not finding the handle, he turned and scrambled for purchase on the wall, but his shoes slipped, and the slate tore his hands open. Arthur's voice was familiar and soothing but forgotten and disruptive.

'I merely greeted you! There is no need to throw yourself off a cliff.'

Benjamin swivelled back to Arthur. There was no air left in his lungs, nothing with which to say – what? What was he going to say? The truth clawed at his throat, sweat mingled with rain and stung his eyes. Ocean-blue eyes that hadn't changed in over a thousand years drowned in concern. He couldn't look away from the man whom he had made Jack promise to find. And why had Ben done that? Arthur frowned, fumbling with his cloak's clasp, allowing the rain to soak his clothing so it clung to his figure. Ben's heart swung from his rib cage. Ben spun, looking for a way out –

'Did something happen? You do look rather pale.'

'*What should I do with my hands, Ambrosius?*'

Laced behind his back didn't feel right, so Benjamin clasped them in front of him, and not liking how that felt, forced them to be still at his side. '*Should I bow?*' Ambrosius shrugged. '*Right. You're right.*' Benjamin bent himself into a low, stiff bow and fell to one knee.

'*Smooth,*' Ambrosius groaned. '*For your next move, swoon. Arthur might catch you.*'

'Get up, for crying out loud!' Arthur's hands seized Benjamin's arms and Benjamin's heart gave up. Full cardiac arrest. His legs turned to jelly, mouth dry, face on fire, an inexplicable pain in his chest. Arthur strained, trying to force him to stand. Having lost control of his limbs and finding himself forgetting how to manage his lanky frame, Benjamin toppled forwards.

'*You took my advice. There's a first time in eternity for everything, after all.*'

'*I'm glad you're enjoying this, Ambrosius. Really, I am.*'

'Good Gods, man. Whatever is the matter?' Arthur circled behind Benjamin. Strong hands rough from the salty sea air, hooked under his arms. With a grunt, Arthur had Benjamin's feet on the floor.

'Leave me be, my lord.'

Arthur let go, surprised. Benjamin splashed down and tipped onto his side. The smell of wet grass and decomposing leaves filled his nostrils. Benjamin flattened himself into the ground. The rain bounced mud into his mouth, but the ground didn't swallow him whole.

'Benjamin?'

The soft thud of knees hitting the ground beside him made him feel like a fool.

'You were –' Benjamin swallowed the truth and squeezed his eyes shut. '*Merlin!*'

'I see,' Arthur said in the voice that probed for answers without asking a question. There was a swoosh of thick wool and Arthur's cloak enveloped him, wrapping him in a familiar musk of resin, mint, woodsmoke and warm spices. It took Ben right back to feasts, to warm nights spent together, to hunts. To things that Ben had tried to forget. The weight of Arthur's hand, rubbing slow circles on Benjamin's back summoned a sob that had built up in his chest.

Jack.

Benjamin wanted Jack. Jack who loved him fiercely and proudly.

'Won't you come inside? If you insist on lying on the floor, I can put a rug in front of the fire. Or we could retire to bed.'

'The ground is fine, thank you.' Benjamin muttered, his words muffled by the sodden grass. The rain, having worked its way through to his skin, sent shivers racing through his body. There was nowhere to hide. He rolled over and faced his past. 'Arthur ... How long have you been here?'

8

DEATH CUP

PURGATORY

'Well, let me see.' Arthur carefully took in his dishevelled physician, how he flinched at Arthur's touch, the strange attire that adorned the too-thin body, the haunted eyes fixed on the ground, the twitch of his nervous hands. War, Arthur supposed, was a hard atrocity to bear witness to for one as sympathetic as his physician. If Arthur knew no better, he would think Benjamin was disappointed to see him. Arthur had doubted his own eyes, when the gate revealed his physician staring at the storm clouds. It had been a duller existence, without Benjamin. And the manner in which they – he – had left matters before the battle, had been weighing on Arthur's mind for some time. Well, for 'a year.'

'A year?!' His physician spluttered, laughing like a child.

'At least.' Arthur smiled, hoping to rescue Benjamin from the brink of hysteria. Having lost Benjamin during the battle,

Arthur had heard hide nor hair from his physician, relying on Merlin to ensure Benjamin's continued welfare. Something that Merlin had clearly been neglecting. Based on appearance, Arthur assumed that Benjamin had forgone eating. No doubt to ensure others were fed. 'Merlin promised your eventual arrival. He is not with you?'

'No,' Benjamin said with such venom that Arthur was taken aback. 'A year? Are you certain, my lord?' Benjamin raised himself onto his elbows, silently begging Arthur to declare it was not so.

'Quite certain.' Arthur pulled the cloak around Benjamin's shoulder. His physician dropped himself back to the ground, dislodging the cloak again. 'Tell me about the war!' Benjamin shook his head, consumed by such sadness that his usual green eyes, flecked with brown, looked grey. 'I lost consciousness on the battlefield and awoke here, at Tintagel.' Arthur could not recall anything that would inspire such curious behaviour in Benjamin. He had always floundered in the depths of Benjamin's emotion, but this was something more than Benjamin's typical melancholia. 'Come inside, else Death will catch you!'

'The weather bothers me no longer, my lord.'
There it was again.
The careful formality that denied any familiarity between them. But why, when no souls were present to deceive? A lone raven circled above them and banked towards the horizon, following the waves out to sea. Benjamin's weary eyes traced its path.

'A good night's rest will see you right as rain.' Benjamin stole a glance at Arthur, shaking his head slightly to shift matted hair from his eyes whilst water dripped from his chin. 'Your hair is longer than I remember. The length suits you.' Arthur's fingers grazed Benjamin's hair, a violent flinch his reward. Arthur looked away lest Benjamin spot the tears that formed. He should apologise, though such words were a struggle for Arthur. Benjamin sneezed violently. 'Well –' Arthur pulled the hood of the cloak onto Benjamin's head. 'You may not wish to be cajoled inside, but I am longing for the great hall's fire.' Arthur stood and offered his hand. Benjamin stared, eyes wide, his mouth set in a grim line. 'Suit yourself.' Arthur strode towards the imposing oak doors, its wood stained a deeper shade by the rain.

'Are there others here?'

Arthur turned, his encouraging smile dropped when Benjamin's gaze settled just over his shoulder. If Benjamin were well, he would recognise how Arthur was striving to be kind and compassionate. All the things a king should not be in public. 'The steward and a few servants.' It had been quite an uncomfortable transition. At court, Arthur seldom found a moment of peace. And then Merlin had transported him here, to a castle depleted by war. Perhaps Benjamin was missing court, also. The door groaned as he opened it. 'Come. Let's pack and be on our way.'

'Where do you want to go? You can't leave here.' Benjamin's fingers wrapped and twisted his hair into knots.

'Away from this damned weather! Twelve months of ceaseless rain, stuck atop this cramped morsel of headland – tomorrow, or perhaps the day after, we must return to Caerleon! Merlin can take no issue with travel if I ride with you. Is the war going so badly that I must remain –'

'You know not ...' Benjamin sat up; long arms wrapped around his legs; his eyes shifted to a deep sorrowful blue. 'You won, Arthur –'

'Why was I not informed?' Arthur's voice climbed in outrage.

'Because you're dead!' Benjamin blurted out, tears in his eyes.

'I am most certainly not dead!' Denial flared in Arthur's chest.

'This, all of this –' Benjamin gestured at the brooding castle. 'Is another of Merlin's illusions.'

The cold of the iron handle nipped at Arthur's hand, his sodden tunic clung to his skin, heavy and uncomfortable. The sea roared and Arthur shivered, pressing his other hand against the rough grain of the door. Benjamin was mistaken. His physician stood on legs that looked unable to carry him. But the conviction in his strange, shtriga-like eyes was unwavering. 'And what of you? Speak!'

Benjamin looked away. A quick stab of guilt reminded Arthur that much of Benjamin's silence was his fault. Arthur had forced his physician to keep the biggest parts of himself secret.

'My lord –'

'Enough, Benjamin!' His physician startled and stared at the ground. 'Cease with your *my lords*. We are alone and I have crept around my own castle long enough. What has happened? Speak freely, I implore you.'

'I, I don't, uh,' his physician stuttered, looking pained.

'Benjamin!' Arthur closed the gap quickly, paying no mind to how Benjamin shrank away from him. Patience was something that one expected of a ruler, but his year alone – or more, judging by Benjamin's reaction – had eroded his forbearance. Arthur refused the urge to shake Benjamin, until his concerns tumbled out alongside the truth. 'Do you have any idea as to how infuriating it is, to be severed from your own war efforts? To be abandoned?'

'Yes.' Benjamin stood tall, for just a moment. 'More than you'll ever know.' He shook his head and looked longingly at the edge of the cliff.

'I am sick to death of pacing Tintagel's draughty halls, alone and wondering at the fate of my realm. And you, who I have missed dearly, eventually arrive dressed bizarrely; you speak as though you have allowed your tongue to rust. You refuse to call me by my name nor look me in the eye, and recoil from my touch!' Tears cut streaks down Benjamin's face. Arthur grabbed his physician's chin. 'Look at me, love.' Benjamin locked his gaze on Arthur's nose. 'Are you alive or dead?'

'It's complicated ...'

'The truth, Benjamin.' Scars that looked ancient but were new to Arthur, contorted on Benjamin's face.

'The truth ... 'tis an awful thing. It wounds, my lord. Ask me no more, for I shan't wound you with it.' Benjamin pulled free and took himself into the great hall. 'I suddenly find myself in need of alcohol.'

Arthur pulled the door shut on the hostile elements, not that it would prevent the wind from finding its way in through the gaps in the stonework. The torches would still be aflame if Arthur had not had to coax his physician inside. Benjamin strode through the darkness with ease whilst Arthur coaxed a spark from a flint. The torch flared to life, and, for a split second, the light reflected from eyes set into skin so pale, Arthur would have mistaken Benjamin for a ghost. His physician coughed, to mask his discomfort and continued on his way. For the first time, Arthur felt uncomfortable in Benjamin's presence. Whatever had happened to him on the battlefield? 'Are you still sulking over Merlin turning you into a goat?'

'It was over a thousand years ago!' Benjamin's angry footsteps confidently rounded a corner and faded into the darkness, forcing Arthur to jog to catch up.

'How long?!'

Arthur emerged into the mercifully warm and well-lit great hall. Benjamin stared, fixated on a tapestry of Merlin cloaked in his aquamarine magic, sealing the realms. Worry creased Arthur's forehead and ironed out his smile. The fire and the candlelight gave Benjamin a little more colour, though he still looked in need of a physician himself. Arthur dragged a bench in front of the fire and forced Benjamin to sit beside him. Their shoulders pressed together for a moment, sending a jolt of nervous excitement through Arthur. Benjamin shuffled away, just enough to break contact.

'Merlin trapped you here over a thousand years.'

'A thousand years have not passed, I assure you.' Arthur laughed, but Benjamin remained pensive. 'If that be the case, we would have long since expired.' The fire crackled and popped, sending shadows chasing across the heavy tapestries of red and gold. His golden dragon seemed to fly around the room, hopping from one field of red to another.

'One thousand, four hundred and eighty-eight.' Arthur heard each and every one of those years spent waiting, in Benjamin's quiet voice. It brooked no argument. That would explain why nerves toyed with his physician. He needed time to readjust. 'Tell me, does time change one's eye colour? Yours are grey when once they were green.' Fear flashed across Benjamin's face before he fixed his gaze on the flagstone. So, it was not a trick of the light. If something looked like shtriga, it most likely was. 'This spell of Merlin's has snared you also?'

'So it would seem,' Benjamin informed the floor.

'Did Merlin harm you?'

'In more ways than one.'

Arthur jumped up to pour them some wine, lest Benjamin see the fury burning in his soul. 'What does Ambrosius make of all of this?'

'He doesn't think we're in Purgatory proper. It's some sort of extension. I can't open a portal here. We're going to have to find the crossing point. I must return. There are –' Benjamin hesitated, 'people waiting.'

'Who could be waiting? Those we know must be long gone.'

'I don't like leaving Merlin in-charge and unchecked,' Benjamin answered too quickly.

Sorting out this rift between warlock and physician would be Arthur's first order of business. He couldn't have the pair out of sorts. Second would be to learn how Benjamin had filled his days, and with whom? That Benjamin would have experienced loneliness, Arthur did not doubt. Still, the idea that his physician had made a new life with somebody else ... 'Why would *you* want to be anywhere else, when you can be here? With me, as you always wished.'

Benjamin downed his drink and helped himself to the jug. 'If I stay, I'm signing Gaia's death warrant.'

'Merlin has managed without me. I dare say we can sit here a while more.'

'No, I've managed so far. Without either of you.'
Arthur wrestled the jug from Benjamin. His physician had gotten stronger, it seemed.

'Merlin killed Mórrígan with Fate's dagger. In Merlin's defence, she had destroyed a few realms.'

'Goodness.' Arthur leaned against the table for support, exhausted from trying to remain calm and patient for Benjamin's sake.

'The crossing point will take us to Styx or Hades. I can portal to Gaia from there. Finding the crossing-point won't be easy. Especially in this weather.' Benjamin peered out of the window. 'If you were Merlin, where would you hide the exit? Merlin is a firm believer in hiding in plain sight.'

Arthur shrugged; Ambrosius would suss it out, he had no doubt. 'What became of my Galloglass?'

'Merlin neglected to tell me that I had to exercise them regularly. And by exercise, I mean send them into battle. They went rogue.' His physician shrugged apologetically.

'Damn him! They were my finest soldiers. As a matter of fact, I asked him to make you into one.'

A strange look crossed Benjamin's face, 'I'm not sure that would have been better. Look at me, Arthur; look long and hard.' The King blinked in surprise at the sudden use of his name.

'Magic or not, you look a little too well preserved. Your hair is still black. And your eyes, the colour ... it perturbs me. I have been striving not to acknowledge it.'

'You recognised the changes in me; I saw it in your eyes.'

'Benjamin ... do not shatter my heart.'

'Look at me, Arthur; look long and hard.'
Arthur could not. Doing so would reveal another way in which he failed Benjamin.

'You wanted to know, Arthur.' Benjamin set his jaw, nostrils flared, daring Arthur to accept him whilst steeling himself for rejection.

'You need sleep, Benjamin, that is all.' The smoke from the fire stung Arthur's eyes, clawed at his throat

'I sleep no more. Merlin's passiveness saw to that.' Benjamin drew a deep, shuddering breath. 'You didn't lose me on the battlefield. I went missing days before ... Mórrígan came to me, distraught. Said that Merlin was fatally injured.'
Arthur closed his eyes, able to picture Benjamin snatching up his satchel and pushing past Mórrígan, anxious to help.

'Arwan was waiting for me at Merlin's cottage. He and Mórrígan –'

'If I had been there –'

'You would have died at my hands, Arthur. That was their aim. Merlin could have stopped it, but ...' Tears cut tracks down the dirt on Benjamin's distraught face.

Arthur passed his hand over his mouth to try and mask his horror. His focus had been in all the wrong places, on the war. Benjamin had been a distraction he could not accommodate.

'I tried to stay away. So, I didn't harm you.' Benjamin's voice dropped to a whisper. 'But I couldn't, I had to ... I'd just found you, at Camlann, when, when, you, and I couldn't stop him, couldn't ...' Benjamin's grief strangled his words, he buried his face in his hands, stifling a sob that tore at Arthur's composure. The cold stone bit into Arthur's knee as he knelt, searching Benjamin's strange eyes, wishing he could see the gentle green gaze again.

'Merlin gave me your talisman – Guardianship does not suit me. But there was no alternative. Nor was there an opportunity to settle my quarrel with Awran and Mórrígan. It was time to heal. So, I allowed sleeping dogs to lie.'

Damn Merlin for robbing Arthur of the chance to rip War's throat out. Events had hardened Benjamin. Yet another piece of the man he loved gone for good. The storm threw open doors and crashed against the windows, howling in sympathy for his poor physician who had tried so hard, just to be let down by those closest to him.

'Arthur? Say something ... please?'

The plea for acceptance broke Arthur's heart. And the cruelty of the timing was cosmic. Arthur had pined for his physician, and he had the audacity to return at a time when the universe seemed to be collapsing in on itself.

'Were you lonely, Benjamin?'

'My bones often ached for Caerleon.'

'And for me?' Arthur was not sure if it was worry or suspicion that lent an edge to his voice.

Benjamin's mouth opened, but no words came out.

''Tis a simple question.'

Benjamin's eyes flashed to black and grey, changing colour so quickly, Arthur could not keep up. 'I cried enough to raise the dead. *My lord*.'

'My Gods, we're back to that! Shall I send for more wine?'

'No.' Benjamin strode towards the door. 'It's not about what we want, my lord.'

Arthur cut him off, grabbed his arms and pushed Benjamin back towards the bench.

'All those who are here, they were somebody else before. It's as if they've a second face, just beneath the surface. My mind, it conjured you up often, but never my wife.' His physician turned away in disbelief. 'I needed you, Benjamin. I love you.'

And the man who had promised his heart to Arthur, turned to him, with the look of an unwilling traitor in his green eyes.

'I love another.'

The words jarred in Arthur's very being, like a sword colliding with bone.

9

FALLING APART

Tintagel, Gaia

T he wind whipped across the ruins perched precariously where the land met with the sea and sky. It was the kind of wind that refused to leave once it had settled deep into a vampire's bones. Behind them, hills rolled away into the distance; in front, there was nothing but darkness and the ever-present call of the waves. There was a certain something about this place. Even Jack could feel magic humming faintly, as if it were buried within the soil.

'Must we do this in the middle of a storm?' A gust of wind shoved Jack in the direction of the steep drop to where the waves threw themselves into the cove. April looked back and shrugged, unable to hear him over the rain drumming off the rock. The wind was a voice thief, lying in wait. They were about halfway to the very top. Not that things would improve once they got there. The windy, narrow, sometimes a mud slide, always littered with little pebbles keen to turn an ankle, path kept trying to trip them. Jack caught April as she slipped over for the hundredth time and shot a murderous look at the back of Merlin's head. He must have been a mountain goat in a past life. 'Is this safe?'

'This path has been here for thousands of years!'

'That's not what I meant!' There was a huge skill gap between levitating stones and rescuing souls.

'If you prefer to risk becoming trapped alongside Arthur and Benjamin, then I can indeed complete the spell alone.'

'No. Ta muchly.' Jack was inevitably going to get caught up in *that*, but he wasn't rushing towards it with open arms. Nor did Jack want to think about the two of them together. A sharp tug on his sleeve brought him back from his trajectory towards the ancient stone ruins, such was the pull of the "don't climb on the wall" sign.

'Why didn't we portal to the top?' Jack added extra whine for Merlin's benefit.

'We are attempting to force our way into Purgatory to retrieve two souls, without drawing the curiosity of certain beings.' Merlin's mood had tipped from unhinged neutral chaotic to bonkers evil chaotic somewhere on the journey.

'Like Death?' April stumbled and glared at Jack, seeming to guess at his wanting to pick her up and speed things along. Jack threw his hands up in defence and skirted around them both, preferring to be in the lead.

'Among others, yes.' Merlin pulled the hood of his cloak over his eyes, squinting up at the sky.

'Death doesn't like you.' April huffed, her cheeks flushed red and still annoyed at Merlin for jumping out at her in the remains of the great hall that sat below them.

The rescue was going just swell.

'Death is too impatient and far too untrusting. I have no intention of leaving the universe at odds.'

'Oh, good. I was concerned.' Jack shook his head at Merlin's arrogance, the path turned back on itself again. Bringing Ben back to fix the imbalance seemed like a child's plan. If Charon, the Guardian of Styx, listened to every plea of "I shouldn't be here", there would be no souls in Hades. Death's laws were too rigid to be so easily broken. 'Get a move on, Merlin. The rain certainly isn't going to wait for us.' A cackle like none Jack had ever heard erupted from Merlin, scaring the life out of him. 'And the crazy is back, wonderful.' Merlin took a step towards Jack but the bottom of his already-tattered cloak, which had materialised somewhere during the bridge crossing, snagged on a low bit of rock and a new rip was added to the butchered garment. 'This. This is why nobody wears cloaks nowadays.'

'At least we'll be able to find our way back. Just follow the bits of robe,' April muttered as she stomped past, woefully out of breath. She slipped through a gap in the ruins and edged towards the point where the grass ended and pitch-black nothingness began.

Jack left Merlin to fuss over his wounded cloak. 'April, if you're not comfortable with the spell, don't do it. It's not your responsibility to help Ben. And ... if you're the price for getting him back, I'm not going to pay it.' April took his arm and pulled him along, shaking her head at his concern. 'Do you have a strong enough handle on Eilir?'

April nodded and Jack remembered the tree. And the state of his apartment. He had no basis for his hand-me-down concern that April and Eilir would get a taste for the bigger, darker, spells, but Jack could almost hear Ben fretting. The snap of a cloak being snatched by the wind turned his head. Merlin was perched rather precariously on the crumbling ancient wall, looking out to sea.

'Oi! If you're going to jump, kindly wait until Ben is back.'

'There's something comforting about black clouds and angry sea. And just listen to the wind! It will take what it wants from you. You cannot stop it.' Merlin tipped his head back, listening to it howling out the secrets of the ghost of a castle. 'Blow winds! Rip away my afflictions. There's no harm you can do to me that my own hands cannot – have not already done. Jump? Mayhap I'll fly.'

A strong gust of wind caught Merlin square in the back. He wobbled. Jack rushed forwards, catching Merlin around the waist, suspending him above the drop for a heartbeat.

'Alright, everybody back on the path.' Jack slowly let go of Merlin. The warlock regained his balance and laughed that terrifying laugh.

'Come on April, leave the madman to yell at the sea.'

Sky poked through the gaps in the bluey-green statue of Arthur that stood watch, peeking out from under its low hood, with nothing but the occasional seagull for company. After his confinement in Purgatory, the real Arthur would be in just as many pieces. And what would seeing Arthur again do to Ben? He might be hanging by a thread himself. 'I'm not sure when I opened my daycare for broken, wayward ancient beings, but I am at capacity.' Huffing and puffing came from the bottom of the path. 'I am not carrying you, warlock.' Jack was on the verge of making a hypocrite of himself when Merlin ambled into sight.

'Have a stomp in the rain, Jack. Howl at the wind, you'll feel much better for it.' Merlin dropped his hands to his knees, surveying the statue on its little patch of dirt, surrounded by layers of brown stone turned grey by the rain. 'My knees aren't what they were. Nor my back, for that matter. Or my shoulders –'

'Merlin!' April clapped in the warlock's face. 'Focus!'

'You've 18 and a half minutes to retrieve them.'

'That's so specific!' Jack turned away instead of knocking Merlin out. 'I'd heard that Purgatory had a cell phone tower installed. I'll give Ben a call, see where he's at.'

'If you would pause your sarcasm.' Chalk scratched across stone as Merlin etched a crude circle, marking it at intervals with runes. 'I would inform you that they are confined to a re-creation of Tintagel.'

Jack looked about the crumbled ruins, the bridge that connected them to the mainland, the caves were somewhere below them. 'They could be anywhere!'

'And yet I suspect they will be wherever is warmest.' April caught his arm as he raised it. He shook her off, but

Merlin's insinuation wasn't so easy to shake. Jack craned his neck, trying to read the inscriptions that Merlin added. 'Spell casting is 80% arts and crafts, isn't it? If you lot want to draw so badly, I'll get you some paper.'

'What's the matter, lad?'

'Eighteen. Minutes! To search the entire site and convince somebody I've never met, that the world he thinks is real, isn't.'

'Eighteen and a half. Benjamin should have made progress on that matter. Come, the hour is upon us.' Merlin took hold of April's arm and dragged her out beyond the statue, almost to the edge. 'Just, about.' Merlin pulled Jack this way and that by his arms, fussing over millimetres.

'I thought that the hour was upon us?'

'There.' Merlin didn't let go, he stared up into Jack's face, a knowing smile on his lips.

'I'm not nervous,' Jack lied.

'Of course not. You are ashamed.'

'Of what?'

'Upon learning of Benjamin's continued existence, your first thought wasn't one of joy –'

'That's not true, Merlin,' Jack lied for a second time.

'Relief. That was your first thought, lad.' Jack felt his face redden, he wanted so badly to punch Merlin.

'Benjamin's return means that you are no longer Guardian. And Arthur's return relieves Benjamin of responsibility. It's understandable.' Merlin cut off his protest. 'I'm not judging.' Except that Merlin's tone insisted he was doing just that. Merlin returned to marking runes.

Jack couldn't remember what he'd felt first.

Everything had hit him at once. He'd been a little too preoccupied with the fact that Ben was with Arthur, but having seen Tintagel, Jack was reassured that they weren't exactly cosy. Even with a roof and complete walls, the place was desolate. And it felt reasonable that Jack should be feeling uncomfortable with the situation. Fear. It had been fear that, Jack would find Ben, only to lose him again. 'Ben is alive. That's all that matters.'

'Right you are, lad.'

'You'll understand, Merlin, if I am reserved on the matter. Until I see Ben myself, I won't allow myself to hope.'

'As you please. You know –' Merlin considered a rune, rubbed it out with his hand, redid it. 'Not everybody is designed to thrive in responsibility.' Merlin looked up from his rune-work and, for the briefest moment, the warlock acknowledged just how difficult this had all been for Jack. 'Benjamin is an old hand at this. Now, April.' Merlin's joints creaked as he straightened up. 'You must hold the portal until all three are returned.'

'Where are their bodies?' Jack met April's worried eyes over Merlin's head.

'You're smearing my ruins,' Merlin grumbled and pushed Jack back to his mark. 'Stay out of the circle, unless you wish to be disintegrated when the pathway opens. Concentrate on getting back in time.'

April's magic flickered in her hands. Jack wished there was another option, but Merlin had begun the spell, his head tipped towards the sky.

'From the highest point –'

A crack of thunder drowned out Merlin's spell. The sound of a blade tearing through fabric filled his ears; the rock beneath his feet morphed into the solid flagstones of a castle corridor.

Tintagel before it lost its roof, Jack presumed. Wall sconces flickered but didn't illuminate much – just a dark castle corridor with too many doors. Behind him, the real Tintagel waited, framed in embers of the aquamarine and jade. The jade was considerably fainter than the aquamarine. Every fibre of his being was screaming at him to put an end to this madness.

'Be careful of that which you cannot see, lad.' Merlin's voice whispered in his mind. 'I'll keep April safe.'

With nothing else to distract him and the clock ticking, Jack set off.

10

ALL LOVERS HELL
TINTAGEL, PURGATORY

C old, rough scales slithered past Jack's ankles.

It was all the motivation Jack needed to run, his footsteps bouncing around him, rough stone scraping at exposed skin. In need of a plan, Jack rattled anything that looked like a door handle.

Locked. All of them.

Jack's clammy hand slipped off another handle and impaled itself on the door's unfinished wooden relief. White-hot pain slammed him into the door, wood gouged at his cheek. Splinters were the worst.

'Son of a – oh come on!' Jack's blood was smeared over a carving of Arthur and what looked suspiciously like Ben. Panic prickled at the back of his mind, startling his breath into quick, short gasps for air. The portal had removed itself to the far end of the hall that seemed much longer than it had a second ago.

'Magic is the worst. Magic and splinters.' Jack tripped on the uneven floor and landed on the ground, inches away from something that looked rather like a snake. The sound of a body dragging itself across the floor was more concerning. 'Magic is intent and want,' Jack mumbled to himself. If he pictured a staircase – a thunderous crash that was not the sea filled the hallway, followed by two disembodied voices raised in discord, punched through the big arched doors at the end of the hallway. The slithering thing, cold and now slimy, wrapped around Jack's ankle; claws, long and brittle, sunk into his leg, the other scaly hand snatching at his jacket. An arm comprised entirely of rotting flesh curled around Jack's waist. He threw his weight forwards, but instead of disentangling himself, Jack fell backwards into the only unlocked door in the universe's longest corridor. The rotting face of his assailant snarled at him, unable to cross the threshold. As Jack's foot slipped over the edge of the step, he realised he wasn't in a room.

Flailing arms were not enough.
Jack rolled and bounced down spiralling stone steps, grabbing for purchase whilst the voices rushed to meet him.

'How could you betray me?'
Arthur, Jack presumed, and he sounded incandescent with rage.

'That's not – you'd been gone for so long! It was miserable. I was miserable!'
Ben!

'Was it so easy to set aside the life we had built together?'

'The life we built together? We must have been existing in

different realities!' Jack rounded yet another turn and came rolling and tumbling right into the middle of the argument.

'Jack?!'

Before he could register what was happening, Ben pulled him to his feet. Jack stumbled towards the safety of a bench. 'Stairs. Lots of ... stairs. Dizzy.'

Ben knelt in front of him, his hand on Jack's knee. Relief crumbled Jack's focus. He grabbed the hand, pressing his forehead against Ben's.

'Are you going to introduce us?'

The coldness in the voice brought Jack back to himself. He tentatively opened his eyes to find Arthur glaring at him.

'You must be King Arthur.' Jack extended his hand, trying to be polite for Ben's sake. Arthur impaled Jack with his piercing blue eyes. He slumped back, his shoulder burning. He must have acquired some more splinters on his way down.

'Alright?' Ben sat beside him at an unmistakably respectable distance, his hands safely in his lap, his head bowed. Arthur's ability to cower Ben was enough for Jack to hate the handsome King.

'Should've set a timer. Damn it!' Not that Jack had any time in which to start an argument. Ben frowned, darting a glance at Arthur. 'We've got 10 minutes tops.' Long wooden benches and tables filled the hall, all dressed with fresh flowers, red velvet runners and groaning under the weight of a feast. There was only one set of doors – giant oak arches studded with metal rivets. 'I've just come from a long corridor, bedrooms? Big wall hanging with a dragon, crest of arms. How do we get back there? There was a rotting corpse. Shifter maybe?'

'That would be my seneschal,' Arthur replied in a haughty voice that almost made Jack feel small and insignificant.

'Did you forget to feed your seneschal? He's quite bony.' Jack kept staring at the older, distinguished man to whom he'd been comparing himself for hundreds of years.

'George does have particularly cold hands. It is as if Death has touched you.' Arthur shuddered.

'It's more likely to be a gatekeeper. Death probably wanted somebody to keep an eye on you, Arthur. The gatekeeper has been impersonating your visitors and staff.' Ben clenched and unclenched his hands, trying and failing to summon Ambrosius, his eyes shifting colour rapidly.

'Merlin didn't tell me there'd be a gatekeeper. Just pushed me through the backdoor to keep Death off my tail.' Jack blinked, and blinked again, as another door faded in and out of view. He sprinted to it, waiting for the door handle to solidify. He heaved but the door wouldn't budge, just faded rapidly to nothing. Ben, who was moving slower than normal, added his strength. The door creaked open just enough for them to slide through.

'Let's go, Ben –'

Arthur slammed the door shut, pulling Ben to stand beside him. 'Benjamin has chosen to stay.'

'Has he?' Jack looked pointedly at Ben, who, judging by the way the shtriga was eyeing up the closest window, wanted to be anywhere else, preferably on his own. Jack pulled his phone out to try and guesstimate the time. Cracks shot off in every direction on the screen.

'Why did you bring your phone?' Ben yanked his arm free of Arthur.

'Because there wasn't a cloakroom. Let's go.' Jack grabbed Ben's hand; Arthur's sharp intake of breath didn't go unnoticed.

'Benjamin?' Arthur's siren song found them on the second step.

Jack had to fight to keep a hold of Ben.

'This isn't real, Arthur!' Ben looked pleadingly to Jack.

'Listen to me.' Jack spoke urgently and without slowing down. 'I need you – April, who's out there in the real world, casting a spell with Merlin, needs you.'

'Benjamin!' Arthur's outraged voice followed them; Jack tried to speed up, but Ben dug his heels in.

'We can't leave him!' Tears littered Ben's eyes. 'Jack –'

'Benjamin!' Arthur was on the stairs. 'I did not dismiss you!'

'Wow! He seems like quite the catch.'

'Benjamin! Leave and you will regret it.'

'Why are you letting him speak to you like that?' Jack could have cried as the top of the staircase came into view.

'It's fine. He's overwhelmed. I told him that I'd met somebody else.'

Jack shook his head in wonder. 'Of all the times you could've picked to start being open about our relationship, you pick this one?!' Jack paused at the threshold, arm out to slow Ben. 'On three? One, two ... three!'

The door cracked against the stone wall; Jack darted into a silent corridor that stretched further still.

'*Which way? I don't see a portal.*'

And just like that, Jack felt complete again.

The flames in the wall sconces flickered and extinguished, dropping them into total darkness. Scrabbling noises came from behind. Ben whirled and pinned something against the wall.

'Unhand me!' Arthur shoved Ben off him and inserted himself between the couple. Jack's teeth ground the silence between them. The only thing heavier than the tension was the threat of attack. Not that Arthur cared. He strode into the hallway, head up, hands on hips, ever the hero. The caress of ice-cold fingers grazing the back of Jack's neck froze him to the spot. 'Ben? Please tell me that's you rubbing my neck?'

The gatekeeper glitched into its wraith form and shot past them, wrapping its silvery-white translucent self around Arthur, dragging the King up the hall. Ben knocked Jack to the ground in his rush to stop the gatekeeper. He dived and caught Arthur's legs. A door creaked open to admit the gatekeeper as it steadily pulled Arthur and Ben towards the unknown. Jack stumbled up and ran to separate Ben from Arthur.

'Help Arthur!' Ben hissed.

'You first, your ex–boyfriend last.'

'Jack!'

'Ugh, fine!'

'No, look – portal!'

Jade and aquamarine magic cut through the air, peeling it back on itself. And it was close enough to give Jack hope. The magic shot down and raced through the grouting in the stonework, flowing like water towards them, pulsating. Jack circled behind the snarling wraith. 'Hey, gatekeeper?' It turned and collided with Jack's fist. Sufficiently stunned, it loosened its grip and Jack hauled Arthur free, throwing him head-first into the portal. Benjamin was being tossed about like a ragdoll, too tired to fight back. Arthur was half-in, half-out the portal. 'Go! Merlin is on the other side.'

'Benjamin –'

'Isn't leaving without you. And I'm not leaving without him.' Jack didn't wait to see if Arthur did as he was told. 'Ben!' His partner threw out his hand. The gatekeeper caught Jack's wrist; loose, dead flesh rubbed against Jack's skin and he gagged. Sensing its chance, the gatekeeper pulled Ben into the nothingness that lay inside the doorway, with a determination borne of somebody who only knew the one job and now the task was at hand.

Ben's boots slipped on the stone, now so inexplicably smooth that he couldn't find purchase. Out of the corner of his eye, Ben spied the doorway hurtling towards him. He counted two breaths and went limp in its disturbing grip. The gatekeeper flew backwards, free from Ben's resistance, just as they came level with the doorframe. Wood dug into his fingertips; he threw his weight backwards, kicking the gatekeeper loose. It shrieked, claws tearing Ben's shirt and back to bits. One more kick and it tumbled into the darkness. Jack rushed forwards, rescuing him from the brink of nothingness and Ben slammed the door shut.

'The portal!' Jack's grip tightened, forcing Ben to run, his feet dragging and stumbling along in a half-jog. The edges of the portal were fraying, his view of Tintagel – the real Tintagel – dimming by the second. Ben dug deep, looking for his magic that had been quiet for far too long.

'Ambrosius?' Silence, not even a twitch. 'Ambrosius?' A faint prickle of pins and needles as his magic tried and failed to form.

Jack laughed in relief, but the view was shrinking as the portal sealed itself rapidly. Ben took one last look at Jack's delighted face, brought Jack's hand to his lips and pushed his vampire through the portal a second or two before it closed.

The gatekeeper wailed behind Ben.

11

DRAWN

TINTAGEL, GAIA

April's entire being shook with the effort of holding open a collapsing portal. The first sign of trouble was the man who flew out of it and started yelling at Merlin in a grand do-as I-say voice. Eilir, tired from overexertion, wanted nothing to do with the blonde-haired man. April was inclined to agree.

'Merlin!' the furious King yelled. 'You hold this portal until Benjamin –'

'How dare you speak his name!' Pure hatred consumed April, and her voice was Eilir's.

Arthur swivelled to stare at her. April returned fire with her own unimpressed glare.

'No, no, no!' Jack stumbled from the portal, tripped over his own feet, and shot back up just as the pull of the collapsing portal wrenched itself from April's grip and sealed for another year.

Jack turned slowly and stalked towards Merlin. 'Open it!'

'Does nobody listen to me? Hmph!'

Jack launched the nearest candle into the sea.

'Does that make you feel better?' Merlin asked sarcastically. 'You are a vampire. You understand how Purgatory works.'

Jack charged Merlin and came up against Arthur's protective arm. 'Get Ben back!'

'I'm ... trying to reopen ... the portal.' April stumbled over the words of the spell. She couldn't take the look of despair on Jack's drawn face. Eilir struggled valiantly, but she couldn't catch the right edge, like trying to open a plastic carrier bag with numb fingers. Merlin erased the circle from the ground with a wave of his hand.

'There's trouble to be had by mispronouncing a spell. Benjamin will be fine. He knows his way through the under realms. Oh! Hopefully he has a coin on him.'

'What for?' April asked, exasperated.

'The Ferryman, April.' Merlin blinked at her in surprise. 'Now, Arthur –'

The King's fist caught Merlin and sent him staggering backwards. April's hands flew to cover her delighted smile.

'You can see the future and yet you did not see that coming?' Arthur had a temper it seemed.

'Ah. Benjamin has been regaling you with stories.' Merlin wiped gingerly at the blood trickling from his nose. 'Did you see that, Jack? Arthur did what you've been wanting to do for months.'

April closed her eyes, listening for the splash Merlin would make when Jack threw him into the sea. It did not come. Instead, Jack pushed past her, heading towards the path that dipped back down into the ruins, and froze, his attention drawn to the lower ruins.

'There's somebody down there!'

'Who's mad enough to be out in this?' April peered over Jack's shoulder. Jack gripped her arm so tightly she stamped on his foot. Jack eased off but didn't let go. 'See?' Where the well is. Or was. Whatever.'

April squinted into the night, even with Eilir helping, she wasn't convinced that something was stirring. Merlin's magic bounced around the place, not at all tired from the spell, whereas April felt like she'd run a marathon. But when Emrys and Eilir came into contact with one another, there was a strange shyness on Emrys' part.

'There's nobody down there, Jack. Meanwhile, things are getting awkward over there.'

Arthur's attention was wandering around the ruins. April hoped Tintagel wasn't one of his favourites. 'I have never been as disappointed with another as I am with you, Merlin.' Arthur's gaze landed on her, and she shivered under the intensity of those blue eyes. 'And who are you, my lady? Forgive Merlin, he seems to have misplaced his manners.' His tone was nothing but courteous, insisting they could be friends. That everything would be fine. Even though April felt like telling Arthur to jump off the cliff.

'April is a friend of Benjamin's.'

'The pleasure is mine.' The slight furrow of his eyebrows

suggested that Arthur thought she was familiar.

'And Jack you've met. He is also –'

'If you say friend, Merlin, I will dropkick you into the Celtic Ocean.' Jack was still frowning at imaginary dog walkers on the beach.

'What has become of my castle, Merlin?'

'Nothing lasts forever.'

'Perhaps with regards to castles. But I must disagree, some things do last forever.' Arthur looked pointedly at Jack whose middle finger began to extend. April forced his arm down. He turned back to the ruins.

'Dog walkers usually have dogs, and they don't move that quickly. They're in the gatehouse, no the courtyard now and – Ben?'

April followed Jack's pointing finger and saw the silhouette. They watched it exit where a door had once stood. The silhouette descended a set of stairs and without breaking its stride, jumped over the edge of the cliff.

Jack jumped over the edge.

April ran towards the edge to check that he was alright. Emrys wrapped around her like rope. Eilir squirmed, bumping up against the fuzzy calm blue magic, whichever way she turned. It felt like Emrys had grounded Eilir.

'Where do you think you're going?'

'Wherever I want to go!' April pulled at the magic restraining her, desperate to follow and not enjoying being left alone with Merlin and Arthur.

'Vampires excel at stupidity. If they fall off a cliff, it's of little consequence to them. You'll break your neck. Hmph!'

'Merlin!' Arthur swatted the warlock around the head and Merlin reluctantly let April go.

'That's a projection. The real Benjamin must have found the crossing point –' Merlin darted off, moving as well as April or Jack.

Arthur rushed after Merlin, keen to be involved. 'What's the matter?'

'Jack and Benjamin might try to use the crossing point at the same time. No, that won't do at all. Stay here, the both of you.' Without another word, Merlin vanished into thin air.

'It bothers me when he does that,' Arthur grumbled.

'Yeah, it's annoying.' Emrys was still crowding Eilir. 'Worse still, you can't be sure he's actually gone. I don't trust people who can make themselves invisible.'

Arthur arched his eyebrows at her in mild amusement, still giving her that curious look of vague recognition. At least that's why she hoped he was staring. 'Merlin's your friend, not mine. I tolerate him for Ben's sake.'

'Why do you call him that, Ben? It sounds childish. Does ... Jack call him Ben?' Arthur's tone was polite and measured.

'Ben prefers Ben. Benjamin doesn't suit him. Not the him from now.'

'*Loneliness hurts just the same as physical pain. Arthur's hiding it well, but it's devouring him.*' Eilir struggled, pushing at Emrys.

'*Well, you know, Ben sounds childish.*' With a great effort, Eilir

101

managed to push Emrys off of them. 'Yes, Eilir!'

'Eilir?' Arthur repeated puzzled.

'My magic.' April turned to leave, turned back, bowed awkwardly to the King. 'My lord, or whatever.' And bolted down the hill with the fall to her death awaiting her over the side.

'Get as low down as you can.' Eilir picked that moment to appear on her shoulder, sending April into cardiac arrest. 'There, in the courtyard, by the bridge.'

'That's still not very low,' April panted. 'Have you seen the drop?'

'I'm aware of it, but I have an idea.'

'And that is?'

'Jump.' Eilir disappeared from her shoulder.

That didn't sound like a good idea, but there was the courtyard. She passed through the remains of the archway; the new bridge lay ahead stretching over to the mainland. 'Can't we take the death-stairs?'

'*It'll take too long, and Arthur is catching up. Climb onto the stonework.*'

'*But the sign says –*'

A shower of stones and curses announced Arthur's arrival just as Eilir's pins and needles shot through April's whole body.

'*Jump!*'

And, Gods help her, jump she did.

The ground rushed towards her. April twisted in the air, her stomach somersaulting as the wind rushed past, roaring in her ears and forcing her eyes shut. April screamed but before her panic could settle in, Eilir was there, slowing her fall.

Beside her, the imposing cliffs rose up and the remains of the castle watched her silently. Below, the aquamarine glow of Emrys bloomed out of the cave's mouth.

Eilir deposited April beside the huge boulders on the pebble beach, just outside the cave and she rushed into the dark cave, stumbling and gasping in shock at the frigid water that covered her knees. Eilir's jade energy appeared as a ball of light that floated just ahead of her. A huge wash of water slammed into her back, pulling her under, the shock of the cold stealing her breath. April flayed about, trying to find the surface, her body bumping into, and being raked over, rocks smoothed by the tide. Something grabbed her jacket. The watery glow of her magic, pulsating above her picked out the outline of her rescuer. She broke the surface and came face-to-face with a disgruntled Merlin. She sucked in a desperate breath and coughed out water, her lungs burning. Merlin dived under the surface.

'April!' Ahead of her, Jack clung to a huge boulder jutting out from the side of the cave, cut off from the entrance by the rapidly rising water. 'My foot is trapped!' Between them, the water churned in a whirlpool keen on devouring them all. Merlin surfaced and shook his head at Jack. April started to wade forwards, but Merlin held his hand up. This – she'd seen this in a premonition.

'They tried to use the crossing at the same time. And travelling in different directions! The resulting surge of magic has caused the tide to turn.' Merlin bobbed about, looking behind April.

'Where's Arthur?'

'Who cares?' Jack grunted, his wet hands slipping on the rock. 'I can't hold on much longer.'

April vaulted over a cluster of above-the-tide rocks at the edge of the cave, thrusting her bokken out for Jack to grab hold of. 'Little help, Merlin?'

'I think you'll manage.' The warlock smiled at her and vanished.

'Oh for –'

'April! Imagine pulling me free.'

She focused every atom in her body on her goal. Eilir's glow encircled her sword arm, travelling down the bokken to Jack. Eilir found where Jack was trapped and snipped him free of the fabric of Purgatory. April pulled back; her feet went out from under her. She splashed down in the water just before Jack landed on top of her.

'And if anybody was wondering, "would Jack follow Ben – or an approximation of Ben – into another universe?" The answer is, yes!' April squirmed, kicking at Jack until he rolled off of her.

'And in case you were wondering folks, if I jump off a cliff, yes, April will follow me!' Jack thrashed his way back to his feet. 'There are three things that I hate most in this world: Merlin, cats, and wet clothes. This jacket is ruined! Okay, four things: saltwater.' Jack splashed his way around the whirlpool. 'Let's just leave that there. Merlin can deal with it. Where did he magic himself off to in such a hurry?'

'At a guess.' April accepted his extended hand. 'To find

Arthur. I left him behind.'

'Good,' Jack said with too much conviction. April raised her eyebrows. 'I mean, oh, no, you abandoned the King in his castle-that's-not-a-castle-anymore, in a world he doesn't recognise, during a storm. How could you? Bad hunter!'

'Gees, I get it.' April jammed her sword into its sodden case. 'Did you catch them kissing or something?' Jack stared at the whirlpool, his arms crossed. April froze, praying her sarcasm hadn't been prophetic. 'Forget I asked. Let's go.' They sloshed their way out of the cave, grateful to be reunited with the pebble beach.

'I found a letter that Ben had written to Arthur and, apparently I'm the jealous type. Who knew?' Jack tried to laugh it off.

'I *knew* you were snooping around!' Whatever had happened in Purgatory must be bad if Jack was willing to admit to snooping in order to divert her questions.

'Alright, climb down off your high horse, will you? Or better yet, be a dear and magic up a horse so neither of us has to walk back up that hill.' Jack tipped his phone upside down, sighing at the stream of water that ran out of the charging port.

'You can carry me no problem.'

'Have you seen how steep and long it is?!'
April just stood there, water dripping from her hair, looking all cold and tired, knowing that Jack would cave. The vampire grumbled to himself and picked her up. His shoulders bunched up with tension.

'Ben's been with you for over half a century.'

'It's not Ben that concerns me.' Jack straightened up, trying to hold his head high and nearly lost his balance. April tried not to shiver as the night air hit her wet skin and clothes. But Jack noticed and started to run – full vampire speed.

The long and very steep hill was almost too much for Jack, vampire-strength and all. At least Merlin was waiting at the top. With Arthur. He stopped beside Merlin and let April down, his hands hovering beside her as she wobbled about. 'You're still not used to the speed? And you! What the hell, Merlin?'

'April could manage perfectly well, and somebody had to find Arthur.' Merlin gathered what was left of his cloak about him.

'What madness possessed you? Jumping from such a height!' Arthur demanded, locking gazes with April. Jack sucked in a breath, eager to see her bring Arthur down a privileged peg or three. Although he'd happily see to it himself, if Arthur gave him a reason. Although Merlin might beat Jack to the punch. The warlock was glaring at Arthur, aquamarine magic dancing at his fingertips.

'There was no need for you to endanger yourself with me present.' Arthur puffed out his chest.

'I thought your condescension sounded childish. And in case you hadn't noticed, neither Jack nor I are damsels in distress.'

'Regardless. There's no place on the battlefield for women.' April's eyes widened in disbelief, unable to compute the arrogance. Merlin shot Jack a concerned look. She was shaking but that could be attributed to her unintentional swim in the cave.

'You will choose a course of action that includes myself next time,' Arthur concluded, his entire body followed the progress of a car as its lights rushed towards them and swept round the bend in the road.

'That'll depend on whether or not you can keep up with me.' Arthur bristled at the insinuation. His kingly belief that he was important in resolving any crisis was an old habit. 'Last I checked, I saved Jack. Little old me, all on my own.'
Merlin inserted himself between the rowing pair, pushing Arthur back from April. It was a small shove, easy to miss, but a shove all the same.

'There is no more that can be done here, tonight, *Arthur*. Let us retire to somewhere dry, *Jack*. We can portal from the beach. It's best to do so out of sight of people, *April*.'

As they walked back down the hill a lone figure all bundled up in a parka pushed their way through the group, trailing their hands over Arthur's arm.

'Away with you, urchin.' Merlin stepped forwards and the figure hurried off without a word.
The urchin stuffed their hands into their jacket pockets and walked purposefully away. Jack felt uneasy. But Merlin pressed on, seemingly unbothered by coincidences.

12

REMEMBRANCE

I t was the oldest trick in the book.

Hood pulled low to obscure the eyes.

Walk with purpose and a bowed head, bump into the victim.

Never break stride, never glance up or back, offer no apology.

It was in the confusion that the sleight of hand took place.

A nudge of the sleeve. A brush of the skin.

And just like that, Barqan was in Arthur's head. Her magic expanded in her mind, connecting with her poison as it sung in Arthur's veins.

Once Arthur had fallen asleep, Barqan was about her business with the brisk efficiency of somebody who could not afford another mistake. Barqan crept through his dreams of battles, of a life once lived, of Benjamin – she winced as Benjamin pulled away from Arthur in Purgatory. She thought he had better sense – and manners – than to reject Arthur outright.

What a disaster the shtriga was.

How unusual it must be for Arthur to be losing; how alien it must be to be challenged for Benjamin's affection. Paranoia screamed at Arthur's insecurities, winding them up into a frenzy of fortuitous white-hot hatred. Fate's brief had been simple: sew enough discord to separate Arthur from the pack. And here Arthur was, already dreaming of all the ways he could make Jack disappear.

One good look.

That's all it had taken for Arthur to realise that he could not beat the vampire. Jack had found the time to look at Benjamin as if the shtriga was the entire universe. Even in the middle of a mission. Even when faced with his predecessor. Benjamin would keep his distance from Arthur now, Barqan was certain of that. And that distance would erode the King's already fragile confidence. The odds of Benjamin returning were slim, Arthur had decided. The idea pulsed through his mind, a recurring thought that pulled him deeper and deeper into himself. The King fancied low odds, it seemed. Barqan pushed on. There were plenty of points to latch onto in Arthur's subconscious. It was rougher than Barqan had expected, the edges sharpened by resentment and uncertainty.

The sound of a hostile Arthur accusing Merlin boomed around her, just before she saw the punch land. He couldn't quite work out what it was Merlin had done, he just knew that it was worthy of his disapproval.

And on top of all of that, he was in a Gaia that was much changed. Arthur could not imagine being able to move as easily here. As Jack did. As Merlin did. As Benjamin no doubt did. They had all adjusted, grown together. The twenty-first century ... it was one long inhale, never still – unrelenting, it squeezed Arthur's throat. Benjamin seemed colder. He was not so easily persuaded by Arthur now. A pang of guilt stabbed Arthur deep enough to prick Barqan's concentration. Arthur believed that he could have sheltered Benjamin from all of it. Arthur's distress pulled her back in. Purgatory – it had, for the briefest moment, been perfect. Everything Arthur had wanted, in the place he wanted it to be.

The devastation at finding it had not been real – unspeakable. Barqan settled in-between imagined scenes of Benjamin, riding beside Jack, of Jack reading whilst Benjamin ground herbs in his humid workshop, of Arthur staking Jack, and another in which Arthur strangled Merlin.

Merlin should have killed Arthur.

Mortals weren't designed to cope with time. They obsessed, tore their memories apart until they were left with confetti, they spotted objects in the debris, assigned meaning to what was left. Merlin had gifted Arthur with all of the time in the world to dwell.

Death would have been a mercy.

Barqan caught a hold of a passing unhappy thought about Merlin and melted into it. Inside, Arthur was wondering why his advisor had gone to such lengths to send him away.

'The warlock tries too hard; perhaps a lighter touch would serve him better.' Barqan materialised behind Arthur. His shoulders were up and tense, hoping for a fight. 'Or perhaps Merlin sought reassurance from his King. Reassurance that he craved and never received.'

'Barqan.' Arthur jumped, instantly dismissing her as a part of his dream. All the better, for he'd speak honestly within his own mind. 'Merlin chooses the hardest path. Each time, without fail.'

'I question where Merlin's loyalties lie.' Barqan conjured up a chair in the vastness of Arthur's subconscious and guided Arthur to sit.

'It was my understanding that he was finished with Fate.' Arthur shifted, uncomfortable at the notion of Merlin lying to him.

'Theirs is a complicated relationship.' Barqan did not have enough fingers and toes on which to count the number of times she had been sent to fetch him home. 'Merlin has gone a long time without a commander. Taking control of a war-torn realm after your apparent death was no mean feat.'
Arthur leaned forwards, watching her intently. It was a curious thing, to have the ear of a King.

'Ensconcing you in Purgatory was a little drastic. I wonder if Merlin did what was most convenient for him.'

'How so?' Arthur's eyes were wide, scared of the truth.

And the trap snared the rabbit. 'All these years, you have been left to slumber in Purgatory, blind to Merlin's schemes.'

'He prefers clean hands. He has no desire to rule,' said the King, though his head nodded in agreement that Merlin could indeed do that.

'Why, in his humble opinion, he is master of the universe. An ambition out of reach for most. When I heard that the wise King Arthur had appointed Merlin as royal advisor, I thought to myself, that would prove to be Merlin's greatest trick. Do not let it be your greatest mistake.' A low, slow rumble rocked Arthur's subconscious. The less-than-certain King turned away, but his doubt was rocking his subconscious. Memories crashed around them, shattering like glass and allowing other paranoias to mix in. 'You know, it was Merlin who introduced Benjamin to Jack. Why, I asked myself, would Merlin do such a thing, knowing that you would return.' Arthur's head whipped round. 'Still, I suppose you mind not. You did not marry Benjamin.'

With a small smile, Barqan slipped out of the dream and back to Avalon.

***

'Say that you do succeed in turning Arthur against his advisor, what use is that to you? Merlin is still the key to Gaia.' Arawn reclined on an ornate gold chaise longue in Fate's rose garden, enjoying the late afternoon sun whilst she took great care in pruning roses. His long black robe draped over the side of the chair, puddling in a pool of darkness underneath him. The deer skull – complete with horns – that he wore as a mask to terrify mortals, completed his outfit. That he had entered Avalon wearing it suggested to Fate that Arawn was getting a little too comfortable in his temporary position.

Replacing War had been harder than expected.

Fate took two deep breaths, she was remembering why they hadn't spoken in several hundred years. 'Merlin continues to think that he can play two games: his and mine. Arthur is a distraction to be utilised.'

'It is far from me to tell you your business, Fate.'

'But you will, regardless.' For Arawn enjoyed the scratchy rise and fall of his Welsh accent, so thick it twisted his English into something that sounded exotic.

He was alone in his belief that others enjoyed listening to him.

'A more proactive approach would be best. If you take him for a fool then he has already won.' Fate gathered the roses into her arms, a thorn pricked her thumb. She watched the blood bead, sensing Arawn's sudden interest. This god lived for suffering in any form. 'Though it may not seem like it to your inexperienced eyes, Merlin is a predictable creature. He will return. He always does.'

'Fine. You have the warlock where you want him, and soon you'll have influence over Arthur. What next, Fate? You've destroyed three realms and Chaos hasn't so much as blinked in surprise. For what it's worth, I'm not particularly interested in all of that. I for one quite liked the old arrangement.'

'That's because you, along with the other death gods, like to count your currency, and the souls all travel downwards. Chaos is good for your business.' Fate magicked the roses inside the palace and faced Arawn, hands on hips. 'It occurs to me that we have too many death gods.'

'Look.' Arawn stood, all shadows and sharp angles. 'I'd rather be in Gaia, of course, and that's why I am here. If Benjamin hadn't have gotten away –'

'You'd have taken Gaia for your own, yes, I know.'

'It should have worked,' Arawn grumbled. 'I blame Merlin.'

'We all do. Merlin will continue to be the universe's scapegoat, even in death.'

'So, we use the old goat one last time to draw Chaos out?'

'And wherever Merlin goes, Arthur and Benjamin will follow.'

13

SNUFF

PURGATORY

B en's entire body collided with the far wall.

The decorative hanging did little to cushion the blow. The gatekeeper levitated in front of its door, the only exit since the portal and stairs down to the great hall had abandoned him.

'You're stronger than you look.' Ben leaned against the damp stonework, prompting the gatekeeper to let out an unholy screech. 'Alright! I'm just resting.'

The wraith returned to levitating in silence, trying to hold Ben captive with its dead-eyed stare. 'As nice as this is, I won't be sitting in this hallway for eternity.' Big talk given that Ben had zero options, and the gatekeeper knew it. It was safe to assume that Merlin wasn't going to, or perhaps couldn't, open another portal.

The obvious option was to take a tumble into the Nothingness.

'Maybe it wouldn't be so bad. It would be quiet. No arguing.'

The space behind the gatekeeper shimmered but there wasn't a portal. The wraith screeched a quieter screech and pointed long, thin razor-sharp claws at him.

'I didn't move! You're persistent, I'll give you that.' The faintest prickle of pins and needles ran down his arms. '*One, clean shot. Ambrosius. That's all I need.*'

Ambrosius nodded weakly, and they inhaled as one.

The burnt-orange ball of magic torpedoed the wraith in its chest, sending it cartwheeling into the Nothingness from whence it came. Ben slumped against the wall, just as tired as Ambrosius. Living in limbo was a draining, all-consuming experience. He had to get home. April casting spells with Merlin? No good could come of that. Using the wall for support, Ben walked himself back to his feet and came face-to-face with the door to the Nothingness. In the back of his mind, he heard April enquiring as to whether or not he had been born in a barn and shut it. Ambrosius popped into life on Ben's shoulder, swaying with exhaustion. His little hands clinging to Ben's collar. Ben turned towards where the portal had been and began walking. The faintest sound of claws scratching and tapping on a thick oak door to his right stopped him.

'*That wasn't me.*' Ambrosius held up his tiny hands as evidence.

The door crashed open and out shot the gatekeeper, all claws and teeth. It collided with Ben, constricting its cold form around him. They toppled to the ground; Ben dragged himself free, but he was too slow to dodge the gatekeeper's questing hands. Ben's feet slipped into nothing, he grabbed the doorframe and kicked the gatekeeper hard in its side, sending it back into the Nothingness. The gatekeeper's grip loosened, and Ben hauled himself back onto solid ground, slamming the door shut. The gatekeeper clawed and hissed, pulling at the handle with a strength to rival Ben's. The space where the portal had been taunted him with a clear view of regular chairs and the hunting scenes painstakingly stitched on the wall hangings. A horrid thought snuck up on him:

Merlin had traded Ben's life for Arthur's.
And what the hell had Merlin put Jack through? Presenting Ben as dead and then dangling him at arm's length so Jack and April would retrieve Arthur. '*I am going to kill him.*' But first, Ben had to beat the gatekeeper to the crossing point and make it to Styx.

'*The stairs are back!*'

'*Alright!*' Ben took the uneven stairs four, six, at a time – whatever he could jump in the confined spiral tower. There was a deafening thud, wood splintered, and the gatekeeper, surprised at the sudden lack of resistance, tumbled into the stairwell. Ben tuned out its screeching as he tripped into the great hall. He burst through a side door and tore across the courtyard. His eyes fell on the steps cut into the cliff. He skidded to a halt at the top step. The tide had already swallowed the beach.

'If I were going to put a crossing point anywhere at Tintagel,' Ambrosius offered groggily, 'I'd put it at the very top or the very bottom.'

'This is Merlin's reconstruction –'

117

'And if we had an ego the size of Merlin, we'd put it –'

'– In Merlin's cave.' Ben sprinted to the other side of the courtyard and jumped, plummeting to the giant boulders that littered the beach below. He fumbled the landing, pitching head-first into the cold waves. Ben sloshed and lurched towards the mouth of the cave.

'Bored of the stairs were you, Ben?'

'We're being pursued, if you hadn't noticed!' Ben paused just inside the entrance, trying to see the shimmer of air that would give the crossing point away.

'Now your hands are all torn up and you're going to have to wade through salt water.'

'I'll heal.' Ben snuck a quick glance, not quite trusting his body after War had stabbed him.

'Shame about the tide. You're not the strongest swimmer.'

'You're a bother when you're tired, Ambrosius.' His magic huffed in reply. 'Where's the gatekeeper?'

'It's trying to break through some warding. That's a bit of luck, hey? There's no warding at our Tintagel.'

'That's because there's nothing left of our Tintagel.' Ben waded further into the dark cave. 'I'd rather not have seen it in such a state, but Jack had insisted on going.'

'And he got told off for climbing on the walls!' Ambrosius laughed.

'Only because you egged him on!' Ben shook his head, fighting a smile.

'Happier times.'

'When we thought Arthur was dead. There –' Ben pointed his magic towards a patch of darkness that looked a little brighter than the rest of the darkness.

'Whirlpool. It's under the surface.' Ben climbed over the ancient rock, slipped and pitched forwards into the water, inches from the unnatural glow of the whirlpool. 'Why are these things never vertical?'

Ambrosius laughed. The laughter was music to Ben's ears. Although Ben acknowledged that it took a lot of energy just to maintain that level of cheerfulness. The gods knew Ben couldn't manage it.

'Light up the cave?'

Still chuckling to himself, Ambrosius hopped into the air, chasing the shadows off the dark stone walls. The tide wasn't supposed to be in. Ben edged around the whirlpool clockwise and then turned back on himself, peering into the inky blackness of Styx's permanent night.

'I could be looking at sky, sea or land.' Ben didn't care for Styx. Five rivers and each one wanted to relieve you of your soul if you so much as dipped a little toe. 'For all I know, I'm staring into an abyss.'

'As a general rule, I wouldn't stare at an abyss, real or not, for long. It might answer you.' Ambrosius' light dimmed and flickered. Ben beckoned with his hand and his magic extinguished himself with relief.

'It's going to take days to get home.' Not that Ben was in a rush to deal with that mess.

'Have you thought about what you'll do?' Ambrosius knew full well that it had been the sole occupant of Ben's thoughts since learning of Arthur's true fate.

It was an impossible choice.

'Date them both. Assuming Arthur doesn't kill Jack.'

'No!' Ben swayed in the cold breeze.. 'It's not ... traditional.'

'The traditional boat has long since sailed, hit a reef, and disappeared beneath the waves. There were no survivors.' Ambrosius sent pins and needles up and down Ben's arms.

Neither of them had anticipated Arthur's reaction. Rage disguised as love. Arthur had mastered that early on in their relationship. Their time apart had unearthed the startling difference in how they felt about one another. Ben loved Arthur enough to let him go, and had it been the other way around, he would have. His refusal to stay had been taken as a betrayal. The air had felt thick after Ben's confession. He hadn't been unfaithful to Arthur, but that was how Arthur felt. Then again, perhaps that was Ben's survivor's guilt talking. He felt like he should feel bad, but ... he didn't. Jack was all that mattered. Ambrosius pressed against Ben's consciousness, trying to console him.

With a deep breath and a tired heart, Ben dived beneath the water, swam into the empty air nestled inside the crossing point, and dropped into a free fall.

14

BITTER END

STYX

B en landed face-first in the middle of Styx's brooding and mud-choked floodplains.

A gaggle of silvery souls scattered like seagulls startled by his crashing into their dimly-lit afterlife. The air in Styx was thin, designed to strangle any lingering thoughts of making it out alive. Black clouds suffocated the weak sun where it hung low in the sky, defeated. Banks of dense, unnatural fog swept through the fields without warning, swallowing the thousands of abandoned wooden boats that had fallen foul of the mud. The ghostly crews were long gone, but the echoes of their desperate cries for rescue assaulted him. In the distance, mountains rose through the clouds and disappeared from view. Ben's muscles burned with the effort of standing. He shook the mud from his hands, despairing at the state of his clothing. The braver ghosts were starting to poke their heads up from behind the boats. Some were nothing more than outlines painted onto the air, waiting for the next breeze to blow them from this realm into the Nothingness. These were the souls who'd found themselves stuck, or else had given up, choosing – knowingly or not – to fade from memory, from existence altogether. Just breaking down into atoms over hundreds of years, to be returned to the universe. The ghosts of black tulips sprouted in sporadic clumps. If Ben were to in-spect them closely, they would let go of their colour to reveal pearlescent outlines. A subtle reminder that nothing lived on the Elysian Fields of Styx. And if there was one place Ben didn't want to be out of place in, it was Styx. Should Death's little reapers find him, he'd be dragged off to Purgatory or the Nothingness and he wouldn't be coming back. A shudder sent chills through Ben's body. It was hard to grasp the air in Styx; Ambrosius groaned but cut through the atmosphere as best he could. The burnt-orange embers tore a jagged rip barely big enough to squeeze a foot into.

'I know you're tired Ambrosius, but that's messy.' The rip glitched and closed in on itself. Ambrosius' regret flooded Ben's mind.

'It was a valiant effort.' Ben looked out at the dark floodplains that stretched off far into the distance. They were miles from anything useful.

'We could go to Elysium.' Ambrosius indicated at the glow of industrial floodlights in the distance. Sounds of mining drifted to them, reminding Ben of the overbearing heat from the furnaces in the overcrowded mine.

'No. We might bump into Hades. Plus I have no desire to visit the Crossroads. It's a glorified sorting office for all of the realms. And without a physical body, we could be sorted off to Tartarus.'

The rivers lay still, like sheets of dark glass. There was Acheron, the river of pain; Lethe, the river of forgetfulness; Phlegethon – the river of fire; and Cocytus – the river of wailing. The river of Forgetfulness was looking pretty appealing right about now. Connecting them all and encircling the under realm, was the river Styx. As sure as the sun would rise in Gaia, Ben would find Charon the ferryman somewhere along the shoreline.

The only way out was up. Leaving Styx with sans magic meant using the footbridge. And getting to the footbridge involved crossing the river via one of two paths. Ben's choices were:

Sneaking past Hades' overgrown, three-headed guard dog, Cerberus, or

bargain with the ferryman who never said yes.

Ben had done enough fighting for one day. His limbs felt like somebody had tied kettlebells to them and he resigned himself to having to drag them all over the under realms and beyond, searching for Charon.

The combination of shale that passed for a beach in Styx, was a little more than Ben's weary feet could manage. He paused, hands on his knees.

Some distance ahead, he thought he saw Charon. A tall, dark smudge beside the water and mountains.

Ben resumed his trek, passing thousands of monochrome spirits loitering along the shore. Poor things had been laid to rest without rite and without coin so now they were damned to wait on the shore for a hundred years, watching the more fortunate ones be whisked away to the sorting office.

Ben stumbled; shale dug at his knees. The far-off figure kept its solitary watch over the relentless stream of boats constructed of bones emerging from the thick mist that clung to mountains and hung low over the surface. The ferryman had waded out to where the shallows dropped off, the tide lapping round his legs, robe fanning out behind him on the water of a river wide enough to be mistaken for an ocean.

Charon's lantern skimmed the surface, its candle flickering in the night, hood pulled low over his face, as always. Ben had seen Styx's Guardian's face twice. Frigid water lapped at his feet, creeping in through tiny tears to numb his toes. With a deep breath, he dipped a boot; the silhouette of something long and scaly darted to the surface. Ben jumped back onto the beach, shale crunching underfoot.

'Charon?!'

The ferryman turned deliberately slowly, and returned to shore without a splash. Unfazed by the fact that any number of night-mares could be swimming about down there. Charon set down his lantern, ignoring the languishing soul crawling towards it. He began rummaging through Ben's pockets.

'Let us have it, Benjamin.' Charon's voice sounded like gravel and dirt falling on a coffin lid.

'Don't tell me that you two want my talisman as well?' Charon pulled up one of Ben's legs, forcing the boot off and upending it. He sighed in irritation, threw the boot over his shoulder and made for the other one. Ben hopped out of reach. Charon looked him up and down through the thick wool of his hood and pried Ben's mouth open.

'You must have a coin,' Charon stated incredulously.

'I don't!' Even without being able to see them, Ben knew that Charon had raised his eyebrows. 'I have no coin on my person.'

'Oh.' Charon stepped back. 'How unfortunate. I do not relish the idea of spending one hundred years in your company,' the ferryman said not unkindly.

'I'm not dead!'

'My apologies. You smelt as if you were.' Charon picked up his lantern and stepped over a soul on his way to the shoreline, returning to his never-ending watch.

'Well now I'm offended ...' Ben looked about for his boot.

'And you are without a body.'

'Of that, I am aware. I'm also traveling in the opposite direction.' Ben's heart sank. A soul was dragging his boot towards Charon. Ben hopped and hobbled over the beach, the sharp shingle slashing at his exposed foot. 'He'll not accept the boot, I'm afraid.' The doomed ghost looked at him with sad, pleading eyes; Ben pulled the boot gently away. 'I must cross, Charon.' He jammed his foot back into the boot and joined the ferryman, astonished at the thousands of boats bobbing along.

Impassive and inscrutable, that was Charon.

Given that the Guardian was surrounded by so much waste and devastation, it was perhaps sensible to keep a distance from emotions.

'Guardians have been passing through Styx lately.'

'Annwn, Erebus, and Tuonela have been destroyed.' Guardians only visited Charon once they'd expired.

'The gods are rebelling again?' Charon asked with the interest of somebody who knew that he should be, but in actual fact, was wholly uninterested.

'Worse than when the supernatural clans rebelled. Styx is safe, I suppose. The dead have to go somewhere.'

'Nothing is safe. Nothing is sacred. Annwn's gone you say? Curious, Arawn has not crossed the shore.'

Ben swayed under the weight of a memory older than Jack. He grabbed Charon's shoulder to steady himself. If Arawn wasn't dead –

'Unfinished business. Best let that go.' Charon stole a quick glance at him. 'If Arawn had failed, think of all you would have missed. I speak of Jack –'

'I understood!' The candle in Charon's lantern flickered in response. Ben peered down and realised that the flame was grey with specs of black. Charon's magic. 'Is there something that I should know, Charon?'

'Not yet.'

'Will you tell me what it is when I should know?' Ambrosius fluttered into view on Ben's shoulder, having picked up on Ben's mounting frustration.

'You will know by then, thus rendering my informing you, useless. I will have no truck with pointless activities.'

Ben closed his eyes and bit down on a sigh that was determined to be heard.

'Am I to assume that you were attempting to rescue your King?' Charon shifted his lantern to the other side; the glow of his magic growing. Ambrosius jumped to Ben's other shoulder, curious.

'Unintentionally. Merlin stabbed me and sent me to a hell of his design.'

'Leaving it until your temporary demise is poor form.' Charon tilted his head to the side, pondering that.

Ben counted to three. 'I'm in a hurry. So, if you could call your boat over, that would be much appreciated.'

'Why should I help you?' Charon turned his hooded face to stare Ben down.

'Let me see, oh – ' Ben clicked his fingers. 'If I fail to return, Fate will destroy my realm and your quiet beachfront apartment will exceed capacity.'

Charon had grown tired of being a God and volunteered to be Styx's Guardian for "some peace and solitude." Doing Death's dirty work provided Charon with an excuse to ignore, and never see, his siblings. Although Ben found it interesting that Charon hadn't strayed too far from the family business.

'You can portal from here, Benjamin.'

'I'm not sure where to portal to. Frankly, I don't want to overshoot my body and end up as an astral-projection for the rest of my days.' Not to mention how both he and Ambrosius were fighting a losing battle against unconsciousness. 'Being out of body is draining.'

Charon set his lantern down again, a definite sign of refusal. The ferryman could not be rushed, only paid.

'Are you well, Benjamin?' Charon eyed Benjamin through the netting of his hood. Benjamin was not usually covered in so much mud, despite the weather of his realm. And his aura – black mixed with burnt-orange, spoke volumes. The toll of the exertion involved in his making it this far had all but drained him. Benjamin's legs looked set to give out at any moment. The prospect of having to mind the sick shtriga was almost enough to encourage Charon to grant his fellow Guardian passage.

'A wraith gatekeeper chased me all around Purgatory Tintagel.' Benjamin sagged forwards. Charon steadied him, noticing how Ambrosius appeared almost translucent. The chatterbox-magic had yet to utter a word. Charon extended a finger, but Ambrosius curled into a ball on Ben's shoulder and vanished. Benjamin stared at the horizon, struggling to focus his vision. He swayed and pitched forwards. Charon caught him, noting how flecks of Emrys' aquamarine magic was woven in with Ambrosius' orange, turning it a muddy-brown. Ambrosius was strong enough to cope with a few days out-of-body, and yet, it was so depleted that the curse keeping Benjamin alive was weakening. Charon's own magic could not decipher if Emrys' presence was designed to help or hinder.

'Press Merlin for answers. I do not wish to see you back on my shores before your time.' Charon lifted his lantern, oblivious to its considerable weight. 'Illuminare.' Even the glow of his magic could not properly cut through the murky, dark light of the underworld.

'That's Italian, not Greek.'

Charon watched his longboat float itself indolently towards them, the curved prow caused no disturbance to the water. Benjamin had once remarked that skulls had no business being buoyant.

'Rest will see to it. Ambrosius will be fine.' Benjamin nodded in agreement with himself.

'Expectations make you lonely, Benjamin.' Time and experience never succeeded to extinguish the shtriga's hope for a simple solution. But Charon was being impatient with the young Guardian. Benjamin was outside of his realm, without a body, and perhaps distraught over Arthur. It might even go some way to explaining the unhappy aura. That the Guardian wished to return home at all was admirable.

'What are you suggesting?' Benjamin mumbled, his eyes closed, his face pinched.

He was a decent Guardian. Better than Merlin or Arthur. Charon could not send Benjamin back unprepared.

'I have known Merlin longer than I have not. That your magic should be so depleted after his return to you, does not seem coincidental.'

Benjamin's face was an amusing mix of startled comprehension and surprise. It was well known Charon did not get involved unless his realm or way of life was directly threatened.

'I am quietly aware of what happens above and below me. In Gaia alone, seven thousand people die, per hour. I meet them all. Some talk. Not that it serves them.' The latest batch of boats bobbed into view on the horizon. 'And you, Benjamin, are distracting me from the new arrivals. Which of Merlin's webs are you trapped in this time?'

'Wish I knew.' Benjamin's whirling thoughts grounded on rock. 'Why didn't you tell me? If you knew where Arthur was?'

'Death would not have approved.'

Benjamin nodded his understanding.

'For what it is worth – ' Charon hooked an arm around Benjamin's side and prepared to put him in the boat. 'I considered your freedom from Arthur's – and Merlin's – influence, for the best.'

'You were right.'

Charon froze. 'You surprise me.'

'Time lent me clarity on some things. And ...'

'And Jack opened your eyes to others.'

Benjamin's head dropped to his chest. Charon turned back to his watch;

Benjamin would catch his breath on his own.

'Once you are reunited with your body, Ambrosius will feel better. As for the rest, it has a way of working itself out.' Benjamin snorted in reply. 'Arthur's return was not for your benefit. Keep Merlin and Arthur in your sight.'

Benjamin's wide eyes did not look reassured. And rightly so. Concern was practical where Merlin was concerned. Charon had no sight of what was to come, only what was and what had been; however, it was apparent that Benjamin would fail to cross the bridge unaided.

'Cerberus will accompany you.'

'That's kind of you but Cerberus can stay.'
Under his hood, Charon's lips nearly twitched into a smile. Nobody except he cherished the company of a three-headed dog. Charon brought the boat a little closer to the shore than usual. 'You are a shade still accustomed to having a body. Cerberus will see off anything whose curiosity brings it too close.' Charon waded through the water and lowered Benjamin into the boat.

'Your realm is without a God. Mórrígan …'
Guilt, real and imagined, weighed heavily on the shoulders of one too young for such a burden.

'Hades will oversee us until a replacement can be found. Mind you, it has been like this for over a century. Between Mórrígan's plotting with and against Fate, her preoccupation with conquest, revenge, and her questionable obsession with Merlin, Mórrígan spared no time to tend to Styx.'
Benjamin grunted in agreement, curling into a ball as best he could on the boat's narrow planks.

'The Gods are fools if they rise against Chaos, but cowards if they give in. Fate is right to stand her ground, but wrong in her methods.' Charon disliked the shivers rocking Benjamin's body, arms wrapped round himself, eyes screwed shut. Ambrosius was curled up on Benjamin's shoulder, looking paler and paler. Charon manifested a blanket; Benjamin didn't stir as he was tucked in. 'Merlin has visited with Chaos.'

''T's not good ...' Benjamin burrowed into the blanket, seeking warmth.

'Remaining impartial is becoming more challenging. Do not forget Cerberus.'

The black dog bounded up behind him, its wagging tail thumping the ground and sending up showers of shale. The right head, with the white spot around its left eye, spotted Benjamin and Cerberus pawed at the ground, eager to be given the command. The middle head, which featured no markings other than elderly scars, was sniffing at the beach and the left, with a white circle around its right eye, was focused on Charon, waiting. Charon pointed at the little boat.

The ginormous dog gave a deafening but excited bark that rumbled across the entire realm and shot past the ferryman. Benjamin lifted his head in time to see Cerberus flying through the air, shrinking to a more acceptable size as he went. Benjamin lacked the energy to stop Cerberus' three heads licking his face. Charon did not encourage such displays of affection from the hound. So, it was hardly surprising that the dog got carried away upon sighting a friend. Charon assumed Benjamin would not mind. He'd never dismissed the dog before. Content, the hound padded around in a quick circle, rocking the boat, and settled down on top of the Guardian, all three heads nudging at Benjamin, concerned, intrigued and eager for attention.

'Bad dog!' Benjamin mumbled whilst burying himself in Cerberus' long fur. Cerberus woofed happily, one head on

Benjamin's shoulder.

Charon lifted his hood a little, revealing a thin mouth and the tip of his nose, and let out a dry, crackly cackle.

When you ferried the dead, there wasn't much amusement to be had.

15

PENDULUM

C haron's disused laugh followed Ben as he bobbed along the river, towards the island where the bridge out to the upper realms began.

'At least one of us is having a good time,' Ben grumbled and scratched the middle head behind the ears. The other two, affronted, butted the middle head in an attempt to get Benjamin's attention. 'Alright! I only have two hands. Watch the claws!' Cerberus retracted his razor-sharp claws and whimpered an apology. 'Good dog.'

The boat docked itself against a neglected wooden jetty, listing to one side, forcing the passengers out onto the rotting structure. The smell of sulphur hung around them, making Ben gag. Ahead of him rose the steep, almost vertical incline, of the bridge.

'You might have to carry me Cerberus.' The middle head huffed in response. 'I've been walking since Purgatory!'

The middle head remained unsympathetic and a little offended at Ben's suggestion to ride him like a horse, despite the outer two whining in disagreement.

'Never mind. After you.' Cerberus stepped onto the bridge, looking back to where Ben still sat on the jetty. 'I'm coming!' Cerberus tilted all three heads to one side, huffed again, and padded back to him. The right head nuzzled Ben's shoulder, dipping low enough to allow Ben to wrap his arms around the dog's neck for support.

On the crowded bridge, souls drifted past Ben in varying states of distress. He tried not to stare at the wide eyes of freshly-made ghosts who would never follow in his footsteps. Ahead of him, a tall and imposing figure stood out as they confidently bobbed, weaved and swaggered their way through the crowd.

Ben groaned; he was not in the mood to interact with the altitudinous, suit-wearing purple God whose melodious voice, distorted by irritation, reached Ben.

'I appreciate that this is all new to you, but, well, how to put this delicately, *you are in the way!* It's bad enough that this bridge is so full.'

Hades, Lord of the under realms.

Ben might have had a chance to sneak past if he weren't using Cerberus to stay upright. It wasn't so much that Hades rushed everywhere, more that this particular slow-moving shade preferred to meander. The bridge into Styx wasn't built to accommodate meandering.

'Kindly hurry up,' Hades begged the shade; his affronted gaze finally spotted Benjamin. 'You!' Hades raised an accusing finger.

135

'Well met, Hades.' Cerberus growled softly.

'How dare you, a Guardian, kill a god! When I get over there – would you please hurry along?' Hades looked up at Ben and mimed pushing the shade out of the way.

'Just go around, Hades.'

Hades shot Ben a dark look and gestured at the souls who crowded around him, drawn to the warmth of a body still alive. 'I am somewhat boxed in at the moment.' Ben took the opportunity to dig deep for what little energy he had left.

'Merlin killed Mórrígan. I may have helped. And you hated Mórrígan!'

'It's the audacity that irks me. The example you have set –'

'In case you hadn't noticed,' Ben yelled over the fearful shades that drifted past with darted glances at him, 'two, possibly three Guardians and their realms are dead. Did you really expect me to step aside and allow War to do as she pleased?' The ambling shade slipped past Ben, leaving him face to face with Hades who stood, hands on hips, blocking the way ahead. Ben would have crossed his arms in defiance, but he was afraid he'd collapse if he let go of the hound. Cerberus gave a louder warning growl.

'How did you get the *dog*?' Hades reached out to pet Cerberus' left head but all three snapped at his fingers. 'Charon never lets Cerberus leave his side!'

'Apparently the *dog* is here to keep me safe from anything that wishes me harm.'

'Like me?' Hades stared down at Ben for a moment before his eyebrows rose and a cheeky grin lit up his chiselled face.

'It's good to see you, Hades.'

Hades pulled him in for a crushing bear hug that picked Ben up off the ground. He smiled properly for the first time in days, allowing the exhaustion to creep back in.

Hades set him back on his feet, poking and prodding at Ben's form. 'Why don't you have a body?' The impossibly tall God frowned, concerned.

Ben considered lying, but Hades would find out sooner or later. He also couldn't handle the gentle concern in Hades' eyes, so Ben looked out across the vista of Styx. The rivers seemed to glow from this height. He swore he could make out Charon stood on the shore.

'Merlin stabbed me.'

'The little runt!' Hades' anger shook the bridge, dislodging some shades who fell off the bridge, screaming. 'Want me to drag him to Tartarus for you?'

'It's not the worst thing he's done –'

'Oh, Benny. Should I ask?' Hades let go of his arms and Ben promptly fell forwards. Hades caught him by the shoulders and held him upright. His feet brushed the floor as he came eye-to-eye with Hades.

'He "killed" Arthur. Trapped him in Purgatory. Suppose you knew.' Ben's voice dipped as the pinprick of what promised to be a cracking headache pinched him above his eyes.

'Benjamin – ' Hades sounded offended, downright hurt at the accusation. 'If I had known ... my offer of throwing Merlin in a cell in Tartarus still stands.' Ben had to doubletake a ghost drifting past because it looked a lot like Jack.

'Are you alright, Benny?'

'It's been a long year ... have you had trouble with Fate?'

'Aside from having to adopt Styx, no. As if I don't have enough to do!' Hades, seeing that Cerberus was distracted by an attempt to catch his tail, tried to stroke the dog again. The dog growled. 'Fine! As for Fate, I suppose she has a reason for leaving Styx and Hades intact.'

'What could Fate possibly want with billions of deceased souls?' Ben wondered.

'No idea! But she can have them!'

Hades felt shafted by his assignment to the under realms. He had admitted to Ben, whilst drinking late into the night, that he didn't want to be a God. It was the family business and that was that. Just a massive inconvenience to Hades' true ambitions of wandering about the universe playing the lyre. And it was the mutual understanding of having to be something they did not want to be that had bonded them.

'Arawn should be dead, but Charon says he hasn't arrived yet.'

'Arawn,' Hades scoffed. 'Last I saw, he was lingering in Avalon. That rascal is always up to something. I remember when ...'

Ben tried to focus on Hades' history lesson, but the headache was becoming the centre of his being and blurring his vision. Ben felt himself sway, acutely aware of the drop below. He supposed that Mórrígan hadn't been interested in risk assessments when she'd run the place. His legs buckled and he blacked out.

16

BAD TIME

B en's feet and lower legs were on fire.
He couldn't move them.

His heavy eyelids batted open, and to his great surprise, Ben found himself staring at the tiny plaster mountain range of his bedroom's artex ceiling. The terracotta-coloured walls were aflame with the low evening sun that filtered in through a crack in the mismatched curtains. One had a garish seventies floral pattern, the other navy blue. The armchairs, usually burdened with laundry revealed their faded brown linen. The oak dresser, chest of drawers and wardrobe were shut all the way and had they been relieved of their clutter.

It was unnerving.

The reason for his immobility spilled over both ends of Ben's bed, fast asleep. Ben tried to push himself upright but collapsed back onto the pillows, awakening Cerberus who raised his now-singular head.

''S alright Cerberus.'

The hound accepted this and dropped his head back down; the bed groaned under the weight of the enormous dog whose tail was sweeping the floor.

'That can't be comfortable?' Cerberus replied with a dog-sigh.

'Yeah, I guess it's better than the floor. Did you bring me home?' The dog yawned, his tail thumping the floor. 'Good boy!'

'I brought you home, thank you kindly.' Hades poked his head around the door.

'You're a good boy too, Hades.'

The Lord of the under realms strode into Ben's room. The sleeves of his crisp white shirt were rolled up past the elbow, the top buttons undone and the pinstripe tie nowhere to be seen. Ben couldn't recall the last time he'd seen Hades so casually dressed. The armchair screeched in protest as Hades dragged it over to the bedside and hopped into it, his long legs hanging over one arm. No matter where Hades was, he always looked like he belonged.

'I tried sending Cerberus back, but he wouldn't go.' Cerberus raised his great head to give Hades a look. 'Oh, don't glare at me, you'd have taken Benny back to Charon if I hadn't been there.' Cerberus rolled over and showed his back to them. 'Bad dog.' Disappointed, Hades shook his head. 'Do you see the disrespect I have to endure?'

'Terrible.'

The largely one-sided debate as to who Cerberus belonged to had been going on for millennia. Hades had found the puppy wandering through Styx, alone and frightened. Much like the puppy, the Lord of the under realms was fierce and scary, but he had a soft heart. If you asked Cerberus, the hound would tell you that he belonged to no one.

'You've been asleep for two days.' Hades settled a pillow behind Ben's back, helping him to sit up. 'Merlin is still running around with Fate's dagger. He has resurrected your thought-to-be-deceased royal-pain-in-the-arse boyfriend. And dumped him on your current boyfriend. Who is technically deceased –'

'You spoke to Jack?!'

'Briefly – why doesn't he like me?' Hades had a need to be liked that was bordering on pathological.

'Jack likes you fine. He so rarely meets his match in sarcastic wit.' It was a lie and they both knew it. Hades was, in Jack's opinion, loud, arrogant, cocky and in love with himself.

'Charon thought Merlin was interfering with Ambrosius somehow.'

'Charon loves a conspiracy theory.' Concern rearranged Hades' face into harsh lines that framed his soft brown eyes. Compassion hadn't helped Hades in early life, not during the wars, not after. So, the God had stomped on it and folded it up until it was small enough to hide in his breast pocket, only bringing it out when absolutely essential.

'I attributed your looking unwell to your misadventures in Purgatory. Merlin *is* messing with your head though.' Opening a portal vexed Hades, so Ben wasn't inclined to take his diagnosis.

'Did you not stop to think about how much this has taken from you? Merlin's return alone –'

'At least I'm not dead.' Hades huffed at Ben's attempt to drive the conversation away from actually being a conversation. 'You're immortal, not impervious to … Jack told me what happened. Charon told me what happened after that. Benny, it's –'

'It's going to get worse before it gets better.' The thought that he was going to have to face the others, filled Ben with a kind of anxious dread that he could taste. They'd want to talk about it, all of them. They'd all be judging him, expecting him to side with them. His stomach flipped.

'What happens if Ambrosius is too tired to feed the curse, hurm?' Hades nagged. 'You'd die human. Maybe that's better. Maybe it's worse.'

'If anybody should know the answer to that, it's you! And this isn't making me feel better!' Cerberus raised an ear in Ben's direction and sighed. Ben agreed with that summary.

'It's subjective! You'll linger on in one realm or another until you forget everything that made you, you. Some people would rather forget.' Hades shrugged. Death wasn't a thing that Gods worried about.

As a shtriga, he shouldn't either. If it were to happen then Ben would have to suck it up and slip into the Nothingness like an immortal who was stupid enough to be killed. Again.

'I was going to go, once you'd woken. But I can't leave you like this.'

The vibration of Ben's phone echoed from the bowels of the

bedside table.

Ben found his thumb hovering over the call button on Jack's name. The moth-eaten grey carpet was visible. April and Jack might have a point about redecorating.

'Thanks for tidying up in here.'

'I didn't tidy up.'

Jack must have been sorting through his things. Ben's miserable reflection watched him from the mirror on the dresser, his eyes grey and stormy. Perhaps Jack was keeping a distance until Hades left. Perhaps not.

'My staying is not solely for your benefit. I wouldn't mind putting Merlin in his place.' Nonchalant threats did nothing to mask the anger.

'You're not letting this pass, are you?' The fierce loyalty was one of Ben's favourite things about Hades.

'Not a chance. Besides, we can't have all of the realms collapsing in on themselves. The old boy on the shore won't know what's hit him.'

'You don't give Charon enough credit.' Ben frowned. April had been texting him and the phone was complaining about a lack of storage. No texts from Jack though.

'True. Consider though, the fact that all of the realms were built to work together, in sync. Each has its own role. The disappearance of realms upsets that balance. Whenever the balance tips, the under realms take the hit. Some souls are getting trapped, and some aren't even being reaped.' Hades swatted at Ben's phone hand.

He put his phone in his lap and forced himself to focus.

'Life and death are a cycle; the rites are important to ensure that the living can do so in peace. I can't allow this to continue.'

'Who'd have thought that you would turn out to be the most sensible God of all.'

Hades chuckled, he lived to surprise people. Ben flipped onto his texts and sent April a short note.

'Everything goes to hell if I can't run the under realms properly. Pardon the pun. I'd like to send some souls to Avalon. Right now, the majority are ending up in Tartarus.'

'True or not, that's what Jack refers to as a humble brag.' Hades scowled, trying to subtly look at the screen.

The early years of their friendship had been dominated by Hades relentless complaining about Merlin appointing Artemis as his Guardian.

It had been tough on them both.

Hades' long-term on-again/off-again partner had been appointed as his Guardian, right after the spectacular breakup that had lasted a year and caused significant damage to two realms.

'Artemis can't let the thing with Persephone go.'

'You married another woman.' Ben's phone buzzed.

Hades dragged his hands roughly over his face. 'Do I need to explain it in interpretative dance? Because words seem unable to convey that I did not kidnap Persephone! Nor did I force her to marry me.'

'Uh-huh, she just jumped into your chariot.' Ben was only teasing, but he noticed that Hades wasn't wearing his wedding ring.

'She did actually.' Hades swung his legs back to the ground, sitting at the edge of his seat. 'Zeus was going to – I had no choice. But did Artemis see it like that? No.' Hades slumped back; the chair rocked with his weight. Sunlight glinted off the elusive molten gold fused to the obsidian wedding band hidden beneath Hades' shirt.

The Gods' lives were never easy, stuck as they were in one another's orbits. Fate's escape plan had given them freedom, but they didn't know how to moderate themselves.

'Sometimes I wish that Artemis would turn herself into a constellation.'

It was easier to say than the truth which was that Hades would fall to pieces without Artemis. Ben kept listening for the front door. Hoping that Jack would let himself in, calling out "it's only me!" as his vampire always did.

'Long story short, a hunter called April is on her way.' Ben's arms wobbled but couldn't take the weight of him trying to get up. He flopped onto his side.

'You didn't call Jack?!' Hades made to stop him.

'No.'

'You waited for Arthur's ghost. Which is more than most would do.' The bed bounced as Hades plonked himself down next to Ben.

'It's not a sin to be lonely, Benny.' Hades grabbed Ben's phone, forcing him to look at the God. 'Please don't tear yourself apart trying to see this from everybody's point of view.'

Ben nodded so Hades would return his phone. He sucked in a shaky breath and finally began to type to Jack.

'I wish I had your patience, always looking for the good in people that are terrible for me.'

Ben's mouth twitched, keen to point out that Artemis hadn't been Hades' best option. Gods and mortals alike could not help who they loved.

A frantic hammering on the door drew Cerberus from the bed, barking. He padded off to investigate, looking back impatiently at Hades.

'You'd best let April in. She can and will kick the door down.'

'I'm coming!' Hades cried out in answer to both April and the dog.

Left alone, the little voice in the back of Ben's head whispered that he was going to have to cut himself in half to keep both Jack and Arthur happy and why could neither of them accept that Ben had both a past, a present and, in Arthur's case, a future?

The front door crashed into the wall, no doubt punching a nice hole in the plaster.

'Oi!' Hades' indignant cry did nothing to slow the rapid thud of booted feet trekking mud into Ben's carpets. And then April was standing in the doorway, dithering between delight and anger. 'Why haven't you replied?! Jack is out of his mind with worry.'

'I was asleep?' Ben looked to Hades for confirmation. 'I was asleep.'

'For two days?' She crossed her arms, radiating disapproval.

Her aura was stronger.

'He was. I've been bored, waiting for him to wake up.'

April jumped at the sight of the 6'5 purple God towering over her. She hurried over to Ben's side, sneaking glances at Hades over her shoulder.

'April, I don't know how to explain this to you right now. I don't want to see anybody.'

'You mean Arthur and Merlin.'

Why was everybody jumping to conclusions, Ben wondered.

'I get what you mean –'

'No, you don't,' Ben muttered bitterly.

April noticed the pointed look that Hades and Ben exchanged. He wished he hadn't mentioned it.

'Merlin has been visiting Chaos in Tartarus. Which is cause for concern. And, you know, the other stuff.'

'You didn't tell me that!' Hades rounded on Ben. 'Plucking souls from Purgatory, letting realms fall, stealing Fate's dagger. Death won't stand for this, mark my words, Benny.'

'Forget Merlin, how did you get back?' April forced a hug on Ben.

Exhaustion flooded him and strangled his voice.

Hades cleared his throat, 'I found Benny crawling out of Styx. I considered telling Cerberus to leave him, but then I'd have doomed myself to at least a hundred years of Ben's moping.'

April released Ben and turned back to find Hades and Cerberus standing at the foot of the bed.

'Cerberus is the dog, right?'

'Correct.' Hades puffed out his chest, ever the proud dog parent.

April's hands went unconsciously to her side.

'This one doesn't bite.' Ben held his hand out; Cerberus trotted over and nudged Ben's hand onto his head, his tail wagging.

'Cerbi is friendly!' Hades smiled his biggest, bestest smile. Which involved a lot of sharp, jagged teeth. April scooted closer to Ben, her shoulder pressing into his.

'Hades doesn't bite, either. He just doesn't know how to interact with living creatures.' Hades tried to rearrange his smile. 'Charon asked Cerberus to accompany me home.' Ben patted her on the shoulder, not quite over the trauma of the hellhound incident either.

'Most people bring back magnets from their adventures. Not a giant dog and – ' April looked Hades up and down ' – whoever or whatever he is.'

'We've not been introduced.' Hades extended his hand, a business card materialising between his index and middle fingers. 'Hades, Lord of the under realms.'

April didn't take the card, her eyes narrowing. 'He's purple.' Hades looked down at his hands, uncertain as to April's point. Ben groaned as he pushed himself to the edge of the bed and swung his legs over the side. The exertion set the room spinning.

'He looks like somebody put Papa Smurf in the wash, red trousers and all.'

'That sounds like an insult, but I've never come across a Smurf before?' Hades couldn't quite stop looking at April.

Ben assumed that, like he had been, Hades was curious about her aura.

'It'll be something on TV.' Ben leaned forwards; eyes closed. It did not stop the vertigo. 'April and Jack consume programmes like their existence depends on it.'

'Speaking of Jack, he's been a mess, and Arthur – who is gross, by the way – isn't helping. It's all I can do to stop Jack from doing something stupid.' April frowned at the floor.

Shame.

That was the only word for the ugly feeling in his stomach. April shouldn't have been in that position. His phone buzzed and flashed at him. 'It's Jack.'

'We'll give you some space.' Hades held the door open for April, watching her slip out of the room. 'Doesn't April remind you of Artemis?'

'Because they both have a strong sense of justice, swords, a dislike for the majority of men, in particular Merlin and yourself?' The call ended. If Ben kept talking, the anxiety might not eat him alive before Jack arrived.

'Well, yes that. April's aura, what is she?'

'Not sure. She has magic.' Ben pinched his eyes shut. Hades retook his seat and Ben was unspeakably grateful that he wasn't leaving him alone. 'Fate has it in for her.'

'Fate has it in for everybody who isn't Fate. We're all to blame for the state of her existence.' Hades squeezed Ben's shoulder. 'Breathe.'

Ben wanted very much to take a breath in, but the universe

seemed hellbent on suffocating him.

'Not that it's my business, but did … Arthur do anything?'

'Not exactly.' Ben felt so tired. He didn't think that feeding would resolve it.

'That's not a solid no.'

'We argued – well, Arthur argued. He's furious, Hades.'

'Arthur has not been your partner in a very long time, he will have to deal with it.'

Ben prodded Ambrosius, looking for a portal, but his magic rolled away. 'Fate tried to have April killed.'

'What do you expect me to do about that?'

Ben gave Hades his best attempt at puppy-dog eyes.

'Fine! You might not like the answer, mind.'

'If I at least know what April has done or, is about to do, I can –'

'Help? Benny.' Hades gave him a long, hard look that suggested he'd lost his mind. 'If Fate is scared of April –'

'I'd have less to worry about if I understood what's going on. I'd wager that Merlin knows. Somebody put her in my path for a reason.'

'Exactly my point –'

The front door crashed into the wall again. 'Where is he?!'

'Ah, Romeo has arrived.'

17

SPIDER BITES

H ades flattened himself against the wall as Jack shouldered his way past the God.

'What are you doing here?!' Jack spun around on the stairs, his breathing indicative of a panic attack.

'I brought your boyfriend back. You're welcome.' Jack's mouth opened and shut, not sure where to start. 'Go on up. He's not feeling well, mind you.' The vampire took the remaining stairs two at a time. 'Ah, young love.' Hades watched Jack round the corner and, not for the first time, felt a pang of jealousy. A clatter of pans followed by some delightful swearing startled Cerberus into a barking fit. 'The hunter-mage-witch!'
April came hurrying out of the kitchen, Cerberus following her, tail a-wagging, shamelessly seeking attention and food.

'The damn dog prefers everybody to me.'
April threw him a quick, wide-eyed "make the dog stop" look.

'Cerberus, heel.' The hound took one look at Hades, woofed,

and trotted off to the kitchen. 'Or go to the kitchen, whatever you prefer.' Hades leaned on the banister and considered the girl who terrified Fate. 'He never listens to me.' April shrugged. 'Does nobody in this house care for my plight?' April's eyeroll was spectacular. '*You* are just like *Benny*.'

'Are you going to loiter on the stairs and listen to them?' April ventured to the bottom step, her head to one side.

'I can guess what they're saying. "*I thought you were dead! Don't ever do that again. I love you.*"' Hades mimed throwing up. 'No, I've got some thinking to do whilst they sort themselves out.'

Hades had stuck his neck out twice before and had lost his head on both occasions. He'd barely survived Fate's war with Chaos. And then there was the mess with Persephone. After that, he'd tried to avoid getting caught up in other people's catastrophes. But Benny wouldn't ask if he wasn't desperate. And Ben had never turned Hades away.

'I could make it to the end of time itself and I'd still not be able to figure out how Benny always manages to be in the wrong place at the right time. Coffee?'

April nodded but appeared to be stuck to the floor.

'Would you prefer if I went first?' Another nod. 'Come on – yikes – those cabinets! This place hasn't changed since my last visit.' He looked about in mild disgust.

'I suggested redecorating.'

'Ha! Fire is the only cure. I can't believe Benny lives like this.' Hades sat himself down at the rickety table, concerned he might get a splinter. Or break the chair.

'He spends most of his time at Jack's.' April edged around Cerberus who'd conveniently plonked himself by the cafetiere. 'How do you know them?'

'I argued with Merlin. A lot. After he and Arthur "died," I argued with Benny. A lot. Couldn't get rid of him, a real nuisance.' Hades smiled. That Benny wasn't a God had also helped their friendship.

'What do you need to think about?' April stared at the mugs, searching for a way through.

'Guardian-related nonsense.'

April crept up behind the hound and was stretching one arm out so far, Hades was just waiting for a pop. Or the inevitable. 'Cerberus won't hurt you. But if you pour boiling hot coffee on him, he might very well bark at you.' April rested her chin on her fists, much like Benny did when he couldn't decide what to do. Cerberus rolled onto his back, caught April's eye and thumped his tail, stomach on display. The creature had no shame.

'He seems to have taken quite a liking to you. Cerberus that is. Ben too.'

April reached out slowly but snatched her hand back. Cerberus whined sadly and flopped back onto his side, sniffing at the kickboards, hot on the trail of crumbs.

'You're the third god I've met.' April stepped in-between Cerberus' legs, her body shaking as she held her breath and retrieved the cafetiere. It was the only way she'd get over her fear. 'Maybe the fourth – does Death count as a God?'

'You've met Death?!' Hades sat up a little straighter. Very few lived to tell the tale of an encounter with Death.

'Fate brought him along to intimidate me. Apparently it wasn't my time.'

'Death knows best. And Death prefers they. Benjamin tells me you've recently discovered your magic. How's that working out for you?'

'Fine.' Talking about Eilir with anybody other than Jack was uncomfortably weird: like April would be judged, somehow, for having magic or having magic and not knowing how to use it, or she might say the wrong thing to the wrong person. Jack hadn't exactly told her to keep her magic a secret, but he hadn't encouraged her to speak openly either.

'It took Benny a while to nail the more complicated stuff. Try not to turn yourself into a goat.' Hades' booming laugh took April by surprise. The rickety chair struggled to accommodate the God's giant frame as it shook. He pulled her mug towrds him, still chuckling. Coffee splashed into the cups, some of it escaped to form little dark puddles on the table.

'Ben never mentioned that he's friends with the purple Lord of the under realms.'

'Oh, well.' The chair groaned as Hades leaned back. 'I imagine that's because I sit just behind Merlin on Jack's list of "Benny's friends he doesn't like."'

April caught herself staring at the strong, seemingly chiselled-from-marble face and shook herself free. Maybe that list should be called "Benny's friends who intimidate Jack."

'That's quite the achievement.'

'It's not a very long list. There aren't many of us to choose from. So – ' Hades settled his crossed arms on the table, chin resting atop of them. 'What can you do with your magic?'

Eilir tapped on her mind, '*We do not need to fear Hades.*'

'Okay.' April scrunched her eyes shut, her focus on trying to levitate the coffee cup.

'Aw, well aren't you a sweet little bundle of energy!'
April opened her eyes in horror to see that Hades wasn't addressing her, rather Eilir. At least April assumed the tiny jade bundle of embers that stood next to the cafetiere with hands on hips, was Eilir.

'Eilir's never manifested herself like this.'
April's magic turned at her name, minuscule eyes looked up at her as if they were seeing April for the first time. Not knowing how to introduce herself to her own magic, April extended her index finger, which Eilir took in her tiny hands.

'Reckon we can move that there cafetiere?'
Eilir nodded and without turning to look at said item, lifted the cafetiere into the air for five seconds.

Hades glanced up at her and laughed. 'You stick your tongue out when you concentrate.'
April pulled her hood over her head, willing it to turn into an invisibility cloak.

'You be careful now, with great power comes great responsibility.'

'You mean like Spiderman?!'

'What's a Spiderman?' Hades looked genuinely curious.

'Never mind.' April frowned. 'There has to be a reason for me having magic. A purpose.' She held her hand out – like she'd seen Ben do – Eilir hopped up.

'Not necessarily. It could be inherited. Perhaps spending time in stressful situations with Benny brought it to the surface.' Eilir jumped down and scampered over to Hades. The God did a double take and looked closely at Eilir. Everybody kept looking at her – and Eilir - as if they knew them. Which was weird and something she desperately wanted to talk to Ben about. It seemed natural that Ben would replace Merlin as her teacher, once he felt better. April was relieved, but Eilir turned sad eyes to her.

'Okay, but why does Fate see me as such a threat? She's not scared of Merlin.'

'Fate relies on Merlin's infatuation.' Hades rolled his eyes. Love seemed to be a trivial pursuit for gods. 'Premonitions?'

'They're more frequent now.' The image of Merlin stood over Ben stopped by to haunt her. 'I saw.' She hesitated. 'I saw Merlin with Ben, but before I'd had the misfortune of meeting Merlin.' And there was the new premonition. The one that she was seeing every night, the one with Merlin and the tree. 'Two have come to pass.'

'Come to pass – you sound like Merlin. Please don't start speaking in rhyme.'

'Who has time to rhyme?'

Hades glared at her, daring her to do it again. Hades had shown her nothing but his good-natured self, but in that moment, April glimpsed the God behind the myths. He did not like Merlin.

'I never know what they mean until it's too late.' There was something lurking at the edges of April's magic, she could feel it. Like her future was hiding, just out of sight and if she could find it, she could be useful. She could stop Jack from ever losing Ben again.

'You'll learn to read them over time, but here's the thing: you can't change the outcome.'

That was frustratingly on track with how things had been going. Although it made April feel better about the whole Ben-being-stabbed–thing. Cerberus rolled over with a dog-sigh. 'Fate said she couldn't see the end of my story.'

'Ah!' Hades' smile wasn't cruel, but it wasn't reassuring either. 'You're a total enigma with magic and prophetic sight? We have a winner!'

'That's it?' April was pressed against the table, her chair tipping forwards.

'What were you expecting? To be told that you're special?' Hades crossed his fingers, hoping that April wouldn't see through his bluff. Fate couldn't see her death and Death didn't take her. Whatever came next for April was bigger than them all.

'Am I overthinking this? It's possible that I'm being paranoid.'

Outwardly, April seemed to be coping well. But Hades could see the strain of everything bunching up at the corners of her eyes. The strain of trying to keep Jack from falling apart, the guilt over not preventing Benny's "death," the uncertainty of her newfound magic. It was close to pulling her out to sea.

'A little paranoia isn't such a bad thing, given your line of work.'

'I suppose. Merlin's been teaching me spells.'

Fate was right to be scared.

The idea of Merlin teaching anybody, anything unsettled Hades, let alone somebody whose life was unknown to the one who wrote history.

'Merlin's a terrible tutor. Not enough patience, too much resentment.' And a terrible influence. Merlin had done a sterling job breaking Ben.

'Merlin asked me to retrieve Arthur with him.' April sounded a little too proud of helping. 'The spells that he wanted to teach me ... it's like he doesn't think I'd use this stuff against him?'

'No use trying to understand a mad man's logic.' Cerberus batted at something that Hades couldn't see. Whatever it was, it vanished under the cupboards and the dog whined. And whined. With a sigh, Hades got up to have a look. 'There's nothing there.' The hound disagreed, pawing at the kickboards. 'I'm not removing them so that I can tell you there's nothing there.' The dog huffed sadly. 'You can have a treat but then nothing more until dinner.' Cerberus jumped to his feet, licking at Hades' hand.

'Do you know why an oak tree is significant to Merlin?' Hades opened the fridge, the impatient hound on his heels. Cerberus jumped and snatched the chicken from Hades' hand.

'Merlin was trapped in an ancient oak tree, and here's the plot twist, his jailor was a student to whom he'd imparted all of his wizardly knowledge. I think she was called Vivienne.'
April turned the colour of somebody who was about to faint.

'It's a story. Hey, breathe.'
April swapped her rapid, shallow breaths for deeper ones, but they still sounded too much like hyperventilating for Hades' liking. She pushed away from the table. 'I need to talk to Jack and Ben.' She said in a small voice that told him she was wary of coincidences and consequences.

'Now's not a good time.' April thought about it, wringing her hands. 'Look, I'm here to help Ben, and you being all worked up will undo my efforts.' He softened his voice. 'What's bothering you?'

'It's probably a coincidence.'

'More than likely.' He tried to smile, very aware that he towered over April.

'When Eilir – my magic – named herself, she gave me two names.'

Hades winced. 'Don't say –'

'Vivienne.'

'You said it.' Hades poured her a cup of coffee as a distraction. 'You probably don't want to hear the other part of the story ...'

'Jack told me. He's like a million years old and, and Merlin!'

Hades chuckled. 'The last I checked; Merlin was still menacing this universe with his presence. And he doesn't have tree branches for limbs.'

April smiled at that, but she was still dangerously close to tears, trying desperately to work out why the name had popped into her head. Something thudded against the floor upstairs, Hades poked Cerberus in the ribs and the dog rose and stretched, his claws tapping on the floor. 'Big stretch!' Cerberus huffed at Hades and padded upstairs.

'There are too many myths about Arthur and Merlin. This one is just that, a myth. It never happened.'
There had been a Vivienne in Merlin's life once upon a very long time ago. Hades settled back into his chair, resigned to the fact that he was going to have to stick his neck out for Ben.

'For now, keep your cards close to your chest. Do not, and I cannot stress this enough, mention it to Merlin.'
Although coincidence was Merlin's middle name. The name was significant, Hades knew it. And Eilir appeared to be warming up. If April was going to make it to that oak tree and whatever followed, she'd need Artemis' help.

Hades didn't like how that tasted.

18

ULTRAVIOLET

'What happened? Are you hurt?' Jack's frantic questions pushed the door open. 'What are you wearing?'

Ben looked up from the jumper he'd been folding. 'I needed to change.'

'And you thought that a cross between Victorian and medieval fashion was the way to go?' Jack spluttered, furious.

Ben turned and caught his reflection in the mirror. The brown, tweed waistcoat wasn't so old. Nor was the high collared white shirt. The royal blue woollen overcoat, that swept down to the floor, had looked fine when he'd put it on.

'Arthur's been back for five minutes and you're dressing to make *him* feel more comfortable?' Jack stood in the doorway, solid and present, his bottom lip quivering. Ben pulled him into a bone-crushing hug that tried to convey everything that they felt but couldn't articulate and the things that should have been a given. Ben closed his eyes and buried his face in Jack's hair, glad to be back where he belonged. He'd been foolish to worry about Jack rejecting him.

'I don't hate the waistcoat.' Jack sniffed, his fingers worrying at a button on the not-so-offensive garment.

'This isn't for Arthur's benefit. I really don't own that many outfits.'

'I know. It's just ... you've not worn any of this the entire time I've known you, and you were dead and then you weren't, and April – she trashed my kitchen and set a tree on fire, and, and, you were going to stay with Arthur –'

'That's what Merlin had you think?' Jack gave a small nod against Ben's shoulder.

'I will kill him.'

'Good, he's in the mood for a quarrel.'

Ben tipped Jack's chin up and kissed his vampire. Ben had sensed Merlin's utter desperation when his magic had wrapped around his and ripped him from his body.

'Trouble has a way of bending around that man. He keeps summoning it up and inviting it in for us to deal with. As a matter of fact, I left him in my apartment with his latest acquisition.'

Ben's stomach flipped. He'd thought – hoped – that Merlin would take Arthur away. But then again, Benjamin had spent hundreds of years petitioning anybody who'd listen for Arthur's return. Was he supposed to be feeling grateful? Because at no point had that feeling made itself known. Benjamin should have been careful about what he'd wished for.

'Merlin has to keep moving, Jack. We all do. Otherwise, the

guilt catches up.' Ben squeezed his eyes shut. 'It catches up.' Jack heard and understood, he hugged Ben tighter. Ben sucked in a shuddery breath. He didn't deserve such understanding from Jack.

'I'm not sure what to say ...' or how to fix it and have everybody leave happily.

'Should I be concerned?' Jack pulled back slightly.
Ben took his face into both hands, stubble grazed his fingers.

'From the moment I awoke in Purgatory, I wanted to get back to *you*. I was worried about *you*. When Arthur found me, my thoughts were for *you* and only *you*.'

Jack retreated into the hug. 'Arthur isn't what I imagined. Based on your stories.'

'He's not as I remember him. Either Purgatory changed him, or perhaps I embellished his memory over time. Maybe I just forgot the bad bits ...'
The strains of Hades and April's conversation came to them. Ben was confident that April would like Hades, but a small part of him worried that their personalities would clash.

'I've asked Hades to stay.'

'Ugh, what a mix of personalities. The dog also?' Jack winced, maybe he hadn't meant to sound so bitter and tired of it all. 'Suppose it's good to have a God around. He's the least terrible of the lot.'
Jack and Hades had last seen each other in the nineties. Hades had accidentally killed Jack's electronic pet that lived on a screen. Ben didn't believe for a second that Jack was over it.

'So, you'll be nice to Hades, whilst he's here?'

'Fine.' Jack paused. 'Were you really going to stay? With Arthur?'

Ben sighed. All this time and Jack still hadn't learnt not to rush through every moment. He looked down into those big, wounded eyes and knew that lying would only cause more friction later on.

'In the moment, I considered it, yes.' Ben didn't miss Jack's flinch. 'But it was only a moment, and I felt awful.'

Jack didn't know if he wanted to know at what point the desire to stay had left. Was it when Ben realised that time had rubbed the shine off of his once great King? Or was it when Jack arrived? Because Ben had looked guilty as hell.

'Why?'

'Jack –'

'I want to understand.' Really it was so he could torture himself.

'Arthur.' Ben struggled with his words and eye contact, 'Arthur was unlike anybody I had ever met – at that point. He was older, he was sophisticated ... I was young, Jack, impressionable and inexperienced.'

Ben looked older in that moment. His pale blue eyes hadn't changed colour in a while and his skin was clammy. Exhaustion shook his body; he'd have fallen if Jack weren't holding him. He fished an armchair closer and guided Ben into it. Jack knelt beside the chair, watching his partner's rapid breathing with unease. Yes, Jack was hurt. But he could tell by the way Ben was wringing his hands in the folds of the ridiculous jacket-coat-thing that there was nothing Jack could say that would injure Ben more than his own thoughts. Jack gently separated Ben's hands from the jacket; the shtriga's eyes closed. He'd felt Ben's presence the moment he'd opened the front door. And nothing had felt better. Jack squeezed Ben's arm; he jolted upright, eyes wide.

'It's alright, it's just me, Ben. We don't have to talk about it now.'

'No. We do.' Ben took Jack's hands in his, holding on tight, head pressed against Jack's. 'Arthur had the right words, every time. I thought that what I wanted was what I needed.' Well, there was something to be said for that, Jack supposed. Arthur didn't seem capable of a platonic friendship.

'I shouldn't have pushed you to find Merlin –'

'None of this is your fault, Jack.' Ben sounded so sincere, so earnest, that Jack nearly believed him.

'Okay.' And perhaps that was all that either of them could bear to say on the matter. 'Arthur doesn't have the right words where April's concerned. He said something misogynistic, so she hit him round the head with her wooden sword! Merlin's been trying to explain to Arthur why he can't say stuff like that ever since.'

'Is that so?' Ben's smile had nothing to do with Arthur. He seemed to be enjoying just listening to Jack talk. And Jack was happy to oblige.

'*Merlin* has been banging on about calling the remaining

Guardians together. Oh, speaking of – ' Jack pulled the sword talisman from his pocket and hung it around Ben's neck as if it were made of wood. 'You can take this back and all of the crazy that comes with it.'

Ben stared at the little sword, a tremor running through him. 'You should have given this to Arthur.'

He should have, but Jack was only talking to Arthur when he absolutely had to. And even then, he'd been outsourcing it to Merlin or April.

'Arthur is benched until Merlin says so. And we must all dance to the warlock's tune.'

Cerberus' sharp barks pierced the quiet from downstairs. Claws scrabbled on the wood floors as the hound charged from the kitchen to the hallway.

'Regardless of what you might think, I left my feelings for Arthur behind a long time ago.'

Jack closed his eyes. 'I saw your letters to Arthur. And you do not get over things quickly.'

'That's true because I'm certainly not over you, nor will I be any time soon. I'm not looking to rekindle –'

'Rekindle what?' Arthur strode into the room as if he belonged there. Jack scrambled to his feet, stepping in front of Ben, not knowing if he wanted to punch the King or drag Ben away.

'Nothing, Arthur.' Ben almost sounded certain.

19

SOME OF IT WAS TRUE

J ack shouldered his way past Merlin who was loitering by the
front door. Jack was not in the mood to make small talk with
the man who kept ruining his life.

The kitchen was warm from the heat of bodies and the oven. The
kettle was gurgling, and the soaking wet dog had tracked muddy
paw prints in from the back garden. Jack intercepted the cafetiere
from Hades' grabbing mitts. He wanted a cigarette more than
anything, but he had enough to argue with Ben about. Hades
tracked the cafetiere's movement, a mix of lust and pity in the
God's eyes. Jack assumed – hoped – that the lust was for the
coffee. Not that he wanted the pity. Sure, there were a couple
of things to work out, but Ben was back, and the rest was just
a matter of time.

'I've been waiting for you to conclude your reunion. What a
waste of time.' Merlin stood like an oversized draught excluder
in the kitchen doorway.

'It must be nice, not feeling anything.' Hades swung back on his chair, daring gravity to drag him down.

One of these days, Hades was going to slow down just a little. And when he did, every rule he'd bent to suit him, every near miss, every miscalculation, every risk he'd ever taken, was going to bury him. He had an unsettling amount of influence over Ben. Cerberus was curled up under the cabinets, watching Merlin intently. Jack leaned over to fetch a mug and Cerberus' tail wagged hopefully.

'Ignore him, Jack. He's been fed and is trying his luck.' The dog whined in Hades' face and moved to sit next to April. Jack clapped Hades on the back as he took a seat at the table.

'You haven't called the remaining Guardians yet, have you Jack?' Merlin tried to impale him a look of impatience.

'No. And thank you kindly for bringing Arthur with you. So thoughtful.' Merlin glared at him, his little fists clenching and uncurling at his side. Jack topped April's mug up and surrendered the pot to Hades who captured it so aggressively that the burnt black, almost a sludge, liquid spilled onto his trousers. Hades stared at the stain, grumbling under his breath.

'Oh!' Jack grabbed April's arm. 'This is a teachable moment. April, make it disappear.'

'The stain or Merlin?'

'Dealer's choice.'

April summoned Eilir with more ease than before. The jade magic curled around her hands but didn't go near the stain until the third attempt. April was sweating with the strain of fighting

Eilir, but the stain vanished.

Hades nodded his thanks and eyed up Merlin. 'Tell us – plainly – what's going on.'

'Of all of us, Hades, I'd expect you to already know.' Merlin's gaze shuffled around the room until it landed on April, making the hunter squirm in her seat.

'As usual, warlock, you are the only one playing with a full deck.' Hades was starting to glow. An echo was creeping into his voice that sounded like cries for mercy on dark foggy nights. It sent chills down Jack's spine. He'd never seen Hades in his death god form.

'Chaos allowed you to win. They have been toying with all of you, playing a long game.'

The chair groaned in protest as Hades' height doubled. He'd turned a deeper shade of purple, his skin aflame with his golden magic that trailed behind him when he moved and flared in tune with his irritation. His eyes caved in on themselves, forming black holes that would steal a person away to the under realms, if their gaze lingered for too long. Hades' pinstripe suit dissolved into a toga as black as the night sky and flowed like clouds, revealing a toned and ripped physique.

April coughed and Jack realised he'd been staring.

'Cease your peacocking, Hades. I've seen it all before, and believe me – ' Merlin looked the god up and down. ' – I've seen better. Where will you Gods go when there are no realms left? You go home, Hades. To Tartarus. To Chaos.'

Understanding washed the colour and cockiness from Hades'

face. He held his God form, not willing to admit that Merlin was right.

'Why would Fate back herself into a corner like that?' Jack laid both of his hands, palms up, on the table. April understood and her hands ducked into her lap, ready to draw Eilir.

'She thinks it's upsetting Chaos, to lose their playgrounds. She thinks it's some sort of poetic gesture about everything dying eventually. But really, she's doing all of the heavy lifting.'
Hades grabbed Jack's arm with a strength that threatened to break every bone if his words weren't taken seriously. 'Call the Guardians together, now.'

'That bad?' April asked.

'Living in a monotonous grey world, I can cope with. Living in a barren landscape with my squabbling siblings and extended family is a stretch though I'd manage. But all of that and a mad dictator prone to eating or tearing Gods apart? Tried it a couple of times, wasn't for me.' Hades looked to Jack.

'There are already enough people in this house who I don't like.' Jack pried his arm free. 'The last time we helped you, Merlin, you killed Ben.'

The kitchen was retreating from April's vision.
The debate, though getting heated, faded until it was the low murmur of a TV in another room. Was it Ben's kitchen that brought on the kaleidoscope of colour in which blurry figures lived in a time that had yet to arrive? April didn't know.
Eilir was humming a melody that sounded familiar, but April

couldn't place it. It was sombre, gentle, slow in places, climbing and twisting through trills in others.

It sounded like loss.

Clouds, irritated by her presence gave way and April hurtled towards the tops of trees in a sprawling wooded park. The wind bit and tore at her skin. '

Eilir!'

April's descent halted sharply, her nose brushing against the tip of the highest leaf. The furious squawking and flapping of an upset bird assaulted April's ears. Bark cut and splintered in her hands as she caught a sturdy looking branch, the speed of her fall swung her into and over it. Eilir sang-mumbled something about a man by the lake shore. April caught her breath before she pulled herself up, her hands tiny against the giant trunk of the ancient tree. Below, Ben, Jack, herself, Hades and a woman who dressed like a Roman hunting God in sandals and armoured top and skirt, stood in a circle around Merlin.

Eilir's humming grew louder.

April reached one foot to the branch below, but her other foot slipped on the rain-soaked bark, her tenuous grip on the branch above, severed. She crashed through branches until one pushed the wind from her lungs. A creak. A sharp snap. The frosty, winter-hardened ground rushed towards her. April's flailing hands brushed the cold grass, and she was back in the kitchen.

'I think we should do it,' April said in the cold tone that always made Jack look at her in a strange, questioning way. 'Trust me?'

'You? Yes. Hades? Sometimes. Merlin? Never.'

Merlin nodded in approval and rocked back on his heels. His knowing smile acknowledged the premonition whilst Eilir continued to sing her haunting song.

'All right,' Jack agreed reluctantly.

'I'm glad you agree, lad. Because I've already summoned them.'

'You threw up a bat signal without asking me?!' Jack's mug was rising into the air.

April tensed; Jack's volatile state was threatening to spark a fresh argument, and she was tired of being stuck in the middle of bickering adults. She had hoped that Jack would lay low with Ben. Him stewing in the kitchen and glaring at Merlin wasn't going to help Jack sort through everything that was picking apart his stitching.

'You're hangry. Why aren't you upstairs?'

'Arthur kicked me out.'

April opened her mouth but realised she didn't know what to say to that. To any of it.

'It might be best if you don't flaunt your relationship to Arthur,' Hades cautioned Jack. 'He never appreciated other people paying attention to Ben.' He was slowly reverting to his usual form. As impressive as Hades-the-death god was, April felt more comfortable with the purple-guy-in-the-suit.

'Hmph!' Merlin pulled out his talisman, consulting it as if it were a pocket watch.

'I was working on the assumption that they would be late, and we cannot be late.'

'Perhaps it has something to do with the caller?' Jack suggested. April kicked him under the table.

'The last time you called a meeting, Merlin, only three Guardians showed up. And one of them was Arthur,' Hades piled on.

Because what April needed was Jack *and* Hades teaming up to wind up Merlin.

'Hmph. Artemis is always late. It's rude.'

Hades stilled. 'She'll get here, whenever she sees fit –'

'Oh, do not stop on my account.' Arthur strode into the kitchen as if it were his to command.

Jack slipped out from behind the table and stalked out of the room, Merlin following close behind. April had a bad feeling and rushed after them. Everybody needed to take a minute and step back from one another. Merlin cut Jack off at the bottom of the stairs. Jack roughly pushed Merlin aside. He put one foot on the stairs, and Merlin spoke the Gods' honest truth.

'If you both keep pushing Benjamin, he'll choose neither of you.'

The banister groaned as Jack's grip tightened. 'Call the Guardians, tell them to meet somewhere else.'

April pulled Merlin by the arm, but the warlock looked at her sadly.

'Alas, my child, I cannot afford Benjamin time to adjust. Nor Jack time to calm down.'

Jack's head dropped to his chest. 'Why did you have to drag me into this?'

173

'Would you rather have lived and died without meeting Benjamin?'

'If you'd have left us all alone, we would have both died not feeling like we're shaking apart.' Jack laughed harshly. 'Perhaps in that universe, there's a Jack and a Ben who are strangers and are happier for it.'

'They always met,' Merlin said carelessly. 'I've never been particularly interested in the other universes.'
April thought a universe where the two didn't know each other would be a dull one.

'Can you make Ben forget Arthur?' Jack blurted out, his gaze darting to April, aware that Arthur and the others could probably hear all of the conversation.

'Do you ask me that to save yourself the pain of Benjamin's decision, or, because you think that you know what's best?'

'Yes. No. I don't know!' Jack sunk down and sat on a step, picking at threads in the tired carpet. 'I don't want to take Arthur away from him, not completely, but ...' Would either be happy, knowing that Arthur was out there? April couldn't see them inviting the King round for dinner. They had to reach some sort of decision. Otherwise, Jack was going to leave again.
Merlin slipped past Jack and disappeared upstairs.

20

REMNANTS

'I'm coming in, Benjamin.' Merlin paused on the landing, watching dust drift in the afternoon sun creeping in from the landing window.

'I'd rather you didn't, but my wants and needs have never stopped you before, so knock yourself out.'

Merlin looked to the ceiling, wondering why he couldn't catch a break. Jack was right, he was in dire need of courage and a heart. As a young man he had discarded his heart, metaphorically speaking, when it began to slow him down. He couldn't understand why he had held onto it for so long. Merlin pushed the door open and realised that he hadn't considered what to say. Benjamin was curled up in the armchair, smothered by a blanket, looking like death warmed up.

'Jack is crying on the stairs. But I don't want to talk about that _'

'I'd very much like to talk about that!' Benjamin struggled to sit up.

'April's had another premonition.' Merlin sunk down onto the bed.

'She told you?' Benjamin won his battle, but he was now drenched in sweat and looking even paler than before.

'Not exactly.' Merlin sent Emrys to fetch a cluster of photos that stood proudly on top of the chest of drawers. He flicked through moments of Jack and Benjamin's life. 'April's trying to get everybody to play nicely – it's adorable.' Merlin's smile broke around the fact that his child detested him. Not that she realised who he was to her. Eilir was puzzling it out, Emrys was certain of that.

'Arthur is trying to hold court in the kitchen, not that anybody is paying attention – and you know how he gets when nobody pays him attention. Hades has sided with Jack. It's only a matter of time before they are duelling at dawn, or whatever it was Arthur used to do.'

'You don't remember?' Sadness weighed Benjamin's voice down.

'If you're telling me that you've not forgotten a single moment, then you are a liar! Forgetting, it's very efficient.' If he couldn't recall it, Merlin could not feel it. He set the photos aside and noticed the carpet beneath his feet. 'This is the tidiest I have ever seen your chamber.'

'Cleaning only interests me when I am procrastinating.' Benjamin began folding the blanket.

'Or avoiding a difficult decision?'

'I've not really had a chance to talk to Jack. There's always somebody else around.'

'Well, now there's nothing left to sort, you can go downstairs. Ignoring the problem won't tidy it away.'

Benjamin shook his head, looking at his phone. He was tedious company these days.

'What about Jack? He's looking for a resolution on his own. Emotions really do make a mess of straightforward situations.'

'Straightforward?' Ben choked on his laughter.

'I advised Jack that you wouldn't be able to sort this out overnight.'

Benjamin blinked in surprise, almost driving Merlin from the room. What a sad state of affairs, for Benjamin to be shocked that Merlin cared for him.

'You assume that I am rooting for Arthur. You are wrong.' Merlin marched to the window and pulled open the curtains, ignoring Benjamin's hiss of disapproval.

'You yourself proved that I never truly knew you. That's the worst of it, Merlin.'

A flash of red flittered from the fence to an upturned plastic garden chair and back to the fence.

'You should have bird feeders.' Benjamin's frustration prodded at Emrys. 'The robins are hungry. And look at the state of the grass!' Benjamin pulled the curtains shut with an aggressive snap.

Merlin dragged his hand over his face. 'Arthur means Jack harm. I'm less certain that that harm won't extend to you. Purgatory has changed him. Take care.'

'You should have let us both die.' Benjamin shook his head, disgusted with Merlin.

'I don't really like myself without either of you.' Merlin snuck a glance at his talisman, impatient for it to start glowing. 'Jack is the only choice.' Benjamin looked up with hopeful eyes. 'But you committed yourself to Arthur. Declared your love in the presence of witnesses. And you scold me for lying –'

'It wasn't a marriage in any way, shape or form.' Benjamin dropped onto the bed, blinking rapidly.

'Shape and form do not come into it. You made a promise that the Gods heard. Arthur considered it binding. That I do recall.' Merlin had held his tongue despite knowing that Arthur could never be all that Benjamin needed him to be. He had watched the ceremony through tears of regret, knowing where their paths would end.

'Neither of you were being completely honest with yourselves or the other. Oh, you cared deeply for each other, but love? You broke your vows before you'd even made them.'

Ben curled up on the bed, trying to take up as little space as possible, hoping to hide from the consequences.

'Promises can be broken, Benjamin. It's how you go about breaking them that matters. They wish only to know who stands where. What's in your heart?'

'Jack?' Merlin hadn't expected the answer to sound like a question. He turned and saw the vampire in the doorway, tears streaming down his face.

'They're arriving,' Jack croaked out before turning and fleeing.

21

YOU HAVE STOLEN MY HEART

April was terrified of Artemis.

The God of Hunting had arrived like thunder on a hot day.

Hades had stood, bowed, and Artemis had begun shouting in a language whose origin April couldn't even guess.

Artemis was all grace and muscle that probably had something to do with firing the longbow that sat on her back, beside a quiver bristling with arrows. Her doe-brown eyes were as sharp as a hawk's. Her armoured top looked the same as the one she wore in April's premonitions, but the skirt had been swapped out for sandy coloured linen trousers that almost hid her sandals.

Arthur sat at the table, content amongst an argument whose volume rivalled the blitz. Feeling like the two Gods had something to work out, April slipped from the room and sought the safety of Jack's company. He hadn't moved from the stairs.

'What's their deal?' April winced at what sounded like Hades being slammed into a wall. Perhaps this gathering would cause enough damage to force Ben to redecorate.

'On again, off again.'

'Are they currently off?'

'Hard to tell, best not to ask. Actually, they're off. Hades married somebody else.'

'Oh –'

'Put the chair down, Artemis – ouch!'

Jack stood, uncertain about intervening. April pulled him back onto the stairs. The poor guy had his own relationship to fix, let alone getting involved in whatever Hades and Artemis had going on.

'You'll like Artemis.'

April shot him a questioning glance, her attention mostly fixed on the door, just in case trouble spilled out.

'Just wait until Arthur says something condescending to you.' Jack stretched, fixing a smile to his forlorn face. 'I'd best fetch Merlin.'

'What? No, I'm not going back in there by myself.'

'You'll be fine.' Jack gently pushed her towards the kitchen as he started his slow, drawn-out climb to Ben's room. 'Don't hide behind Hades.'

'Have you seen the size of him? If he stands in front of the fridge, it disappears.' April sucked in a deep breath that gave away her uncertainty, pushed her shoulders back and entered the kitchen with what she hoped was something close to self-confidence.

Hades glanced in her direction and was promptly slapped in the face with enough force to drive him back a couple of steps.

'What?' Hades clamped his hands over the slap mark. 'I was merely looking to see who it was.'

'There was no need to stare!' Artemis raised her spear. April caught a glimpse of the miniature spear – Artemis' talisman, tied at the point where wood and metal met.

'I wasn't staring! For the love of – this is April.' Hades pulled her over, it was difficult not to feel like a human shield. 'She's a friend of Benjamin's, she's not a friend of Merlin and she's mortal. Try not to be tyrannical.'

'Oh, because I am expressing my opinion, I am a ghoul.' Artemis' voice was steel striking against flint.

'No, because you're throwing things about the room.' Hades pinched the bridge of his nose. 'Your strong convictions are but one of the reasons I fell in love with you. I don't love it when you cause damage to our friend's home.'

'What did Hades do?' April froze as Artemis turned slowly to glare at her. Hades' eyes flicked between April, his Guardian and the backdoor. 'Not that he needs to have done anything to justify slapping him.'

There was a heavy pause. Artemis' laughter startled April and Hades both. He joined in, jabbing April in the back, prompting her to add her own uncertain laughter. Artemis wiped a tear from her eye.

'So, you are the cause of all the fuss?'

'What?' April and Hades chorused.

'Hecate tasked Fae's best warlocks to try and decipher what April is. And how to stop her magical abilities from growing.'

'I can just about move a cafetiere. I told Fate and Death the same thing.' April caught the look loaded with shared understanding that passed between Hades and Artemis. A jolt of static shot through the air, tingeing it. April spotted the beginnings of a portal opening above the table.

A lady with hair greyed by time, handbag perched over one arm, dressed in hunting boots and a knee-length tweed skirt and matching blazer, strode out into the middle of Ben's kitchen table.

'Still getting the hang of portals are we Hecate?' Hades hurried to offer his hand, beaming at the newcomer, just about keeping the laughter from his voice. 'It's only been sixty-odd millennia, I suppose.'

'I have had no cause to leave Fae in centuries and these portals are modern contraptions. I had to ask a mage to open this one.'

'So how are you getting back?' Hades asked in disbelief.

It was the most bizarre scene, an elderly woman, dressed for an afternoon in the country, stood on a table, still not quite matching Hades in height, chatting away like it was a regular occurrence.

'I was hoping that one of you would be gracious enough to open a return portal for me.'

'Hades would be glad to do just that,' Artemis answered in a tone that dared him to disagree.

'I would, I was going to offer – no need to bully me into it! We were just talking about you, actually,' Hades helped the slightly disorientated Guardian down. Arthur drew back a chair with a bow.

'Arthur! You're back,' Hecate carefully unfolded her glasses and popped them on her nose to inspect the King. 'Tell me, for my memory isn't what it was, did you die?'

'Hecate.' Hades danced her away from that subject. 'Artemis tells us that you've been having your magic folk look into diminishing the powers of a certain young mage.'

April shrank into a chair, not feeling so bold and desperate for Jack to return. She had no business being the centre of attention. Not when those paying attention included Death.

'Oh, yes. Nyx ordered me, I am afraid. You know how it is. One cannot ignore the wishes of the God of the realm.' Hecate frowned at the King and the Gods, completely ignoring the mortal in the room. 'Do you know her?'

Three pairs of awkward eyes pinned April in place.

'Nyx is an interesting personality.' Merlin announced his entrance with his know-it-all tone, causing everybody present to roll their eyes. Ben and Cerberus followed. No Jack though. Judging by Ben's sorry expression, things hadn't gone well.

Arthur watched Ben's every move. There was a glint to his eyes that reminded April of a lion watching a distracted antelope. Ben flattened himself against the wall closest to the door, his back slightly turned towards Arthur. Which, April thought, should have been reassuring but for the fact that Arthur looked ready to fight.

'Nyx –'

Another portal opened in the wall beside the door, interrupting Merlin. A hooded man with a lamp stepped through. Cerberus gave an acknowledging bark from where he sat beside Ben. Charon, April guessed. Eilir twisted in her mind, wanting to manifest so she could greet him. April let go of Eilir, but Merlin turned to smile disconcertingly at her. He was aiming for encouraging, she thought.

'Nyx is Chaos' daughter, and mother of, amongst others, Fate.' The Ferryman set down his lantern with a clunk. 'What of her?'

April would have been surprised by that but she was distracted by the rather quiet Jack who crept in, his face tear-marked and ashen.

'You know.' Hades tried to catch Ben's eye, but Ben was trying to force eye contact with Jack. 'It explains a lot.'

'And what is that, dear?' Hecate asked, knitting appearing in her hands.

'Fate is obsessed with April.'

Hecate looked from Hades to April, knitting needles clacking together.

'She's the mage whose powers you're trying and failing to strip,' Hades explained patiently.

'Oh. I am sorry dear. It's nothing personal, you understand?'

'I really wish I understood half of what's happening, but it's alright.' It was difficult to dislike Hecate when she reminded

April of her grandmother.

Merlin looked around the room. 'I didn't invite Barqan. And I am uncertain as to where Menoetius' loyalties lie, given that he is Guardian of Tartarus. I suppose the remaining Gods will not attend.'

Charon's head turned this way and that, looking about Ben's kitchen. April had to sit on her hands to resist the temptation to pull back the hood. It must have tiny eyeholes. Because how else was he navigating the kitchen without tripping over the dog or taking himself out with the table? The Ferryman prodded at the saltshaker and chuckled to himself, his attention briefly returning to April as if the inanimate object had offered up a memory of her fighting Barqan. As he turned toward her, April caught a glimpse of teeth that resembled tombstones.

'What is it child?'

She jumped. 'Nothing.'

'Hurm.' Charon returned to his inspection of Ben's countertops. 'Why have you called us here, Merlin? To this deserted house.' There was a distinct tone of boredom in Charon's voice, and maybe a little disdain.

'This is my home, Charon, as you know full well.'

'You can do better than this, Benjamin. April agrees with me.' She did. But how did Charon know her name? Meanwhile, Eilir was delighted by the amount of magic in the room, to be surrounded by friends.

'I'm getting around to it!' Ben moved a pot to cover a charred, brown stain on the worktop that had almost certainly been caused by a hot pan melting the laminated wood.

'And why call us now? It's a little late in the day, do you not think, for a team effort.' Artemis rounded on Merlin.

'Everything is happening as and when it should.' Merlin huffed. 'The question is, who is Fate most scared of? April or Chaos?'

'Chaos. Every time.' Hades sounded too serious, as if he were trying to divert Merlin's attention from April. Ben must have said something to him.

'So, we must squash the fear before Fate destroys the entire universe?' Artemis asked, eyebrows raised.

'Precisely.'

The fizz of another portal opening dispensed another new and equally terrifying individual.

'Kind of you to come,' Hades said evenly. 'What news from Tartarus?'

April turned slightly to her right and jumped when she found Jack occupying the seat that had been empty a second before the portal had opened.

'Chaos grows weary of childish games. Return home.' Menoetius' deep voice echoed around the kitchen that didn't have an echo usually. April wanted to know why this one was navy blue. And why he bore a striking resemblance to a bull. Menoetius' head dropped to one side as he took her in. Jack sat up a little straighter, pushing back on his chair, ready to attack or defend, whichever came first.

'The girl comes back with me.'

'No.'

Every head in the room swivelled to look at Ben.

April couldn't have been happier to see a spark of the old Benjamin. And she absolutely wasn't going anywhere with the new Guardian.

'You do not look so well Benjamin,' Menoetius sneered. 'And is that Arthur, I see? Well, blow me down, it is! The King is back in his own realm and flanked by Merlin, so there is no need for your frankly pathetic services as Guardian to continue.'

Up until this unpleasant storm had arrived, April had been suspecting Ben of over-exaggerating how little the other Guardians liked him. She wasn't saying that it was all in his head, just that, perhaps, he'd been reading too much into it. Because nobody had shown Ben any more disrespect than they had to each other. Less so, in fact. Although the meeting was still young and Hades was gouging holes in Ben's tabletop with a jagged blade that seemed destined for Menoetius.

'April stays where she belongs.' Artemis casually flipped her spear so that it was primed and ready to launch. It sat, perfectly balanced in her hand. She wouldn't miss her target. 'I seem to recall you being disgraced and reduced to a Guardian, Menoetius. Or did I dream that?'

'No, that happened,' Hades confirmed. 'I'd like to say it was because he kept losing my cattle, but he was stupid enough to challenge Chaos, was killed and then demoted.'

Menoetius drew his magic; an angry red ball of flame aimed for Hades' head. Artemis' spear whistled through the air, pinning the offending hand to the wall.

'Why have you come, Menoetius?' Artemis stalked over to him. Menoetius was just about containing any expression of pain. 'There is a rift in the family. It is disrupting the natural order of things.'

April had heard something similar before. Perhaps Fate wasn't the biggest threat. Personally, if April had to pick one ancient being to avoid annoying, it would be Death.

'What does it have to do with April?' Ben asked.

Menoetius' smile suggested that though he be fallen, he still kept the secrets of Gods more powerful than he.

'Don't you see? How they are all interlinked? Fate, Merlin, Death and April.'

'Tell us,' Artemis demanded before looking at April. 'Of all the people to get mixed up with, you had to entangle yourself with Merlin?'

'None of that is by choice.'

Artemis was about to say something – possibly lecture her – but Menoetius ripped the spear from his hand with a grunt and took his leave.

'We need to ask the right questions of the right people.' Merlin shook his sleeves out and crossed his hands in front of him. 'The only person who can answer our questions and, coincidently, the only person who can end this, is Chaos.'

'There it is.' April realised that they were all looking at her. Eilir's laughter filled her head.

'You want all of us to speak to Chaos?' Ben asked, coming to stand behind Jack. The vampire kept his gaze fixed ahead, his jaw straining under the tension.

'No. April and I will speak to Chaos.'

'Absolutely not.' The back of April's chair snapped under Ben's grip.

'April and I will speak to Chaos about healing the rift between them and Fate,' Merlin repeated, as if adding more words and still not asking April was going to make a difference.

'That is a terrible idea. Jack?' Ben spluttered. The vampire had transferred his attention to his phone. 'You have nothing to say?' Jack swallowed loudly, still not making eye contact with Ben. 'Merlin, I don't think that's a very good idea.'
April was starting to feel like she might end up having two Christmases. Out of the corner of her eye, she caught Arthur smirking at the rift he'd caused. Pins and needles trailed down her arms. April allowed Eilir to form in her hands. Arthur just laughed and returned his attention to Ben.

'April?' Ben tapped her on the shoulder. 'If you don't want to go?'

'I, I think that I have to,' April said shakily. She couldn't ignore the premonition. She couldn't forget the mournful tune that Eilir had sung. She had to get to that point. Maybe this was the way to it, maybe it wasn't.

'If you're sure? Jack asked.

'Not really, but I think it's where I'm meant to be.' April caught Merlin watching her, a ghost of a smile on his face.
She couldn't figure out the look in his eyes. Determined but sad,

unhinged but completely aware.

And proud. Merlin looked proud of her.

'What about the rest of us?' Hecate asked.

'You can continue to crochet for now –'

'Knitting, dear.'

'There's no difference.'

'I assure you, there is.' Hecate peered over the top of her glasses at Merlin.

'Do not be late the next time I call.' Merlin held up his talisman as if it were the answer to all of their problems. 'When next I call, we shall combine our talismans and our magic.'

'To do what, exactly?' Charon appeared behind Hades, making him jump out of his skin. 'The combined power would be enough to kill a God or three. But Chaos? No. We are also two talismans short.'

'Just the one, actually.' Merlin held up Menoetius' coin tied in a leather cord.

The fact that Merlin excelled at pickpocketing surprised April not at all.

'Merlin – ' Artemis collected her spear from the floor. 'Are you going to kill Fate?' April couldn't quite make out her tone.

Merlin calmly pushed his chair back. Even standing up, he was too short to meet Artemis' steady gaze on the same level.

'If it comes to that.'

Chills ran down April's spine. How could he commit to killing his wife with so little thought? She was about to enquire when Merlin asked her, in a gruff voice:

'Are you ready to leave?' Without waiting for an answer, Merlin opened a portal.

April hesitated for a moment. Jack slipped something into her pocket. Her hand found the familiar shape of a dagger. She nodded her understanding and without looking back, she joined Merlin at the portal.

'Hey, Merlin,' Jack called just before they were about to step inside. 'If something happens to April.' It was the sincerest thing that the vampire had said all day.

'Slow painful death, yes, yes.' Merlin and Jack weighed each other up, nodding in mutual understanding.

With nothing left to delay her, April plunged into darkness.

22

HOPE IS A DANGEROUS LITTLE THING

J ack was almost relieved, as the portal swallowed the warlock.

'He'll be back,' Ben said, seeming to know what Jack was thinking. Then again, if Ben knew what was currently running through Jack's mind, he'd not be making small talk.

Of all of the eyes on Jack, he was acutely aware of Arthur's venomous stare. Ben pulled out the chair next to him and reached for Jack's hand under the table. Jack snatched his away. If Ben wanted to acknowledge Jack as his partner, he could damn well do it in public and not hiding under the table so his other boyfriend couldn't see. It was horribly unfamiliar, being this angry with Ben *and* being unable to let any of his barbed thoughts fly. Arthur's attention had turned to Ben, a stern look upon his face.

Jack couldn't compete with a king, so he wouldn't.

He was sure that, if they had enough time alone, Ben could find the words that would fix everything. But the words had to come from Ben. Jack hadn't broken anything. Not yet anyway. If Ben loved him, as he claimed to, he should just tell Arthur to leave. Jack had been patient with Ben, had accepted his grief and even his love for Arthur. He had made room for it in their relationship, in fact. But the actual man, present and correct? Jack couldn't clear that much space.

'*I can't do this.*' Jack left without waiting for a reply. He felt Ben reaching out for him, so he slammed the mental door shut right before he slammed the front door behind him.

Hades watched Jack brush past Ben, fearing that his friend had made the wrong choice, if he'd even had the chance to do so.

Ben, with his head hung low, retreated slowly upstairs, whilst Arthur grinned like the cat who got the cream. Beside Hades, Artemis' fingers were drumming on the table. No doubt she had some choice words for Arthur. Not that she'd let those particular arrows fly until she'd gathered all of the facts.

'So, Arthur. It's been a while.' The King had the decency to jump a little and look embarrassed. That was satisfying, but not enough to sate Hades' need to defend.

'I was in Purgatory.'

'We knew.' Charon answered and Hades turned slowly to fix the hooded man with a stare that he hoped conveyed how unimpressed he was and how unhelpful the ferryman was being. Of all the times Charon could have picked to start mixing in –

'And you did nothing?!'

'It was not our place.' Cerberus nudged Charon in the leg over and over again until Charon relented and petted the dog. Hades couldn't get used to seeing Cerberus with one head.

'Nothing is where I left it. I understand little of my surroundings. The miniature suns, for example.' Arthur frowned at the ceiling.

'Miniature – oh, light bulbs.' Hades covered Artemis' hand with his own. They hadn't seen each other in months. Maybe years. Time lost all meaning when he was away from her. He wanted so badly to talk to Artemis, to be captivated by her, but she was still repulsed by his very existence. So that wasn't on the cards any time soon.

'Benjamin remains relatively unchanged,' Arthur noted.

'Of course. The two of you were written in the stars.' Charon was full of surprises today.

'And how do you plan to spend what's left of your life?' It wasn't like Arthur was going to don his armour, ride into parliament and demand the return of his realm. There was something about the way Arthur kept staring up and slightly off to the right, as if he were close to tuning into a radio station but the frequency wouldn't pull free of white noise, that had Hades feeling suspicious. Truth be told, Hades had heard enough of Arthur and Benny's "courtship" from others, Charon included, to have formed a deep prejudice against the King.

'First, I must acquire a sword and a horse. I will see that Benjamin is safe –'

'Benny can look after himself. He has good people around him now.' Hades insisted.

'His name is Benjamin,' Arthur replied tartly. 'Merlin has embarked upon a diplomatic mission with nobody but the girl –'

'April,' Artemis and Charon choroused.

'For assistance. If Merlin seeks a peace treaty, who better to negotiate that than Gaia's King? Really – ' Arthur laughed to himself. 'What do women know about such matters?'

Artemis' spear flashed into her hands; Hades grabbed her arm. Artemis slowly lowered the spear, leaning it against the table.

'Merlin couldn't negotiate his way out of an empty room without starting a minor war. Believe me, April will lead negotiations.' Hades considered nudging the spear away, but he'd likely find himself at the other end of it before his foot made contact.

'I must speak with Benjamin. Excuse me.' Arthur's polite smile was anything but reassuring. The King bowed his head and exited.

'We shouldn't leave him alone with Benny,' Hades said softly, staring after Arthur.

'What harm could it do to let two old friends talk?' Hecate held what looked to be the bottom half of a jumper up to the light, admiring the garish yellow. Hades felt sorry for whomever it was destined for. It looked itchy. Hecate caught his eye and beamed at him. 'The jumper is for you, dear.'

'Thank you? Hecate, you do realise that Arthur and Benjamin were ... involved with one another?'

Hecate stopped knitting. 'Well that explains an awful lot.'

Hades exhaled, relieved and surprised at the quick acceptance.

'Arthur is behaving very strangely, Hecate. I'm concerned he'll pressure Benny into a decision he wouldn't ordinarily make.'

Hecate considered this, needles clacking together. 'Benjamin is a smart young man; he'll see through it all.' She stood, balancing her handbag in the crook of her arm, and looking expectantly at Hades.

'Try not to dance on any more tables.' Hecate tutted fondly and swatted the younger God around the ear as he offered her his arm, opening a portal back to Fae with his free hand.

'If I didn't know better – ' Hecate turned back at the opening. ' – I would think that Merlin, though he is fond of the young mage, views her as a threat.'

'He does,' Artemis agreed. 'As evidenced by his clumsy attempt at politeness.'
And now that Hades really thought about it, introducing April to Chaos seemed suspect. They could easily cause April to do something a little more advanced than levitating.

'Well, that's simple.' Hecate packed her knitting away.

'Obviously, but for Charon's benefit, why don't you explain it?' Hades smiled.

'With magic such as April's, she could be Merlin's undoing.' Hecate thought for a moment. 'I shan't continue to strip her of her magic, but I will keep up the pretence. April should see a dramatic improvement.'

'Everything is happening as it should ...' Hades really should have stepped in when Merlin insisted April go with him.

'I should say so. Lovely to see you all. Behave yourself, young man.' Hecate patted Hades on the cheek and entered the portal. What sounded like choking brought Hades back to the table.

'I don't think I've ever heard you laugh, old man.' Hades tried to lift Charon's hood with one finger but was slapped away. 'I just want to be sure that you are laughing. It's terrifying; never do so in my presence, again.'

'You call me old like time will never catch up to you.' Charon's laughter died down. 'I have stood on the shore for aeons; I know countless universes by the souls they send. They each tell their own story, but really they all boil down to one of seven. I can no more change their stories than you can.'

This. This was why conversing with Charon was, at times, tedious. Hades thought to keep his tone level. 'Your point, Charon.'

'Why would the likes of Fate, Chaos and Merlin fear a child?' Charon drew the last word out. 'Why else would Death spare her, if not for her heritage?'

'Are you saying that April is? No ...' It was so ridiculous that Hades couldn't give his suspicion life. Coincidences were Merlin's middle name.

'We've all vaguely recognised both April and Eilir. Her aura is unique, because she is no mere mage, Hades.'

'And Hecate is about to remove the tourniquet on Eilir.' Artemis gathered up her spear and bow. 'This is not a peace mission.' Artemis' almond eyes were focused and serious. Whatever lay between them was set aside for the time being. She looked every bit the fierce hunter who had haunted his mind since the day they met.

'I'll get Benny and the royal prat.' Hades took the stairs two at a time, feeling uneasy in the stillness of the upstairs rooms. 'Benjamin? Have you killed Arthur? Please say yes.' Hades threw the door open to find an empty room. The chair by the window was on its side.

Hades checked the house twice over, unwilling to accept that Ben and Arthur were nowhere to be found. He was stomping down the stairs when the front door opened.

'Benny?'

'No. Jack.' The vampire shook his wet jacket out. 'Something the matter?'

Artemis and Charon appeared from their search of the living room, like a choir of bad luck dispensers.

'Arthur has left,' Charon stated bluntly. 'We suspect that he coerced Benjamin into joining.'

Jack dropped his phone in his haste to call Ben.

The dial tone wailed, cutting through the silence.

The automated voicemail announcement made Hades feel sick.

Jack tried again.

And again.

And again.

Hades gently freed the phone from Jack's hand.

The vampire pulled his coat back on as if he knew where he was going.

'It's my fault. Arthur said he needed a sword and a horse. That he needed to get Ben to safety.' Hades appreciated that that wasn't a clue, but it was all he had. 'Jack ...' Hades looked back to Charon who nodded his approval. 'Hecate is going to return April's magic to her. She could go full mage–witch–whatever whilst she's with Merlin and Chaos.'

'That's good, right?'

'Well ... we think – we don't know, but we think – ' Hades took a deep breath and exhaled the words in a rush. 'Merlin is April's father.'

Jack stared at him for a long minute. 'I'm going to need you to say that again, Hades. It sounded like you said –'

'I must return to Styx.' Charon lit his lantern with a click of his fingers. 'If you wish to find Benjamin, follow Cerberus.' The ferryman melted back into the wall and was gone.

'Hades and I will go after Arthur and Benjamin.' Artemis notched an arrow, and Hades couldn't look away. 'Will you await April's return here, Jack?'

'I'm coming with you! April can look after herself.' Jack almost sounded like he believed that.

23

MULHOLLAND DRIVE

B enjamin's companionship had been hard won. Arthur had worn his physician down.

Much like when Arthur had wanted to hunt. It would take two hours of persistently asking over and over until Benjamin threw down his book in defeat. He would stomp off to change his clothing, but his mood would always lighten by the end of the ride. Sometimes, Arthur would refrain from killing an animal for Benjamin's sake.

But today, no matter what Arthur did or said, his physician refused to warm to him.

It felt like a punishment when Benjamin insisted they journey in the bizarre horseless carriage.

'I appreciate you taking me ... when did you learn to, what did you call it, drive? It is quite clever. I should like to have a go. Although I doubt my ability to manage it quite so well ... we are journeying to Uffington for a horse –'

'Are you kidding me?' Benjamin's voice boomed in the confined space.

'Pardon?' If Arthur had willingly and purposefully left Benjamin behind, then this charade would be acceptable – for a short while. Arthur observed Benjamin's deathly-tight grip on the wheel, the muddy brown of his conflicted eyes, and tried to fathom why this was a decision at all. The little voice in the back of his head whispered that Jack had stolen what was rightfully Arthur's, and the anger refreshed.

'You don't need a horse!' Where Benjamin had once spoken unreservedly and with affection, he now spoke in short, clipped sentences. 'You insisted that April's in trouble.'

'She is! Merlin has taken matters into his own hands, and her with him.' Benjamin's grip tightened further still on the wheel and the voice in Arthur's head said: *'Benjamin wishes he were strangling you so he would be free of his vows.'*

'It should be I who brokers peace –'

'You don't need a horse.' Benjamin's voice was low. Arthur could not recall a time he'd witnessed the physician so furious.

'A king must have a horse. What's more, it's said that the horse will dance on the downs upon my return. I am returned. I have Excalibur.' The weight of the steel was reassuring. A comfort even with Benjamin behaving as he was. Arthur drew the sword ever so slightly. They bounced over a bump; Arthur grabbed the handle protruding from the door. The sheath fell away, revealing the runes, talismans, and other symbols that Merlin had insisted Arthur have engraved on the blade to assist with some spell or other. He raised the sword to his eye, looking down the blade as best he could in the cramped space. Benjamin snatched the sword by the blade; Arthur cried out in warning, but the razor-sharp edges did not cause so much as a scratch. Benjamin threw it behind them; the ruby in the pommel vanished as the sheath joined it. Benjamin had returned to wrapping strands of his already knotted and tortured hair around his finger.

'I am returned; I have my sword. The horse should be dancing.'

'The horse is a chalk painting on a hill. It's older than us!' Benjamin glanced over. His tone sharp and authoritative. 'I've never heard of this legend.'

'April found hundreds of stories about me on the magic silver box.' Arthur puffed out his chest with pride, pleased that his kingly efforts had been chronicled extensively. 'I'd have brought Merlin, but he's gallivanting about in the under realms.'
Benjamin's head was shaking from side to side so violently, Arthur feared it would tumble off.

'So, you didn't need me, exactly. Anybody with magic would have done.'
The hurt and disappointment that was etched into every line of Benjamin's face was all too familiar.

'How else will the horse be brought to life?' Arthur regretted it as soon as he had said it. His surly manner was not going to improve matters. The tablet that Benjamin repeatedly prodded at flashed and danced about on the shelf; the vampire's face smiled at them. Benjamin's expression softened briefly, relief glistening in his eyes, but he did not accept the communication request. The way Benjamin looked at Jack ... he had never once looked at Arthur quite like that. His heart wouldn't settle from its erratic rhythm.

He wasn't losing Benjamin.

He had lost him.

'*And to a better man. A man who is not ashamed or afraid. The blame is yours,*' the voice in the back of Arthur's mind insisted.

'Do you disregard me because you love me still?'

'I detest you.' For the briefest of horrifying, soul-destroying moments, Arthur believed Benjamin.

'This would be so much easier if I felt nothing at all for you, Arthur.'

'You do not hate me!' Arthur laughed nervously, staring at the trees as they blurred by. The people in the other carriages passed, unaware of the significance of what was happening just feet away from them. Benjamin slowed them down; the ticking sound filled the car again. They turned onto an uneven surface that rattled his bones.

'I do. Truly.'

Arthur dropped his eyes to where his hands had come to rest in his lap, willing himself not to cry.

Benjamin brought them to a halt in the shadow of a tall hill cloaked in the silver of a winter frost, his gaze stubbornly fixed straight ahead.

'I fall in love with you every time you smile.' Arthur offered Benjamin his own smile. With that trick and with that line,

Arthur had never failed before. Benjamin glanced over in disdain and returned his attention to the fields and countryside that was much changed. The first drops of rain hit the glass of the carriage.

'What does Jack offer you that I cannot?' In the blink of an eye, the rain pelted the carriage. Arthur covered his ears, nearly missing the strangled sound that Benjamin made. Arthur's anger snowballed into pure fury that, though unfair, could not be slowed. 'Need I remind you of the promise you made in a willow grove –'

'Are you so miserable that you'd condemn me to an eternity of isolation, Arthur?'

'You presumed! And I waited!'

'You didn't know what you were waiting for!' Benjamin pulled the key free and threw it on the shelf, next to the tablet that buzzed again. 'You should be ashamed, Arthur.'

'Look who speaks!'

Benjamin threw open the door. Arthur pulled him back into the car, dismayed at how Benjamin squashed himself into the door, trying to enforce space.

'Of all people, you should have recognised Merlin's work,' Arthur shouted, spittle landing on Benjamin's arm. 'You should have known better!' In the blink of an eye, each and every one of their shared years were dashed on the rocks.

Finished before they had even begun.

Arthur had no place in his own realm if Benjamin did not want him there. The little voice whispered that this would not have happened had Merlin not parted them. And then there was Benjamin's audacity to build a new life from the ashes of his previous one.

'Untangling a relationship of 867 years isn't as simple as you're making it out to be. It's not a case of deciding who gets to keep the kettle and who gets the sofa.' Benjamin yanked his arm free. That hurt more than anything else, to see Benjamin recoil as if touched by poison ivy.

'This is Merlin's doing!'

Benjamin let out a dark laugh. 'This isn't all on Merlin.'

'You, you are the one who has taken a new lover!'

Benjamin slammed his hand onto the wheel, triggering a loud sound that sounded like a horn in the middle of a battle.

From nowhere, April's shrill voice, lecturing him on the ways of the world, came unbidden to mind. What an obnoxious woman. Too many opinions. The Gods help whoever had the misfortune to marry her.

'Fine! We will be wed, just as you wanted.'

'The timing of this is cosmic.' There was that strange, tortured laugh again. 'I was this close to asking Jack to marry me. And then, person by person, bit by bit, my past started showing up.' Benjamin punched the wheel so hard, a pillow emerged from it.

'I knew you were jealous of my marriage!'

'For crying –' Benjamin finally looked him in the eye and Arthur recoiled from the ice-cold blue orbs. 'I was, but I understood; hells I attended the ceremony!' Tears tracked down Benjamin's cheeks, his hands clasped together as if he were begging.

'My relationship with Jack is not an attempt at punishing you.'

'What other motivation could there be?'

'That I love Jack!'

'Is Jack better than me?' Arthur had ridden into battle, had fought to the death many a time, had faced monsters. But nothing terrified Arthur more than the beat in-between question and answer.

'Yes.'

Ben threw open his door, it hit the end of its hinge, ricocheting back into his shoulder. He stormed off to the other side of the gravelled area where he stared up at a map. Behind that, the winding path cut a track through fields and well-hidden burial mounds, all the way up to the hilltop with the chalk horse leaping over the ancient landscape. The tablet glowed in Benjamin's hands as he prodded at it, no doubt attempting to reach Jack.

Arthur grappled with the handle, cursing the strange material until it popped open, releasing him from the metal cage with wheels. His legs carried him on a collision course with Benjamin; his approaching footsteps drove Benjamin's head down, as he collapsed in on himself.

'If you wanted to marry me, Arthur, you could have. You were the King!' Benjamin's voice was flat, his body tense.

'You broke my heart, Arthur! You broke my heart.'

The corner of Arthur's mouth twitched. One foot fell in front of the other, and he threw Benjamin up against the map, one fist raised.

'Hit me, if it'll make you feel better.' Benjamin's stormy eyes taunted Arthur.

'Had I been free of my responsibilities, I would have done all of those things and more.' Arthur's fingers twisted themselves into the unusual, soft fabric of Benjamin's jacket, the physician allowed Arthur to pull him forwards and slam him back against the wooden map, not at all worried about any damage the King could do. Arthur's grip tightened as the threatened punch inched closer. His vision blurred in and out, like somebody else was trying to focus his eyes for him. There was a glee that wasn't his, at the idea of hitting Benjamin. Or perhaps it was. The blazing fire inside of him was burning away his good sense.

'Who are these people who cannot call you by your name? *Benny! Ben!* They could never care for you as I do.' Arthur's accusations arched through the air like poorly fletched arrows fired by careless archers. 'Was I such a terrible partner that you took another, without a second thought?'

'Was two hundred years of mourning not enough?!'
Arthur's fist collided with Benjamin's hand. The rain had darkened Benjamin's long hair. It clung to his face, getting in the physician's eyes.

'We made vows.' Arthur ripped his fist free and raised it again. 'You're mine, do you understand? Not some vampire's floozy.'
Benjamin shoved Arthur off him with that freakish shtriga strength. Arthur threw the punch. Blood poured from Benjamin's nose, mixing with the rain dripping from his hair.
Arthur pressed forwards. Benjamin held his hands up, not wanting a fight. But Arthur wanted him to fight for him like he was

for Benjamin.

'I don't love you, Arthur.'

Arthur's weathered hands pulled the shtriga forwards with a strength that caught them both by surprise. Benjamin anchored himself on the map with one hand, his other wrestled to free himself from Arthur's steel grasp. Arthur threw his weight against Benjamin's chest, pinning him to the map, his hands either side of Benjamin's head.

'Arth –'

Arthur's rough kiss stole the words from Benjamin's unwilling mouth.

Ben wasn't sure how he'd gotten here. Over Arthur's shoulder, he spied Cerberus sprinting towards him on silent paws, fangs bared in a silent growl. Ben went limp in Arthur's grip, trying to ignore the King's wandering hands. Ambrosius struggled to manifest, lacking the strength. Cerberus leapt through the air, claws reaching for Arthur.

Excalibur tore into the dog's neck.

The hound let out an anguished yelp and collapsed.

He shoved Arthur away, desperate to help Cerberus. Arthur's vice-like grip clamped down, twisting Ben's arm, forcing him to the ground, tugging at his clothes, pushing his coat onto his shoulders. He clawed and pushed Arthur's hands away, pulled his coat back onto one shoulder, kicked backwards and bit Arthur's arm attached to the hand wrapped around his throat. Ben drove an elbow into Arthur's chest and rolled, forcing the

King off him. Stones crunched as Arthur scrambled back to his feet and advanced rapidly.

His lungs weren't letting him breathe. Ben caught Arthur's punch and threw him to the other side of the car park. Ringing filled Ben's ears, fighting his hammering heart for attention. Oxygen was a sea, and he was on the seabed. Arthur wouldn't ... This was white-hot anger at not getting what he wanted. This was pure aggression; this was an attempt to dominate and control, and in all their years together, Arthur had never once forced ... it had never been so rough. Pins and needles coursed through Ben as Ambrosius succeeded in opening a portal.

'Ben!'

Jack, Hades and Artemis were staring at him in dumbfounded shock. They had caught the end of it, at the very least. A curious mix of fear and embarrassment inspired Ben to portal away from questions he couldn't answer.

Jack pushed at Hades' outstretched arms, but the God didn't budge. 'We can't ignore this!'

He would never find a better reason to rip Arthur's pretty head from his body.

'Easy – hey!' Hades spun and grabbed Jack by his shoulders. The God's eyes were flickering black orbs. He pointed to where Artemis knelt, stroking the whimpering dog's fur. 'I want to kill Arthur every bit as much as you do, but Merlin brought him back for a purpose. More's the point, do you want to be the person who upsets Death's natural order further?'

'Hades is correct.' Artemis tied a bit of cloth around Cerberus' wound. 'Ensure that you are justified in using force against a Guardian. And then use all that you can muster.' She stood, glancing at where Ben had been moments ago. 'I had best check on April. Can you both manage here?' Hades nodded and Artemis left in a swirl of skirts.

'Come on, Charon will banish me if Cerberus dies.' Hades dragged Jack with him to heal the dog. 'Benny will come home when he's ready.'
There was something reassuring about how Hades was struggling to contain his God form. Jack eyed up the idling car, an idea forming.

'Stay.' Hades said sharply. Arthur groaned, his arms and legs scrabbling in the dirt, trying to get up.

'Me, Arthur or the dog?'

'All of you.' Hades strode over to where Arthur was attempting to crawl away, and stamped on his back, flattening the King against the ground. 'Let's be clear, Arthur, I am not ignoring what I saw and what I can still see,' Hades said in a low, menacing voice. 'You are no longer welcome here – speak and I will rip your tongue out. If you remain in Gaia, Jack will –'

Tyres crunched on gravel; Hades looked up in time to see brake lights disappearing. Hades tore a hasty portal. 'You're going somewhere where Jack can't find you and you can't find Benny.' Arthur's eyes widened in fear and silent pleading. 'I'm not sending you to Purgatory, although you might wish I had.'

And with that, Hades hauled the King through the portal.

14/02/1895

Dear Arthur,

I believed in us. You didn't.

Your wedding vows said so.

I wonder if you realised how you hid yourself from me? Always blaming your queen.

Why wouldn't you let me leave, Arthur? Instead, you had me creeping about in the shadows of your marriage. Why did we do that, when the entire court knew?

Our last night together, the fire was still roaring when you left. You said: 'She is my wife, Benjamin. It's where I am expected to be the night before I leave for battle.'

I watched you go, not trusting myself to answer. You should have stabbed me. It would have been cleaner. Of course, Merlin chose that moment to barge in. He was still grieving from Vivienne's death and using it as an excuse to darken my doorstep more than usual. I watch the door a lot these days, expecting Merlin to storm in.

Your apology – a day later – wasn't strong enough to close that particular wound. It took me a long time – many hours of staring at the door, unable to move, lest one of you, by some miracle, reappeared, to realise why we argued so much in those last few months; you could forget but not forgive. I can forgive but I'll never forget.

As you will never read this letter, nor will you ever meet him, I see no harm in telling you this: I have met a person who is proud of me – of our relationship. Imagine that? I am only sorry that you could never feel this way, for I was proud of you.

Benjamin.

P.S. I still don't enjoy cities – too crowded, but autonomy is an advantage now.

24

SPACE INVADER

JACK'S FLAT

B en emerged from the bathroom and his tenth shower. His skin was still trying to crawl off his body.

An engine that sounded close to insisting it could go no further, rattled and spluttered to a stop. Something crawled up from his stomach and grabbed a hold of his lungs; he backed into the bathroom, damp fingers slipped on the lock once, twice, a third time. It slammed home. Ben slid down the slippery, cold tiles, flinching at every sound: the door to the building opening and closing, the footsteps climbing the stairs two at a time, the key in the lock, the chamber releasing with a hiss, the apartment door sweeping over the laminate, the slow footsteps that moved through the empty rooms, finally coming to rest outside the bathroom door.

The door handle rattling.

'Ben?' Jack's voice was rough with concern.

Ben buried his head in his hands, struggling to find his own voice in amongst the roaring of doubt and self-loathing. If he could repeat the tale, what would Jack say? That Ben had been wrong, naive – that he deserved it. Ambrosius had tucked himself away in a corner of Ben's mind, ashamed that he'd been unable to help. They'd tried to put themselves back together in the mirror. Nothing looked right anymore, nothing looked like him.

Jack's head lightly banged against the uncaring wood of the door. 'I'm going to sit out here for as long as it takes; you know that, right?'

The shower head dripped slowly. Ben could never turn it off properly. Too many dials and buttons.

'April and Merlin aren't back yet, if you wanted to go back to yours – you don't have to, but if you did, – it doesn't feel like a train station anymore.

Artemis has gone to check on April. She'll kick Merlin into the next universe if he's caused any harm.' Nerves had a way of speeding up Jack's speech.

Poor April.

She'd been trying so damn hard to hold them all together. Ben had been wondering about wishes and why clever people didn't make them. If granted, wishes soured over time. Ben should have let the dust settle, instead of believing it to be something long overdue. Perhaps that was part of the problem: Ben had felt obliged to be grateful.

'Alright. I'll stop talking at you if you promise you're not going to portal away. Deal?'

Portalling was pointless. Wherever he went, Merlin and Hades would be able to follow.

'Jack? Benny?'

Ben listened for the sound of four sets of claws tapping on laminate, around the sound of Jack scrambling to his feet, but there were none. He tipped his head back against the tiles, praying that the hound had not died on his behalf. Jack shooed the God into another room, but not far enough away that Ben couldn't hear them.

'He won't come out.' Jack said anxiously.

Hades' heavy steps approached the bathroom door, Ambrosius began cutting through the air. Ben shook his head. It was the one thing that Jack had asked.

'Arthur wanted you back, and you said?'

'No.' Ben's voice croaked.

'So he attacked you?' Anger distorted Jack's voice.

'I told him the truth. That I don't love him ... he was so strong. Magic, maybe?'

It was wishful thinking – a reasonable explanation for an unfathomable thing.

'I don't know.' He could hear the doubt in Hades' voice, the confusion as to why a shtriga hadn't managed to fend off a mortal, and it drove him right back into his silence.

'What's the plan, Benny?'

It wasn't a plan as such, but Ben wanted to stay put until everybody had forgotten about it.

If he closed his eyes, he saw Arthur's callous, barbarous eyes.

215

Ben was just now realising that he recognised the look. He'd been seeing it since the start of their courtship. Arthur had never used physical force; no, it wasn't that obvious.

Whenever Ben had wanted out, Arthur would remind him just how special he was. Arthur would make promises that he had no business making. And once Ben had forgotten why he wanted to leave, Arthur would shun him. The loneliness would eat at Ben, would drive him insane, trying to fathom what he could have done wrong. Days, weeks, sometimes even months later, Ben would pass Arthur in a crowded hallway and Arthur would smile just for him, as if Ben was the only person at court. He'd touch Ben's arm, whisper a combination of words that sounded like an apology.

And the cycle would start again.

Nobody but Arthur could tear Ben down and rebuild him like that. The worst of it all was that Ben couldn't decide if he actually liked it, or if Arthur had conditioned him into craving it. As if Ben found acceptance and belonging in Arthur's cruelty. And why didn't Ben fight Arthur off today?

Had Arthur really been that strong?

It had certainly felt like it. Either way, Ben had frozen. He wanted to say that shock had paralysed him, but Ben thought now that he had grown accustomed to Arthur taking what he wanted from him. Ben had been raging at Merlin for playing mind games when, in fact, Arthur had been doing the exact same thing.

'*You had your doubts about Arthur since he returned.*' Ambrosius tied himself in worried knots. In the living room, Jack and

Hades traded back and forth over what to do.

'Still, I wouldn't be here if I'd just learnt to let Arthur go –'

'It's just you and I now, Benny.' Hades' voice boomed throughout the apartment.

He jumped, nearly crying out. He'd not heard Jack leave.

'There are plenty of uncomfortable chairs in my own realm, I don't need to sit on the floor in yours. I'll be on the sofa whenever you're ready.'

'Where has Jack gone?'

Hades stopped mid-stride, surprise almost tripping him up, judging by the muffled bang.

'He's gone to wait for April and Merlin at yours. He'll return once she's back.'

Ben gathered his legs under him but wobbled at the thought of leaving the bathroom. He slid out of the shower and onto the bathmat, rolled onto his side and drew his legs into his chest, arms wrapped around himself.

Ben really didn't want to be alone.

Even if he really did want to be alone.

Being alone is what had gotten him into this mess in the first place. Death had told him, a long time ago, that he'd had a lucky escape. Ben hadn't been kind or courteous in his reply. He owed Death an apology. Ben felt like the living embodiment of infinite stupidity. Whatever Arthur felt for Ben, it wasn't love. It wasn't even compassion. Ben's tears were warm on his face.

'I almost convinced myself that I'd dreamed it.'

Contrary to what he'd said, Hades returned to his post outside the bathroom. 'I wish that were the case, Benny.'

'It was my fault –'

'You wouldn't choose him, so he took the choice away from you. There's no excuse for that. Absolutely none.'

'I shouldn't have let Arthur think that I was coming back.'

'One of the first things you said to him was that you were with somebody else. Arthur – and Jack – decided it was a competition. *You* were worrying about doing the right thing, which isn't the same as choosing between them.'

Ben spotted a stain underneath the sink that resembled Australia. Jack mustn't know of its existence. He'd never stand for such a blemish in his pristine apartment.

The vows that Ben couldn't keep.

Merlin should have shared that insight at the time. Another thing that Merlin could have prevented but didn't.

'I am going to make damn sure that Arthur never comes home.' Conviction had never sounded so much like intent. Hades tried the door handle. 'You can see the irony of you shutting yourself in a small room, right?' The door handle rattled. 'Come on Benny.'

'Not yet.'

'Well ... good talk.' Hades grunted as he pushed himself up from the floor.

'You're getting old.'

'Ha!' Hades sounded a little too far away and Ben's panic flipped.

'Hades?!'

Footsteps came closer and his panic breathed out. 'What?' The door handle rattled frantically.

'Nothing, I – what did you do, with Arthur?' Ben forced himself to breathe slowly.

The handle stilled. 'I threw Arthur into a pit in Tartarus,' Hades sounded a little too proud. None of the Gods went anywhere near Tartarus.

'What?!'

'It seemed like a rational thing to do at the time –'

'No! You went to Tartarus and you didn't look for April?' Ben scrambled up. He didn't know what to do, but he should do something.

'There are thousands of pits down there! I didn't bump into them. And I was a tad busy trying not to get caught by Chaos.' A gentle thud announced Hades leaning against the doorframe. He had gone back to the place he feared most. All to keep Ben safe.

Ambrosius popped up on Ben's shoulder, pacing back and forth. Merlin could free Arthur. Ben exhaled sharply, tried to take another breath as quietly as he could. Ben sunk into his frown, Arthur had been the best man he'd ever met but ...

'All of those years ... Arthur had a temper, yes, but was this there all along? memory is a fickle thing. I hid *all* of the bad parts in my mind. Pulled the dust sheets over them. And I still had to deal with what was left, the lies I told myself.' Ben held his hand out for Ambrosius.

'What, in all of the universes, are you talking about, Benny?'

219

'I have to admit the part I played in my own suffering.' After hours conducting a forensic examination of the last few days, Ben had placed a time of death on Arthur as he remembered him. If he'd even existed in the first place. 'I'm telling you Hades, there was something magical at work in Arthur. I didn't recognise him.'

'Benny ... We've all done it. Spent a little too much time on somebody who could never be all that we wished. It's a funny kind of grief.' Hades spoke a little too loudly, but Ben still heard the rustling of something sliding between the lock and the door. Ambrosius wrapped himself around the handle and snapped the card in half.

'That's not what this is.' Ben picked at the frayed edge of the towel he'd draped over the heater.

'Oh yes, it is. You're mourning something that once was, something that should have been, and something that happened.' Hades gave the door a subtle kick and he gave up. His footsteps travelled to the end of the hall, paused and began to sprint towards the door.

'I've been a fool for a very long time,' Ben sighed.

The footsteps stopped abruptly. 'Some people exist to be fools; you are not amongst them. But, if you are going to take this up as a hobby, don't be the same fool twice. If you want to lie on the bathroom floor, crack on. But there's a lot happening out here. People are relying on you.' Hades' voice drifted down the corridor, away from the bathroom.

It was true that Arthur had taken a part of him that he was

never going to get back. But Ben would, eventually, bury this and accept that he'd also be burying a piece of himself. His hand came to rest on the lock.

'Now's as good a time as any, Ben. It'll be easier to be in the living room when Jack returns, rather than you joining the group.'

'I'm not sure why that makes sense, but you're right.' It was something that Ben could control. He took a deep breath and unlocked the door. Specks of dust floated lazily in the sunlight and, seeing no reason for retreat, he crept into the hallway.

Hades was sprawled on the sofa, legs hooked over the arm, reading. Ben settled himself in the armchair, listening to the consistent turning of pages, the familiar rattle of the boiler, a tap dripping and started to feel okay. Until Hades flipped another page and said: 'Jack's been gone an awful long time.'

'Please do not feel obliged to stay. What trouble could I get into in the apartment?'

Hades flicked the page over, his eyebrows raised doubtfully. 'You'd find something. Or something would find you. Either way, I'm halfway through this, so, if you don't mind?'

'Be my guest.' Ben looked over at the bookshelf, maybe reading wasn't such a bad idea, but he couldn't hold his attention long enough to even take in the book titles.

'Here.' Still reading, Hades chucked one of his discarded books over, his shot went wide, and it landed behind the armchair.

'Never take up cricket.' Ben glanced down at the cover. 'Hilarious.' He stormed into the kitchen and threw Jack's copy of

The Once and Future King into the bin. 'Why did he buy it?'

From behind the safety of pages, Hades chuckled. 'Research?'

'Too soon!'

'I know.' Hades closed his book and looked up. 'But the wheels don't stop turning because yours have come off. If the others aren't back soon, we're going to have to search for them ... April's premonitions –'

'She's had another?' Guilt punched him in the gut. Ben folded himself back into the chair just as the rain and wind returned to batter at the windows. Ben found himself looking at the front door for the hundredth time, willing Jack to return with April in tow.

'Yup. She's enroute for a showdown with Merlin. Hecate put a stop to Nyx stripping April's magic, so she might go super-witch in the near future. Super-mage?' Hades returned his attention to his book.

'I'm going to need more information than that!'

'One more chapter.'

Ben knew him well enough to know it would be the rest of the book. 'Don't make me slap the book from your hand.'

'Alright! Jeez.' Hades slammed a bookmark into place.

'Merlin and an oak tree – do you know what her magic is called?'

Ben shook his head, ashamed.

'Eilir. Only Eilir gave April two names. The other is, Vivienne.' Hades peeked at the next page of his book. Hades set his book aside and sat up straight.

'That's a coincidence. Merlin's daughter was called Vivienne. I'm just now realising that April reminds me of her.' Ambrosius tugged on Ben's ear, recognition and understanding radiating through the core of his magic. 'April's not ... no! She can't be his Vivienne?' Ben waited for Hades to laugh, but there was no humour in the God's black eyes. 'You're certain?'

'Charon says so. I'd hazard a guess that Death knows. And I can't shake what Merlin said –'

'Everything is happening as it should.'

25

SHAKE WITH ME

TARTARUS

Tartarus seemed to be comprised entirely of mountains that zigzagged up into the clouds. April hadn't spotted much in the way of vegetation in the grey world. It was rock everywhere she looked. The shrill, lone cry of a seagull in the grey-black smudges that made up the sky, drew April's attention to the sound of waves breaking somewhere behind the imposing rock-face. She kept peeking into the shadows, expecting something to crawl out of the thousands of grate-covered pits littering the ground. She was trying to ignore the yelling and screeching that came from them.

'It looks like a somebody put every game of Whac-A-Mole in existence in prison.'

'Moles do not scream like that.' Merlin was as surefooted as an irritating mountain goat.

She wasn't going to have any ankles left at the end of this trek.

'We appear to be marching towards a mountain.'

'It's a fell. At best it's a particularly large hill. It's smaller than Snowdon.' Merlin's mood had been deteriorating with every step. Maybe he had a blister.

'It takes eight hours to climb Snowdon!'

'Seven at most. Hmph! We need to go up, so up we shall go!' April would never know because seven hours of hiking was seven too many. She wouldn't be walking up this *particularly large hill* if she didn't expect there to be answers at the top.

An assumption that came care of the premonitions.

April was starting to think they held no meaning other than that she no longer had freedom of choice. She was certain that the reason for that was currently untangling his robe from an isolated tree branch protruding from the ground.

'Everything was fine until you came along and stomped all over my life.' She felt Merlin roll his eyes.

'I wasn't aware that you were satisfied with your life prior to my *stomping all over* it.' Merlin tugged his robe free with so much force, he sent himself stumbling towards the edge of the path and the drop below. Sadly, he stopped himself in time, toes protruding into thin air.

'You're a real douche bag, Merlin.'

'Yes, I am.' He spun around and stalked towards her.

April reached for Eilir, not liking the wild look in Merlin's eyes, his breath hot and rancid.

'You were a disaster, trying to kill demons with a wooden sword because they killed your boyfriend. It was an embarrassment.' Merlin's nails dug into her arms. 'I wasn't going to watch whilst you dug your own grave. Do you think I'd trust anybody other than Benjamin with your wellbeing?'

April shivered in the cold breeze. 'Why does Eilir recognise you? Why does *my* magic crave *your* attention?'

'Eilir is trying to find her way back home. Aren't we all?' Merlin smiled wistfully.

April resettled her sword over her shoulder, trying to understand – because Eilir wasn't telling her – why Merlin felt like home for her magic. Sometimes, when she wasn't worrying about the boys or the world ending or why Fate wanted to kill her, or trying to understand why Death let her go, April wondered what shape her life would have taken if Merlin, disguised as Melvin the hunter, hadn't interfered.

'I did right by you, child. Remember that the next time you curse me.'

'Who am I to you that you feel so obliged to look after me? If you can call pushing me towards danger, caring.'

Merlin's eyes grabbed a hold of hers and shifted from side to side before he turned on his heel and continued his determined march towards the summit, powered by something that he wouldn't – couldn't – say.

'If you're hoping that, by confronting Chaos, you'll redeem yourself to Ben, you're going to be disappointed.'

Merlin stopped again, half looking over his shoulder. 'You craft and wield your judgement better than you do magic. Clever, dressing it up to look like Benjamin to play on my insecurities.

But you are smart enough to know it won't work.' Merlin closed the gap. 'Contrary to what you might think, your destiny is not to try and reignite that which has long since died.'

'That which what?'

'My consciousness, April!' Merlin's voice bounced off walls of rock. 'If it pleases you to think that I do these things out of guilt, then by all means continue wasting your time.' Merlin returned his gaze to the horizon. April slapped him. As hard as she could. He covered the slap mark with one hand, nodding as if he understood why he deserved it.

'I see so much of Benjamin in you, though there's much of me also.' Merlin set off without checking to see if she followed. Of all the unfathomable statements to leave Merlin's mouth, that was the weirdest. Behind April, the air sizzled and ripped. She spun, drawing Eilir as the cries from the pits climbed in volume. One sandaled foot stepped out, followed by another. Artemis nodded a greeting, her eyes fixed on Merlin's receding frame.

'Has he forgotten that you are both capable of opening portals?'

'According to Merlin, the not-a-mountain is smaller than Snowdon.'

Artemis eyed the climb ahead of them and holstered her spear. 'He is deluded.'

'That's what I said! I've not accepted that I am going for a hike in hell.'

'You do not know how to open a portal?'

April shook her head, feeling a little self-conscious. Ben wasn't

227

up for it, and Merlin didn't take requests. Artemis turned April to look up the path.

'Think of your destination. Let Eilir weave into the atmosphere and cut downwards with your fingers, like so.' Artemis punched her thumb and forefinger together, and pulled the air in front of her downwards. 'Hold the destination in mind until we are both through.'

It would have been useful if April's premonitions had shown her that scene.

All she could picture was a slab of grey rock that protruded out into the abyss. Eilir hummed in her head, pins and needles ablaze, but April couldn't catch the air – or whatever she was meant to be doing. She imagined waiting at the top for Merlin to bob into view, and how satisfying that would – Eilir caught an edge and dug in, pushing the air apart. It felt like she was cutting wood against the grain with a blunt spoon. April pulled her hand down with the other one, tearing a portal large enough for them to step through. Artemis nodded her approval. April hid her smile.

The inside of the portal was as breathtaking as the first time she'd fallen through one. Artemis stepped through and the light rushed past April. Something knocked the wind from her, and she assumed that Artemis had arrived at the top. Eilir was trying to mentally drag her into the portal, her entire body on fire with her magic's impatience.

Atop the mountain, April spotted the ocean on the other side of the ridgeline. A river weaved its way between tall cliffs and dark forests, rushing towards the point where it became so much more than what it was. April had the overwhelming urge to walk the pristine beach. Beside her, Artemis pointed up. The clouds, which had been in their appointed place a moment before, were now swirling about the mountain.

'Did I do that?'

'No.' Artemis pointed to where Merlin stood, toe-to-toe with the drop, the wind whipping at his robes. The rat must have portalled the second he was out of sight.

The clouds dipped to circle Merlin. The cold and the rain drove April back into the solid wall of rock behind her. Generally speaking, April was good with heights, but she drew a line when the clouds were below her. Artemis' sharp eyes were locked on the sky. Merlin sent two balls of aquamarine magic chasing each other up into the air, lighting up the clouds like flares. The two strands of magic collided with one another.

A deep rumble came from the core of the realm and grew to shake the entire world.

It sounded like laughter.

The clouds were sucked sharply downwards as if somebody was collecting them with a vacuum cleaner. Eilir thrashed about in her head, pins and needles erupted in both arms, wanting to open a portal.

'Everything is happening as it should.' Merlin held April's gaze. 'Just as it should.' His childish giggle was unnerving and at odds with his smile. He looked resigned to what was happening and a little bit relieved that it was. He returned his attention to the clouds, leaning forwards, one foot free of the ground.

April clutched at whatever courage hadn't fled and pushed off from the rock to look over the edge. The clouds were knitting together and rising up until the cloud-figure towered above them. The cloud's face, with puffy cheeks, bushy eyebrows, and storm clouds for eyes, looked a lot like the Stay Puft Marshmallow Man. With his magic in his hands, his shoulders back and head held high, Merlin was a defiant ant facing off against the gargantuan cloud-figure with a cocky confidence that April would never know.

'Merlin.' Chaos' voice was a deep roll of thunder that bounced off the rock, echoing back to them from another dimension. The cloud-eyes crinkled in elated delight and the mountain shook once more with their laughter. 'I expected you sooner.'
April hadn't considered that there might be people out there who actually wanted to see Merlin.

'I had some loose ends to tie up first.' Merlin's measured voice caused her heart to beat faster for fear that she was one of his wayward ends.

'No matter. You brought Artemis! I am delighted to see you, child.' The God stared coldly down the length of a notched arrow. The bow looked so primitive, so inconsequential compared to Chaos.

'Artemis is here to ensure that I do not cause the mage harm. She will not remain. Chaos, do you hear me?'

'A parent wishes to have their children home, you should understand that, Merlin.' The cloud-eyes lingered on April. Emrys flared to life in Merlin's hands. Eilir jumped to life in April's hands, startling her and causing Chaos to laugh in delight.

'You agreed to the Gods leaving.' Merlin's voice had a sharp edge to it that cut April free from Chaos' attention.

She caught a glimpse of Arthur's imposing advisor who would not be defied. She could clearly see the charismatic young man with a smile that inspired people to follow him. This, Eilir wanted her to know, was the Merlin Ben spoke of, before all of the double-crossing and failed marriages, the Merlin that Eilir recognised with delight that April could not ignore. Her magic knew Merlin, somehow.

And that terrified her.

'I ensured they wanted for nothing!' The cloud sounded offended.

'Whilst denying them everything,' Merlin insisted.

'I denied them nothing.' Chaos sulked. 'Tell him, Artemis.'

'So long as we gave you absolute loyalty, respect and adoration, we were safe.' The arrow shook slightly, desperate to fly free from the bow.

'There you go! See Merlin?'

'And that is a perfect example of how you only hear what you want to hear.' Artemis recentred her aim for what April presumed was Chaos' heart. 'Travel was forbidden, you forbade marriages, destroyed children whose birth you did not approve of. The other realms were a haven and we sought out the love of other beings – for affection that should have come from you.'

'I was pleasantly surprised when they fashioned themselves into Gods,' the cloud continued as if Artemis hadn't spoken.

'But such blatant disrespect cannot be ignored! And I miss the company.'

'Ha!' Merlin snorted. 'You like the idea of company, but you detest the fact that company has the audacity to talk to you.'

'Noise bothers me if I cannot control it.' Chaos stretched up into the sky, their fingertips brushing stars. 'I am not actively pursuing them, you know?'

'No,' Merlin conceded. 'But you have been reaching out to Fate and she feels backed into a corner. You know how she gets.' Chaos nodded knowingly. April's mouth dropped open, but she thought better of asking how destroying worlds was just one of those things Fate did when she was in a mood.

Chaos sighed an overly dramatic sigh, tightly clasped cloud-hands came to rest against their lips, as if in prayer. 'It pleases me to watch them in their realms, so I propose we leave them as they are. If you return Fate to me.'

April could have laughed aloud; she'd gladly pay Chaos' price but the task was impossible. Merlin stared impassively at Chaos. If he had concerns about using his wife as a hostage, April couldn't tell.

'Whatever is the matter?' Chaos asked in genuine confusion. 'This would neatly tie up those pesky loose ends. I speak to you as a warlock, not as a Guardian.' Chaos leaned forwards, the enormous cloud-head almost touching Merlin's. 'You, like I, have looked ahead. The outcome is already decided. There is no time to waste so I shall not squander it persuading you. Deny me and you will leave a far greater mess behind.' Merlin inclined his head in agreement. 'You have caused much mayhem, Merlin. If only you had more years ahead of you than you do.'

'I've had time enough, hmph. Those closest to me can't take much more of my antics.'

'What?' April asked sharply.
The swirling storm-cloud eyes found hers and Chaos floated past Merlin, their hands pulling the giant cloud-body up and onto the ledge, head coming to rest on their arms.

'You are April. And Eilir.'
Artemis' shoulder brushed against hers. She was still terrified, but April thought there might be a chance of getting out alive.

'She is so young!' Chaos glanced at Merlin, but the warlock was watching April with eyes that carried an odd look of relief, resentment, resignation and, curiously of all, tears.

'Do not let that fool you,' Merlin said stiffly, pride riding the undercurrent of his voice. 'April is going to run rings around us all.'

'Such is the way of nature. The youth repair what we elders break.' Chaos extended a cotton wool hand to April. An arrow sailed through the air and through the forearm. It was ignored along with a flock of birds that flew in one side of Chaos' head and out the other.

'Beauty often aligns itself with ugliness, and so you, April, have found yourself inexplicably linked to Merlin through no fault of your own. You must not feel guilty about what is to come.'
Artemis, well-versed in Merlin and Chaos' double-talk paused

midway through notching another arrow. She replaced the arrow in the quiver and took a step back. Merlin shuffled his feet, picking at a loose thread on his cloak. April had nothing to feel guilty about, but the supposed adults couldn't make eye contact with her. The tree. This had to have something to do with the tree. And Vivienne.

'Ah!' Chaos chuckled, tufts of cloud shifting with the laughter. 'You haven't told her?'

The warlock's fingers twitched, Emrys running over his knuckles like a coin.

'Merlin is still deciding which end of your sword he would rather meet with.'

It was the straightest answer that April had heard in a long time. And it came from Chaos! April's sword felt heavier than one made of steel. It was too much, to have ancient beings allude to her destiny, to imply that April should be in a rush to figure it all out alone. If that's what they wanted, then they needed to dispense with the riddles. April drew Eilir but Merlin stepped between the delighted cloud and her.

'Damn you, Chaos!' Merlin shouted at the cloud. He took a moment before turning to April, but she could still see fear in his eyes. His body shook with it.

'This is not how I wanted to tell you, April.' Merlin took her hands in his firm but gentle grip. 'Eilir has been trying to remind you of who you are. She started with your name.'

'Vivienne?'

The name sounded unfamiliar and odd but entirely right, all at once.

It resonated with Eilir. Her magic was bouncing about inside her head, making it rock, making her feel seasick. The pins and needles were strong and getting stronger. Snatches of unfamiliar memories were pushing through into her head. Spells that Merlin had taught her thousands of years ago came flooding into her being. But that couldn't be, not unless ...

'Your daughter was called Vivienne.'
Merlin nodded stiffly, looking at her in a peculiarly affectionate way. Ben said that there was no such thing as a coincidence. Only Fate.

'No.' April felt sick.

'This is not a debatable matter, April.' Merlin looked to Artemis for support but the God shook her head. Given Artemis' family drama, that was fair.

'We cannot discuss the mechanics of it right this second, but you are Vivienne. Like it or not.'

'I don't like it; I don't like it at all!'
There was a twang and a snap and the grey, bleak realm lit up with her jade magic. April grabbed a hold of Eilir and reined in her magic, the darkness rushed back in to reclaim Tartarus.

'Vivienne?' Chaos called. 'When you find yourself debating if death is a punishment or a mercy, you mustn't hesitate. There is as much courage in killing as there is in sparing a life –'

'Enough, Chaos! Leave her be.' Merlin sounded strained. The clouds broke apart, flying back to their rightful place in the night sky. Artemis returned her bow to its place over her shoulder; the spear appeared in her hand instead. Merlin leaned over the edge at an alarming angle, dragging April with him.

'We should be away. Much has happened in your absence.' Artemis hauled Merlin back from the edge. 'And the shadows are awakening.'

Merlin nodded and dropped April's hands, cutting open a portal.

'Two questions. One, how do we get Fate to return? And, two, are you sick? Whose life am I sparing?'

'That is three questions –'

'How did Chaos know my name?' April grabbed a handful of his robe as Merlin dared to walk away from her.

'Chaos knows everything except when to hold their tongue.' Merlin turned back to her, his voice low. 'And some things aren't for Chaos to understand.' He nudged her towards the portal, Ben's kitchen appeared in glimpses as the portal waved in the air. Merlin kept insisting she own her destiny, but judging by the worry etched into his face, he didn't understand what that meant.

'Go, April. Benjamin will be worried –'

'No!' April tried to shut Merlin's portal, but Emrys forced Eilir back.

'Get in the portal!' Merlin spun her around and with his hand on her shoulder, marched her towards the portal. 'Now, young lady! Do as you are told, for a change.'

'Why are you like this? I'm glad that Ben's home. I can't stand learning magic from an old fool.'

The portal shut with a snap. Merlin staggered back, as if April had shot him.

'You are an inconvenience that repeatedly breaks my heart!' Merlin squeezed her arms, his head shaking back and forth. Eilir curled up into an anxious ball, scared of disappointing Merlin.

'How and when have I –'

'Be content with who you currently are. You won't like what comes next.' Merlin turned sharply and opened another portal. April ran in front of him, forgetting about the drop. He closed the portal and marched down the trail. Artemis held an arm out. Merlin hit it and ricocheted back to April like a pinball. His foul breath accosted her, his warm spittle landing on her cheek.

'Given time and tuition, you will rival Benjamin and myself.'

'That wasn't so hard, was it?' April's voice was strong but her heart was pounding in her chest, scared to hear the rest.

'Chaos doesn't know you; they know the things you will do. They know who you will become. Let's keep it that way.' Artemis opened her own portal so she'd have somewhere to look that wasn't at them.

'And who will I become, Merlin?'

'Cease asking questions that dwarf you.'

'Merlin!'

The warlock nodded slowly, the faraway look in his eyes pushed April back a step, but Merlin rushed forwards and folded her into an uncomfortable hug.

'The girl who asked far too many questions of those trying to protect her.' His voice was loud against her ear, despite his quiet tones. 'At the crucial moment, keep a steady hand and do what must be done.' Merlin pulled back, looking into her eyes like he knew she'd understand. 'So, Eilir remembers? That's, that's –' Merlin's giggle overtook his speech; it built into a laugh that rocked his entire body. April disregarded the urge to push Merlin over the edge.

'I brought you here so you could see what you have been overlooking the entire time.'

Artemis had walked out to the very tip of the ledge and appeared to be in communion with the clouds. 'You have your name, Vivienne. Your destiny issued. Cease chasing ignorance when you know your path.' Artemis turned and April couldn't breathe at the sight of a God with sunset-burning eyes, lips drawn back to show teeth as sharp as any bear's, cheeks scratched by brambles, her silver-grey hair brushing the ground, a wolf pelt draped across her shoulder.

The weight of Artemis' scrutiny set Eilir set ablaze with conviction. The oak tree filled her vision once more. *I tried to warn you.*

'Let's get you home, child.' Merlin stared into the portal, trying to hide his tears.

Child. Vivienne. Oh Gods. Merlin was her – no she couldn't give it life. April's voice fought to find its way through the blockage of her breath.

'Let your tongue taste the truth for once, Merlin. Am I going to kill you?'

'Yes.'

26

TO MY ILK

April landed in Ben's kitchen and collapsed into the nearest chair.

'No one is home, hmph.' The portal popped shut behind Merlin. He set about exploring cupboards that cried in protest of being opened so violently. April's stomach was a heavy knot of nausea that craved acknowledgment of the fact that Merlin was, inexplicably, her father. On the one hand, it would explain Eilir. On the other hand, Merlin could very well be lying. But if he were her father, who was her mother? April kept waiting for a second portal, but it seemed like Artemis had gone elsewhere. April dropped her head onto her arms, trying to fathom how, in the near future, she was going to permanently still the hands aggressively rummaging through Ben's cutlery drawer.

'What are you looking for, Merlin?'

'Whisky. Or rum. But, as this is Benjamin's house, I will settle for a forgotten bottle of wine that somebody bought him in the forties.'

'That's a drawer …'

'It's a drawer – I know it's a drawer! I seek a corkscrew. So, when I acquire the wine, there shan't be any delays.'

April beat him to the fridge and forced a bottle of coke on him.

Merlin looked dubiously from her, to the bottle, back to her and opened it. The short sharp hiss of gas made him jump. He gave it a cautious sniff. 'There's no alcohol in here.' He held the bottle out to her, offended by the fizzing liquid.

'It's alcoholic.' April held her breath.

'It smells like somebody burnt a potion.' Merlin tipped the bottle from side to side, watching the dark liquid slosh about with a level of scepticism usually reserved for people who smile all of the time.

'Give it a go!'

Merlin shrugged, extended the bottle to her, downed it, and reached for another.

'Wow! Slow down!'

'Time is not on my side, child.'

'Fair point.' It wasn't like Merlin could get drunk off carbonated water and sugar. 'You could leave Gaia?' Merlin shook his head, trying to sip his drink to appease her. 'I can't hurt you if you're not here.'

'Yes. You can. But you know not what you do.'

Merlin was too calm for somebody about to take a trip to the great beyond. 'You've known all along.' Merlin nodded, a strangled look on his face as the downed coke tried to resurface, and belched.

They were just edging around the obvious. And it wasn't a very wide circle in which to manoeuvre. April reached for her phone.

'Do not summon Benjamin, I beg you. He has enough on his mind. And I, cannot stomach another of his lectures.' Merlin took a swig from the bottle. 'What was your last premonition?'

'I can't control them!' Best dodge that particular subject.

'Practice! You don't practice,' Merlin grumbled. 'There will always be the odd vision that breaks through, unbidden; its message too important to ignore. The ressst.' Merlin gestured with his bottle, spilling a little. If Merlin had twigged and magicked the pop into something stronger, April had missed the spell. 'The rest, heh. The rest are floating out there, waiting for you to reach out and decide what it is you desire to see... Dooo youuu have the courage to se, se, che? Tree?' He shook his head, trying to clear the way to his words. 'Focus on what you want to, want to kn-kno-know and wh-y. Then traverse time... see beyond the veil... all that falls in-between.' Merlin stood, tripped over his own foot, spun, and looked about for his attacker, swaying like a metronome.

'Where's my hat?'

'You didn't have a hat.' April rose, wishing that Jack was here to pin the warlock down –

'Drunk already. Have you no shame, Merlin?' Artemis strode into the kitchen, eyebrows raised, her disgust not at all hidden. Eilir jumped, they'd not noticed the portal.

'I shall fetch Hades. Try and keep him here.' Artemis was gone before April could nod. She prodded Merlin back into his chair.

'Perhaps you'd like to tell me who my mother really is. An explanation on *the mechanics of it* would also be appreciated.'

'My Gods, child! Just when I believe your curiosity has reached its limit, you push through. Hmph.' Merlin's sadness weighed his shoulders down. He held his hand out for Emrys. The little figure, who seemed more blue than green this time, hugged Merlin's thumb. Merlin blew Emrys in the direction of the back door, aquamarine embers covered the surface, fixing the damage.

'Curiosity can get you killed, April. And I want you to live, child. You must. Live. Do better than me.' For the briefest moment, Merlin's guard dropped enough to show April a wrecked, vulnerable man who was quite unrecognisable. 'Questions bring answers, answers bring clarity, and clarity brings disappointment.' His head flopped from side to side, weighing up the pros and cons. 'Shhhh, sh, be quiet, and I'll tell you a secret, so I won't have to think on it ever again.' Merlin's nails dug into her shoulders. The manic laugh that chilled her filled the room. Eilir bristled, straining to remove them from the situation.

'April.' Merlin clacked his tongue at the bitter aftertaste of the name. 'Never did grow on me. I thought it might ... only a name. It never sounded right, didn't quite fit as snugly as your others. I couldn't change it.' His drunken mind stumbled over itself as he visibly tried to gather his thoughts. 'Couldn't ask *her* to change it ... would have drawn attention to you. She couldn't see you this time round.

Fate's irrational fear of April.

Merlin's romantic history.

Vivienne.

Her chair hit the floor, the countertop bumped into her back; Merlin came with her, his fingernails drawing blood as they waltzed about the kitchen, keeping time with the fridge's insistent beeping.

'It was as if my heart were simultaneously being torn apart and reassembled. How could she not feel it?! I did. Every time you returned. I *felt* it.' Merlin cradled her face in his hands, taking in every detail. 'Pretty. Like your mother. Fie! Why waste breath on Fate? I've followed you for – ' Merlin scrunched up his face in concentration, eyes fluttering shut and then open again, alight with the answer. 'Nine hundred years or so.'

'I'm going to call Jack –'

Merlin slapped the phone from her hand and took hold of her shoulders once more.

'Fate and I had a baby girl. She wasn't long for this life. We both knew it. Only one of us took action.' April had never heard such bitterness before. 'Part mage, part God. She would be reborn. It's the imbalance of mortal and immortal genes, you see. We called you Vivienne.'

April dug her fingers under Merlin's, but she couldn't break his grip on her.

'Fate is my mother, and you are my father ...'

'Sshh, don't tell anybody. It's a secret. Heh.' Merlin moved her to one side so he could gain access to the fridge, not the least bit bothered by the bombshell he'd just dropped.

'Benjamin has known you in all of your lives.' Merlin looked up, his face illuminated by the fridge light. 'He never quite figures it out though. I gave his intelligence too much credit. Perhaps he's long-sighted, can't spot what's right in front of him.' Merlin shut the fridge, lost his balance and hugged the fridge for support. 'Or beside him.'

'Well, I can't kill you now, can I Merlin?' Homicide was bad enough but patricide? That was going to take some counselling to get over.

'You will have no choice.' Merlin's words crawled along. 'Another's blood will stain your hands before mine. Some would argue that the judgement you render me is infinitely worse.' He smiled at her ruthlessly. 'Benjamin won't hold it against you. I will write him a letter. How novel, to finally reply to his tsunami of thoughts.'

There was so much Merlin and Ben said only in words they thought the other would never read.

'You're really drunk. That or this is one hell of a sugar rush.'

'Drunk I may be, but serious I am.'

'Okay Yoda. Why didn't you tell me earlier? Like one of my past lives, earlier?' There was a sentence that she never thought she'd say.

'You were happy. The truth would have robbed you of that.' Merlin spoke with so much sincerity, he almost sounded sober. 'More's the point, I would have led Fate straight to you. The first time you died in my arms ...' Merlin held an imaginary child close to his chest. 'Benjamin is a far better father than any figure I could have cut.' April searched every line of Merlin's face, looking for wrinkles, comparing nose shapes, eye colour, hair, anything that told her they had the same blood.

'Is that the time?' He peered at the oven clock that thought it was 0200. 'Cloak?' Merlin shouted, twisted and spun about. He landed in a heap on the floor, the cloak appeared on top of him.

'Where do we go from here?' She'd just found where she fitted into all of this, and now Merlin was going to leave? April snatched his cloak from him.

'I am going to Avalon.' Merlin stood, pulling his cloak back gently and fastened it around his shoulders.

'Wow, you just keep building on your one single, terrible idea, don't you?'

'Five minutes in my company is all it will take for a centuries-long argument to begin, and that, should buy you time.' April lurched forwards to steady Merlin as he wobbled back over to the fridge, delighted to find more bottles, which promptly vanished. 'Most magicians keep cards up their sleeves.' The air popped and a sliver of Avalon shimmered in its hazy summer heat. April grabbed a hold of Merlin's sleeve, pulling him back. He smiled through his tears and shook his head. 'What can I do to stop this?'

'Everything that I could not.' Merlin took her hands in his, he chuckled at her bemused expression. 'My daughter. My Vivienne. Smile, April – you and your curiosity are going to save the world.'

Merlin kissed her on her forehead whilst freeing his hands. He didn't look away as the portal sealed, cutting them off from one another once more.

27

UP AGAINST

April slipped back into a chair, stunned.

The kitchen clock's tick tock mocked her.

Her ... parents ... ruined everything they touched. At least she didn't look like them. But she'd always know.

It didn't change who she was. Or did it?

Merlin was the worst person she'd ever met. She didn't believe that he'd ever been anything but, especially after learning how he had manufactured his friendship with Ben. And Fate ... shame and disgrace burned in April. She'd never behave as her parents had ...

Ben might as well have been her father. It was his sense of justice that ran through her.

She pulled her phone out. Eilir tapped on her mind. April imagined her magic on the table, and for once, Eilir popped into view on the first try.

'Call Jack. Benjamin never hears his phone.'

'Right.' The dialling tone pierced the quiet. 'Did you really remember who Merlin is – was – to us?'

'I couldn't quite place him. Emrys felt so very different to when I last encountered him. But, after a while, Emrys felt like family. Like home. And Merlin was –'

'You're back?' Jack's voice sounded gruff, like he'd been crying or yelling at the galaxy, or both.

'I'm at Ben's. Is he with you?'

'Long story, but no. He's at my place. Is Merlin with you?'

'Long story, but no.' Her voice cracked and betrayed her. 'Merlin's ...' the words stuck in her throat. 'Can you both come home?'

'Two minutes.'

No sooner had April ended the call, Jack let himself in; his footsteps snuck into the living room and back to the hall. The cupboard under the stairs opened and shut just before his dishevelled blonde hair popped round the doorframe, falling across his scratch-marked face.

'I don't know how to say this.' Eilir hugged April's little finger.

'Well, we know you're not breaking up with me.' He patted her shoulder, curiosity and concern burning in his eyes. She'd been worried about telling Jack before he'd arrived. Now she was terrified. 'Merlin is ...' She forced herself to breathe. 'He's, my father.'

'Oh.' Jack rocked back on his heels, trying to hold his tongue.

'Oh?!' April had expected a little more than that!

'Charon worked it out.' Jack fell into the chair beside her. 'Was he mumbling? He mumbles.'

'Vivienne is ... me. Merlin and Fate's dau – nope, I can't say it. Ben has known me in every one of my lives – without realising it.'

'Now that I can believe.' Jack closed his eyes, trying to digest it all. 'My condolences on your parentage. Reincarnation.' Jack jumped up and busied himself with the mundane task of making coffee.

'Wanna hear the rest?' Jack held his hand up. With an effort that was visible at his temples, Jack looked back to April and dropped his hand.

'I am going to kill Merlin. Chaos implied it. Merlin confirmed it.' Jack gripped the countertop, watching the kettle boil. 'If we get Fate to return to Chaos – everything goes away. Oh, and I gave Merlin a bottle of coke and now he's drunk, somehow.'

'Wish I'd known about that sooner!' Jack laughed in disbelief.

'It's not funny!'

'Sorry! Are you certain that he's drunk?'

'Yes. Unless warlocks can get high from sugar?' Jack shrugged, trying and failing not to laugh.

'I'm freaking out here!' She also felt like she needed to shed her skin. But that wouldn't be enough. She'd still have their DNA at her core, shaping her. She would still be the child of a God who had ordered the deaths of entire planets. And who knew the depth of Merlin's sins?

'Am I like them? Jack, I don't want to be like them! I can't –'

'Hey!' Jack wrapped her in a hug, her breathing slowed down

a little as she inhaled the sweet, sunny, citrus and resinous scent of bergamot, sandalwood and cedar. He'd changed his aftershave again. 'You are your own person. That's what we love about you. Sounds like Merlin won't be a problem for much longer.'

'Don't joke!' April was close to pulling her hair out. 'Ben won't talk to me again.'

Jack stiffened up and his mouth clamped down into a thin, hard line. Fear gripped April.

Ben adored Jack like nothing April had seen before. But the way Jack was staring at the floor, his foot tapping erratically, had April worrying. And trying to desperately keep from rushing Jack into what was clearly a difficult answer.

'Arthur, um, Arthur attacked Ben.' Judging by the way Jack was blinking back tears, they weren't talking about a fist fight.

'Is he hurt?'

'Physically? No. But Ben isn't doing too well. Hades chucked Arthur in a pit in Tartarus.'

'I saw those pits. Arthur's not getting out.' She squeezed Jack's hand.

'I should be so lucky – Chaos knows that none of the Gods will go back, right?'

April nodded.

'And Chaos has convinced Merlin to fetch Fate back, right?'

April nodded.

'Merlin knows that he doesn't have a chance in all of the hells, right?'

April nodded.

'Merlin has gone to Avalon, hasn't he?'

April nodded.

'Merlin should be able to recognise a trap –' Jack darted from the kitchen. An almighty crash drew April to the living room. The coffee table was on the opposite side of the room, its legs poking into the air. A bookcase tipped and toppled to the ground beside her. April choked on the ensuing dust cloud.

'Merlin's taken the talismans!' Ben hid them in a book. Damn it!' Jack flipped the coffee table back to its feet and dug through its drawer. A notebook slammed onto the top. 'Pen, I need a pen.' April spotted one beside her foot and rushed to give it to Jack before he took the sofa apart. Jack scrawled a hasty note for Ben.

'So, we're going to save Merlin from his recklessness by recklessly chasing after him? We should wait for the others.' April didn't have a good feeling about this.

'No time. They'll not be far behind us.'

'I can't portal to other realms yet and you can't do it at all.'

'There are other ways in, if you know where to look. Just get us to Glastonbury.'

***

Ben's house was deathly quiet.

Stood on the landing, worry tapped Ben on the shoulder. Jack wouldn't disappear. Not now, he wouldn't do that to Ben. Then again, Jack would be forgiven for finding the situation too much to handle.

'There's a note in what used to be the living room,' Hades called up to him. Ben hurried downstairs and met Artemis in the hall. She handed him the note, dread in her eyes.

'Damn it, Merlin! Avalon?' Ben read it and read it again.

'I hope Fate doesn't kill him; I want that privilege.' Hades said with the cockiness of a boxer entering the ring. 'Artemis, how do you feel about fighting Fate?'

'It would be my pleasure.' The God of the Hunt smiled darkly. Ben flipped the note over and his legs buckled. He reached behind him for any surface to sit on and found the windowsill. What could possibly happen that would force April to kill Merlin. Ambrosius pricked at Ben's skin. For all of his faults, Merlin had strived to be a good father. Ben could not imagine him doing something that would threaten said child. That April was Vivienne seemed so obvious now. She had been the answer to a riddle perched on the edge of his tongue for months. Her unusual aura was that of a demigod.

'Merlin's either swaggering to his death, or Fate's bed. Are you listening Ben?'

'Did you read the back?'

Hades snatched the note from Ben's unresisting hands. 'Oh, wait. She's going to kill him?!' He and Artemis exchanged a worried glance that seemed to be about Benjamin.

'Promise me.' Artemis took Ben's hands. 'That you will not interfere. Do not stand between April and Merlin.'

'Preventing Merlin's death isn't as big an ask as you think.' Standing by whilst April pulled the trigger was another matter. She would carry that with her for the rest of her days, whether or not her actions were justified. Hades returned the bookcase to its feet and set about depositing items to wherever he deemed to be their rightful place. Which seemed to be the wicker bin.

'I know that you're desperate to redecorate my house, Hades, but it'll have to wait. We need to stop them before they find the crossing in Glastonbury.'

'Oh, I will have my way with this place – you can't deny me now. However, they'll still be searching for the crossing point.' Hades came upon a jar filled with multicoloured sand and threw it in the bin. Ben didn't care for it either, but he retrieved it. Jack had bought it on a trip and *he* would care if it vanished. 'You are a ridiculous creature, Benjamin.'

'I informed Jack of its location some time ago. I suspect he wasn't paying attention. He was reading at the time. Neither will know how to use the crossing point, if they find it.'

Ben threw open a portal and turned in time to see Hades drop the jar back into the bin.

28

THE VIEW HERE

GLASTONBURY

A pril's feet were complaining.
They stepped out of a pub and into the dark, biting cold of a December evening. The pavements glistened in the street-lights. April glanced back up at the King on the pub's sign. Wherever she looked in this town, Arthur and Merlin stared at her from shop windows, signs, and artwork. The pub had been packed to the gills with armour and crystals and a cape that was in far too good a condition to be Merlin's, as they claimed. The town's colourful mix and match of buildings were trying their best to sleep through winter, even if the gleam of frost suited them. People weaved along the narrow, old paths, going about the last few bits of Christmas shopping. It didn't matter how many galleries they looked around, this painting wasn't anywhere to be found. Jack dragged them into another gift shop whose display window featured hundreds of miniature

Merlins in navy blue robes, clutching wooden staffs crowned with a crystal ball. They were surrounded by a miniature army of fairies, dragons, trolls – anything mystical that came covered in glitter. The shop bell dinged and the air, thick with incenses, tried to choke April. She wandered amongst the shelves, half-listening to Jack asking the lady dressed in a green druid's robe, about a painting of the Tor, surrounded by a lake. Even if they did find it, April wasn't convinced that they'd be able to use it. Not without calling Ben for help. Which Jack didn't want to do. Jack was choosing to ignore the fact that he'd gotten himself stuck in a crossing point just days earlier. She rounded a corner and bumped into the vampire snapping an Arthur figure in half. He shook his head and, dejected, they returned to the street.

April really needed somebody to teach her inter-realm portalling. Eilir had refused to try. Something about the consequences of getting it wrong resulting in death. Jack's phone appeared in his hand. Again. She was keeping him from Ben, not that he'd turn back. And he had to move at her speed. April had to be the only demigod who didn't have super-human speed and strength. She added it to the list of things to ask her parents, when they found them in Avalon.

'Oh! I get it – the lake is the way into Avalon. Wait, are we going to have to swim? I had that sandwich.'

'For the last time, the lake is long gone. And the sandwich would be the least of your problems. How many of the cake-things do you have left from that bakery?'

April was suddenly very interested in a poster about pottery classes in the post office window.

'What about the art exhibition at the abbey?' She pointed to the pottery flyer's neighbour. The reflection of Christmas lights blinked in the window, framing the posters. The shop across the road had a mannequin wearing star-speckled robes and sporting a long white beard. One thing was clear: nobody had a clue about the real deal. Here, Merlin and Arthur were local heroes. Legends. Folklore. They were kind and brave and all of the things the real ones weren't.

'This place is one big Merlin gift shop.' Her laughter stuttered and halted. And it was so obvious that a passer-by gave her a sympathetic look, and Jack a glare.

'She's alright, she's, eh.' Jack waved the man along. 'So, are we going to talk about it?' He pushed his arm through hers and started walking them in the direction of the abbey.

'Do you want to drag up my dead boyfriend again?' And then she remembered who she was talking to. 'Don't dig him up.'

'Obviously!'

In this town, April had zero chance of forgetting about Merlin, and Jack had zero chance of forgetting about Arthur.

'Learned or inherited – people grow to be variations of their parents.' Of all the worries and thoughts, that was the loudest. April's parents – the people who had raised her in this life, were timid folk who hadn't wanted to so much as disturb a puddle. They had been generous, caring people, but people with whom April had little in common. Which was contributing to her general feeling of being a ticking timebomb. And when the inevitable happened, who would she be? Killing her own father ... that was straight out of a playbook co-written by her parents.

'Merlin is a disease, granted, but you can't catch his personality by osmosis.' Jack had been aiming potshots at Merlin since they'd arrived, but it wasn't helping with his mood. She should ask, but April was riding her own stormy waters and was dangerously close to being dragged under by the weight of everybody else's troubles.

'What does it mean to be a demigod?'

'That you will spend the rest of eternity bothering me with questions.' Jack's smile hardly pulled his lips up. I assume it's why you're stuck in a reincarnation loop.'

Jack's quickened pace suggested that he wasn't the one to answer such questions. The ancient sadness that had caught in Merlin's throat, came back to haunt her. She preferred not knowing, she'd decided that about two seconds after Merlin had vanished. Perhaps if her memories of her past lives came back, she might feel some sort of connection to Merlin. But she couldn't remember, and so she couldn't imagine the pain of being separated from a parent who loved her. And who would she have been, if she'd been able to grow under Merlin's guidance?

Somebody that April wouldn't recognise, that was for sure.

'You *can't* slip your genes, kid. You *could* explode, trying to think yourself free of your parents. Or you can see it as a fun bit of trivia.' They rounded the corner and found themselves enclosed by ancient masonry on either side of the steeper-than-it-looked slope. 'Family is just an excuse to inflict trauma on people who feel obliged to live through it. Ben and I like having you around, so, you know, you do have a family. Whether or not we have the same blood.' Jack coughed, pulling his jacket collar up to hide how he'd turned red. 'We're going to have to run. Sorry.'

They darted past the ticket office, through the little exhibition in a school hall-type building. Branches brushed past April as they bolted through the cobbled courtyard garden and into the Lady Chapel, with walls and floors but no roof, and out into the muted greens of the grounds. Jack slowed, not that there was anybody around to see them, and set April down. She wobbled, staring up at the grey stone pillars of the archway that reached for the sky, searching for its missing piece. Small, stone archways with grass sprouting from the top of them, marched down either side of the entranceway. This was all that was left of the once great abbey. Inside the broken walls, the shadows stretched across the grass. The only sounds that resided here were natural; the past breathed, untroubled by the present. It was as if the ground was waiting for the monks to return. Lavender mixed with the sickly-sweet scent of roses that April couldn't see. They wandered through the ruins, coming to rest at a tiny gravestone crammed with writing. Clumps of grass poked out from damp soil that had been hastily removed from, and then returned to the grave.

'Well, I guess we know where Merlin stashed Arthur and Ben's bodies.' April ignored the strangled sound Jack made. 'The painting isn't going to be out here, is it?'

'Where's the exhibition then, if you're so smart?'

'You were so determined to not pay, that you ran through it,

Jack.'

The art exhibition was painting after painting of Arthurian legend scenes.

And hot.

April ducked under the end of a scarf, only to be caught in the face with a discarded mitten. She ignored the mumbled apology and pressed on to where Jack stood, his temples pulsing, jaw working.

'What's up? Oh.' Jack was glaring at a painting of Arthur sat upon his throne that was surprisingly accurate in its portrayal. 'Come on, there are loads of landscapey paintings over there.' Because Jack looked to be seconds away from yanking the frame off the wall and sticking his foot through the canvas. 'I don't think the art world and the magic world collaborated on this with the sole purpose of winding you up.'

Jack's teeth ground in reply but he allowed April to haul him away, glaring at the painting over his shoulder as she pushed through the crowd of vaguely interested people. Out of the corner of her eye, a familiar face stopped her in her tracks, but not Jack who, still staring at the Arthur painting, collided with her.

'What? What happened?' Jack emerged from his hatred. 'People are staring at us.' He followed her pointing finger to read the gold plaque. 'Merlin and Vivienne In The Forest. Ugh, we're surrounded, April.'

'Yes but look at the painting.' April couldn't breathe, couldn't move, couldn't look away. The snake-like roots of the oak tree reached for her from the canvas, the solid tree trunk so tall it grew past the top of the frame. Sat in the shadow of it, with his back against the trunk, was Merlin who held Vivienne in his arms, her head against his shoulder. Beside them, a sheathed sword leaned against the tree. Merlin looked content. It was a peaceful scene, but it had April shaking.

'Add a beard to real-life Merlin and you've found your wizard.'

'And Vivienne?' Because as far as April was concerned, she was staring at her likeness clothed in a ridiculous purple dress with long, trailing sleeves.

'Her hair's a different colour. And you don't wear dresses.' Jack leaned in for a better look and pursed his lips. 'Nah, she looks nothing like you.'

'This is my premonition.' Jack's eyes widened in horror and disgust. 'No, not Merlin holding me like that. But us, the oak tree.' The room swayed, spinning away from her whilst the painting anchored her to the spot.

'The art world and the magic world aren't collaborating to paint your premonitions, as interesting as they are. Oh! Hello.' Jack pulled her down the line to an old oil painting of Arthur dying on the banks of the lake. 'What a shame.' Jack pointed at the wound, drawing a dark glare from a man who had been pretending to understand the painting. Jack replied with his biggest, bestest fake grin, until the man ushered away his family. 'Go, go, go.' Jack pushed her forwards.

'I didn't realise art galleries were this stressful.'

'Just when you're looking for magic paintings.' Jack stared impatiently up at it, waiting for something to happen. But the female mourners continued to mourn and the boat carrying Arthur's cure remained just out of reach of the shore.

'That's a lot of crying ladies.' April snapped a stealthy photo of the painting.

'Arthur's queen.' Jack pointed to a regal lady, draped in a gold cloak, who cradled the dying King's head in her lap. 'The person to Arthur's left, who's trying to heal him, looks a lot like Ben, but wearing a circlet crown.'

'Ben wasn't with Arthur when he died.'

'And Arthur never openly acknowledged their relationship, let alone give Ben a circlet. Artistic interpretation, I guess.' Jack shrugged. 'The silvery floating thing on the right, that you almost can't see, is Death. The young lady by the tree looks like.' Jack cleared his throat. The young lady by the tree had red hair and her eyes. On the other side of it, Merlin and Fate were arguing at the shoreline.

April's heart squeezed tightly, its rhythm off. It was too hot in the room to breathe. Behind her parents, and on the far side of the lake, stood a conical-shaped hill wrapped in a pearlescent mist. Sat atop the hill, rising from the mist, painted in a foreboding grey-black, with unhappy dark clouds above it sat a lone wooden church tower.

'It's the Tor.' Which April recognised from the various interpretations of it dotted around the town.

'Uh–huh.' Jack handed her his phone; he'd pulled up a copy of the painting. 'The Tor isn't in any of these photos. There's a generic fell, but no Tor.' He backed up from the painting and

261

crouched down. 'Magic is like water; you can't see what's going on below the surface. You have to catch it in the right ... light ... Ah! There!'

April copied Jack's bobbing about. The painting's colours exploded under Eilir's sight. Everything hummed with a kind of magic that she now recognised as Emrys. And the flat blue smudge had become a shimmering deep blue lake, sunlight bouncing off the surface. April's eyes tracked up the painting to the wooden door set into the side of the hill. 'How are we supposed to fit through that? Somebody's looking out through the tiny windows!'

'Most likely,' Jack said as if seeing a miniature person moving in a painting was an everyday occurrence. 'You're going to have to open the door for us.'

'Oh sure, allow me!' They had successfully cleared out the gallery, apart from a mildly concerned attendant.

'So much sarcasm from one so small.'

"*If you grow agitated with Eilir – or yourself - who knows where you'll end up.*" A much younger Ben towered over her, his smile not quite hiding something that prickled behind his eyes. He scooped her up and April felt like nothing bad could happen. "*You are more than capable of wielding your magic.*"

April shook the memory away, tears clouding her vision. Ben had been the only adult to show her nothing but love and patience. Eilir beamed with joy at the old scene and turned her attention to the door. April's fingers jumped over the bumps of the canvas, the old paint flaking under the pressure. Eilir flowed into the painting, swimming through the lake, climbing over the grass and encircling the door's handle. 'Say I can open it, what's on the other side?'

'A dark tunnel.'

'We're going to get lost, aren't we?'

'No. So long as we pick the correct fork.' Jack's smile was not reassuring.

April couldn't even begin to imagine them standing in Avalon. So, she imagined the only thing she knew she'd recognise. Merlin. April's heart and magic stuttered, so she tried to focus on finding him, and not what finding him meant. 'I don't think it's working.'

'It's working!' April opened her eyes to the sight of a hill ascending in front of her. Night had tucked the Tor in with a low cover of fog, Eilir's jade-coloured embers clinging to the grassy bank. Thick oak doors with an intricately carved woodland scene and heavy iron handles appeared from nowhere. April stared, mesmerised by the details of the miniature forest animals that beckoned her into the world they guarded. She walked towards the doors with more confidence than she felt, only for Jack to pull her back.

'Calm down! I have no issue with you wasting Merlin; hells, I'll do it for you, but a little caution every now and then, that's all I ask.'

'If this is the beginning of the end, I can't run from my –'

'Don't say it!' Jack pleaded.

Running away was a Merlin move, so April wasn't going to do that. 'If you need to get back to Ben ...'

'Give us a light.' Jack pulled the heavy doors open and April couldn't have loved him more if she tried.

Eilir's glow didn't stretch very far in the tunnel's never-ending darkness. It twisted its way underneath the ground, descending in long steps to the centre of the earth, but they never seemed to arrive anywhere. There was a constant smell of damp soil that made April think of graves. April was done with steps, magical doors, steep hills, warlocks and destinies. Around them, creepy hands scuttled away from the intruding light. 'Ugh, I still don't like the creepy hands.'

'Nobody likes them.' Jack pushed ahead of her as they emerged into a large hall with a high ceiling. Fanning out in a circle were nine other tunnels, three of which had caved in. Jack walked out into the middle of the circle, slowly turning to look at each entrance before he was face-to-face with April. 'Maybe they're laid out in realm order?'

'Makes sense. Gaia is the second but do we count to our left or right?' April joined Jack, looking at the tunnels either side of Gaia's. 'We could try them both.'

Jack's head was whipping back and forth, looking for even the smallest difference. The pressure of choosing and getting it right first time pushed April to pick one. 'Where are you going?' Jack grabbed her collar.

'We can't stand here forever.'

'When faced with the choice of three, ask me.' The new, squeaky voice made the both of them jump. April instinctively put her back to Jack's.

'Fairies. Fantastic.' Jack put the slightest pressure on April, and she realised he wanted her to edge back towards the tunnel they'd entered through.

'Fairies are cute, right?'

'Does that look cute?' Jack pointed to a jagged ledge above the tunnels.

'Not so much.'

They had metallic green scales for a start, and too many sharp pointy teeth for their black lips to close around properly. Their wings didn't seem big enough to carry them around. She'd have missed it completely if it weren't for Eilir and as April looked, more and more emerged from the walls, like lizards in robes and with wings.

'We're journeying to Avalon,' Jack said. 'We're not looking for trouble.'

'It is you who entered our domain; we will decide what transpires here.'

'Merlin has drained me of my patience for magical beings who speak in riddles. What do we need to say or do for you to let us pass?' Jack gripped her arm, ready to run.

'Youth always rushes.' The original fairy tutted; the others nodded in agreement. 'What moves right but never left? Left is right, and right is left. One is right, and one is wrong.' The fairies dispersed, flying low in a swarm. April realised they resembled bugs.

'What moves right but not left?' April repeated.

'I don't know,' Jack groaned. 'Electronegativity?' Jack glanced at his watch.

'That's it! A clock! The hands of a clock only move to the right!'

'And Avalon is shrouded in the mists of time!' Jack smiled. 'Left is right and right is wrong ...'

Above them, the fairies giggled. It sounded like beads bouncing off a stone floor. April shuddered.

'Right is wrong so left must be right – as in correct! Ha!' Jack pushed her into the tunnel.

'Was that too easy?'

'Who cares? In the left tunnel we go.'

29

MY ENEMY / BIRDCAGE

AVALON

'Not again.' Merlin couldn't look at the latest victim of his horticultural homicide.

'Fate cares more for you than she ever did for Vivienne. She never so much as shed a tear for Vivienne.'

The rose garden shook in the breeze, not accepting his flimsy apology. Fate didn't quite know how to handle precious, delicate things. He'd done his best, but it was tricky keeping Vivienne alive. His daughter took after him – charging through life, not looking where she was going. He turned away from the glass palace that was throwing the midday sun into his eyes but was glad of the sun-drenched soil that warmed his aching body. The city strained to be heard on the breeze. He'd lost track of days, but if it were Wednesday, then the market would be in full swing. Merlin plucked a rose, too drunk to care about the scolding he would receive.

If he didn't leave the rose garden, nothing could move forwards.

And Vivienne – April – wouldn't … the liquid in the bottles sloshed around, well, in two of the bottles.

He'd given up everything for her.

Benjamin would tell him that was sole responsibility as a parent. Children lived to surpass their parents, and April would be a better servant to the realm than Merlin ever could. It was for the best. The drink fizzed in his mouth, tickling his throat.

Dutch courage was the only thing strong enough to get him through the next couple of days.

There was a certain numbness that Merlin could only find at the bottom of a bottle, and he'd been craving it for some time now. At the house, Merlin had buzzed with the energy of the universe, ready to take Fate on. Now he was here, well … he dug his fingers into the cool soil, recognising his own work in the mix of soil. His wedding ring, bruised by time and loosed by dirt, slipped off of his finger and into the earth. Merlin buried it in the damp clay. They should have let each other go. A long time ago. But he never could walk away once he had given his heart to something.

'Well, Emrys, we were so caught up in trying to move the world along, we forgot to enjoy it. It'll be a relief I think, to sleep. Perhaps, next time, we will plot our own course. I should like that.' Groaning, Merlin tried to stand and found himself to be completely lethargic. The bottle's label blurred and doubled, tripled. 'How much have I had to drink?'

'Judging by the state of you, too much.'

Merlin tried to bow to the shadow that fell over him. 'Hello, Fate.'

'You should be ashamed of yourself.'

'As should you!' Merlin hiccupped. He hadn't meant to be so quarrelsome. Best to get it all out now, though.

'Excuse me?' Fate replied, her voice quietly furious.

'At best, your conduct has been unruly.' Fate took a threatening step towards him. 'Allow me to speak. I've got to leave some of it behind. There's only so much room in one's grave and I should like to rest comfortably.' Merlin crawled to the wall encasing the garden and pulled himself into an upright position. 'I understand your refusal to return to Tartarus but making the rest of us suffer – poor form, love. Your selfishness has cost the lives of your siblings. And their realms. Was that really easier than picking up the phone every once in a while? Backfiring on you now, isn't it?'

The sun began to set on another day. Merlin blinked and blinked again. It had been noon a few moments ago. His grip on the neck of the bottle slipped, and the sweet contents spilled to the ground. He scrambled at the dirt, but it was too late. All was lost.

'Go home, Fate. Do not make me drag you to Tartarus.'

'To live for eternity in a realm devoid of sunlight, passing judgement on Gods who step out of line? I think not. I will destroy the realms so Chaos has no entertainment and then I will be gone to a new universe where they cannot find me.'

Merlin pitched forwards onto his side. 'Could we reschedule this argument?'

'Suit yourself. Your departure is not imminent. I am not letting you loose to further derail my plans –' Fate frowned. 'You are still here.'

'Running is pointless.' Emrys popped into existence and fell off his shoulder.

Merlin and his magic laughed at one another, unable to help themselves. Fate perched on the wall, backlit by the fading sun in a pastel sky. Perhaps it was the light, but Merlin thought he could see faint outlines of crow's feet at the corners of lavender eyes that were paler than he recalled.

'You've got me now, Fate. Nobody will pester you. Cease with the destruction.'

'How altruistic of you.' Fate wrapped her magic around Merlin.

'Do not squeeze me, woman! I'll be sick on your roses! Can you not see how drunk –' Bile rose in Merlin's throat.

With a tut, Fate turned sharply on her heel, her magic jerking Merlin with her to the palace. He bumped along the flagstone path, noticing the first beads of dew forming on the top of the grass. Merlin waved sadly to the roses.

'Do you ever think of Vivienne?'

'Sometimes,' Fate replied in a bored voice, but there was something that almost sounded like kindness there. 'Do you?'

'Every day.' The wind howled across the sea, throwing waves against the breakers.

'You masked the spell well, love.' Fate's step faltered.

'Vivienne would have made a fine demigod, a fearsome

huntress.' Fate kept her tone cool and business-like.

Merlin smiled from pure happiness. It hurt. He hadn't done it in years. As his lips parted to show coffee-stained teeth, his best-kept secret fell out.

'Vivienne did just that! Across multiple lives.' A nervous giggle shook him free of Fate's grip.

Looking at the drunken father of her child, lying on his back, covered in mud and compost, and clutching a bag of who-knew-what, Fate reminded herself that faking a death was Merlin's speciality. Tears prickled at the edges of her eyes and a sob scratched its way up her throat. They had drifted apart after Vivienne's death, and whilst she had always loved Merlin, she had not cared for anything more than Vivienne. Without her, Fate had turned away from her duties, from the realms, no longer putting effort into creation. How could she, when the one life that mattered to her was nowhere to be found? The majority of the stories turned sour; the worlds dropped into disrepair.

'You and I have done so much damage to one another. Un-speakable acts borne of every emotion and motivation possible. If you've kept her from me – ' Fate heard her voice crack. Her magic battled to suppress her desperation to leave, to search the universes for Vivienne.

'At first, I thought you weren't ready to leave your grief – or guilt – behind.' Merlin took another swig from his bottle. 'But when you failed to broach the subject after the fourth regenera-tion, I knew you couldn't see her.'

Fate's breath caught in her throat. 'I did not harm our child,

Merlin!'

'Shout louder, I might believe you ... what sort of a life would a child of ours have? None.' Merlin had a horrible habit of answering for her, of assuming he knew Fate's mind on every matter. Well, Merlin couldn't have landed wider off the mark if he'd closed his eyes and fired.

'Neither of us possess parental instincts.' It was said with such sincerity that Fate almost agreed with him. 'Vivienne had a chance to enjoy life rather than entering the pantheon. At least I thought she did.'

'How so?' Fate closed the short distance, towering over Merlin.

'Responsibility found her. It's the funniest thing! Our little girl grew up.'

Five words pierced her heart, cutting deeper than any blade. Fate hauled Merlin up by his shoulders, slamming him against the wall.

The warlock smiled his irritating, coy smile and returned his gaze to the horizon. Fate was untethered and alone in a strange blue ocean, her rage free to do whatever damage it needed.

'You left Vivienne with mortals? With Benjamin?'

'And a damn-sight better job they did. I watched from afar.' Merlin shrugged. 'Sometime around Vivienne's third birthday, I realised that our opposing truths were doing nothing but harm to our child. Now, I can disagree with your truth and still love you. And I still love you, Fate. More than I should. But there was much too much of you in our daughter. One of you is sufficient.'

Fate's rings tore Merlin's skin open. The following punch shattered bones.

She should have felt something, seeing Merlin sprawled on the floor, trying to stop the flow of blood from his nose, from wounds she had inflicted. Feeling would return later. She grabbed Merlin's collar and dragged him all the way into the palace.

'Oh Fate, my love, we were never going to end in anything other than misery.'

Barqan was exiting the palace as Fate passed, a resigned Merlin sweeping the floor behind her. Like the majority of creation, Barqan had never understood the dynamics of their relationship. She averted her eyes and hoped that neither would –

'Barqan!' Fate barked.

She fixed a blank look to her face and turned, not at all prepared to join their circus.

'Good day, Fate. Merlin.'

The warlock gave her an absurd little wave, Barqan acquiesced in the fact that there would be days of marital discord and plastered a subservient smile on her tired face.

'Merlin will be staying with us.'

Barqan's eyes slid to Merlin who winked back. 'Where would you wish for Merlin to reside?'

'The more uncomfortable the space, the better.'

That rather depended on whose point of view Barqan was supposed to adopt. There was a hate in Merlin's eyes that suggested sharing a room with Fate would be worse than death. That said, the warlock was lying calmly on the floor, not so much as twitching against Fate's magic wrapped around his.

'Emrys likes it.' Merlin winked again.

'That's …' Barqan positioned herself where she couldn't make eye contact with the warlock, lest she throw up. 'If Merlin remains, somebody will come for him. He's been visiting Chaos an awful lot.'

'Has your hearing failed you, Barqan? Lock him up and see to it quickly.' Fate left Merlin where he lay, freeing him from her magic. 'He can keep the bottles. Whatever it is, it seems to make him more amicable.'

'Don't go too far, love. They'll be here soon. The time is upon us!' Merlin pointed at Fate's receding back. 'Rude. Suppose you've more important, Guardian tasks to be doing, rather than babysit me.'

Barqan searched Merlin's expression for any sign of him knowing of her involvement in the destruction of realms, but it seemed the warlock was sober enough to keep some cards close to his chest.

'Are you planning a daring escape, warlock?'

'Walking is a terrible idea. Why do you ask?'

'This is the first time I've witnessed you in a calm state, Merlin. It is disconcerting.'

'I am leaning into old age. You are going to have to carry me.' Barqan reluctantly stored her spear on her back and, after a deep breath – that she regretted – she grabbed Merlin's waiting wrists. He went limp as soon as she took his weight.

'Should I be arming myself? Other beings live here besides Fate and myself.' As wearisome as he was, Merlin's sight was to be respected. Not that he owed her any assistance. His cloak tightened around his neck; she was on the verge of stopping when Emrys remedied the situation.

'You should always be armed, my dear djinn!' Merlin cackled, but he watched her with cold, hard eyes. 'Don't get involved, Barqan. Actually, do. For once, be a Guardian. Gods aren't always godly.'

'What, if not that, do you think I do with my time? I have ensured Avalon's safety.'

'So you have.'

Barqan dropped Merlin's wrists, her heart racing.

'Did you think I wouldn't notice your magic on Arthur? That I failed to recognise you in Tintagel?' Merlin propped himself up on his elbow.

Barqan forced her head high, trying to stop the shaking. She had done some questionable things of late, but Arthur's actions …

A portion of the blame was hers.

She had fought for control of Arthur; she had tried to blind him just long enough for Benjamin to flee, but Arthur's rage had taken control at that point. She'd had no choice but to look away. 'If you knew, Merlin, why allow it to happen?! Benjamin – you could have prevented that!' Merlin's eyes went wide, as if intervening hadn't crossed his mind. Emrys' anger was palpable; it collided with her magic, searching for an answer she could not give. She'd thought that by having control of Arthur, she would be able to put the brakes on Fate's plans if she crossed lines. Not that there were many remaining lines for Fate to trespass.

'Arthur's behaviour.' Barqan caught her reflection in one of the hundreds of mirrors that adorned the palace. She had disgraced herself in Fate's service. 'I miscalculated the effect my spell would have when mixed with the effects of Purgatory.'

'Only you can understand the impact of your spells, Barqan. Yours is a dark kind of magic; it plays on insecurities and desires. As for your explanation, that is owed to Benjamin.' Merlin caught her wringing her hands and softened. 'He's the forgiving kind, so, I think you'll be alright. He won't forget though. He has a long memory for even the slightest harm you cause him. He's still angry about the goat incident –'

'So why tell me?' Barqan snatched up Merlin's arms and resumed pulling.

Merlin pursed his lips, thinking. 'I've looked as far as I can into Benjamin's story. That was never meant to happen, Barqan. The irony, of course, is that it was an anomaly that I could have prevented, had I known it was coming. As could you, seeing as you were in Arthur's head at the time.'

Barqan pressed her lips tightly together and thanked the universe that she had arrived at the door to Merlin's chambers. The glass door bore etchings of his life with Fate that hadn't been there yesterday. It creaked and groaned open.

Merlin craned his neck, his face unreadable as he considered his prison. 'Fie! Damn Fate for redecorating – she knows how I detest modern décor.' Barqan wondered how Merlin could focus on something so banal when he was trapped. 'There's still time to assist the other Guardians, Barqan.'

'Time ran out when I killed Keres, Lamia and Cerri.' She swung Merlin into the room. He landed in a heap on the rug, craning his neck backwards to see her.

'If I were to change allegiances now, what would happen to Avalon?' Her entire being was centred around protecting her home. She'd inherited the role, and it had denied her the chance to be a proper queen to her people.

'Whilst today it's me, tomorrow it'll be you who falls.' Merlin rolled over, his back to her.

'That sounds like a threat.' Barqan squashed the urge to ask Merlin if he'd seen far into her future.

'Run along, Barqan. Jack and April are arriving. It's rude to not greet your guests.'

30

Hiding Inside the Horrible Weather

Tartarus

The relentless screaming was unbearable.

Worse still was the faint twilight that refused to give way to proper daylight.

Arthur tied a piece of ripped tunic around hands bloodied from attempting to scale the side of the pit. Bitter experience had taught him that, though the grate covering looked achievable, it would grow to touch the sky, the second he began to climb. The walls were constructed entirely of compacted mud; however, they sprouted jagged rocks and branches bristling with thorns when Arthur reached above his head. He had persevered for over an hour before exhaustion grabbed his legs and pulled him back to the bottom of the pit. A lone star shone above. That seemed fitting.

Arthur had never expected to visit Tartarus. Certainly, he had not imagined himself amongst its prisoners. Clouds hurried past and the star winked out again; Arthur pulled his hood up, fearing a storm. Hades had allowed Arthur to retain his cloak. Not that it had prevented the cold from seeping into his bones. It had rained more often than not in Purgatory Tintagel.

Yes, Arthur was quite tired of rain.

And yet he had set about creating his own bad weather.

Arthur had no idea what had possessed him.

His temper had dwarfed his good sense, and turned him inside out. He closed his eyes, deeply ashamed and utterly lost. They should have remained in Tintagel. Yes, everything had been right. Until Jack had tumbled in. Arthur paused, expecting that little voice to pipe up, the one that had been validating his jealousy. It was noticeably silent.

'Gods, perhaps I was possessed.'

'Curious.' A voice rumbled above him, causing Arthur's bones to try and flee his body. 'That is the first peep I have heard from you since you arrived.' The clouds pressed themselves through the grate, the bars cutting neat squares into the face.

'There is no need to keep me under lock and key. Nobody will come for me, Chaos. I am not a fool.' Although Arthur's recent behaviour strongly suggested otherwise.

'Benjamin is welcome to visit. Perhaps we could resolve this issue.' Chaos propped their chin on their hands, ever the inquisitive type.

'So, you know.' No doubt the entire universe knew of his shame by now. 'There is no resolution to be had.' Arthur pulled his cloak tighter, uncomfortable in the stiff blue trousers and the tunic with no arms Jack had thrown at him when he had first returned.

Chaos' eyebrows became one long grey cloud. 'You would deny Benjamin happiness?'

There was that question again.

The same point that Benjamin himself had made. Anger, hot and sticky, crawled over his skin.

'I am not proud of myself, Chaos!' Arthur drove his fist into the mud. 'Benjamin is the one thing worth a damn in the world. There is not one single person who matters more to me. Why is that not enough?'

Chaos nodded sympathetically, their face inches from Arthur's. 'The fact of the matter is remarkably obvious.' Chaos stroked Arthur's hair, and the King looked up through his tears. 'You were too late to be what Benjamin needed, if indeed you could have been that at all.'

Chaos might as well have punched Arthur in the gut.

Benjamin had been free to live as he pleased. Arthur had to divide himself into small pieces to ensure that his realm was safe and content. Benjamin drew the shortest straw because Benjamin understood that Arthur was a King and Guardian, above all else. He had to be. What Arthur had failed to recognise was that understanding had made Benjamin lonely, even when they were in each other's company. Arthur could command people, rally armies, adjudicate, debate, strike deals and negotiate treaties. But when it came to telling Benjamin that he was the reason Arthur continued to fight, well, the words would never come.

Benjamin did not need a king, simply love.

The realisation stuck in Arthur's throat. Perhaps it was time to admit that their relationship had perished before they had reached Camlann. Benjamin had threatened to leave Caerleon on countless occasions. Arthur had dismissed him every time, found some way to appease Benjamin ... Gods, perhaps recent events were not as out of character as Arthur wished to believe. He had no defence, no argument to offer in rebuttal.

Not a single soul seemed prepared to acknowledge Arthur in all of this.

That was the frustrating part. Arthur was expected to step aside, disregard all that had passed between Benjamin and he.

'It was not my intention to hurt Benjamin. He would not listen –'

'Well, I believe you communicated your point.' Chaos smirked.

'And repaired nothing. If there is a way to sever myself from my feelings –'

'It's what Benjamin does next that's important. If he does nothing, let him go. That is not love.'

A chill ran down Arthur's spine that had nothing to do with the cold.

Arthur had been on his way to disturb Benjamin one Cornish summer evening.

The sun had shone all day long, the council meetings had been swift and decisive, training had been enjoyable, and Arthur was feeling particularly content as he crossed the courtyard in search of the one person who would complete the almost perfect day. Benjamin's chambers had been empty. Arthur had taken a moment to sit amongst the shelves of books and herbs and the Gods-knew-what that cluttered the work benches. After a while it seemed logical to enquire at Merlin's cottage. At the white door with black beams, Merlin's voice stopped Arthur from knocking. He stepped back, concerned at the sound of a distraught Benjamin.

'It seems to me, Benjamin, that you have given Arthur ample opportunity, and it is his move. If he does nothing, let him go. Though he be a great King, I question whether he is worth so many tears.'

Recollection would not remind Arthur of his actions. An upset Benjamin had, by then, become a common occurrence. Arthur had learned to ignore him when he gave up trying to fathom why.

Chaos had continued unaware, or perhaps unbothered, by Arthur drifting off in thought.

'The King of Gaia should not be insulted by a vampire.'

Arthur stilled, hearing the unspoken offer. He'd already broken Benjamin's trust and pushed his physician as far away from him as was possible.

Arthur had nothing left to lose.

Neither did Chaos.

But of all the Gods to bargain with, Chaos was the sneakiest.

'Truer words have never been spoken, but my circumstance prevents me from doing so.' Arthur stood, as best he could, given how Chaos was still filling the pit's headroom. He had not run such a successful realm by blindly accepting gifts. Nor had he been successful by brokering terms that favoured the other party.

'You, I can free. Myself, in time and with some assistance. Merlin broke some important seals when he rushed off.'

'If you want me to release you from Tartarus, then you must bind Benjamin to me. And the vampire dies.'

'Is that a request?' Chaos hiked an eyebrow and retreated through the grate.

'Mortals make requests. Not kings.'

'Jealously doesn't befit a king,' Chaos clapped their cloud-hands, and the pit began to warm up.

'But it serves a purpose. Bind Benjamin.'

'Is that not a touch drastic?' Chaos teased.

'You all but suggested it yourself. I shall make damn sure that Benjamin cannot ever leave again.'
Chaos poked their head back through the bars, mischief dancing in the storm-cloud eyes.

'Think of the trouble it would cause. All of that angst, anger, desperate sadness for your magic to feed on, Chaos.'

A fluffy cloud smile stretched across Chaos' face. 'Sounds delightful.'

31

FRIENDS AND ALIBIS

AVALON

Dust drifted through the late afternoon sunlight, a breeze stirring the curtains.

Merlin refused to transfer himself to the four-poster bed, or any of the chairs that cluttered the room. He'd already noted with irritation, the shiny, sleek cabinets and metal tables in place of his beloved workbenches patched together from whatever wood had been lying about. The various bric-à-bac of his workshop – glass jars filled with things he could no longer identify, that sort of thing, were gone.

'She's a spiteful creature,' Merlin grumbled to Emrys. 'This was my only sanctuary in Avalon.'

'You haven't lived here in quite some time. Fate is entitled to decorate her home.' Emrys appeared beside him on the floor. Merlin rolled over, dismissing reasonable logic. 'Where is the stone floor? The talisman mosaic? I can't see the walls for those atrocities –'

'Paintings and carpets.'

'Where are the oak tables, groaning under the weight of books and ingredients? And what is that in the hearth?'

'A wood burning stove.'

'Well, I don't like it! Make it go away. Now. "S too much glass.' Emrys sighed, but the stove remained. 'I need a fire. And I will never be able to find anything in here. Fate is forever moving my belongings. Tidying, she calls it.' Merlin curled into a ball, wondering if there was any point in magicking his surroundings back to the old and familiar. 'My refuge has become a pleasant-smelling, stylish hell. Nobody needs that many cushions on a bed.'

'That's enough, Merlin! Time is running out, and you are wasting it being disgruntled by soft furnishings! Sit up.'

'My armchair has vanished –'

'There is something wrong with this room – and it's not the decor!' Emrys' nerves scratched at Merlin's and his little bundle of magic manifested beside his nose.

Merlin sat, looking at the room from the corner of his eye. Just below the surface, there was indeed the hum of Fate's magic, brimming with her malice and intention. His wife had been crafting illusions. 'We are going to have a horrible time.'

Emrys side-eyed Merlin and the warlock struggled under the doubt and scorn written into every line of Emrys' being. Merlin held out a finger, but Emrys turned his back. He wouldn't be here for long, but it would be just enough time for Fate to torture him with his own imagination. A knot of panic constricted his airway, hiding oxygen from his bloodstream. Emrys stretched in the shaft of light from the window. At least, Merlin thought, his magic would fight to keep him on an even keel. Searing pain shot through him, causing Emrys to double over. A formless presence slid itself under the door, growing until it hit the ceiling. Its heavy breathing filling the room, pounding on Merlin's skull. It wanted him to look, to remember. Looking back was a trap into which Merlin never wanted to fall, let alone be pushed. Two feet stretched from the ceiling, landing in front of him. The rest of the presence dripped into the legs, the torso, the head. The eyes – those quicksilver eyes.

'Benjamin.'

Merlin's body was on fire with his magic as Emrys tried to hold onto the knowledge that this wasn't real.

'I warned you –'

'That something like this would happen; yes, congratulations on your accurate prediction.' Merlin caught himself rushing to offer a defence and let it go. He was only arguing with himself. Benjamin's body contorted, the spell grabbed a hold of Merlin's throat and crushed his windpipe.

'It wasn't enough for you to chase the storm. You had to change the weather. But even you, mighty warlock, cannot calm the sea.'

Merlin's fingers knotted in his hair, scraping against his scalp. His body weighed a ton and it was dragging him down into the Nothingness. He wasn't seeking forgiveness, he wanted sleep.

His eyes tingled with Emrys' efforts to keep them open. Merlin blinked and found Benjamin sat cross-legged in front of him.

'What happens if you ignore your premonition, Merlin?'

'Time. The future. Rivers that, if dammed, burst their banks and forge new paths.' If Merlin stopped it now, if he made a different decision, somebody – Death or Chaos – would intervene. And Merlin would be adrift, never reaching his final destination. They all must come ashore one day. Merlin hadn't noticed when the lines had formed around Benjamin's eyes, or when the grey hairs had appeared.

'April lives this time, Benjamin. Whatever sacrifices are required to ensure her survival, I will gladly make. When it all comes clear, I will be held accountable.' A bubble of nervous laughter drowned out Benjamin's reply.

Merlin had always stood defiant in the face of his destiny. But now that the hours were whittling away ... He'd not been this scared since Vivienne became ill. And with that came the sad truth that Merlin should have been a part of all of her lives and yet, he shouldn't have been a part of her life at all. His assistance was more effective from afar.

Benjamin reappeared by the window, the stained glass bled onto his shirt, marking the spot where Merlin had stabbed him.

Even he, on occasion, misread a premonition. Merlin had to admit that, when it came to sending Benjamin to Arthur in Purgatory, he had gotten it wrong. He had scolded Barqan for not anticipating Arthur's action when he himself had failed to do the same. Benjamin shivered from the cold but did not shut the window. The commotion of April and Jack's arrival found Merlin on the breeze. Benjamin believed himself to be at fault. Merlin could tell from the way Benjamin bowed his head and how he ran his fingers through his hair erratically. Merlin yearned to return to Caerleon, to make sure that Benjamin understood who Arthur was when the crown and armour came off. The smell of death came unwarranted into the room, transporting him back to the battlefield in Wales. A hand grabbed his calf. Merlin yelped, jumping away from Arthur, dying on the floor. Chainmail and armour clunked and rattled in the hallway, never seeming to arrive at the door.

A roaring fire billowed heat into the room, leaving Merlin wishing for the chill of an arctic Avalon night. The smoke stung his eyes; Merlin stumbled, his arms flailing until the sharp corner of a desk drove itself into his hip. Through watery eyes, Merlin took in the opulence of Arthur's chambers. Red velvet curtains were drawn against the arched windows, the bed covered in its red and gold covers adorned with Arthur's dragon crest. Merlin ran his hands over the plump red velvet back of Arthur's chair, pulled out slightly from a desk covered in parchment; sealing wax bubbled over a short candle, as if the King had been called away from his work.

'You were drinking? Merlin, you are full of surprises!' Arthur's voice echoed in the room. The King blinked into view, his face ruddy, golden hair matted and tangled from training.

'I was drunk. Now I am hungover.'

'You should have eaten earlier, when you had the chance.'

Arthur tossed his helmet aside and discarded his gauntlets in much the same manner. He appeared beside Merlin, settled in the chair by the desk.

This was the evening Merlin had introduced Benjamin to Arthur.

Benjamin had turned bright red the instant their eyes had met. Arthur had almost knocked the table over in his haste to greet the physician. The physical contact had almost caused Benjamin to collapse. It was around then that Merlin had begun to wonder about his own marriage.

'Much has happened, Arthur. My mind needs to sort through it in only the way sleep can do.'

'Or you could eat something.' Arthur speared an apple with his dagger and jabbed it in Merlin's face.

This was a young Arthur who had yet to suffer his most bitter defeats. Merlin missed him so.

'Ah. You will be the jury then. Benjamin was particularly judgemental.'

'The trouble, Merlin,' Arthur declared around a mouthful of the rejected apple, 'comes when you abandon too many of the smaller details. They combine to make one hell of a monster.'

Merlin looked for the wine, not needing to be reminded that his concern for the bigger picture had neatly covered up the ramifications of his seemingly inconsequential choices.

'If you'd have taken a disliking to me, think of how much happier we'd all be, Arthur.' Matters of the mind were better left unsaid until the eve of battle. 'I have suffered grief also, sometimes at your hands. But do I complain? No!'

The goblet darted out of Merlin's reach. Smoke curled up from the wax, the burning smell drove Merlin to extinguish the flame.

'It was you who recruited me, Arthur.'

Another apple appeared in Arthur's hand. Arthur stared dispassionately, not one to tolerate self–pity. Least of all from Merlin.

'I am a warlock, not a magician. I could not give you joy without grief. They are one and the same.'

Arthur's cup left his hand and emptied itself, whilst Arthur remained still as could be. The ruby red liquid puddled on the bearskin rug, darkening the fur.

'We can go back and forth all day, pondering an alternative world where your acquaintance had not been worth making, or where I had the foresight to trust that niggle of doubt and had dismissed you from court, yet we cannot escape that the deeds are long since done.'

'Fire at will, Arthur, my skin is tough enough to suffer your slings and arrows –'

Merlin's mouth wouldn't open. He rushed to the mirror on Arthur's dresser and saw delicate silver and gold threads joining his lips. His nervous laughter bubbled up his throat, out of his control and with nowhere to go. For all of his faults, Arthur believed in justice. Even if he admired the head that he must detach from its body.

'The truth is a dangerous gift for a wise man. Even you are not such a fool as to invoke it. It is time to own the monster created by the details you ignored.'

Merlin clawed at his mouth, desperate to draw a breath, he tried to back away from Arthur, but his feet wouldn't move, and he fell to his knees. The last thing Merlin would see of the world would be the disgust and betrayal in his daughter's eyes as she realised that her father amounted to nothing more than his failures. He would take her disappointment with him into the darkness.

Emrys cut his feet free. Merlin crawled away, not stopping until he reached the windowsill – the only thing he could count on for support. He grabbed the splintered wood and hauled himself onto his shaky legs, his back to Arthur.

Merlin no longer wanted to stare his jury in the eyes.

'Victims of this situation there are, but you are not among them.' Arthur's chair thudded over. His steps stopped just short of Merlin; his sword hissed as it was released from its sheath. 'Merlin,' Arthur said sternly. 'Your bones are not kindling and our forgiveness is not the spark that will make or break you.'

Merlin's chest burned; his eyes stung. He crumbled, the windowsill caught his rib cage and knocked the wind from his lungs, trying to remember that it wasn't real.

'It's no longer about you, Merlin. It's about those of us left to deal with your legacy.'

The room slid into its next scene change, smoothly depositing Merlin into one of Benjamin's uncomfortable kitchen chairs.

'He really needs to redecorate.'

'He changed the handles on the cabinets.' April slid into the chair across from him. Merlin stared until April glanced away. He couldn't help it. She looked much like he'd imagined Vivienne would have at that age. The same defiant eyes, the long black hair a neater version of his. His face tingled, and Emrys pushed Fate back enough to cut the threads, freeing Merlin's voice.

'Vivie.' The force of lost time slammed into his gut.

'You couldn't let me go, could you?' April offered him some coffee. He was staring again. He couldn't help it. This was all Merlin had wanted. To sit and talk with her.

'You are a rare and precious gift.'

April gave him a half-smile, her hands fidgeting on the table-top. 'Where did April come from? I wasn't even born in April!'

'You were. Originally that is.'

'Huh.' April nodded. 'If you couldn't tell me, why not Ben?'

'He wouldn't have let me near you! Besides, I wanted you to form your own opinion of me. You'd have felt obliged to pretend to like me once you knew. You were so small. You fitted in my arm, the first time I held you, nothing else mattered.' And just like that glorious moment, Merlin found himself crying freely.

Her first hesitant steps in the woods of Caerleon.

Her first birthday celebration in the great hall of Tintagel.

Her first words in the rose garden of Avalon.

The time she levitated a stool by accident. Her fifth birthday.

Her first death.

Her small body convulsing in his arms as he fought to keep her alive, and all the while, Fate watched on. A dispassionate bystander. He reached for April, but she pulled away. That's what he got for diverting attention away from her reincarnations. Once Merlin had realised that she was stuck in a loop of living twenty years or so, he'd tried to make space for the continual renewing grief. He'd not been able to maintain it. So, Merlin had ensured they would remain strangers. The conviction in her eyes, at that moment, confirmed how she hated him for that alone. His absence had caused April to harden to the point that she was capable of a solitary existence. Perhaps she would one day consider how much Merlin's absence had taught her.

'You'll miss me a little, you know, when you have a question that must be answered that minute.'

She laughed!

He'd forgotten how his soul soared with that rapturous sound. Merlin grabbed her hand and kissed it before she could argue. To his surprise, she didn't pull away. His daughter was kind. A trait that she had learned from Benjamin. Thank the Gods for Benjamin and the strangers who thought she belonged to them. For it was a miracle that April had developed a sense of justice, had grown into a compassionate person. The universe knew that neither he nor Fate could have taught April those skills. There was a reluctance in her sad, emerald-green eyes.

'I never knew what had caused this hole at the core of my being. But it was you. And now, you have to leave.'

'All of this ends with me. Those that seek their revenge will be satisfied, as will those who cannot stand the sight of me. And those who fear my presence in their lives will be free. With one act, you can straighten out everything.'

'Everything except the fact that you are my father.' Her face fell, and Merlin's heart broke for her anew.

'Hmph. You always wanted me to tell you everything that was going to happen, before it happened. I refused. It doesn't do to merge your soul with the inevitable. You'd have only tried to plan around it.'

April's hands flew to her throat, scratching.

She blinked, her head fell back, hair trailing towards the floor. Merlin skidded round the table, in a rush to gather her up in his arms. Her hair was plastered to her hot, flushed face and he couldn't free it. The reassuring warm weight of her body vanished. He crashed to the floor of his chambers. Merlin buried his head in his hands and curled up in a ball on the floor. Merlin had held April in his arms, and she hadn't been breathing and –

'Merlin!' Emrys shouted. 'It's not real! April survives this. She survives *you*.'

'She's dead,' Merlin whispered.

'She lives! This has always been your problem, Merlin. You muddle past, present and future. How have you gotten this far and not learnt that?'

Merlin shrugged, his fingers absent-mindedly combing through his hair, concerned only with the notion that he might have had free will once. Or maybe it had all been an illusion and all of his decisions had been inevitable. But that, that would be letting himself off lightly.

Death was an easy consequence of his actions; living had grown to be too much hassle.

Merlin felt as hollow as a cracked egg.

32

KEEP GOING

AVALON

April's foot slipped over a ledge and she hung in the air like a cartoon character.

Jack pulled her back onto solid ground. April blinked as fast as she could, trying to force her eyes to adjust to the overly bright lights of Avalon.

'The tunnel leads to a mountain ledge? That's poor planning.' April squinted at the town far below. 'We're going to be walking for days!' Then again, maybe that wasn't a bad thing. Merlin could get himself killed in a day.

'Which is why we're going to run.'

The town and the glass palace weren't getting any closer on their own. April held her arms out reluctantly. She buried her face into Jack's back, hoping that would keep dizziness at bay. The air rushed past her as he jumped from the mountain to whatever lay below it – a forest, judging by the branches whipping at them.

'I wasn't made for this,' she mumbled. 'I don't make it past a slow jog on a good day.'

'We're nearly at the edge of town. I'll walk soon.'

Nearly couldn't come quick enough. April forced herself to breathe through the nausea, listening to the bird song in an otherwise quiet town. April imagined that, when Fate found out that she still had a daughter, she was going to be sorely disappointed, perhaps enough so to back off. Although April suspected that being Fate's daughter was only going to double her chances of dying in Avalon.

April had, at times, wished for her parents – the ones who raised her in this life – to be more than they were. And now she had learnt her lesson about making wishes.

'I can feel you overthinking.' Jack shifted his grip on her.

'Huh?'

'You're strangling me.'

April loosened her grip and tried to distract herself by opening her eyes. Jack was still half-running up the windy, steep cobbled streets with houses built into the rock that rose above them, connected by stone walkways painted white, all the time climbing towards the other mountain with its glass palace. It all felt like somebody who'd never visited Greece or Italy had tried to describe them to an architect. The vertigo slammed into her, and she had to close her eyes again. She wanted to ask Jack to stop, but slowing down was like being on a plane that hadn't bothered to reduce its speed for landing. 'I don't know why we rushed to get here; we don't have a plan.'

'You see the people?' Jack asked quietly.

April did. They were dressed in robes with different coloured sashes tied around the waists and draped over one shoulder. There were distinct groups – those with the flaming blue eyes and tribal tattoos standing out against the red–brown ochre skin were djinn.

'*The others are Gods*,' Eilir informed her. '*Lesser Gods, of course.*'

'*Of course.*' April should have guessed. They carried themselves with authority and grace in a way that made her miss Artemis and Hades. They passed a God who seemed to shimmer blue in the sun and wore a turquoise sash over their gold robe. The God, upon spotting her, dipped into a low bow. She side-eyed them, wondering if their loyalty was to Fate and whether it was guided by fear or love.

No matter how hard April tried, she couldn't picture herself spending time in this town of white-and-pastel-coloured buildings. Not that she'd have spent long here. Partly because it seemed Merlin was intent on keeping her on Gaia, partly because Death came calling far too soon. On the surface Avalon looked to be pleasant enough. The kind of place people visited once a year and exclaimed that they would live there, if only they could. 'They remind me of Merlin, only better looking,' April said out-loud. 'They dress just as badly.' Jack laughed quietly, but the tension in his shoulders and back remained. Barqan stepped into their path from a side alley, eyes blazing, spear in hand.

Jack executed a record scratch stop. 'Did we summon you by

mistake?'

Barqan shook her head. 'As neither of you have visited Avalon before, perhaps you will allow me to show you around?'

'Thank you kindly.' Jack forced a smile, his grip on April tightening.

'It is easy to get turned around in the alleys of Avalon, I would not want you to get lost.' Barqan's head tilted to one side, looking at April pointedly. She pretended not to notice. 'Will you put April down? A lady can walk.'

'I quite agree, however April doesn't cope well with our speed. She'll be about as stable as a spinning top running out of steam, won't you April?
April could only groan in agreement.

'*If you're going to be sick,*' Eilir piped up, '*aim at Barqan.*'
April began to laugh and made some sort of spluttering sound instead.

'Will we have to continue at a human pace?' Barqan asked with disgust in her voice.

''Fraid so. Unless you want to portal the three of us. Personally, I'm in no hurry to get up there.'
Agreement and dread flashed across Barqan's face so quickly that April thought it was a trick of her spinning mind.

'We shall walk.'

Jack bowed as best he could, trying not to dislodge April. 'That could be your job when this is all over. Tour guide of Avalon.'

'Very droll.' Barqan marched off, glancing down every

alleyway, watching the shuttered windows with wary suspicion and noting every curious face that passed them. 'It's over for you, not I.'

'We'll see about that,' April replied with conviction that she attributed to Eilir. Her magic was running pins and needles up and down her arms, burning hot with righteous indignation and an eagerness to fight her way out.

'I credited you both with greater intelligence, but seeing as you followed a fool here –'

'And where is the fool?' Jack joined Barqan in looking down alleyways. April wasn't sure if he was trying to wind the djinn up, or if her paranoia had rubbed off.

'Fate locked Merlin in his chambers. He was destroying the flower beds. Again.' Jack hiked up his eyebrows in amused curiosity. 'Fate has no tolerance for his rambled nonsense.'

'How? How has Merlin gotten that drunk? I gave him one bottle of coke! This is not my fault!'
Thoroughly confused, Barqan looked to Jack for clarification.

'Humans enjoy flavoured carbonated water. Merlin isn't drunk, he's on a sugar high. Possibly his first ever. He'll crash soon enough.'

'I did think it strange. Merlin is drunk more often than not and well adapted.' Barqan folded her arms behind her back. The tattoos were sprawling across her skin, ready to do their worst. April assumed the djinn picked sleeveless outfits for intimidation purposes. Eilir was throwing herself against the confines of April's control, desperate to be free, to take April to safety. Jack stumbled on a loose cobble stone, grabbed a sheet hanging over a windowsill and lost his balance. It was Barqan who caught April. She threw a dirty look at Jack and set April down. Right at the foot of thousands of steps carved into the rock, they hugged the hillside, twisting around the corner and out of sight.

April winced. 'Those steps and this heat will finish me off before Fate gets a chance.'

They'd survived the majority of the steps, their reward being a wide, green – and mercifully flat – valley. Grand sandy coloured villas with manicured gardens sat on either side of the olive tree-lined path that wound up towards the next valley. Above them, the palace bounced sunlight in all directions.

Eilir ceased fidgeting for a moment. *'Have you considered that if either parent perishes, you inherit their titles?'*

'Nobody knows who I am!'

'Chaos and Death know.'

Cresting the hill deposited them in a garden full of reds, yellows, blues and purples. Trellises and arbours stretched on for at least a mile in all directions, the perfume suffocating, the view of the town and the water, breathtaking. A lone wooden fishing boat, its white sail unfurled, bobbed over the waves and into the safety of the harbour wall where people waited to unload the day's catch. In the rose garden, April ran her hands through the tapered lavender flowers and the rough rosemary plants, watching bees go about their business. Here, the lavender was thriving as April had never seen. Must be the dry, maritime air. April could picture Fate and Merlin arguing in the gardens and thought that lavender was an ironic choice, given that it represented silence and calm.

It was harder to connect herself with Fate, not after their sole interaction consisted of Fate trying to force Death into reaping April. Merlin was a dumpster fire of a human being but at least he'd made a twisted effort to meet her.

April sat on a stone bench, ornately carved with the talismans, her feet tapping the ground, and wondered how she was supposed to kill a myth. If she separated the man from the story, then the task seemed plausible. Magic was out of the question. Not unless Merlin were to roll over and accept his fate. She wobbled, fighting the persistent dizziness. Jack's hand found her shoulder. He plonked himself down, unable to make small talk with Barqan any longer. The sunlight picked out a scar under Jack's eye that April hadn't noticed before.

'I expected more of my daughter. You are essentially human. I blame your father.' Fate emerged from a crossroads in the garden and stopped, one hand over her heart. Eilir shook within April, determined to stand strong but very much scared of the mother who had berated Vivienne endlessly. Fate gathered her skirts and stepped neatly over a flowerbed, closing the distance quickly.

'Avalon could be the last realm standing and I still wouldn't live here, with you!' April said in that voice she'd come to realise was Vivienne's. Fate snatched at April's wrist. April pulled back so violently, she nearly toppled over the bench. Barqan caught her once again. Eilir slipped over April's hands like gloves.

'Wow!' Jack's hands were up, advocating for peace. 'We came

301

to relieve you of Merlin. Nobody is staying here against their will, and nobody is using their magic.'

'Leave, vampire. My daughter and I have much to discuss –'

'No. We don't. Everything is happening as it should.'

'April, don't start,' Jack begged her.

'She cannot claim parentage. Reincarnation – I was raised by everybody but her. I don't even remember the girl they see in me.' April had been patient with Jack when he was self-destructing, now it was his turn.

'I can show you who you are.' Fate held her hand out in offering. 'Do you not want to know?'

'I know who I am. I'm not human, nor am I an immortal creature. Most of all, thank God, I am not your daughter.'

Fate shook her head, fighting to keep her mouth in a straight line. She closed her eyes, inhaled and threw Jack violently into the rose bushes. Judging by the grumbling and groaning as April hauled him up, nothing but his pride had been injured. He emerged from the bush, pulling thorns from his leg. Now that she looked, there was plenty of wood in the garden and Jack was ready to get hurt on her behalf.

'How quickly you write off somebody whose acquaintance you have yet to make.'

April blinked; sheltered in the shade of a nearby olive tree, stood Merlin, sober and smiling, whilst he played with the daughter he loved enough to deceive Fate. But Fate had locked her outside of the palace overnight. Vivienne had hidden in a greenhouse, cold and frightened until Merlin had found her.

'Your room is as you left it. Darling, we have a chance to start again, without your father's interference. Together we can create new worlds, new lives to replace those lost.'

'New lives do nothing for those you interrupted!' Eilir was pulsating and growing to envelop April's body like a second skin. She threw Eilir into the atmosphere, scrambling for a point at which to open a portal. Long delicate fingers brushed through April's hair. She turned to find Fate standing all too close. April pushed Jack back until he bumped up against the wall.

'You adored Merlin and paid me no mind,' Fate sneered, all pretence of motherly love gone. 'You were content to wallow in Gaia. Your father encouraged it.'

'Children go through phases,' Barqan cut in.

'Magic calls to magic, Barqan. Merlin's tutelage no doubt included spells and the encouragement to undo me.'
April tried again to open a portal, but Eilir kept getting caught on a prickly energy that April assumed to be Fate's magic. It sensed April trying to leave and it closed around them. April snatched Eilir back, holding her magic close.

'Your illness was strange, that Merlin could not heal you, stranger still.' Suspicion moved Barqan slowly. Her spear found its way into her hands as she put herself between April and Fate. 'Merlin exhausted all options, April. He begged Death, petitioned Gods, consulted healers.'
Fate had one delicate hand pressed to her chest, the other against her hip as if she'd seen a mother grieve once and was trying to imitate it.

'Each supposed cure only worked against the child.' Barqan shook her head in disgust, though her eyes were wide with fear at having said too much. 'There is not much that Merlin cannot see, but love blinds him of common sense and alcohol strips him clean of his instincts.' Barqan spoke with authority, but the slight tremor in her hands gave her away.

'You lost a child?' April wasn't sure if she'd known Barqan's child, but she felt for the Guardian all the same.

Barqan inclined her head, sorrow dimming the flames in her eyes. 'My daughter has yet to return from the Nothingness. I only had to witness her death once. How Merlin endured all of your deaths ... He was a devoted father, April. It is everything that came after that ...'

Memories began to drop into place like Tetris blocks that Eilir was frantically moving into place. Memories of Fate refusing Vivienne a hug. Merlin, laughing whilst he taught her to cast spells, and Fate, stood to one side, thin-lipped and unamused. Fate had been resentful – jealous, even, of Vivienne. Eilir kept dropping April into memories, wanting to show her everything, all at once. Merlin wasn't innocent, but he'd had the good sense to keep a child away from a mother who confused control and manipulation for love. And he'd subjected himself to years of heartbreak for her. Eilir was fuming, her pins and needles relentless. April's heart was doing somersaults. Her throat was a traffic jam of all the half-formed thoughts and things she wanted to say. And if Barqan was right, Fate sabotaged Merlin's efforts to save

Vivienne. Gods were petty and Chaos had pitted them against one another. Violence had become the only means of survival. It was better to remove the competition. April had been an issue that, unless resolved, would grow to steal all that Fate had fought for. April's face burned with certainty that she never wanted to know the mother who refused to raise her because of a future that might have come to pass.

'I want to see my father.' Fate's chin jutted out defiantly.

'No! I would never endanger your life, Vivienne.' There was no feeling, no light in Fate's eyes.

'My name is April.' She sent a warning shot of magic to the left of Fate.

'Barqan, will you fetch Merlin, please?'
The djinn jumped aside, narrowly avoiding a portal that opened in the middle of the group.

33

THE MEMORY OF BATTLE

'Ben!' April would have hugged him but Jack pushed her over in his efforts to embrace his partner.

'Merlin putting himself in danger is one thing. Merlin putting the both of you in danger, quite another.' Ben moved a little too slowly for April's liking.

Perhaps it had something to do with the craters under his eyes.

Artemis prowled around the edge of the group, locking eyes with Barqan who laid down her spear without protest. Fate stared right back, a dagger appearing in her hand.

Ben's expression was full of wonder for a friend he'd never lost. A portal opened beside her; Ben nudged her towards it. 'Go home, April.'

'None of you will be leaving.' Fate said coolly, closing Ben's portal.

Ambrosius flared, pulsing in Ben's hands. Artemis handed her spear to Hades and drew her bow. The setting sun cast long shadows through the garden; Artemis stepped into one and, for a second, the God was transformed into a wolf made of shadow and light, a crescent moon crown on her head, shoulder to shoulder with Hades whose golden magic shimmered over his body. Barqan joined them, practically composed of blue fire and black tattoos. The air was fizzing with the combination of magics working against Fate's.

'What about Merlin?' April shrunk back, finding herself under the incredulous stares of four Gods, one Guardian and Jack.

'*Parents or not, you don't owe Merlin anything.*' Ben's gentle voice sounded in her head, Ambrosius connecting with Eilir. Goosebumps prickled all over her, as if she'd been hugged by a ghost. '*Go home with Jack; leave Merlin to the rest of us.*'

'*I'm meant to be here.*'

Ben groaned, afraid to ask, but reopened his portal, just in case.

'Fine. You wish to see the fool?' Fate snapped her fingers. 'Barqan!'

Barqan reappeared, half-dragging a dishevelled Merlin behind her –hunched over and shuffling his feet. He looked every bit a thief on his way to the gallows. When he found April in the group, a grin tried to stretch across his tear-stained face.

'We're all exactly where we are supposed to be, Vivie.' Merlin's words calmed her a little.

Standing across from her mother, with her father slumped in between them, Eilir's pins and needles broke out across April's entire body, keen to remind her.

The park laid itself over the rose garden. She shivered in the snow whilst Jack tried to teach her magic, blinked and found herself watching Benjamin run from Barqan, April on his back. Benjamin dissolved into a memory of Merlin, pretending to be a hunter, watched on in approval as April succeeded in killing her first vampire.

An argument between Fate and the Guardians cracked like thunder around April.

In her mind's eye, she sat in front of a canvas, paintbrush in hand whilst the sound of birdsong called to her through the open balcony doors overlooking a Victorian London. The canvas morphed into a piano on stage, and then April was five years old; she was Vivienne and Merlin had far less white in his groomed hair that touched his shoulders. The room, dim and muggy, smelt of amber, spice and something she couldn't place. Through the smoke, Merlin leaned forwards to take her little face in his rough hands: "*One day, far from now, you are going to save us all. And I will be so very proud of you. And when you wonder, as you surely will, why Death leaves you untouched, remember that you have not lived long enough to do what you must. Be brave, for all our sakes.*" Eilir couldn't stop, couldn't slow down. Her magic vibrated so violently, April thought they were going to separate.

Ben and Jack collided with her, knocking her out of the way of a ball of Fate's magic. Fate slammed her magic – a death spell – into Hades. He staggered backwards. Artemis tackled Fate to the ground and all the while, Merlin laughed his broken, child-like laugh.

'*Oh, April. Let it happen.*' Merlin's death had arrived, and he was relieved.

Propelled by Fate, Artemis slammed into April's back. The world turned a shade of jade. The orange of Ben's magic streaked across the garden, criss-crossing with Hades' gold, Artemis' forest green and Barqan's reddish yellow magic. April had expected Barqan's magic to be black, like the ink of her tattoos. The magics left trails in their wakes, clouds of orange embers mixed with silver and green. The memory of impacts from head-on collisions. The harbour and the town were awash with every colour imaginable, and some April couldn't name. Encasing it all was the pulsating glow of Emrys. Ambrosius smashed into Fate's magic in a shower of orange embers, sending the spell spiralling into the sky at such a speed, it punched through Merlin's warding and left the atmosphere. Eilir slipped past April's control, an electric current flowing in April's veins until she was a creature comprised entirely of flame and magic. Merlin's disconcerting laughter wrapped itself around April, echoing in her mind. She caught his knowing smile right before the hammer dropped and every memory she'd ever repressed or forgotten, from every life she'd lived, returned home. Including the time she said, 'love you, bye,' whilst ordering a pizza. And spells. Things that April hadn't realised magic could do were now possibilities – if she wanted to. Merlin crawled to her like her life depended on it. He took her hands, his blue-green magic blended with Eilir's jade.

'I suppose you're feeling quite tragic. This is what we've both been waiting for.'

It was roses and willow trees all the way to the palace. And this wasn't an English park in the grip of winter. April hadn't imagined having quite so large an audience for it either. The pressure to follow through, to finish something that had begun lifetimes ago, howled in her head, pressing against her ear drums, magnifying the beating of her own heart.

'What happens next?'

'My child.' Merlin gripped the side of her face. *'You already know.'*

He rummaged inside his robes and pulled out all ten of the talismans. The sword sat atop the shield, winking at her. All of the death and sacrifice – she couldn't remember what it had all been for. And this, this moment could not have been the sole reason for her existence. Merlin beamed with pride, not that the wide smile hid the torment in his eyes. It was the same manic sadness he'd worn when he'd killed Ben.

Eilir weaved her way through the talismans, fusing with Emrys, lending Eilir even more strength, more than she'd ever known. And Emrys was bolstered by Eilir. Merlin kissed her forehead and shrugged off his frailty as if it were an ill-fitting jacket. He settled himself cross-legged on the ground, his eyes closing as he let loose a spell from cracked lips. From deep within Avalon's core, an ominous rumble shook the ground. Hands separated her from Merlin, and April spun, breaking free of the grip, not quite understanding why she wanted to stay beside him. Barqan lunged at Merlin; with a flick of his hand he threw her to the ground. Another rumble sent statues toppling, and in the town below, April heard screams. Eilir charged forwards and collided with Fate's spell. The impact knocked the wind from her lungs. Out of the corner of her eye, April saw Fate break free of Artemis' grasp. She snatched up Barqan's fallen spear and made a beeline for Merlin. Ben grabbed Merlin by his shoulders, shaking him, but he would not be moved. Another shockwave knocked them all off-balance. Fate was the first up, sending an attack spell that caught Ben square in the chest. He collapsed back into Jack's arms. Another shot struck down Hades. April drew as much of her magic as she could and launched Eilir at Fate, with April's permission to cause harm. Fate blocked it and returned it to April. A blast of gold knocked the whirling ball of silver and jade off course. Fate didn't see the blow from Artemis' spear that drove her to her knees. April's wide eyes found the Huntress'. Artemis gestured at the motionless bodies of Ben, Hades and Barqan, at the cracks racing up the side of the glass palace. Sat crossed-legged amongst the carnage, Merlin stared at her, his gaze unwavering.

'Merlin started this when he left Avalon. You must be the one to end it, April.' Artemis was breathing heavily, blood dripped down her arm from a fresh wound.

April drove Eilir into Fate's chest, consuming the God.

Fate convulsed on the ground and then she moved no more. If she'd screamed or protested her death, April didn't hear. Avalon groaned under the strain of it's imminent demise. April stepped back to brace herself only for her foot to slip over the edge of a crevasse that hadn't been there before. Gravity pulled April into the chasm. Her flailing arms caught Artemis' spear.

'Open a portal.' Artemis' voice refused any protests of ability, so April did as she was told. 'Good. Hold it.' Artemis threw Ben and Hades in first and slung Barqan over her shoulder.

'What about Merlin?' He was still sat cross-legged as foliage and glass rained down around him, the ground fracturing and splitting open.

'With any luck, the ground will literally swallow him whole. Come on!' Jack grabbed April's wrist.

'We can't leave him.'

Jack's sound of disgust told her that he thought they could, but the vampire understood that when April said "can't", she wasn't speaking out of loyalty or love. She was speaking from knowledge gifted to her by her premonitions. He jogged back to Merlin, but the warlock had, apparently, glued himself to the floor.

Seeing Jack's struggle, Artemis thrust the point of her spear into Merlin's back. And still, Merlin stayed.

'Damn yourself, Merlin, by all means. But will you condemn your daughter to the worst death possible because of your arrogance?'

Merlin glanced at Artemis but returned his gaze to April and allowed Jack to topple him onto his side. Artemis grabbed one arm, Jack the other and they dragged him to the mouth of the portal.

'I had to do it,' Merlin said right before Artemis sent him

through with a sandaled foot.

Screams of those trapped built up around them, travelling on the wind. She was going to hear the screams for the rest of her life.

As they left, April thought she could hear rocks falling to the ground, blocking the cave entrance to Avalon's tunnel.

34

SHHHH! GOLF IS ON

BEN'S HOUSE

The cold linoleum of Ben's kitchen floor pressed itself against April's cheek.

She'd let his magic mix with hers.

She'd let Merlin cast his spell.

April had thought that the talismans were to help her kill Merlin, but he'd needed Eilir to help Emrys to destroy Avalon.

And honestly, shouldn't she know better by now?

Through the tangle of table and chair legs, April spied Ben; the peeling laminate of the cupboard doors scratched against his shirt as he leaned over and pulled Jack into his arms. Across from them, Barqan hugged her knees and watched Artemis desperately shaking and – gently – slapping an unresponsive Hades. Pain shot through April, convening in one eye. Eilir was unusually quiet, still mixing violently with Emrys, tearing up her insides. Failure roared in her ears and her heart was jamming itself into her throat, causing her to gasp for air like a sailor drowning on the shore. April hadn't felt entirely out of place in the new memories. He'd played the grieving father well, but Merlin would only ever be a frustrated director pushing his unruly cast into their lights. Missed marks would not be tolerated. April curled into a ball, as if by making herself as small as possible, the universe and all of the dead of Avalon wouldn't be able to find her.

And Fate.

April had killed Fate. A God. The one who wrote time.

Her mother.

A sob tore its way free of her turmoil and its exhale brought her into a tighter ball. Everything was just white noise in her head, and she'd killed her mother, and her father had killed all of those people, and Hades wasn't moving, and what happened now there was no Fate and –

'April! April, it's alright,' Jack yelled from the shore. She wanted to disagree, but the words got stuck, adding another blockage to her windpipe. April was being ridiculous. Hades might be dead, and she hadn't checked, she had just curled up in a corner and devoted her entire concentration to trying not to implode. Violent shivers rocked her despite the sweat dripping down her face because the room was an inferno.

'Look at me! We're home. You got us out of there. We didn't know that Merlin was going to do that.'

But there were so many souls she left behind.

'Hey.' Ben knelt beside her with a grunt of pain. He gently pried her out of her hedgehog impersonation and into a hug that

315

loosened the clamp around her lungs, just enough for her to draw a shallow breath. If she focused on the fading notes of cedarwood aftershave, and the solid form of Ben. The screams tore through her mind. In front of her, Jack glitched and became Fate, withering in pain as Eilir squeezed until Fate's heart stopped. The nausea, the dizziness, the pins and needles and the lack of oxygen came together in a crescendo that pitched her forwards into darkness.

April tasted copper.
She screwed her eyes shut, not ready to wake up and begin hyperventilating all over again. Somewhere behind her, a radiator whined as it rattled into life. Jack was grumbling. Tired, lumpy cushions moulded around her. April couldn't remember how she'd gotten onto the sofa. And when she stretched out a little, her feet prodded something fleshy.

'Have you awoken?' A page flicked over, striving to hide the strain in Benjamin's voice. 'I'm content to pretend that you are not stirring.'
April peaked through half-open eyes. In the pale twilight, Ben looked every one of his years.

'Hades is most annoyed about the hole in his offensively expensive shirt, but he will make a full recovery.' Another page turned.

'Eight hundred-plus years and I am just learning that you have a weird vendetta against shirts made after the Victorian era.' Jack crouched on the end of the sofa, by her feet. April shifted to the side so he could sit down.

'It was a bold colour choice. And Merlin is in the kitchen.' April's eyes shot open. 'Don't look at me like that! You should see the state of him.' Ambrosius was curled up on Ben's shoulder. He looked pale. April hoped that Emrys had not mixed with Ambrosius as well. When Merlin fired the spell, April had thought she'd felt Emrys drawing on the magic of all those present, but Eilir especially. And had Eilir not found her magical feet, Emrys would have drained her completely. That might not have been a problem for April if Eilir ceased to be, but without Ambrosius, Ben would die.

'Merlin's not going anywhere. Least of all because Barqan and Artemis are tearing him apart – verbally of course.'

'Hades and I were just debating what to do with Merlin.' Artemis came striding in, staring at April in a way that made her want to faint again. 'We thought the decision should be left to you.'

'Why?' April's voice croaked, prompting Jack to force a glass of water into her hand, pushing her shoulders so she sat up, squeezed in-between Jack and Ben. 'He was my father once, perhaps. There's nothing in the name now.'

'I speak not of family ties.' April sat up as straight as she could. Artemis seemed the type who didn't tolerate slouching. 'Rather obligation and duty. Your mother's office falls to you.' And that was why Ben looked a thousand years older. It wasn't just concern that had painted thicker lines onto his face. Nor was it dread or fear. No, Ben was struggling with the awful weight of accepting something that, no matter how much he wished it wasn't so, was unequivocable. It was fate.

She was Fate.

'No way. No. Nope.' April shook her head and immediately regretted it. If she sat perfectly still, she could stay in the denial stage and avoid throwing up in front of Artemis.

'Some days, it takes me two hours to decide which pair of identical-looking jeans I'll wear. I can't be deciding whether Gary gets to cross the road or bump into the love of his life two years next Tuesday!' April couldn't read Hades' expression as he let the windowsill take his weight, but judging by the way he sat as close to Artemis as possible, and kept haunting the edge of the room, Hades was longing for home.

'There is no decision to be made, you forced your own hand,' Artemis insisted.

'You, my dear, are banned from delivering news,' Hades cut in, a restraining hand on her arm. 'What Artemis is trying to say, is that, as the demigod who caused the position to be open, *and* the daughter of Fate, you are the natural successor.'
April pulled a face that disagreed. There were other Gods, one of them had to be better qualified for the job.

'The role passes down at the moment of death.' Strands of silver still marred Hades' golden aura, though they were faint and growing fainter as he fought against the last of Fate's residual magic. The hole in the shirt revealed glimpses of a healing tear to his chest. Hades caught April looking and crossed his arms over his chest.

'Sure. But think of it like this: I don't want it and I'm not going to do it. Where would I live? Avalon –'

'You can stay here, or you can create a new realm.' Ben rubbed her shoulder, a sad understanding in his eyes.

'Do I really have to do this?' April appreciated the irony of asking Ben.

'I'm afraid so,' Ben said gently. 'The alternatives don't bear thinking about. What if Merlin takes over?' April wanted to agree with Ben, but she had lost control of her limbs. A tall, featureless figure comprised of shadows stepped in front of April and arrested her with the sense of calm it brought with it. It slipped into the gap its calmness had created in her mind.

'Merlin is not long for this world, his opportunities to man-ufacture mischief have all passed.' The words left April's mouth, but they weren't hers.

Ben eyes widened in recognition of Vivienne's voice reaching forwards through the mists of time.

'There is only one punishment worthy of my father's black deeds.' April was willing to bet on her cat's life that this had something to do with trees.

'Vivienne?' Ben laughed in wonder. 'I thought I'd caught glimpses of you. I assumed it was all in my head.'
April felt herself smile. It was a beaming smile, so full of joy and love. She was surprised that her muscles knew the shape.

'Is your imagination so cruel as to torment you thus? By only looking at one side of the dice, you failed to recognise the others that make up my whole. Now it seems I must gain a new face.'

Ben's eyes broke from their search of hers and closed in resignation.

'You can no more keep April from this, than you can the sun from rising.'

'What are you going to do with Merlin?' Ben was bouncing from one disaster to the next with hardly a moment to breathe in-between. It was all he could do to not bury his head in his hands. April tried to insert her own voice back into her throat, but Vivienne was not prepared to share. Perhaps it wasn't a bad thing. April wasn't sure she had the stomach for it. And Vivienne seemed quite keen to deal with the unpleasantness.

'Artemis, please bring my father through.'

'Very well.' Artemis headed for the kitchen, collecting her spear from where it rested in the doorway., just in case there was an excuse to prod Merlin with it.

'This will be the last tranquil moment for the foreseeable future.'

'Are you going to put April back on any time soon?' Jack asked. 'This is weird.'

'It's the most natural thing in the universe.' Ben missed the look that Jack gave him because he couldn't look away from her. 'Fate has three faces, remember?'

'Who's the third one?!' Concern lit up Jack's face.

'Vivienne. April as we know her. And April as Fate.'

Artemis returned with Merlin shuffling along in front of her. She indicated to the armchair, but Merlin sank to his knees in the middle of the room. Artemis settled into the chair instead.

'Am I to join Merlin for judgement?' Barqan asked with a steady voice, having followed the pair in.

'Not yet.' April tripped back into the lead, surprised by Vivienne's quick departure.

'Everything is happening as it should.' Merlin rearranged his robes, calm and collected.

'Of all the secrets that you have kept, that business in Avalon, is perhaps the worst.' Vivienne was still weaving through April's thinking. Vivienne's disgust sat heavy in April, but it weighed a little less than Vivienne's compassion for the father who had been with her at the end.

'If you had known, you would have subscribed yourself to the outcome and adopted the accompanying turmoil. It wouldn't have mattered that you, April, do not consider us to be your parents, you'd tangle yourself in the sentimentality of it all.'
April had never thought Merlin capable of feeling fear. But it was starting to creep into his voice.

'Eilir is now blended with Emrys. Use it wisely and use it quickly. It won't last.'

'What do we do with him?' April asked the room but looked only to Ben.

'This is your decision to make, April,' Artemis said solemnly, spear balanced across her knees.

'You are a God! It's easy for –'

'As are you!'
April bit her lip, turning back to Merlin. Those eyes, that looked a little less predator-ish, had been waiting for the ending for

who-knew-how-long.

'Ben?' April instantly regretted trying to palm it off. He was so emotionally and physically spent, that he was leaning into the cushions, his arm stretched along the back of the sofa, reaching for Jack.

'You are Fate now,' Artemis snapped. 'I suggest you make haste in adjusting to the idea of planning for others. Starting with Merlin.' Artemis indicated with her spear, just in case there was any confusion.
April looked to Ben, desperate for his guidance; he shrugged, fighting to keep his eyes open.

'I don't have the answer, April. At least not your answer.'
The only answer she could think of, well, it was coming from Vivienne, and it seemed a little much.

'But seeing as you keep staring at me like that, Merlin would only find a way to slip past Death.' Ben snatched a glance at Merlin, his eyes hadn't changed from the shade of sad grey clouds in a while. Ambrosius was pulsating slow enough that even Hades was looking over in concern.

'Living is the hardest part, have you worked out why?' Ben was starting to sound like Merlin. 'Life is suffering. It comes to everybody in the end, it's how we deal with it that's important.' Ben shrugged.

'Chaos said there's courage in not taking a life. Death doesn't always look like Death.' April casually flicked her wrist, sending Eilir to check that Emrys wasn't draining Ben. 'I've had this responsibility for five minutes, and I am officially over it,' she complained to fill the expectant silence of immortal beings. It was going to be a long time before she could lump herself in with the likes of them.

'You are thinking like a mortal.' Hades rubbed his eyes. 'The reasons that lead you to take a life may be complicated, but the actual act?' He shrugged. 'It's easy. Merlin has had a long existence. He's written infinite tragedies in the blood of innocents. And if you can't look, close your eyes before you strike.'

'I think Chaos meant that – ' Ben frowned, considering it. 'When you strip it of all of its parts, the thing at the centre of existence, the motor that propels it forward, is balance.'

'So, I should balance the scales?' Ben and Artemis nodded. 'Shouldn't he have a trial?' At the very least, Merlin owed them all an explanation. April wasn't so foolish as to believe that it would heal any wounds, and she'd grown to not believe in closure, but answers were priceless.

'Why delay the inevitable?' Fatigue sharpened Hades' tone with exasperation. 'I can see it in your face, you've already decided.'

'Because it's fair.' And because it bought April some more time.

Death was a kindness Merlin didn't deserve, but maybe Vivienne's idea, which April hadn't really thought through, was too harsh a punishment.

'Let Merlin stand trial in my court.' Hades spoke slowly, watching the others reactions. 'I will go ahead to make the necessary preparations.'

Wood and plaster collided as the front door crashed open, jolting them all into alertness. Except Merlin, who continued to look at April with impatient eyes.

'Where is the vampire!?'
Ben recoiled into the sofa cushions at the sound of Arthur's voice. Hades was a blur of movement, reappearing in the doorway, blocking Arthur's way with Artemis' spear. Artemis was calmly notching an arrow, one eye on Jack who, had it not been for Artemis' proximity, would have charged. His fangs tore free of their fleshy cage. They really didn't suit Jack.

'How did you get out? Away with you!' Hades pushed Arthur to the floor. The King bounced back up and collided with Hades' outstretched arm.

'Chaos released me.' Arthur strained against Hades as he sought his prey. 'Benjamin?! I am sorry.'
Arthur didn't sound sorry. He sounded the kind of angry that usually ended up with somebody dead. Ben stared back, paralysed, veins bulging in his temple. Irritated by the lack of response, Arthur spun away and snatched up a piece of the much-abused door, hastily breaking bits off until it tapered to a spike. April reached for Eilir.

'What are you going to do with that?' Artemis asked, eyeing up the would-be stake.

'Something that I should have done the moment I saw *him*.'
Ben put himself in front of Jack, Ambrosius a pulsating, tempestuous ball of energy that wanted nothing more than to eradicate the threat.

'You have done quite enough, Arthur.' Hades grabbed Arthur by the throat.

A defeated sigh halted the escalating drama.

'It is not entirely Arthur's fault.' Barqan stepped forwards, her tattoos morphing and crawling on her skin, alive with their power and poison. 'Fate had me poison him, so she had a means to gather information and a way to erode the bonds of the group.' Contrition burned in Barqan's eyes as everybody but Arthur stilled to listen. 'I can free him from the fever dream, but the poison has been in his veins for so long, I am not certain if he will survive.'

Hades drove his foot into Arthur's chest, propelling him back into the wall. 'Are you saying that his actions haven't been his own?'

'That particular action was not born of my influence. Arthur still had control over what he said and did. However, I feel that the constant scratching on his mind might have aggravated him. Not that that excuses him.' Barqan ducked under Hades' arm and with one quick caress of his face, put Arthur into a deep sleep. 'Love changes but people do not. Arthur will never stop thinking of you as his partner, Benjamin.'

Ben nodded and flopped onto the sofa. April was dying to ask what on earth had happened, but they were all staring at her again. Personally, April wanted to see more of the mini-drama.

'Damn it!' Hades shouted. 'Merlin!' The room was missing its elephant. Hades drove his fist into the wall, all the way up to his elbow.

325

'Because I don't have enough to redecorate?' Ben sounded genuinely scared that this time, he was going to have to do some DIY.

'It'll buff out?' Hades brushed at the crumbling edges of plasterboard as if smoothing it out would lessen the damage.

'Merlin's taken the talismans as well,' Jack called from the kitchen.

35

LET'S GET DANGEROUS

OXFORD

'Running from those who know your habits is a pointless exercise.'

Emrys popped up in Merlin's hand as the sun drifted towards its bed. They had watched the sun rise from the rooftop, disappointed that it hadn't lent any warmth to the day. They had stayed put, content to watch the students, outnumbered by tourists at this time of year, who remained in the city going about their business. Oxford always smelt smoky in winter. It was the cold. The kind that stung your eyes and stole your breath. And it brought with it the unexplainable smell of wood fires.

'Hiding in plain sight won't save us from the one who seeks us.' Emrys blinked out of view and reappeared on Merlin's shoulder, holding the warlock's ear for balance.

'Let me alone.' With an aching back and creaky hips, Merlin lowered himself onto the cold stone. The blank page stared at him, issuing a challenge he was not fit to undertake.

Four of the letters would be burnt upon delivery. One would sit forgotten in a drawer, another lost down the side of a bookcase. One would be carried, forgotten, inside robes. One would never be opened, much to the recipient's detriment. One would be dismissed directly in front of Merlin. One would be carried with its recipient for the rest of time.

Merlin rummaged in his robes and produced a stick of crimson wax with a wick running through it. He nudged Emrys and his stubborn magic stretched his hand up to the wick. Flame engulfed Emrys' hand and the wick caught light. Liquid wax splattered across the snow-white paper. Merlin pressed his signet ring – a shield with a black cat at the centre of it – into the puddle of wax, watching the crimson liquid ooze around the edges of the ring. The soft thud of feet dropped onto the roof behind him.

'You took your time. I shall die once, and once only.'

'Who knows with you, Merlin.' Death sat, hands folded in their lap. 'I assume that you knew I would be the one collecting you.'

'Aye. And I have long thought it terribly cold that they did not come themselves.' The wind picked up, snatching at any loose item of clothing and paper. Mercifully it carried Death's stench away from Merlin.

'A privilege you do not deserve. I arrived a while ago. Alas, your affairs are in disarray. Despite your advanced warning.' Death gestured at the small pile of letters and the mound of discarded pages.

'Letters do not count as *affairs in disarray*.' Death narrowed their eyes. 'This is not an attempt to stall matters, I assure you.' Merlin watched Death watching the living. They must all seem so messy, to Death. There were more grey and pitch black auras down there than Merlin wished to see. Once the aura reached the black of night, the reapers would come. The only thing that had changed since Fate's death was lack of new life.

'At first I thought you might jump.' Death nodded towards the drop. 'One last attempt to circumnavigate your destiny.'

'I considered it. Curiosity, mostly.'

'But you did not.'

'Death is death.' Merlin shrugged, holding out his hand. When Emrys moved across Merlin's bare skin, he left a trail of tingling behind. 'It matters not how I get there. Predictable experiments waste letter-writing time.'

'With the exception of concealing Vivienne from her mother and depositing her with Benjamin; that is your wisest decision.' Death nodded their approval whilst poking at the pile of letters, blatantly reading the names Merlin had scrawled across the front.

'Wise decisions – they are a rare thing. I did my best. It wasn't good enough.'

'Are you thinking out-loud or are you canvassing opinion?' There was no need for Death's tone. Merlin was well aware of how the others had stacked his perceived failures, and their misfortune, outside his door.

'Memory and thought. An ouroboros that takes me round in a circle of life and death, and I am balanced somewhere in between the two ...'

'You are rambling, Merlin.' Seeing the way that Merlin's face crumpled up, Death relented a little. 'When faced with a tough decision, you cannot always choose the morally correct path.'

'They'll never understand.' Merlin frowned at his letters. He could hear how tired and strained he sounded. It was hard to find the energy to be the person that others expected him to be at the best of times. He certainly had nothing left in the tank on the eve of his death. Merlin held the letters out to Death hopefully.

'It is you I have come for, not your correspondence!'

'It is not that arduous a task!' Death stared incredulously at Merlin. 'Fine, then we are going via the Post Office. For stamps. Unless you have some on you? Second class will be fine.'

'In a matter of hours, you will cease to exist as you understand existing, and you are concerned with postage?' Death pushed Merlin's letter-wielding hand away.

'One of them is for you.'

'You try me, warlock!' Death stood. 'You have lived an extraordinary life. Different to every other soul I have reaped. Tell me, is it the end that you deserve?'

Merlin's legs would not cooperate. Perhaps it was for the best. He wouldn't want Death to see how he was shaking.

'My opinion is not large enough to derail the inevitable, nor can it persuade you.' Death had little patience for games, Merlin admired that, but he was too set in his ways to be offering straight answers.

'I would very much like to find a place, in one world or another, to which I can fix myself. Since I can remember, I have been but a transient in time and space, always travelling, never arriving. Me thinks you know a little about that, Death.'

'I have not yet tired of my thankless task. That is where you and I differ. It seems like yesterday when a young, sure-footed and contemptibly arrogant warlock convinced the Gods that he was their equal.' Death's chuckle sent shivers down Merlin's spine. 'You could have persuaded the stars to align, when you weren't busy building Stonehenge. Why did you do that?'

'To baffle supposedly intelligent people for centuries. Intelligence doesn't always grant you sight.' Merlin's words rung with the hollow echo of influence long gone. If he listened, he could sometimes hear the battle cries, conversations with Arthur and even Fate, before it had turned sour. Merlin closed his eyes to better see the reflections of everything that he couldn't change, and realised that he could spend forever here, picking up one regret after another in his hall-of-mirrors-mind.

Death waited for nobody. Let alone arrogant warlocks looking for stamps.

Below, an American tour guide assembled her group in the quadrangle of the college. 'Now, not far from here, at the castle, Geoffrey of Monmouth penned a book that chronicled Britain's history. He included the fabulous tales of King Arthur and his wizard Merlin.' Her booming voice continued to recount the tales, although her audience were gazing into the distance.

'I am a warlock, you ill-informed clotpole!' Merlin's cries went unheard.

331

Geoffrey. Merlin huffed, his breath appearing in the freezing air. It was remarkable, how such a dull man had created such a wondrous tale. It was nonsense. And the nonsense that followed – the tales of heroic nights and Guinevere, was sculpted by bards wishing to please bored ladies at court. Merlin was often portrayed as a foolish old man. He was the villain in some retellings, and good in others. The one constant in his many narratives was Arthur.

It was almost an accurate eulogy.

Merlin's eyes battered open, and he made no attempt to hide the tears that crept free.

'Are you not prepared?' Death looked away, embarrassed to see Merlin weep.

'Knowing what comes next does not make it an easier pill to swallow, Death.

As somebody who will never die, you cannot comprehend that.' Merlin took one last look at the sunset. 'I wanted five minutes alone with the world before. Promise me something?'

'I have never once fallen for your clever words, and I do not intend to start now.'

'It's nothing so sinister!' Merlin stood and turned Death to look at the glorious colours of a sky on fire. 'Look at the sky.'

Death raised an eyebrow at the simpleness of the cliched request. 'I have seen thousands of sunsets, why do you want me to stare at more?'

'Because I want you to understand what it is you take when you collect a soul.'

Death turned their gaze back to the sky. 'Very well. Have you wasted enough of my time?'

'Yes,' Merlin laughed. 'I have wasted two lifetimes worth of time – yours and mine. And, if it is not too much trouble, there's a post office on the next street.'

36

BROKEN DOWN IN A TIME MACHINE

HADES

I t was dark, damp and cold and raining in Hades.
The rain seemed to whip up the smell of rotting corpses and sulphur. The place reeked more so than usual.

The bridge was slippery underfoot, not that Merlin would fall. Death's grip was far too tight for that, as the bundle of bones in a robe navigated them around slow-moving spirits.

'Lately.' Merlin peered into the gloom, 'I've been telling myself to be grateful for small mercies.' Including, but not limited to, not being imprisoned among the ghosts. Keeping time with Charon would be enough to send Merlin over the edge of the bridge voluntarily.

'And there they all are. Ready for circle time.' Gathered at the foot of the bridge, watching Merlin's grand entrance, were the remaining Guardians and a handful of the remaining Gods.

Their names eluded him, but he recalled the faces. Curiosity and individual vendettas had drawn them from wherever they had been hiding. 'They seek answers when there are none.'

'Fashion something, Merlin. It will be a terribly short trial, otherwise.'

A soul cried out in the darkness; Merlin whipped his head around, trying to find the sound, straining against Death's grip, heart thumping. A firm shove from Death kept him moving forwards, and down.

Always downwards.

Benjamin's arms were crossed, no doubt to stop his hands from worrying. He was an awful fidgeter when uncomfortable. Jack stood beside Benjamin, his attention largely on Arthur who hung back, an unwelcome guest at an already unpleasant event. April's eyes were wide with what Merlin assumed was terror. Though she stood fast.

'Where did you find him?' Hades made it sound as if Merlin were a lost dog.

'A rooftop.'

Merlin shot Death a look to remind them that small details were important.

'I was cataloguing loose ends. It has become a hobby over the years.' A firm shove from Death propelled Merlin to fall at April's feet. 'All of which are neatly tidying themselves up, aren't they, Vivie?' His daughter looked quickly to Artemis, unsure of how to conduct herself in this setting. Artemis hauled Merlin up, nearly disconnecting his arm from its socket. Benjamin couldn't look away, couldn't move.

They could have reached the "waiting room," without passing through the court, but Artemis was enjoying herself. It was an open-air affair, set against the backdrop of the river, for added drama. Eons of use had scorched a circle into the earth, where Merlin would soon take the stand. His back would be to the river, whilst he faced the row of three thrones. For balance, his judges were to be Hades, April and Charon. This was a place where mortals and lesser beings were accused. It was dire, but at least it wasn't Chaos' court.

Small mercies.

The waiting room closely resembled that of an unsuccessful dentist. Laminated wooden chairs and little tables adorned the space, digging trenches into the ancient carpet. The sofa was in the process of shedding fake black leather that stuck to whatever it touched. The lavender shade splashed on the walls felt somewhat ironic. In the far corner sat a cobweb-riddled wooden toddlers' bead maze with multicoloured beads and animal-shaped pieces, attached to coloured wires. Above him, a single florescent tube flickered and blinked, its energy solely devoted to clinging onto life rather than illuminating the room. The leaflet rack nestled in the small gap by the door sat askew. It contained titles such as *So this is your first underworld trial?* And, *Is your heart lighter than a feather?*

Merlin accidentally set the rack on fire.

He leaned against the murky glass of the wide, floor-to-ceiling window, watching the court's light fading to black whenever a sentence was passed. On the cliffs above them, and scattered around the court, mixed in with the shadows, hundreds of hell-hounds stood guard. The unfortunate soul stood in the middle of the scorched circle of dirt looked truly terrified. Emrys was a bundle of anxious energy rocking in his head. It was making Merlin feel seasick. The source of Emrys' anxiety was circling above the court. It flicked between something that, if Merlin squinted, passed as a human with wings, and something that very nearly resembled an owl. Death's latest creation. The flecks of magic in all colours that shone around its mouth-beak suggested it consumed magic and condemned souls.

That fate led to the Nothingness.
Distorted gargoyles dragged themselves through the dirt, eager for the verdict. They couldn't pounce until the gavel fell. In the circle, an older man dropped to his knees, begging mercy. The light dimmed and the old man's screams filled the air. And then they didn't.

The old man's hands groped his now featureless face.

People never really outgrew their fear of the dark and the things it concealed.

By the time the door creaked open, Merlin had watched the light go down on ten people. He sighed but kept his focus on the court.

'Are you trying to cut a hole in the glass with that petulant look, Merlin?' Surprise straightened Merlin's posture. Benjamin stood awkwardly in the threshold. 'They are almost ready for you.'

'You almost sound happy about it.'
Benjamin froze, his anxiety constricted around his entire being, scrambling his thoughts.

'I was joking, Benjamin. Although I do not blame you for not wanting to keep me breathing that bit longer.'
Benjamin screwed his face up in his quest for something to say, gave up and shut the door behind himself. The distressed sofa groaned as Benjamin perched himself on the edge of it.

'It's so cold in here. The devil died from the cold, you know. You should remind Hades of that. Perhaps he can turn a heater on for his next guest. To be warm is a basic right. Charon must be made entirely of ice by now.'
Benjamin's eyes almost brightened, though his mouth couldn't find a smile.

'I'll tell him, but I doubt he's going to install central heating for the shades. As for Charon, the cold is in his bones, the storm in his bloodstream.' Benjamin shrugged out of his jacket and offered it to him.
Merlin drew his cloak about him, flicking one end over his shoulder. He was cold, not in shock.

'An imagined version of you, brought on by a curse, has already chided me, if you wish to save yourself the bother.'
Benjamin started to ask but dismissed his own question with a shake of his head. Merlin sat on the other end of the sofa.

'There was a time, once, when we could fill any silence with chatter. Do you remember?'
Benjamin looked away in time to see the light dim once more and

stared at his boots instead.

'If there is even a modicum of good to be found in this sorry mess, it is that you, Benjamin, have finally learnt to push away those that do not serve you.' Merlin nudged Benjamin's leg and smiled when his assistant looked up. 'I'm proud of who you became.' Benjamin struggled to keep his mouth from quivering. 'Even if it has brought us to hell's waiting room, with nothing left to say to one another.'

Benjamin had to look away before his neck snapped under the strain of continued eye contact. 'Was I so closely watched that my grief for you and Arthur had to be genuine?'

'I suppose the dramatics were more for my benefit. It was novel to attend my own funeral.' The light dimmed behind him, causing Benjamin's tears to glisten like hard-won diamonds.

'Nothing is over, nothing will end, if you don't let go. You taught me that, Merlin.'

The knackered speaker crackled into life, requesting Merlin report to the court reception. Benjamin stood slowly. Merlin caught his assistant's wrist. He turned back, eyebrows raised in a silent question.

'The Egyptians believed that you die twice. Once when you breathe your last, then again, when your name is spoken for the final time.' Merlin tightened his grip. 'Keep saying my name. Even if it's to curse it.'

'Other people will speak your name, so long as they continue to tell stories of Merlin the wizard. But this will be the last time that I say your name. Merlin.'

Benjamin opened the door, letting Merlin go.

With one last look through the window, Merlin drew Emrys into a tight ball at the core of his being. He slowed his breathing, allowing his concentration to ebb and flow with Emrys. His magic radiated warmth throughout his body and flew to the outer reaches of Merlin's being, where he hesitated.

'*Everything is happening as it should, Emrys.*'

Emrys flooded Merlin's mind with sorrow as pins and needles shivered down Merlin's body from head to toe. Behind it came a searing, tearing pain as an unseen knife severed Emrys from Merlin. He cried out involuntarily, his legs buckling under him, panic flooding his mind at not feeling Emrys' presence. Merlin reached for the sofa, to pull himself up. Emrys rushed down the extended arm, cascading to the floor, only to rise up in a narrow column. The aquamarine embers dropped away to reveal a staff crafted from the ghostly-white branches of a dead tree, delicately wound around one another, until the top where they fused together to become a carved dragon's head. Held between pointed teeth, a glowing jade jewel with a burning ball of pure, aquamarine magic.

'What did you do?' Benjamin hauled Merlin to his feet. The horror in his assistant's voice indicated that Benjamin knew exactly what Merlin had done. What his assistant had meant to ask was, why.

Merlin gripped his staff tightly and set off down the beige corridor that felt like a furnace. The peeling plaster revealed damp patches, but there was a distinct lack of doors. They passed a brown fern, wilting in its pot. Behind it, a door of fine white limestone shimmered into view. Merlin brushed away the dust on the bronze plaque and realised with a slight jolt that this was a room of scales.

'Kindly remain out here, Benjamin. The weight of one's heart should be known only to them and the Gods.'

The door opened of its own accord, leaving Merlin little choice but to enter.

37

GLORIOUS SUNSET

T he room was smaller than expected.
    And stuffy.
Merlin had to turn sideways to edge past tables piled high with
ledgers. He held his staff out in front of him, using it to push
low-hanging objects out of his way. Nestled within the paper
maze, Merlin found a petite man bent over a ledger. He had
placed himself underneath the only light source in the room,
giving his bald copper head the illusion of having a halo. His
mouth silently sounding out figures whilst his glass fountain
pen, the colour of sunsets, danced across the page, adding and
subtracting sins and tragedies and regrets. Pointed black dress
shoes that were shined to within an inch of their lives poked
out from beneath the tailored black crushed velvet trousers of
his undertaker's suit. A silver ankh sat over his crisp white shirt,
sleeves rolled up. His jacket lay neatly folded over the chair beside
him, a jackal broach pinned to its lapel.

'Are you going to ignore me, Anubis?'

The God of Death and the Afterlife, held up an impatient, gloved hand before Merlin could chase any sense of the equation from his mind. Merlin pulled the chair away from the desk; it screeched across the floor, almost piercing Anubis' concentration. Anubis closed his eyes in frustration, his head morphing into that of a jackal's. Merlin held his hands up in silent apology and settled into the uncomfortable metal folding chair. Anubis returned to his mortal form and to his work. The office was disorientating in its clutter. Merlin pulled the nearest ledger towards himself, lifting the cover with one finger. Inside, rows of names were tightly packed onto each page, written in red ink. It was an undesirable weight that Anubis had to carry.

So many lives weighed. So many afterlives determined.

The stacks of boxes stretched as far as Merlin could see and yet Anubis did not meet every soul that crossed over. Anubis enjoyed a challenge, and judging by the gleam in his eye, he was relishing digging deep into Merlin's subconscious. A short, sharp woof drew Merlin under the table. He came face to face with a brown sausage dog, perched on a cushion. It was eyeing up his heart like a dog treat.

'There. It does not hurt to wait every once in a while, Merlin. Mayhap you'll learn something in the stillness.' Anubis' round face crinkled into a smile. 'Now that I have a mind to think on it, you have never visited my office.'

'Forgive me, I was unaware you were receiving visitors. Looks like you're still settling in. Or moving out.'

'You only know the theory of what I do here.' Anubis pushed his round spectacles up his nose with one finger. Merlin straightened up, having the uncomfortable feeling that he was being weighed there and then.

'You will weigh my heart against Ma'at, which is to say, you will weigh my truth against yours and find me lacking.'
Anubis set his fountain pen down with careful precision, into its dark red granite holder. The twisted glass infused with orange bounced the light into Merlin's eyes.

'A life is a series of short stories. Protagonists tend to judge themselves far more harshly and accurately than I ever could. Choice and morality are not straightforward. I seek balance.' Anubis placed a feather in Merlin's left hand and guided his right to rest atop the abacus. 'Clarity is priceless.'

A breeze stirred the stale air. The beads on the abacus rattled back and forth as Merlin's truth was laid bare for Anubis. Hundreds of ledgers flew open, the rustling of pages drowned out whatever Anubis was saying. At the edges of the room, at the edges of the plane of existence, stood the reapers. The wispy shadows of blue, silver and black, surrounded him. Fingers dug into his heart, seized it and squeezed. The beads and the pages froze. Dust hung suspended in the air whilst the dog was stuck mid yawn. White light pulsated in the centre of the long slender whisps. They shifted into swirls of electric-blue energy and reformed in front of him. One held the feather, another his heart.

The disapproval was strong.
Merlin's legs ceased to function. He grabbed the nearest solid

object to steady himself and triggered an avalanche of boxes. It consumed him bar the hand holding the feather. It was yanked from his hand, but no assistance was offered. With great difficulty, Merlin clambered free, collecting hundreds of papercuts along the way.

'That paper weighs more than the tree it came from –'
Anubis had his mournful expression on.

'You tried too hard to do the right thing.' Anubis placed the feather on his desk, his sympathy genuine.

'What am I supposed to do with that?!'

'Whatever you please. However, I regret to say, the scales did not tip in your favour.'

'I am shocked! Just as I will be shocked when I am found guilty – and don't tell me that all will be well.'

Anubis pushed Merlin's pointing finger aside. 'I was going to suggest you allow the waves to crash down on you. Mayhap you will wash ashore somewhere quite wonderful.'

'Right and I shall let the wind howl and the rain pour. Go back to counting sins, Anubis. I'll seek enlightenment elsewhere.'

'Inform me if you find it.' Anubis smiled kindly.

'You, I, hmph!' Merlin snatched up his staff and headed for the door, allowing the staff to snag on and dislodge boxes. The door mercifully materialised in the shelves in front of Merlin. He tore it open, prompting a cloud of dust to jump from the boxes it smashed into. 'Oh! You're still here.' Benjamin was leaning against the opposite wall, one foot flush against it, ready to cast off. 'You look like you're about to start snapping your fingers at me.'

Benjamin studied Merlin's face, his eyes rapidly shifting colour. The silver ring with its delicate etchings of dragons shifted over to his left thumb and back to the right. Jack had gifted him that ring a few years into their courtship. Whilst awaiting Jack's arrival at Benjamin's house, Merlin had discovered the ring Arthur had given Benjamin – an ornate gold ring set with a dazzling emerald, the band studied with rubies. Garish. That's the word Merlin had used, and Benjamin had agreed. Not with words, but by the way he covered it with his other hand whenever possible. It had been stuffed inside one of the many crates of letters. A burial, of sorts. With a heavy sigh, Benjamin started walking. Merlin hurried to catch up with Benjamin's long stride.

'Aren't you going to ask how I got on?'

'It is written all over your face,' Benjamin said over his shoulder. The tannoy crackled into life and spat Merlin's name once more.

'Do you remember what it was I told you, just before the last battle?'

Benjamin slowed. 'That I should never let the sun go down on me in an under realm.'

And with that, Merlin pushed through rickety doors with grime-covered frosted glass, and took the stand, his eyes scanning over the surface of the river, watching a fallen leaf float by, jealous of its freedom.

'What are you looking at, warlock?' Charon leaned so far over his throne that Merlin was convinced it would tip.

'Time. Sometimes I catch it drifting past, out of the corner of my eye.'

'And here I was thinking you might prefer to drown.' Overuse of sarcasm. That's why Hades and Benjamin were friends.

'Fall in and you will die. I've lost track of what's down there.' Hades snuck a quick look himself and shuddered at something Merlin couldn't see.

Cerberus stirred at Hades feet. An unusual place to find the hound. He must have sought the reassurance he found in his master's company. 'April has chosen to forgo all of the usual trials. I admit they are archaic, crude and akin to a witch trial, so that's for the best. They warrant an overhaul.'

April nodded with conviction. 'And I see no point subjecting you to them when we both know the outcome.' She paused. 'My premonitions have cost you the chance to talk your way out.'

'The other side of that coin says that, perhaps, I do not want to wriggle free.' Merlin smiled as if he were making dinner plans. 'Shall we begin this witch trial?'

'Very well.' Charon set his lantern down. 'Merlin, you have destroyed a realm and failed in your duties as Guardian. Furthermore, it has been brought to our attention that you wrongfully imprisoned your King and whether directly or indirectly, you were responsible for the turning of Jack and Benjamin.'

'Brought to your attention?! You knew about that all along, Charon!' Merlin stared back in defiance.

'You altered lives without Death's permission. In Jack's case you showed premeditation and in Benjamin's a striking lack of remorse. Not to mention neglect. Do you regret your actions?' Merlin laughed darkly; how could he answer that and not look guilty? All of his decisions would be judged harshly by people who had not had to make them. They had not known the fear that dimmed his intelligence enough to enable him to not offer Benjamin a warning when they parted the night before War's ruse. Nor the crippling power of inevitability. Or how it enveloped him and removed him from himself. Even if he had had forewarning of Vivienne's death – her first death – Merlin would not have changed a single thing. Even when he saw his end, Merlin had not lifted a finger to stop her from reincarnating. If nothing else, this trail would teach April what it was to choose between impossible things.

'Each and every one of you are just where you are supposed to be. I see what is to become and that is my burden to bear, as it shall be April's.' The stubborn line of April's mouth told him that she thought she knew better. Children. 'You, my child, have not had to endure the fear. Not yet.'
April had to look away, tears in her eyes.

'Every fibre of me yearns to be the father you deserved, April. But, to be the father you needed, I had to see you safely to this point. Had I neglected my sight, Gaia would have fallen long ago. And Vivienne would have ended up in her mother's care.'
Hades and Charon exchanged a slightly wide eye look at the prospect of somebody with April's abilities being moulded by Fate.

'I did not breathe life into that which you accuse me of. Except for Jack's turning. I engineered that. It's true. Ask me why it suited me?'

'Why?' April took the bait.

'Benjamin needed something constant to anchor him. I was merely replacing what I had taken – an upgrade, if you will. He had forgotten that he was still entitled to be somebody. And Jack, not that he remembers, took you in April. When he was human. When you perished, Jack was adrift.'

The vampire was staring open mouthed, all bitterness and hatred suspended for the moment.

'As for Avalon, it was a necessary evil, I am afraid. April must rebuild. From scratch.' Benjamin's head was down, but Merlin saw him peeking at the scene. 'You don't want your destinies right now; fine, grow into them. If you are searching for something to burn, use your own failures as kindling.'

April looked to Hades, but his face was a mask. They all claimed to want Merlin's blood, but now that the opportunity had presented itself, they did not want to dirty their hands. Or perhaps Hades was teaching April to think for herself. This would be the moment when she realised that her life would be nothing but difficult decisions and he was the first.

'Have you said enough?'

Merlin smiled at April's phrasing. It was very much like Vivienne to ask two questions within one. Had he said enough to convince his judges? Not at all. Had he said all that he wanted to? Not at all.

'Death always cuts people off midsentence.' A shade

drifted through the court. Cerberus raised his head, but let it pass. 'You've made up your mind?' April nodded. 'Hold us in suspense no longer. What's it to be?'

April leaned forwards, her hands clasped tighter, choosing her words carefully. Her eyebrows scrunched together as she worried about making the wrong decision.

'Sometimes the mistakes we make are fortuitous, other times not. Sometimes mistakes are made in good faith. But you've made too many with too much prior knowledge. If I were speaking to anybody else, I would say that your past isn't a life sentence and you shouldn't let it trap you.'

The sharp intelligence of Vivienne shone in April's eyes. His child would thrive and rebuild all that her parents had broken. And he would see none of it.

The cruelty was deserved.

'I can think of no better prison for you than one of your own making. There's an oak tree in Windsor Great Park.'

'Herne's tree.' Charon was smiling under that hood, Merlin knew it.

'Yes. Merlin will be imprisoned inside the tree. Left to eventually die alone with his memories.'

Merlin bowed his head in acknowledgement of something he had long since accepted.

'Herne will not be pleased.' Charon was right, of course. Herne the Hunter was a prickly character who hated four things:

nobility, change, littering, and Merlin.

Herne's life had been devoted to keeping the grounds of the park and all that roamed there. Falsely accused of murdering a child, found dead in the park, Herne's life disintegrated. Any fool could have seen, if they had cared to look, how this gentle giant placed every other life he met above his own. But fools seek witches to burn in dark times. The shunning did not bother Herne, nor did the cruel words, but the knowledge that his community believed him capable of such a despicable enterprise, did. That is until it did not. One night, the weight became too much to bear, and Herne tossed a rope over the branch of an oak tree in his park, and that was that.

Or so Herne had thought.

The park did not accept his resignation. It burned with the injustice of it all. The oak tree embraced Herne's spirit, shielding him from Death's reapers. When the tree realised that it could not keep Herne hidden forever, it welcomed him, allowing their spirits to fuse. Herne became one with time, and the universe, allowing him to be a part of every story, even though his own was felled much too soon.

As for the park, it belonged to the living during the day and kept its fair share of secrets. The animals of the park understood the importance of the sacred place and remained in death, to assist Herne in protecting it. Once the sun dipped low enough to wash the park in dusk's pastel light, the hunt gathered. With Herne at the helm, the hunt was abroad, seeking to remove any human – or otherwise – heartbeats trapped within. As a result, the park was locked two hours before dusk.

'We are but silent bystanders, removed facilitators. Nothing more, nothing less,' April stated.

Charon nodded approvingly at how April was growing into her new role. 'Merlin set his course when he adopted the belief that he had no control over his actions – even though he is a Guardian, and we move ungoverned by Fate.'

'Well, if nobody has any objections?' Hades looked at each of them in turn.

Benjamin, feeling the pressure of Hades' stare, looked up and shook his head.

'Any last words Merlin?'

The warlock turned from April to Hades. The God shrank back, deterred by Merlin's confident smirk.

'We all end up where we are supposed to.'

38

THE WILD HUNT

WINDSOR GREAT PARK, GAIA

D espite the cold, April's face burned, aware of everybody's eyes on her – Merlin's especially.

The pressure pushed her into a brisk walk. Jade embers encircled and broke the lock on the tall, white wooden gates beside the Ranger's cottage. Eilir navigated her away from the ice-covered sandy coloured path that led to the castle. It wasn't quite dusk yet, but the park felt eerie in the low light. Frozen grass crunched underfoot. The ground vibrated with ancient magic that acknowledged her as Fate. Everything here had its own aura of deep gold. A red-breasted robin hopped along the ground in front of April, pecking for worms. So far, its little chirp was the only sound April had heard. The park hummed with an ancient, powerful energy. April ran a hand across the rough bark of a tree, and it stole her breath.

A newly triumphant King, with a moustache and an

outrageous French accent sat astride a chestnut mare, trotted past on a hunt. The tree insisted it was older still, but April withdrew her hand. She had enough visions rattling about in her brain. Hounds that were little more than dark shadows with red eyes darted between the trees. Here, deep into the deer park, the skeletal branches of ancient oaks patiently awaiting the return of warmer weather; they were planted one on either side of a natural path. The gap between them narrowed as they approached the oldest tree. It towered above the rest, its branches still supporting thousands of leaves.

The group seemed to understand her unvoiced need for silence. Or perhaps they were scared of her. Or maybe they didn't like her, now that she was Fate.

April was over it all.

Merlin was lost in the middle of the pack, the Gods towering over him. Ben was slightly ahead of them, trying to outpace Arthur. April would have felt better if Merlin had rallied against them. His quiet smile was unnerving. Endings didn't seem to apply to him. But that was the point of the sentence – to ensure that Merlin didn't wriggle free. Ben fell into step beside her, making her jump.

'*Are you worried about casting the spell?*'

April kept walking. That bit would be all right, Eilir was confident with it. Merlin had apparently taught the spell to his infant daughter.

'*Or are you hesitant to summon the hunt?*'

April's stride faltered but she quickly recovered. Ben's arm brushed hers, his attention on the trees that lined the pathway.

'*I wouldn't want to summon that ragged band of ghosts and fairies myself. Any prey will do. So long as it's alive and has a soul,*' Ben said wearily.

The hunt sounded like it would take any opportunity for mischief. She didn't doubt that they had unleashed plagues and misery on Gaia.

Yellow eyes arrested April from high up tree branches.

She caught a glimpse of faces and hounds to her left, and she drew Eilir close. Ambrosius engulfed Ben's hands in warning to anything that was stupid enough to approach.

'Here we are.' Merlin nudged his way past the others. Jack a shadow on Merlin's heels. 'This tree has witnessed three thousand sunrises.' He nodded to himself.

'Herne is older than that.' Hades stamped his feet, a smart silk scarf appeared and wrapped itself around his neck.

April pressed trembling hands to the cold bark; all of the sunsets flashed through her mind. Deep within it, she could feel the hum and howl of magic older and stronger than anything she'd connected with. She pushed a little deeper, a pair of wide, hazel and green floating eyes jumped in front of her own.

April snatched her hand away.

Sadness made Merlin's pitch-black eyes look almost human.

'*It's a strange thing.*' He held her gaze easily. '*To be turning myth into legend, legend into history.*' Merlin's smile took twenty years from his face. Or perhaps it was the early evening light. '*Time makes stories of us all.*'

355

'*Are you scared, Merlin?*'

'*Terrified.*' He laughed in relief.

Artemis tapped the tree trunk with her spear, listening for a reply. 'Herne?' Her clear voice carried through the park, chasing birds from trees. Deer shot past them, racing for cover as one hunter called to another.

'Come forth before I sound the horn.'

The tree groaned aloud. Its branches stretched upwards and back until the tree had doubled in height, its branches seeming to scrape the clouds as it stretched. Branches crawled over themselves, knotting together to form arms, the trunk splitting into two legs. April hadn't thought it was possible for a tree to look pissed off, but the moustache set a firm line underneath eyes that were both ancient and displeased.

'I will never know peace.' Herne shook his tree trunk legs free of the ground, revealing feet and toes made of roots. 'There is no need to yell, Artemis,' said the tree whose booming voice was shaking the ground. 'Not when dusk hangs about us, waiting to usher in the night. I do so prefer the night.' Herne crossed his arms, a stray leaf drifted to the ground.

'There's much to hear in the dead of night, if you still yourself.' Artemis bowed. April was glad that somebody present knew the etiquette for conversing with a tree.

'The park rests and everything in it is free to fill its lungs. People are their most honest under the false security of the dark. They wrap themselves in the velvet night, and, with the moon and stars as witness, disclose their hearts.' Herne noticed the rest of the group, his bark eyebrows diving into a frown. 'Why have so many of you called me away from the hunt?'

'Be not fooled, April. Herne was slumbering,' Artemis interjected. The giant tree-man bent down, his face close to hers. 'Such a flimsy thing.' Herne's branches snaked out to brush the hair from April's face. She did her best not to squirm as the mossy bark scratched across her forehead. 'My! She resembles you, Merlin!'

'I do not!' April spluttered, looking to the group for reassurance. Merlin nodded, proud as punch.

'I see you as you were.' Herne straightened back up, towering above them. 'It must be a dark day indeed, for you all to visit me.'

'Merlin should no longer have the opportunity to tamper with the universe.' April's voice rang with a false confidence.

'Absolutely not!' Herne roared and birds shot from the trees. 'The darkest lines on my trunk have been caused by knowing Merlin, it is true. My role in the universe, however, is to observe. To remember. Leave him someplace else!' Herne turned his back on them. 'Merlin carries more sadness than any creature I have ever met. I want no share in that.'

April sympathised completely, but somebody had to have Merlin, and she was not it.

Merlin gently pushed past April and Artemis to tap on Herne's trunk.

'Imagine the stories I can share. I've watched good deeds go unrewarded; I've crafted history. Irritated Death. My story, though often told, is never accurate.'

Herne peeked over his shoulder, his gaze lingering on April. It was a steep price to pay for stories. 'If left free, there will be nothing left to hunt. Your park will be no more,' April stated bluntly.

'Well why didn't you say so? Merlin, have you bid farewell to your companions?'

Merlin looked around the group. 'There is no point trying to force sincerity into worn-out words. Perhaps, one day, Benjamin, you'll return here to tell me that I am not the villain.'

Ben, unable to find a response shook his head. He wanted to be done with Merlin, but he couldn't let go, April thought.

'Here.' Merlin held out his staff to April. 'It belongs with you.'

'I don't want something to remember you by.' She crossed her arms and squirmed, worried that he was about to say something from the heart he purported to have.

'It's functional. Not ornamental!'

April took the offered keepsake, holding it away from her body in case it turned into a snake. If she wasn't mistaken, Emrys was fused with it. Eilir tentatively explored the keepsake, learning the staff's rhythm. April's head vibrated with it. This seemed more final than the trial. It wasn't because he was saying goodbye, although Eilir seemed to be crying for that very reason. It just felt like missed opportunities. All those lessons that Merlin left to others to teach, for fear he'd get them wrong. She'd never truly understand Merlin or where she came from. His decision, for better or for worse, had robbed her of the chance. And he had never had a chance to get to know his own daughter. Merlin met her gaze, seeming to know her thoughts.

'I knew my daughter once. I adored her fiercely. I still do.' Tears ran down Merlin's face, shimmering in the light. 'I met her again, much later on. She was remarkable. And I do not blame her.' April's breath caught in her throat. Herne tapped his tree trunk feet like an impatient orchestra conductor.

'The hunt is readying to leave; the hounds grow restless.' Herne scanned his audience, seeming to realise that some of them were technically still alive. 'You should all be away before the hunt departs.'

Merlin nodded to Herne. 'I am your problem now.'

'With any luck it will be a short internment. Well, Young Fate?' Pins and needle erupted down April's staff arm. Jade magic shot from her hand, engulfing the staff. April raised it but dropped her arm. She gathered up all that had happened, all that Merlin had done to Ben, Jack – to her – and gave it to Eilir. She pointed the staff at Merlin's chest and looked him square in the eye. Jade magic swirled around Merlin and Herne, binding the two. Emrys' aquamarine fused with Eilir, increasing the intensity. April gripped the staff with both hands, struggling with the weight of the spell.

'As you have trapped so many, I now trap you, Merlin.'
Her magic grew and swallowed Merlin. Emrys' aquamarine magic turned to embers and blinked out. Eilir washed back to April, leaving nothing but scorched grass where Merlin has stood. Herne bowed to them and then he was gone, striding into the park. A choir of howls and yips from phantom hounds

greeted him.

Artemis was the first to turn away. 'Merlin never recovered from his discovery that the world is a cruel, disappointing place. He tried to fix it until he inevitably grew to reflect his surroundings. If you must dwell on it, April, consider it an act of mercy.' She envied Artemis' straightforwardness. Maybe one day, she'd be able to separate feelings from actions; but right now, April couldn't tell if the tingling in her stomach was from guilt or Eilir.

'Why'd you keep him on Gaia?' Ben was holding tightly to Jack, his face a blank mask with stormy grey eyes.

'In case I need to remind myself that I am capable of burying my father alive in a tree.'

Ben threw an arm around April's shoulders. 'The world has moved on. As should we. Never speak his name to me again.'

'That's all well and good.' They all jumped as one and turned to see Death occupying the space recently vacated by Herne. 'But Merlin is a rhyme that you cannot quite shake from your mind.' April tried to pull back, but Ben's arm held her in place. She hadn't worked out if becoming Fate had given her any new powers. Not that having powers would make Death any less scary.

'These are for you.' Death handed a letter to each of them. 'Arthur already has his.'

April turned the letter over in her hand, noticing the untidy handwriting. Whoever had written them had neatly folded the letter until it became its own envelope. She brushed her thumb over the wax seal of the shield and the cat, tears gathering in her eyes.

Ben frowned at the stamps. 'Did you steal these from a postman?'

'There was a long, slow-moving queue at the post office,' Death said in all seriousness. 'I did not want to play messenger, but when I suggested Merlin magic them to their recipients, he sent them to me.'

'And how long have you been here?' Jack asked, pocketing his letter.

'Long enough to witness one era end and another begin. Fate suits you, don't you agree?'

April startled and tripped over her answer. 'Thanks? Will I have to deal with many talking trees, or?'

Death made a strange sound that could have been a laugh. 'Very good. Have you not felt the tremors underneath your feet? You have just entombed Chaos' most favourite human.'
April's eyes widened. Chaos had known that Merlin would die, but they hadn't known how or why. Why else would Chaos have allowed her to leave?

'You couldn't have told me that before the trial?'

'The decision had to be your own. Consequences do not cower you. Unlike your father. Seek to beat Chaos at their own game.' Hades tapped Death on the shoulder. 'It sounds like you're asking April to do your dirty work.'

'Those who think themselves above the rest of us will continue to divide people and tear worlds apart.' Death glanced in Artemis' direction, unbothered by either Gods or Benjamin's unease at Death's proximity to April. Hades took a step so he was slightly in front of Artemis. As if that would stop her should she chose violence.

'Not all of the Gods are bad.' April heard how naive she sounded.

'Exceptions do not excuse the majority. The universe does not require Gods to function. Just the two of us, fledgling Fate. We are the two unshakeable forces of life.'

Hades crossed his arms. 'If you bumped me off Death, who will oversee the underworld? You excel at many things, but admin and people management are not among them.'
Artemis and Benjamin turned to stare at Hades, willing him to shut up.

'At the moment, you serve a different purpose by providing counsel to Fate.' Death held out a skeleton hand to April. 'Your inheritance is your parents' legacy, and the legacy is a disaster. Come, rebuild worlds with me.'
April's hesitation was partly due to her not wanting to touch Death and partly because it felt like a setup. If she understood Death correctly, Death believed that the only way to return order to the universe was to kill off the Gods. Hades and Artemis certainly didn't deserve that fate. April didn't really know the others, but she suspected they didn't either. By removing her parents from the equation, April had removed Death's opposing forces, creating an imbalance of a different kind. If April worked with Death, she might be able to save the Gods. At the very least, Hades and Artemis.

Death's hand still hung in the air between them.

Artemis nodded. April hoped that they had been thinking along the same lines. Dread tried to pull her arm down as April took the offered hand. It wasn't cold but she felt the struggle of the millions who had tried to avoid Death's grip.

'The age of the Gods has been declining for centuries, we shall snuff that flame out completely.' Death disappeared before April could reply. She caught Ben sneaking a peak at his letter. It flipped over in his indecisive hands, oblivious to the dust cloud that appeared from nowhere at the other end of the park.

'You had to agree.' Hades took Artemis' spear from her, watching as she stored her bow. 'Show me somebody who isn't scared of Death and I will show you a fool. There's your first bit of counsel.'

'Great, thanks. You might need to do better. At least until we figure out what Death is planning.'

'You've given your word. I will assist you where I can.' Artemis' attention was mostly on the hunt charging about in the distance.

'Thank you.' Reassured to have Artemis on her side, April cracked the wax seal.

23/12/29

Dear Vivie,

I can feel Death standing behind me.

I cannot say for certain what it is they have in mind — my vision blurred at that point — the dark shapes that I saw filled me with dread. Death cannot escape their nature for long.

I did not always recognise you, at first. But I found you eventually. Every time.

I do not know if we will find ourselves together again. So, I will wait for another time, and I hope that it is one in which we know each other properly.

Being without premonitions is both alien and terrifying. Soon I will be without Emrys. I must relinquish him, and regrettably, borrow from Ambrosius, to aid you in casting the spell.

There is much that I want to say to you, and yet I find myself quite unable to put it into words in this moment. So, I will say this: Everything starts and ends with you.

Love,

Your father

'The clouds are bunching together in a weird way.' Jack's face was tilted to the sky.

'Oh yeah. That looks Chaos-shaped.' Hades frowned.
April stuffed the letter into a pocket, trying to hide behind her hair, struggling to breath around the lump in her throat.

'Menoetius joined the hunt.' Artemis grabbed a still-silent Arthur by the arm. 'Hades, portal.'

'There's no need for the tone, dearest.' But Hades complied. Artemis went through with Arthur and Jack. Ben was frowning at the unopened letter as if he could glean its contents without reading it. Hades nudged April closer to the portal. She stepped through, feeling sick at leaving Ben behind.

The portal fizzled out, leaving Hades feeling exposed.

'Bin the letter or cuddle up to it tonight, whichever you prefer, just move.'

Herne had ditched his tree form for his bare-chested woodsman with horns poking out of his long, matted hair, form. The hounds were very definitely of the hell hound variety.

'They won't bother with me, Hades.'

'You are a bucketful of souls on legs. You are *exactly* what they are looking for.'

The hunt changed direction, putting themselves on a collision course with Benjamin. Hades threw open another portal but something big and furry barrelled into him. The portal spluttered and closed. Hooves thudded towards them; Hades caught Herne's eye, but he had no intention of stopping the chaos. Benny rolled to his feet, his back to the hunt. Hades wrapped his arms around Ben's legs, pulling him down, seconds before Herne's horse flew past, its rancid breath warm on Hades' face as he peeked to see if the coast was clear. He rolled them out of the way, feeling the hands of ghostly hunter's brush against his back. Hades opened and closed his hand until his magic flared into life. He launched it at Herne without a spell, just pure intention. The hunt screeched and thundered past them.

Hades dragged Benny up by his collar, his other hand trying and failing to catch an edge in the air.

'I can't open a portal, why?'

'I don't know!' Benny's hands patted his pockets, his eyes scanning the ground.

'You're not going to find the answer about your person!'

'Merlin's letter!' Benny gave Hades his big puppy dog eyes.

'Forget it! This is your realm, do something!'

Two balls of orange magic reached for one another as they arced through the air, exploding on impact. The hunt slowed, their eyes trained on the pulsing orange cloud.

'I didn't mean draw them back to us!'

Benny faced the hunt, his legs slightly bent, hands aglow with Ambrosius and held in front of him, letting the hunt close the distance. When they were close enough to smell, Ben flicked his wrist and sent Ambrosius flying off into the park, the hunt in pursuit.

'Uh, Benny.'

'I didn't think that would work –'

'Benjamin!' Hades spun the Guardian back around. Portals were opening all around them, spitting out Gods, some of whom, Hades hadn't seen since they fled Tartarus.

'Oh hells.' Ben dug at his eyebrow with his thumb, staring up at the clouds.

'Not up there.' Hades twisted Ben's head down. 'There. I think we can assume that the Gods aren't happy.'

'Why?'

'Oh, I don't know. Could be because you and Merlin killed Mórrígan. Or because April killed Fate.' Hades tried to cut the air again. 'Doubt they're fussed about Merlin, but let's add that to the list of misdemeanours anyway.'

'Or because somebody let Chaos out.'

Above them, the clouds were being pulled against their will into the form of a face with tempestuous cloud-eyes. The only person desperate enough was – Arthur.

Chaos dived, corkscrewing their way to the ground, swooping over their heads, coming to a halt somewhere in between them and the Gods.

'Go home. Now.' The tower of clouds commanded the assembled Gods. Perhaps they had come to Gaia for protection. Visible panic rippled through the crowd, but they held their ground. Chaos darted towards the crowd. The Gods scattered whilst Chaos circled them as if the Gods were sheep fleeing their field.

'They don't want to go home, Chaos.'

Hades slowly turned to glare at Benny, watching Chaos out of the corner of his eye.

The cloud-menace stilled, their head tilting to one side. They swirled round and stalked towards Ben.

'That's close enough!' Hades yelled.

Chaos smirked and sped up. Ambrosius shot into the air like a flare, but the spells bounced off of Chaos without the tyrant noticing. Hades sent his own attempt, but he hated using his magic and his grey-black bundle of half-heartedness fell short of the target.

'It was real nice knowing you, Benny.'

'Likewise, Hades.'

'Thanks for getting me killed.'

'Don't mention it.'

Eager for the next book in the Shadows and Regrets series?

Well, fear not; Sounds of Someday will be out in January 2026! Can't wait? Here's a sneak peak at an early draft of the first chapter.

'Benny!' Hades grabbed a fistful of sleeve and hauled the Guardian out of Chaos' path. Ambrosius collided with Chaos and ricocheted off. For a moment, the night sky burned orange. Chaos spiralled into the air, the green and purples of Merlin's warding flashed into view and were gone. 'Well, there goes the warding –'

Benjamin shot to his feet, shouting something unintelligible. Hades chucked his weight into the shtriga, pushing him to the ground. 'Immortality is wasted on you.' Ben's elbow collided with his jaw. 'That had best been an accident –'

The air beside Hades' head fizzled and tore open. One sandaled foot followed another and Artemis' sharp nails dug trenches in his neck as she hauled him, and Benny, through the portal and into the inky blackness of the cosmos. The brilliant white of the star's light had thinned until they were opalescent pearls, the rich colours of the universe muted, sombre shades. And, perhaps more importantly, they weren't hurtling through time and space, towards Gaia.

Ambrosius flared into life, a ball of floating light that backlit Ben.

'It is as if the cosmos is hanging from my feet.' Artemis' voice sounded pinched.

'Just say you're stuck!' Floating about in the universe, between realms, between portals – it wasn't the place to be. Hades did a double take; Benny had a halo. He twisted round and to his dismay, he found light leaking into space, peeling back on itself. A fluffy cloud-hand squeezed through the gap and grabbed blindly for them. Ambrosius wrapped around them – a shield of shimmering orange embers that absorbed every attack Chaos sent. Chaos' arm swept up a galaxies worth of stars, feeling the weight before tossing them into the distance where they collided with their siblings in a shower of sparks and red novas that exploded, showering them in dust. Artemis' and Ben's arms were shaking with the strain of trying to free them. All the while, Chaos was widening the portal, their shoulder was in the process of forcing its way through. Ben's hair was matted to his face, one hand clutching his chest; on Hades' other side, Artemis was morphing in – and – out of her huntress form, whilst Chaos' magic flew around them, prodding and poking at the shield Ben had thrown up. Neither could sustain the level of magic usage for much longer.

Sometimes, the only way out was through.

'We're going to have to fight.' Hades reached for Artemis' hand. She didn't pull away. Maybe there was hope. In the last ten minutes of his existence. 'And here's something I thought would never cross my tongue – Merlin would know what to do.'

Artemis pushed and pushed against Chaos' restraint, but Chaos was bending the universe to suit them. Hades' hand found hers and, though she had heard him speak, her focus had been on her magic. Her mind descrambled Hades' words and Artemis had to accept his logic. Benjamin bumped into her, his magic ricocheting off of Chaos'. Ambrosius' embers glistened all around them, but Benjamin was losing his grip. Exhausted, Artemis reluctantly relaxed her grip on her magic. Though every muscle cried in protest, she freed her spear. If they were going anywhere other than Gaia, she was going to go down fighting. The charred smell of spent magic was inescapable.

Artemis allowed Hades to hold her hand. It was easier than facing his big, wounded eyes.

'Hades?'

'Yes?'

I'm glad you are here. The stubborn words would not be expelled from her throat. 'Ready?'

Seeming to understand what she was asking without asking, Hades squeezed her hand. Benjamin caught her eye, and Artemis realised that Ambrosius was still resisting the pull of Chaos' magic. She nodded once and Benjamin released his hold on the fabric of space and time.

An unseen force snared them round their waists, lurching them forwards, throwing the air from their lungs. Deep space blurred into a night sky burning with stars. She stayed standing with the help of her spear, but Hades and Benjamin met the ground at speed and pitched forwards.

Chaos twirled high into the sky, their manic laughter falling back to earth like freezing rain. At the top of their tight spiral, they clapped their hands and dropped into a nosedive. A fizz and a pop distracted Artemis from hauling Benjamin back to his feet.

'Portal!' Hades pulled her away, his eyes straining to look up and down at once. Chaos rocketed towards them, arms out-stretched.

Artemis attempted to shut the portal, but an unusual force pushed past her, and out of the portal tumbled Jack and April. Chaos snatched April up, Jack's tenuous grip on her boot slipped, and Chaos shot back into the sky. April squirmed, her magic snarling around her, taking pot shots at the God made of clouds. Artemis notched an arrow, but she couldn't find a clear shot. Ambrosius was a blazing inferno in Benjamin's hands, waiting for his chance.

'What do we do?' Jack looked desperately to Artemis.

'My answer will not be to your liking.' Artemis took aim. Some risks had to be taken.

'What? No! Ben!'

'I can catch her.' Benjamin danced about, mirroring Chaos' movements.

'Unbelievable!' Jack scrabbled up the nearest tree.

'Chaos! Are you such a coward as to hide behind a child?' Hades' eyes were dark pits of fury, his golden magic trailed across his body, highlighting the scars.

It took Artemis a second to realise that the feeling prickling her body was panic, so rarely had she experienced the sensation since leaving Chaos.

'Come home. It is remarkably simple. So very easy. Return and I will leave this fledgling Fate to her, well, fate.'

'Fine,' Hades said evenly.

'What are you doing?' Artemis turned her bow onto Hades. 'What. Are. You. Doing?' He would never – and she would never let him.

'Are you sincere?' Chaos tightened their grip around April.

'Yes.' Hades held two fingers behind his back, cutting off Artemis' protest. She lowered her bow, and Benjamin extinguished Ambrosius. 'Just as soon as you set April down. And, to be clear, I mean you put April on her feet, on the ground.'

'And Artemis will come too?'

Artemis had always been Chaos' second favourite. That was the one first place she did not covet. Chaos floated a little closer to the ground, intrigued. Artemis truly hoped that Hades was playing a dangerous game, and nothing more. These days, she could not read him so easily. Distance was a necessity, but it seemed to rile Hades into making reckless choices. And there were people here that he cared too deeply about. Chaos inched a little closer.

'Release April, and – ' Artemis looked to Hades and saw the determination in his clenched fists. 'I will return.'

'Splendid.' Chaos dropped to the ground. Hades closed his fist behind his back.

As Chaos opened their arms to release April, Benjamin and Artemis fired in unison. Artemis' arrow found Chaos' heart. Benjamin's magic shot straight into Chaos' open mouth. Cackling, Chaos pushed up into the sky again, chased by arrows. The bowstring dug groves into Artemis' fingers. Her quiver was running low, but it did not matter. Her magic would replenish it. Hades, still in his God form, leaped up into the tree recently vacated by Jack. He was never going to reach, but the last time they'd heard that cackle, Chaos had devoured a number of Gods, to prevent them from leaving. It was how Hades had acquired his scars.

'Does it not drive you crazy.' Chaos swished about above them with barely a scratch. 'How quickly the night changes?' They dived. The impact sent up a shower of earth and debris, and shook the ground so violently, that they all fell into the crater and into darkness.

PRONUNCIATION GUIDE

Annwn – A-noon

Arawn – Ah-rown

Barqan – Bar-con

Cerberus (Cerbi) - Cer-ber-us

Cerridwen – Ke-RID-wen

Charon – Cha-ruhn

Dirmynd – Dir-mid

Eilir – A-lir

Emrys – Em-riss

Erebus – Eh-ruh-buhs

Frayja – Freya

Gaia – Gi-a

Hecate – Hec-a-te

Kalma – Kal-ma

Keres – K-EE-r-ess

Lamia – Lay-mee-uh

Menoetius – Muh-NEE-sheee-uhs
Mórrígan – Mo-ruh-gn
Shtriga – Stri-ga
Surka – S-car
Tartarus – Tart-arus
Tuonela – Tu-one-la

Milton Keynes UK
Ingram Content Group UK Ltd.
UKHW020024141124
451090UK00001B/3

9 781068 569708